KILLER
CONSPIRACY

LENA DIAZ

SUMMER
STALKER

NICOLE HELM

This book is p...... from independently certified FSC™
paper to ensure responsible forest management.

For more information visit: www.harpercollins.co.uk/green

Printed and bound in Spain
by CPI, Barcelona

MILLS & BOON

First Published in Great Britain 2021
by Mills & Boon, an imprint of HarperCollins*Publishers* Ltd
1 London Bridge Street, London, SE1 9GF

www.harpercollins.co.uk

HarperCollins*Publishers*
1st Floor, Watermarque Building,
Ringsend Road, Dublin 4, Ireland

Killer Conspiracy © 2021 Lena Diaz
Summer Stalker © 2021 Nicole Helm

ISBN: 978-0-263-28333-4

0421

KILLER CONSPIRACY

LENA DIAZ

This book is dedicated to the Secret Service agents on the front line who risk their own lives every day to ensure the safety of our leaders and their families.

Chapter One

Gage Bishop knew that protecting the former president of the United States, especially *this* former president, wasn't likely to go according to plan. Two-termer Earl Manning preferred his own counsel to that of others, including his security detail. That was why he and his family were in a boisterous, drunken crowd of potentially dangerous Fourth of July revelers on a Sunday morning in the middle of downtown Gatlinburg, Tennessee. If something happened to Manning because of this foolishness, it wouldn't keep Bishop awake at night. But he *did* care if something happened to Manning's family, even though he'd tried for years not to. Most days, *Harper* Manning didn't even enter his thoughts. But today, seeing her father, her stepmother, and two younger siblings again, after all this time, meant he couldn't *stop* thinking about her.

It's been six years. She's not even here. Focus on your job.

The former president and his entourage entered a gift shop fifty yards away at Bishop's nine o'clock. Adjusting his dark shades, he took the opportunity to scan the sidewalks and street from his slightly elevated vantage point on the other side of the road. That's when he spotted him: a lone male with a laser-like fascination with the façade of the store Earl Manning and his family had just entered.

He spoke into the mic at his wrist. "Zone three, suspicious white male near aquarium entrance heading north on River Road, blue shorts, white T-shirt, dark brown hair, thirty-five to forty years old."

Bishop began weaving his way through the crowd, zig-zagging to keep the subject in his line of sight.

A click sounded in his ear. "Suspicious male just passed me. I'm on his six," a voice announced.

"I'm on his eight o'clock, ten feet away," another voice said through the earpiece.

Bishop spotted the two Secret Service agents who'd spoken, angling in on their target like border collies herding sheep. He stopped and surveyed the crowd in their vicinity. About forty feet back, another man seemed far too interested in what was happening. He also stopped, his head swiveling as he eyed the agents. Reversing direction, he hurried away.

Manning and his family stepped out of the gift shop. Half a dozen agents were with them, including Randy Faulk and Jack Thompson, two men Bishop had worked with years ago when he'd been with the Secret Service. Backing them up were three of Bishop's current coworkers, fellow Justice Seekers hired to augment the security for this high-profile event in their town.

Static sounded in his ear. "Suspicious male escorted away for questioning. Zone three secure."

That didn't mean the former president was secure, not if the feeling of dread in Bishop's gut was any indication. He reacquired a line of sight on the second suspicious male and started forward. The man wasn't close to Manning and wasn't moving toward him. But that didn't reassure Bishop, given the man's earlier interest. Something was off.

Bishop increased his speed, jogging as he worked to catch up. His prey was now solidly in zone five, the farthest from the former president and the least protected since the security risk had been deemed the lowest.

"Zone five," he said into his mic. "Who's covering zone five?"

There should have been at least one Secret Service agent covering that zone, per the plan. But no one responded.

The subject hiked up an incline then disappeared between two shops perched on the hill.

"Zone five! Repeat, suspicious white male."

A click sounded. "Disturbance in the red zone, zone one. Converge. All available agents."

Bishop had just started up the hill but stopped to look over his shoulder. Red zone meant the area directly around the former president. What appeared to be drunken brawls had broken out at two different locations on the street, both in close proximity to Manning. Agents were running toward the scene like ants at a picnic. Bishop ignored the call. He didn't feel compelled to blindly follow their protocol anymore. Instead he'd follow his instincts, instincts that told him those drunks weren't the true danger.

He turned back as the man he was after ducked into the doorway of a two-story building halfway up the street. Bishop took off running.

"Zone five," he repeated as he sprinted. "Request assistance. White male, green Hawaiian shirt, blue jean shorts, sandy-blond hair, approximately fifty years old." He gave the address of the building where the man had disappeared, two doors away. "Need assistance."

"On my way," one of his fellow Seekers answered. It sounded like Dalton, but they didn't use names in transmissions. "I'm in zone three. ETA one minute."

No one else answered the call. Bishop had a sinking feeling that Dalton's one minute was going to be about a half minute too late. He burst through the doorway into the shop. No customers, no one there to greet him, which had him even more concerned. A thump sounded overhead. He drew his pistol and sprinted for the stairs along the back wall.

"Coming up the hill," Dalton announced, his voice choppy as he ran.

The sound of glass breaking sent Bishop into overdrive. He topped the stairs, sweeping his pistol out in front of him. He checked one door, another, before heading into the last room.

The man in the Hawaiian shirt was on his knees in front of a high-powered rifle on a tripod, aiming it out the window he'd obviously just broken. Bishop shouted for him to stop and aimed his pistol at the guy's torso. The man ignored him.

Bishop was about to squeeze the trigger when he saw movement in a window in the building cater-cornered across the street. A child, probably three or four years old. Too close. Too risky. He couldn't take the shot.

He barreled into the man with the rifle, knocking it skyward just as it fired. The man screamed as Bishop's momentum carried both of them through the window into open air.

Chapter Two

"I'm okay. Enough already." Bishop jerked away from the well-meaning EMTs crouching beside him on the curb. "Thank you," he managed. "But go take care of someone who needs you, all right?"

They exchanged exasperated glances, but retreated toward the roadblock the Secret Service had set up. Twenty feet away, lying across the same curb where Bishop was sitting, was the gunman. He was covered with a sheet, his lifeblood staining the asphalt.

Not far from him, Dalton was talking to a couple of agents, no doubt giving his version of events. He'd arrived just in time to see Bishop and Hawaiian Shirt Guy take a swan dive from the second floor. Luckily for Bishop, he'd landed on top of the suspect. Not so lucky for the suspect.

From behind Bishop, a shadow lengthened across the grass onto the street.

"I was wondering when you'd arrive for your sit rep, Mason."

"How do you always know who's behind you? I swear you really do have eyes in the back of your head."

Bishop didn't bother explaining what to him was obvious. He'd worked with Mason Ford long enough to recognize his footfalls, even the smell of the cologne he sometimes wore. Paying attention to details like that could mean the difference between life and death, both in his former occupation as an agent and his present one working for Mason as a Justice Seeker.

"I see you refused to go to the hospital," Mason said. "You sure you're okay?"

"Thanks to the shooter being my pillow, just a few minor cuts and bruises. I'm fine."

Mason settled onto the grass and stretched his long legs out in front.

Bishop glanced at him before returning his attention to the chaos around them. "I heard Manning survived the close encounter with a couple of town drunks."

"To be fair, I heard one of them had a pocketknife. A patriotic little red, white and blue one made just for the occasion."

Bishop made a derisive sound.

"Situation report," Mason said. "Word is you saved Manning's life."

"A definite downside to this particular assignment but it couldn't be helped."

Mason chuckled. "Old grudges run deep, don't they?"

"You would know."

"On that we agree, my friend. He had a rifle with a scope set up ready to go?"

"He did. Secret Service discovered the dead shopkeeper in a back room. Their theory is the shooter killed him early this morning then locked the place to keep it clear of customers. If he couldn't get Manning on the street, this was his fallback location. Once he realized how heavily the former president was guarded, he retreated here for a Hail Mary. He may have been partnering with Aquarium Guy. That's not clear yet.

"He must have heard me coming after him," Bishop added, "because he didn't waste time raising the window. He broke the glass, hoping to get a quick shot off before I could reach him. Those drunks in the crowd had everyone in motion, making it tough to get a bead on the target. That likely gave me the extra seconds I needed to take out the shooter before he fired. Otherwise…" He shrugged. "Who knows."

"I'll be sure to mention that to the judge when he sentences them for disorderly conduct," he said dryly. "You spoke to the Feds already, gave a statement?"

"As much of one as I'm going to give."

"Understood. I'll run interference on that. But there is one other thing. I know you don't want to speak to Manning but—"

"Don't, Mason."

"Ten minutes. That's all he's asking. It'll be a photo opportunity for him, the magnanimous former president shakes the hand of the former Secret Service agent who once protected his oldest daughter and just saved his life. It will do wonders for his speaker fees."

"Not interested. And I'm not about to shake his hand, in public or anywhere else."

"I warned him you might say that. He wasn't pleased." Bishop shrugged. "He's not used to being told no."

"Again, can't argue with that assessment. But that's not the end of it. He insists he still needs to speak to you, that he knew you were hired to augment security today. Seems he planned to ask for an audience even before the attempt on his life."

Bishop shook his head. "The last time he and I were in a room together, I told him exactly what I thought of him and the bogus lies that got me fired. Does he think I've mellowed over the years? That I won't tell him exactly what I think of him again?"

"He's being secretive, hasn't given me anything beyond the barest details about why he wants to speak with you."

"Corrupt Manning being secretive. Imagine that."

"Work with me, Bishop. I'm just the messenger. And

while the Justice Seekers won't lack work even without the occasional government contract, our reputation could suffer if Manning bad-mouths our company. You of all people know what happens when you get on his bad side."

Bishop fisted his hands. Agents were still swarming the area, interviewing so-called witnesses and searching for evidence. He didn't envy whoever was supposed to be guarding zone five. Or who'd been on the advance prep team for this visit. Secret Service had insisted they be the ones to secure buildings nearby. They'd screwed up, big-time, to have missed securing a second-floor window with a direct line of sight if Manning went to any of the tourist traps along River Road.

"Bishop?"

He sighed heavily. "You're a bajillionaire, Mason. I don't believe for one second that you'd lose sleep over the possibility of Manning lying about your company. There's something else going on." When Mason didn't respond, Bishop studied him from over the top of his shades. "That bad, huh?"

Mason's jaw tightened. "It seems the former president wants to hire the Justice Seekers for a side job. More specifically, he wants to hire *you* to protect someone. Swears you're the only one he trusts."

"*Trusts?* He actually said that with a straight face?"

"I know, I know. Given your past, what he did, what he thinks *you* did, I don't understand it, either. But he wouldn't back down. Says it's urgent. All I'm asking is that you listen to what he has to say before you tell him no."

"Is this an order or a request? Sir?"

"Don't call me sir. And you of all people know I'd never *order* you to do anything."

"Then I respectfully decline. And my shift is over." He pushed to his feet, careful to resist the urge to rub the sore ribs that had taken the brunt of his fall. If Mason even suspected he might have a more serious injury, he'd force him to get medical treatment even if he had to point a gun at him to do it.

"Wait." Mason motioned him to the other side of the street, away from the milling agents.

Bishop reluctantly followed then leaned against the cater-cornered building where he'd seen the child in the window nearly an hour earlier. He crossed his arms, longing for the hot shower waiting for him at home. It would do wonders for his sore muscles and aching ribs. Hopefully it would also wash the stench of Earl Manning from his mind.

Mason crossed his arms, too, his suit jacket pulling tight across his broad shoulders. "You did me a huge favor helping manage security for this event. Your prior experience with the Secret Service was invaluable. All our guys performed admirably, mostly because you planned out every detail—at least, what those agents would allow."

"Stop blowing smoke. Just say it."

Mason turned to face him. "Even though I don't know the details about *why* Manning wants to hire you for bodyguard duty, I do know the identity of the person who needs protection. Bishop, it's Harper."

Chapter Three

Harper headed for the second-floor conference room of the office building where she'd been summoned by her father. She forced a smile for Randy Faulk, the Secret Service agent standing guard outside the door, the same agent who'd protected her years ago, after Gage left. While she had nothing against Faulk, he'd always been more of a friend to her stepmom than to her. They'd just never had the camaraderie that she and Gage'd had. Well, until they didn't.

"Ms. Manning." He gave her a polite smile. "Good to see you again."

"You, too, Mr. Faulk. Is my father inside yet?"

"I'm told he's on his way." He held the door open for her.

She thanked him and sadly wondered why he was relegated to playing doorman for a former president when he'd earned a promotion to the coveted White House detail last year.

When she stepped inside the conference room, she stopped, alarmed to see so many people for what was supposed to be a private meeting. Press passes marked the majority as members of the media. Most of the others she recognized as Secret Service agents, having met them during her father's tenure in office. But the two men standing apart from everyone else, near one of the blinds-covered windows, captured her attention. One in particular had her heart twisting in her chest.

Gage Bishop.

She knew he'd be here. But she hadn't expected that seeing him again would make her feel this unsettled. He was still so mouthwateringly handsome that her nails bit into her palms. Her fingers ached to trace his chiseled jaw, to smooth the tiny crescent-shaped birthmark on his left cheek, to thread through the dark brown hair that she remembered was soft and thick. He was wearing it longer than he used to, though it was still shorter than currently fashionable. The light beard was new, along with the barely there mustache. It seemed impossible, but he was even better looking now than when he'd lived in the pool house behind the Manning family home in Nashville while serving as her full-time bodyguard.

His posture subtly changed moments before his gaze locked on hers. He'd always been able to do that, somehow sense when she entered a room even before he saw her. But where in the past he'd smile or give her a warm greeting, the cold hardness now glittering in his deep blue eyes had her all but shivering before she lost the staring contest and looked away. She moved to the opposite side of the room to lean against the wall while she tamped down the unexpected rush of emotions threatening to shred her self-confidence and resolve.

The door opened again. Everyone fell silent as her father stepped inside with two more agents. Just how much security did one man need? Knowing his ego, he'd probably made a special request for extra protection this trip because of all the media around on Independence Day. Nothing could make a man look more important than when surrounded by a heavy security detail in dark sunglasses with guns bulging beneath their suit jackets. It was like a

Men in Black convention, minus the aliens. And no one was laughing.

His gaze zeroed in on Gage as hers had. But his polite nod went unacknowledged and unreturned. Where Gage had looked at her with cold indifference, he stared at her father with undisguised loathing.

The man standing beside Gage in a nearly matching dove-gray business suit leaned in and said something. Gage gave him a curt nod of agreement then aimed his lethal stare elsewhere.

"Ladies and gentlemen." Her father's practiced smile was at full wattage. "Before I answer your questions about today's events, I need to attend to some private business. It will only take a few moments. Could everyone please clear out except Mr. Ford, Bishop, and my daughter?"

He hadn't even looked her way when he'd entered the room. Had he just assumed she was there because he couldn't imagine her daring to be late after he'd summoned her? Even though she'd made the hour-and-a-half drive from her home outside Knoxville hoping her father could arrange this meeting, the exact location and time hadn't been determined. She'd still been halfway across town when she'd received his cryptic text and had driven like a crazy woman to arrive on time. At twenty-six, it rankled that she still felt compelled to ask *how high* when he told her to jump, even if his order was for her benefit.

When no one made a move to leave, her father said, "Perhaps you don't recognize these gentlemen." He motioned to Gage and the man beside him. "Mr. Ford's company helped provide security today. Bishop is not only one of Mr. Ford's employees, he's a former Secret Service agent. I assure you that I'm perfectly safe with both of them. Now, please excuse us for just a few minutes." This time his tone brooked no argument. But it still took some encouragement by one of the senior agents, Jack Thompson, to usher them out the door.

When the room cleared, Harper was surprised to see one person still sitting at the table, her father's lawyer. She couldn't imagine why he'd be needed on a Fourth of July outing. And they certainly hadn't discussed having him here for *this* meeting.

As Mr. Roth set an old-fashioned briefcase on the table, Harper straightened. What kind of scheme was her father trying to pull now?

"Dad, why is your lawyer here?"

"Just a formality. A simple nondisclosure agreement for Bishop to—"

"I'm not signing anything." Gage straightened away from the wall. "And your ten minutes started ticking the moment you walked in that door. You've got nine minutes left. What do you want?"

Her father's eyes narrowed in warning as he took the power seat at the head of the table and motioned for the others to join him.

Harper reluctantly sat at the other end of the table but avoided the matching power seat. She preferred to blend in rather than take the bull by its horns. Facing the windows, she tried to picture the view behind the blinds: the rows of quaint little shops, vibrant summer flowers spilling over planters lining the sidewalks. Any other time she'd visited Gatlinburg, she'd happily mixed with the tourists, soaked in the friendly small-town atmosphere the area was known for. Instead, this time, she was in a conference room dreading the upcoming discussion.

"Bishop," her father said when Gage and Mr. Ford remained standing. "Won't you please join us?"

"No."

Her father's face reddened. Beside him at the table, Mr. Roth looked as if he was about to faint. He'd probably never seen anyone treat her father with such open disdain. Even Harper's rebellious younger sister, Cynthia, didn't dare treat him that way. Not to his face at least.

Mr. Ford whispered to him again. But this time, Gage refused to concede. He shook his head and remained standing. Ford clasped his shoulder in an obvious show of respect and support before seating himself near the middle of the table. He greeted Harper first.

"Ms. Manning, I'm Mason Ford. I've always admired the work that you and your mother do for the national library literacy program. It's a genuine pleasure to meet you."

She smiled and didn't bother to correct him that Julia was her stepmother, not her mom—God rest her soul.

"Nice to meet you, Mr. Ford. And thank you."

He nodded before introducing himself to the lawyer. Then he finally acknowledged her father. Whether intentional or not, he'd insulted him by making him last in the introductions. She was inclined to think it was on purpose, another subtle show of support for Gage. They were obviously friends, in addition to being boss and employee. She couldn't help but envy the kind of friendship that was worth risking her father's displeasure. He took slights personally and wasn't the type to forgive and forget.

"Let's get this meeting started," her father said, his voice strained.

"Eight minutes," Gage announced.

Her father's perfect plastic smile was ruined by his glare. "I was going to start by thanking you for saving my life earlier today—"

"Don't bother."

Harper sucked in a breath. "What happened? You saved his life?"

"I did my job. It was nothing personal." He checked his watch. "Seven minutes."

"Oh good grief." Her father motioned to the lawyer. "Hurry up. Get him to sign—"

"No," Gage said. "I will not now or ever enter into any kind of contract with you. It wouldn't be worth the paper it's printed on." He crossed the room, surprising Harper by sitting across from her and giving her his full attention. "I'm here as a favor to Mason, not the former president. What's going on, Harper? Why does he think I can help you?" He arched a brow. "Or that I'd even consider it?"

One of the old cracks in her heart split open at the cold bitterness of his less than encouraging word choices. She glanced at her dad, who was openly glaring at him. A lot of unflattering things could be said about her father, most of them true. But when it came to his three children, whether related by blood or marriage, he'd fight to his last breath to protect each and every one of them. Gage's callous attitude toward her had him looking mad enough to start a small war.

When her father's gaze shifted to her, it immediately softened. His mouth curved in a rare genuine smile that was a mixture of sadness and affection. "You don't have to do this, Harper. We can find another way."

"It's okay, Daddy. Don't worry about me. We talked all this out and nothing has changed. But maybe you could step out for a few minutes while I talk to Gage alone. That might make it easier on all of us."

She could sense Gage's puzzlement as he glanced back and forth between them. But thankfully he didn't say anything. If he'd mentioned one more time how many minutes were left, her father would have probably dragged her out of the room, ruining any chance she had to get Gage's help.

She *really* needed his help.

Her father finally nodded with obvious reluctance and pushed back from the table. "Mr. Ford, Mr. Roth, let's step outside. Harper prefers to conduct this conversation in private."

She gave him a grateful smile as he and the lawyer left the room.

Mr. Ford wasn't as accommodating. He crossed to Gage and silently waited.

Without turning, Gage said, "I'll listen to what she has to say. Don't let anyone else back in until we're done."

"You got it."

As soon as the door clicked shut behind Ford, Gage settled back in his chair.

"All right, Harper. It's just you and me. What did your father mean when he said you could find another way? Did you learn that I have money now and you're here to extort me? Or are you here to try to destroy me once and for all by faking *another* pregnancy?"

Chapter Four

Harper jerked back, the sting of his words hitting her like a physical blow. "Wow. You really know how to come out swinging, don't you? When did you become so cruel?"

"When I was accused of something I didn't do and the girl's father destroyed my career and did a heck of a job wrecking my life along with it."

She clasped her hands beneath the table and silently reminded herself what was at stake. Their individual grievances were petty in comparison. "In answer to your earlier question, I didn't know you had money. This isn't about money. *It never was.*"

He didn't look convinced. "Then why am I here? You want something from me. If not money, then what?"

She glanced at her purse on the chair beside hers, wondering if it would be better to just show him the picture. But without an explanation first, she didn't know if he'd even bother to look at it. And if he did, his low opinion of her character would simply be confirmed, in his mind at least. No, she had to be careful, get this right. Because she knew he'd never give her another opportunity.

"It's complicated," she said. "I need to tell you a story first, one that began almost six years ago. There are things that you don't know, or don't understand."

"Six years ago? I've heard this one." His look of scorn practically incinerated her from across the table. "It's about

a Secret Service agent who put his life on the line every
day for two years to protect a young college student whose
father's shenanigans made her a target of violence on nu-
merous occasions. And how did she thank him for being
willing to die to keep her safe? She accused him of getting
her pregnant. Never mind that they'd never even kissed, let
alone had sex. That didn't stop her. She got daddy dearest
to pressure the agent's boss to fire him, then blacklisted
him so that every security job he tried to get lasted a few
weeks at best, before the lies caught up to him and he was
canned again."

The bitterness in his voice had her aching inside. She'd
always known he'd been hurt. They both had. But the past
wasn't something she could fix. The present was what mattered, and what might happen in the future if she couldn't
make him see reason. "You don't understand. Let me explain. I need to tell you about the night that your—"

"It's you who doesn't understand. You never stopped to
think about the damage that your lies could do. Or worse,
you didn't care." He rapped his knuckles on the table. "One
of your father's minions sent a letter to my dad, spreading
the lies about you and me. He was so ashamed of my lack
of honor that he flat-out told me the wrong son had died
in the conflict overseas. He also said that if it was in his
power, he'd send me to die on the other end of that sniper's
bullet instead of Shane."

She drew in a sharp breath. "Oh, Gage. I'm so sorry. I
had no idea that—"

"I haven't talked to my father in five years. His choice.
Not mine. And there's no telling what would have happened to me by now if I hadn't come up with the idea
of incorporating to throw your father off the scent so he
couldn't poison future employers against me. Still, without
references, I was eventually forced to completely switch
career paths to build any kind of career. Thankfully, the

skills I learned working summers for my father in construction paid off. I eventually started my own construction company. That gave me a roof over my head and food on the table. But it was only when I became one of the Justice Seekers that I got my pride back."

"Justice Seekers?"

"My boss's company, the Justice Seekers. He put together a team of former law-enforcement men and women whose careers were destroyed through no fault of their own—like mine. Mason has made it his life's work to give people like me a second chance. I thank God every day that he believed *me*, not the Manning family lies."

The pain that leaked through his angry tirade had her reaching across the table to clasp his hand before she realized what she was doing.

He jerked back as if her touch had scalded him. "I don't know why I even bothered coming in here. Curiosity, I guess. But whatever problem you're having, I'm not the one to solve it. Tell daddy dearest to loosen his purse strings and hire a private security firm to protect you. I'm sure he can more than afford it. But if he won't dole out his own money, maybe he can convince his former VP in the White House to have the Secret Service protect you even though they're not supposed to protect adult children of former presidents. Earl Manning's got plenty of experience breaking the rules and he excels at strong-arming others to do the same."

"Gage, please. You haven't given me a chance—"

"A chance? Like you gave me all those years ago?"

She flinched.

He shoved back from the table and stood, his expression more weary than angry. "I'm sorry, Harper. I truly am. God above knows I never planned on spouting off like this. Or being…cruel, as you said. That's not me. Or at least, it never used to be. All I can say is that seeing you again, bringing up the past, it just…it pushed some buttons I didn't even know I still had. That's not an excuse. It's an explanation. Though admittedly a poor one."

She gave him a wobbly smile and was about to try again, but he held up a hand to stop her.

"Wait. Please." His voice was soft, almost gentle now, filled with regret. "I can't do this. I thought I could. But I can't. I'm not trying to be mean, just realistic. You need to find someone else to help you."

Before she could even try to figure out a response, he was heading for the door. In desperation, she yanked the picture out of her purse and held it up just as he reached for the doorknob. "This is my son, Shane. He—"

"Shane?" He gave her an incredulous look. "You named another man's child after my dead brother?"

His barb buried itself deep in her chest. But she couldn't wallow and feel sorry for herself. This battle was far too important to surrender. Somehow she had to break through that prickly wall he'd erected between them, or they'd both regret it for the rest of their lives.

She hurried over, squeezing between him and the door to block his way. Then she held up the picture. When he didn't look at it, she shook it. "I wasn't trying to hurt you by naming him that. I named him Shane as a tribute, because I knew how much your brother meant to you." She searched his gaze, noted the stubborn tilt of his jaw. "Do you really not remember what happened between us? Not even a little bit?"

His brows drew down in confusion. But he was looking at her, not the photo. "Remember what? Remember the young woman who used to flirt outrageously with me? Remember that I rebuffed you, insisted on keeping things professional? I made vows to God and country to protect you. Allowing myself to act on the attraction between us would have meant breaking those vows. An agent who has a romantic relationship with his charge is a liability. He can't focus, can't be counted on to protect them. What *exactly* do you think I need to remember?"

"The night we made love," she whispered brokenly, no longer able to ignore her own pain, bubbling up from a wound she'd foolishly thought had healed years ago. "It's something I'll never forget. And it destroys me that it meant so little to you that I'm not even a hazy image in your mind."

"Harper—"

"It was the day you found out that your brother had been killed in combat. You got a phone call from your dad when you were driving me home from classes at Belmont University. You called your boss to immediately assign another agent to take over your duties for at least a couple of months. You were all your father had left and you wanted to make sure he was going to be okay. You'd planned on packing that night, then leaving the next morning to help plan the funeral, settle your brother's estate, spend some time with your dad before going back to work. But it was *you* that I was worried about. You seemed so…devastated."

"Don't do this," he whispered. "Don't."

"Don't what?" She searched his gaze. "Tell the truth? Don't tell you that after Agent Faulk arrived and you went to the pool house, I paced my room for hours, worried about you? I couldn't stand the devastation I'd seen in your eyes. I eventually snuck out of the main house to check on you. When you didn't answer my knock, I looked through a window and saw you passed out on the floor, an empty bottle of whiskey on the rug beside you. I debated calling for help. But I didn't know if you'd get in trouble, even though you weren't technically on duty. Instead, I went inside."

She slowly lowered the picture. "I wanted to *help* you. But when I rolled you over, you put your arms around me and kissed me and I…" She let out a shuddering breath.

"I'd wanted you so desperately for so long. And I naïvely thought you wanted me, too, not some random woman in your drunken thoughts who you wouldn't even remember later. I was a fool, in so many ways. Instead of stopping you, as I should have, I jumped in the deep end and haven't come up for air since."

She hated the bitterness and hurt in her voice but there was nothing she could do about it. "Stop looking at me as if I've lost my mind. This is the truth, the truth you've denied for so long that you never once stopped to consider even the possibility that I wasn't lying." She raised the picture again, holding it a few inches from his face.

"Look at him," she demanded. "Ignore me if you want. Hate me if it makes you feel better. Blame me and my family for every bad thing that's happened in your life. But don't you dare ignore him. *Look at him!* Then tell me he's not yours."

Chapter Five

A mixture of confusion and anger crossed Gage's face, but he finally looked at the picture Harper was holding up.

She knew the moment he saw the small crescent moon birthmark on the side of Shane's face, the same birthmark that was on Gage's face. An extremely rare hereditary mark that all the Bishop men shared. She knew because she'd researched the family during the nine months she'd carried the newest generation in her womb. It had been a long trial of loneliness, bitterness and despair. But the real trial had begun the day that Shane was born. She just hadn't realized it at the time.

His hand shook as he took the picture from her.

Harper watched his hungry gaze soak in every detail as he stared at the five-year-old little boy who promised to become every bit as handsome as his father one day. He had the same blue eyes, the same dark brown hair, the same sweet smile that would break hearts when he was older.

If he lives long enough, that is.

Holding back the tears that wanted to fall, she crossed to one of the windows and peered through the blinds at the street below. She was surprised to see her sister out front, laughing at something her latest boyfriend—Dean Everly—was saying. If there'd been an attempt on their father's life, shouldn't the family be on lockdown instead of out in public? Then again, Cynthia had never been a rule follower. And she was a legal adult, a sophomore at Vanderbilt, no longer under Secret Service protection any more than Harper was.

"I didn't know." His deep voice rasped behind her.

She turned, surprised to see his eyes looking bloodshot, as if he'd been on a bender for days. Myriad emotions tumbled across his expression, running the gambit from grief to shock. He took a halting step toward her.

"I didn't know," he repeated.

"I tried to tell you. When I found out that I was pregnant, I knew it would be wrong to keep that a secret. But I didn't know how to contact you. I only told my father because I hoped he could quietly obtain your current address from the Secret Service so I could privately let you know that we were going to have a baby. I never expected him to tell your boss and get you fired, then poison others against you. He told me that he'd confronted you and you made such a scene that your boss found out. Then you disappeared so you wouldn't have to support your child."

He shook his head. "I thought you were lying about the pregnancy because I had no memory of us ever being together. But if I'd known the truth, I never would have run from my responsibilities. I'd have been there for you. For our child. I swear it. I would have been there."

Grief and regret threatened to tear her apart. There was no doubt in her mind that he was telling the truth. It was there in the tone of his voice, the misery and shame in his expression. How different things might have been. If only.

He let out a ragged breath. "I remember getting the call about my brother's death, Agent Faulk arriving at the Manning estate to guard you. I went to the pool house to pack my things. And then… And then…" He shook his head. "I know I drank way more than I should have that night. But I never… I don't remember you being there. I don't." His confused gaze bore into hers. "I would never knowingly disrespect you that way, make love to the woman I was assigned to protect, then turn my back on her after…" His Adam's apple bobbed in his throat. "My whole life I wanted to be in the Secret Service, to serve my country. How could I have broken my vows, crossed that line?" He searched her eyes, as if seeking absolution. "How could I not remember making love to you?"

Tears pricked her vision. She wrapped her arms around her waist to keep from reaching for him, knowing she couldn't bear it if he recoiled again. "As soon as I saw how drunk…" She shook her head. "It's my fault. I should have left. But I… I wanted you so much. I was young and immature. I'd had such a terrible crush on you from the moment we met and you were so determined to keep it professional. But that doesn't excuse my actions. What happened that night is my fault."

"No." He took another step toward her, so close she could feel the heat from his body, see the turmoil in his eyes. "The blame lies with me. You're right that I would have gotten in trouble if you'd called for help and my boss found out I was drunk while still on the Manning estate. And I would have deserved it. I should have waited until I'd left to drown my sorrows, or avoided drinking altogether."

He raked a hand through his hair, making it stick up in spikes. "All this time I thought I'd been wronged, that my honor was intact, when you're the one who was wronged. I am *exactly* what your father said I was. I broke my vows, took advantage of you and didn't even have the decency to realize what I'd done.

"My God, Harper. You carried my child for nine months, went through that experience alone while I yelled at the heavens about how unfair life was, believing I was the one who'd been betrayed. I'm so ashamed of how I treated you. And I'm so deeply, deeply sorry." He winced. "That sounds so pathetic, doesn't it? An apology could never make up for what I've done. For how *you've* suffered."

His complete turnaround had her world tilting on its axis. His apologizing was the last thing she'd ever expected and she didn't know how to even begin to process it. She couldn't. Not now. Maybe not ever. There was too much water under that bridge for either of them to cross. And she wasn't even sure she wanted to, not after all this time. Her battered heart wasn't ready, might not ever be.

Gage's gaze returned to the picture still clutched in his hand, as if drawn by an invisible thread. "How you must hate me to have kept him from me all this time. I've missed everything. His first smile, his first word, his first steps—"

"So have I."

His head shot up. "What do you mean?"

Memories of that awful day had her wanting to curl into a fetal position and shout her own rage to the heavens. Instead, she forced herself to keep it together, to hold on a little while longer, to explain. Time was running out.

"My parents didn't want scandal touching my father's precious political career," she said, bitterness creeping into her voice again. "He was nearing the end of his first term and didn't want anything damaging his chances for reelection. So they rented me a house thirty minutes outside of Nashville and hired a midwife to stay until my due date.

"She did all the grocery shopping. I never went into town, couldn't risk being seen and recognized. And when I went into labor, after I struggled an entire day to bring Shane into the world, the midwife said he was in distress, that he needed care she couldn't provide. She rushed him to the hospital. An hour later, she called to tell me they'd done everything they could to save him, but he didn't make it."

She clutched her hands together. "Two weeks later, I had an urn of ashes on my mantel and a death certificate in the mail. The heartache, the grief, was overwhelming.

I could barely function. It was months before I was able to climb out of that awful pit of despair. But I did. I moved on, went back to school, got my masters…

"You said you started a construction company. Well, I started my own medical illustrations company, albeit a one-woman operation. Things have been going really well since then. I recently even started dating again, after years of Julia doing the mom thing, nagging me to get back in the game." She grimaced, wishing she'd left that last part out.

"Anyway, the reason I asked my father to arrange this meeting with you is that picture you're holding. It arrived six days ago, along with a lock of hair and a ransom note from someone calling himself Sam the Good Samaritan." She shook her head at the ridiculous name. "All this time I thought my little boy was dead. Now I find out that someone stole him, and they're threatening to kill him if I don't get the cash together before he contacts me again."

Gage stared at her a long moment, as if letting everything sink in. Finally, he slid the picture into his jacket pocket then asked, "How much is the ransom demand?"

"Two million dollars."

His eyes widened. "Do you have that kind of money?"

"Not even close. My clients are doctors' offices and publishers of medical textbooks. They aren't inclined to pay extravagant fees no matter how good my illustrations might be. And the work fluctuates, that whole feast or famine sort of thing. After paying taxes, health insurance premiums, and investing in a 401K for my retirement, I've got enough left for a decent living. But I'll never get rich doing what I do.

"All I can figure is that whoever has Shane knows that my father is wealthy and is counting on him to come up with the money." She shrugged. "Say what you will about him. But when I explained what was going on, he immediately said he'd give me the money. His bankers are liquidating assets as we speak."

He stiffened. "No."

She waited for more. When he didn't say anything else, she asked, "No…what?"

"Your father isn't ransoming our son. If we pay the kidnapper, I'll be the one to pay it. And I won't have to liquidate anything."

She stared at him, stunned. "You have two million dollars in the bank? Wait, what do you mean, *if* we pay the kidnapper? We *have* to or he'll—"

"How do you know it's not a trick? A scam? How do you know… Shane…is really alive?"

Harper gave him a brittle smile. "You sound like my dad. The first thing he did was have the ashes in the urn tested. For over five years I've polished and cried over a silver vase packed with firewood ashes." She slumped into one of the nearby chairs and drew her knees up to her chest. "After that, Dad had a private lab verify that the hair came from a live person. I have no idea how they can tell something like that, but that's what they said. Then they ran a paternity test using some of my hair and the lock of hair that supposedly came from Shane. All hush-hush, of course, using a fake name. Dear old Dad is willing to part with his money but never his reputation."

She waved a hand in the air, wishing she could wipe away her words just as easily. "He didn't deserve that. He's been wonderful during this crisis. He's doing everything he can to help me. Anyway, it's not a scam. The test was positive. He's my son."

"Our son." His tone dared her to contradict him. Gone was the anguished man from moments ago. As soon as she'd mentioned the kidnapper, he'd tamped his emotions behind the wall again and was all business, the confident former agent ready to take charge.

"Our son," she reluctantly agreed, feeling an unexpected pang of resentment about sharing the memory of her baby with him when it had been hers alone for so long. "He's alive, has been, all this time. We *both* missed his first smile, his first word, his first steps. Neither of us got to see him as a baby. And if we don't cooperate, and help each other, neither of us will get to see him grow up."

Chapter Six

Harper lowered her legs from her chair and straightened as Gage sat in the chair beside hers and turned to face her. His suit jacket hung open, revealing the pistol holstered to his side. It was a grim reminder of one of the reasons that she'd specifically wanted *him* to help her get Shane back. He was experienced at protecting people. And while it was true that others might have his skill sets, none would be as motivated as a father to save his own son.

"Before agreeing to anything, I need to know what I'm up against. I need the truth."

"The truth? I just told you—"

"Not about the pregnancy. I want to know why you contacted me about the kidnapping. We haven't seen each other since Shane was conceived. No contact of any kind. We don't even know each other, not the people we are today. So why did you track me down to help you?"

She clutched the arms of the chair. "Track you down?"

His jaw tightened. "Since leaving the White House, your father's been to Gatlinburg several times. But he's never requested additional security from a private firm until today. He admitted to my boss that he knew I'd be here. The only way he'd know that is if he'd done some digging, figured out where I live and who I work for. He's smart enough to know that I'd refuse an outright request to talk to either of you. He hired the Justice Seekers explicitly to give him leverage. Don't deny it."

She slowly shook her head. "I won't deny it. You're right."

"That means that you lied earlier when you said you didn't know anything about the Justice Seekers."

Her face flushed with heat. "Do any outsiders really know what that company is? It's not like you hang up a shingle, advertise your services. It seems like a jack-of-all-trades kind of thing, with personal security being only part of it."

When he continued to stare at her, waiting, she let out a deep breath. "Okay. Yes. I lied."

His gaze hardened. "Why was it so important to contact me, to make me a part of this?"

"You *are* the father. You have a right to know what's going on. And you have experience, the kind needed to make sure this goes down the right way. Plus, being totally honest now, part of the background my father learned is that as one of the Seekers you've worked on kidnapping cases before, cases the police had given up on. Both times, you were able to bring the victim home safely."

"Those were adult kidnappings in foreign countries, places where our government couldn't openly go without risking an international incident. It was taking too long through official channels, so their families hired us. Completely different than what we're dealing with here. You and I both know that the FBI is the agency with the most expertise in child abductions in the States. What are they doing on this case? Setting up wire taps? Working with your father to mark the ransom money? Getting assets in place for when the call comes in?"

She cleared her throat. "None of that. The kidnapper's note was quite specific. He said if I tell any officials about the kidnapping, he would…he would kill Shane."

"Kidnappers always say that. You still need to contact the FBI."

"No. I'm not risking my child's life." At the annoyed look that flashed across his face, she corrected herself. "*Our* child's life. The only reason I told my father about it is that I had no choice, no other way to get the money to pay the kidnapper."

"You didn't tell the police?"

"No."

"Secret Service?"

She shook her head. "I can't. For Shane's sake."

"You told *me*."

"It was a gamble. I'd hoped that once you realized that Shane was yours, you'd agree to help. I'm going to follow the kidnapper's instructions, whatever they are. But I also know better than to trust a criminal. I need a backup plan, a way to ensure that this Sam guy won't just take the money and run. I need to know that Shane will be returned safely."

"I'm your insurance policy."

She winced. "I suppose you are. I can't do this alone. I'm too scared I'll mess up. I need you. Shane needs you."

He stared at her, eyes narrowed, as if trying to divine her innermost thoughts. "There's more. What aren't you telling me?"

She squeezed her hands together. "What makes you think there's more?"

He swore. "It's your father, isn't it? He's the real reason you didn't go to the FBI, or anyone else."

Unable to deny it without lying again, she said, "It's complicated."

He crossed his arms, his brow furrowed in a thunderous expression. "There's nothing complicated about his selfishness. He's a narcissistic fool with one goal. Protect his legacy in the history books. His entire political career has been built on a platform of law and order. He doesn't want to ruin his precious reputation by letting anyone find out that he paid millions of dollars to a criminal." He sat forward, resting his forearms on his thighs. "Let me guess. He told you that because of my history, getting fired from the Secret Service, if things went south I could be the scapegoat. He could blame me, say I went rogue, that he was using the money to *trap* the kidnapper, not exchange it for his grandson. He'll paint me as having taken over—without his knowledge, of course. The media would eat that up. And he'd come out looking squeaky clean, once again blaming everything on me."

"You make it sound so ugly."

"Because it is."

"Okay, fine. Yes, the *facts* are what you say. He convinced me my best chance was to work with you, and only you, rather than involve an official agency. But the *reasons* aren't what you said. It's not about making you take the fall."

He cocked a brow. "Enlighten me."

"He's the former president of the United States—"

"And the reason I switched political parties. What else?"

She crossed her arms. "The United States doesn't make deals with kidnappers. If we go down that road, it will open up the current president, future presidents—all of our country's leaders—to danger. The country can't ransom Shane. We can't set that kind of example."

"That's your father talking, not you."

"He's giving me the ransom money. I owe him a debt of gratitude. God knows I'll never be able to pay back that kind of money."

"He's not providing the ransom. I am. Does that change your mind about going along with his wishes? About not contacting the FBI?"

"That would make me the worst kind of hypocrite, one

willing to put others in jeopardy for my own needs. I agree with my father's policy of not allowing the country to officially make deals with criminals. But that doesn't mean I won't do it as a private citizen, quietly, so that other potential future kidnappers don't hear about it. Am I splitting hairs? Justifying my actions in ransoming my son?" She shrugged. "Probably. But I'm doing it anyway. I lost him once. I can't lose him again. That's why I need you. I need you to make sure that when this exchange goes down, it doesn't go bad."

"Without hurting the Manning family reputation, everything on the down-low."

She lifted her chin. "I choose to think of it as following the kidnapper's demands of not involving the authorities, but working with someone who can help ensure it goes as planned. Enough with the recriminations. Will you do it? Will you help me?"

He got up and crossed to one of the windows. He looked down at the street through one of the slats in the blinds as she'd done earlier. Several minutes passed before he finally turned around. But his expression didn't give her any clues. Was he going to tell her to get lost? Or was he going to become her saving grace?

"When is the exchange?"

Did his question mean he was going to help? Or not? "Tuesday. Three days from now, if you count today. He's supposed to send instructions on the day of the exchange."

"So you won't know the exchange location until right before it's supposed to happen." His mouth tightened into a hard line. "Three days doesn't give us much time to plan."

"My fault. I agonized over the decision of whether or not to involve you. My father went ahead and hired the Justice Seekers for security at today's event, just in case I agreed to his suggestion. Is that enough time for you to come up with a plan?"

"It'll have to be. Do you have the ransom note with you?"

"A copy. The original is in my safe at home."

"Let me see it."

She leaned across the table and grabbed her purse, then pulled out the note and handed it to him.

Without looking at it, he shoved it into the same jacket pocket where he'd put Shane's picture. Even though she'd scanned the picture into her computer and had another copy at home, she selfishly wanted to grab the one he had and keep it with her. Since receiving that photograph, she'd never gone anywhere without Shane's likeness. Not having it left her feeling…empty.

"All right," he said. "I'm in. On one condition."

"What's that?"

"You do exactly what I tell you to do, when I tell you to do it."

"Okay."

"Just like that?"

She spread her hands in a helpless gesture. "What choice do I have? As you ferreted out already, other than my original plan to use my father's money, I'm in this alone. I need you. I agree to your terms."

He gave her a curt nod and pulled out his phone. "Give me your number."

She rattled it off as he keyed it in. "Why do you need it? Won't we be together until this is over?"

"Not immediately. If the kidnapper has anyone watching you, and he finds out who I am, he might count that as you contacting the authorities."

"Right." She nervously stood, rubbing her hands up and down her arms. The idea that someone might be watching her had butterflies fluttering in her stomach. "I didn't think about that. How does this play out? What do I do next?"

"You follow my rules. Rule number one, trust me and no one else. That includes your father. You can't tell him anything about my plans. You can only tell him what I tell you to tell him."

"But—"

"That's the deal."

She clenched her hands into fists at her sides. "Fine. I only tell him what you let me tell him."

"Rule number two—"

"How many *rules* are there?"

"Rule number two," he repeated. "Don't tell him that I agreed to work on this case. Tell him that I refused to help, that you're going it alone, just in case he talks to the wrong person and accidentally lets them know you're working with me. Say you'll contact him later with instructions for wiring the money. We'll leave Gatlinburg separately. I don't want the kidnapper seeing us together."

She glanced at the blinds, even though they were closed. "You really think he's watching me?"

"I can give you two million reasons why he should."

Her hands started to shake. She clutched them together to try to hide her nervousness. "Where will we meet after I leave? When?"

"I'll call and let you know."

"Then… I should just…go home?"

"Where had you planned on going originally?"

"Home, I guess. A rural area well outside Knoxville, about an hour and a half from here."

"Up I-40?"

"Yes."

"Stick to your normal routine."

"In case the Good Samaritan is watching me?"

He nodded.

"I don't like this. It doesn't feel right."

"Are you changing your mind? Ready to call someone else for help?"

"Maybe. This isn't how I thought it would work."

He leaned against the wall. "Let me guess. You figured you'd be in charge of everything, make all the decisions. And once you had the kidnapper's instructions on the exchange, you'd call me to tag along behind you?"

She didn't appreciate his condescending tone. "Something like that. As you said, we don't really know each other anymore, if we ever did. I didn't expect you to—"

"Take charge?"

She raised her hands in exasperation. "I just want to make sure it all goes perfectly. That I follow instructions, make the exchange, bring Shane home. I don't want to do something wrong and have Sam realize anyone is helping me. But I'm also afraid to go it alone. It's all so—"

"Complicated?"

She let out a deep sigh.

He tilted her chin, forcing her to meet his gaze. "Two million dollars is a heck of an incentive to make sure he gets his money *and* has a chance to spend it. He'll keep Shane safe, for now, in case he has to offer proof of life. But once he has the money, odds are that he'll try to kill Shane, and you. No witnesses. Clean getaway."

"Oh my God," she whispered.

He dropped his hand. "Don't worry, Harper. Your father may have convinced you that I'd be the perfect fall guy if things go wrong. But you're getting way more than that. My years in the Secret Service were boot camp for what I've done since then. There's not a line I won't cross, a law I won't break, to rescue our child. And when I'm through, this so-called Good Samaritan will never hurt anyone else again."

A cold chill ran down her spine. "What are you saying? What happens to the kidnapper when this is over?"

He didn't answer.

"Maybe this isn't such a good idea. Maybe you shouldn't be a part of this after all."

The look he gave her was chilling. He moved past her but stopped at the door. "Go home, Harper. I need to put some things in place. Then I'll contact you."

"Wait. I need to think this through some more. I haven't made up my mind about whether you should be involved."

His eyes narrowed in warning. "Your decision was made the moment you told me I have a son. I'm in this, whether you want me to be or not."

Chapter Seven

When Bishop reached his black Dodge Charger in the parking lot, he leaned against the driver's door, still reeling from the discovery that he had a child, let alone from seeing Harper again. That long dark hair, those delicious curves and beautiful eyes, a much lighter blue than his own, had haunted his dreams for years. But his dreams were nothing compared to the reality of seeing her in person.

The moment she'd walked into the room, his lungs had seized in his chest. He hadn't seemed able to catch his breath. It had been devastating to realize in that instant that he'd been fooling himself all this time.

He was still crazy in love with her.

When he'd been a Secret Service agent assigned to protect her, keeping his true feelings hidden had been a daily struggle. But he'd persevered, ruthlessly bottling up how he'd felt about her so he could focus on his duty: keeping her safe. Later, after being fired, his life ripped apart because of her lies—or so he'd believed—his bitterness and resentment had easily quashed those softer feelings.

But now?

He raked a shaking hand through his hair. It was as if someone had released the floodgates on the dam of his emotions. He wanted her—*craved* her—in his arms, in his bed. *In his life*. It was a bittersweet irony that just when it seemed that he was free to pursue her, he couldn't. Once again he had to pretend to be unaffected when around her so he could focus on being her protector, and saving their son's life.

Then again, considering the trauma she'd been through—because of him and his rejection of the truth— what was the likelihood that she even wanted him anymore? Hadn't her rejection of his methods at the end of their meeting said as much?

She'd expected the more civilized Secret Service agent she'd been infatuated with years ago. But once she'd seen the harder man he'd become, she'd balked, unsure she even wanted his help. It had been like having a bucket of ice water poured over his head, leaving him bitter and resentful as he'd stalked out of the conference room. He'd regretted his actions halfway to his car, too late to go back to apologize. The conference room was probably already full of media and Secret Service agents again.

He fisted his hand on the roof of the car. It would serve him right if, once he rescued Shane, the mother of his son didn't want him to stick around. He could spend every day of the rest of his life apologizing for not being there for her during her pregnancy and it wouldn't come close to making up for his sins. God knows he didn't deserve her. But that didn't stop him from wanting her, needing her, *aching for her* so badly he didn't know how he was going to survive the next few days, let alone the rest of his life, if she wasn't part of his future.

One thing at a time. Focus on Shane, on saving him. Deal with the rest later.

He inhaled a bracing breath and opened his car door.

"Bishop! Wait up," Jack Thompson's voice called out from across the parking lot behind him. Two sets of footsteps echoing on the asphalt indicated there was someone with him. Both were jogging to catch him before he could escape.

Bishop swore beneath his breath. He should have left

as soon as he'd reached his car. He didn't have the time or patience to deal with Thompson right now, or whoever was with him. But he was here representing the Justice Seekers. Out of respect for his boss, he'd try to "play nice." He reluctantly clicked the door shut and turned around.

To his surprise, it was Randy Faulk standing beside Thompson. Bishop shook the younger agent's hand first. "Faulk, good to see you," he lied. From what Bishop had heard, Faulk had done an admirable job protecting Harper after Bishop had been fired. But he still resented him because of a little green monster perched on his shoulder. He hated that Faulk had gotten to spend years with Harper, watching over her. Years that Bishop had wasted, blaming her for destroying his career.

Shaking Thompson's hand had him feeling like even more of a fraud. They hadn't parted on the best of terms since Thompson was Bishop's former boss's right-hand man. After Hines had fired him, Thompson had escorted Bishop out of the building. Definitely not one of his favorite memories.

"Bishop." Thompson smiled as if they were the best of friends. "I've been looking everywhere for you. I wanted to thank you for helping us out today. And especially for not telling all those reporters that we screwed up."

"Yeah," Faulk added. "The media thinks we're the ones who stopped the assassin. You really saved our butts."

Bishop rested a forearm along the top of his car. "Don't give me too much credit. The company I work for prefers to keep a low profile. No press interviews allowed." It wasn't an entirely accurate assessment since Mason trusted his employees to make their own decisions. Micromanagement wasn't his style. But the white lie was better than the truth—that he didn't have time for reporters because he had a kidnapper to catch.

Still, he couldn't help a little dig at his former nemesis.

"Maybe next time you Secret Service boys will let Justice Seekers clear all the buildings with a line of site to the target like we wanted to do, instead of tying our hands."

Thompson's smile dimmed. He motioned to Faulk. "I hear that press conference is starting up again soon. You should head back before Manning realizes you're not standing sentry duty."

Faulk's face reddened, but he managed to keep his expression respectful, even though he probably wanted to punch Thompson. Instead, he shook Bishop's hand again. "It was good to see you. Really. It's been a long time." He gave him a jaunty salute then jogged across the parking lot to the building.

"What's with him playing doorman?" Bishop asked. "I thought he'd been promoted to White House duty." Not that Bishop kept up with the agency anymore. But knowing who they were working with today had been part of his prep for providing security.

"He made a few mistakes and is paying for it. Got reassigned to the Manning estate, mainly protecting Mrs. Manning. But as you saw back there, Mr. Manning uses him in whatever capacity he sees fit."

"Ouch. Hines never was one to grant second chances. I suppose Faulk is lucky to still have a job."

"Hines retired three years ago."

"Is that so? I figured he'd cling to his desk until someone pried his cold dead fingers off the stapler. Who's the boss now? You?"

Thompson's smile didn't quite reach his eyes this time. "Nah, that job's too administrative for me. I prefer field work, being the guy behind the curtain with the real power."

Bishop didn't believe him for a second. Everyone at the agency knew how desperately he coveted the top job. Apparently, Faulk wasn't the only one who'd screwed up over the years.

"Good luck with the press," Bishop said. "Maybe I'll see you next time Manning's in town."

"You aren't sticking around? I figured you'd be tapped for the internal inquiry into what happened. Your company is key to that since they helped with security. And obviously they'll want to talk to you since you took the perp down."

"My boss will handle it. I already gave a statement and he'll let me know if there are more questions. I've got a scheduling conflict that can't be moved."

"Ah, I see." The confusion on Thompson's face said otherwise. He probably couldn't imagine someone not wanting to be a part of something as historically significant as an attempted assassination investigation. Especially when the person in question was the so-called hero of the day. Thompson would have basked in the limelight if given the chance. The idea of not jumping to answer the agency's questions would have probably given him a stroke.

"Well, thanks again. I just wanted to shake the hand of one of the best agents we've ever had. You were a real golden boy, on the way up. No one climbed the ladder faster than you—which only goes to show how exceptional you were. Judging by the job you did today, that hasn't changed."

Bishop nodded his thanks, surprised by the compliment, especially since the tone sounded genuine.

Thompson pressed his earpiece as if listening to a transmission. But since Bishop didn't hear the telltale static typical of an incoming message, he was willing to bet a year's salary the guy was faking it.

"On my way," he said into the mic on his wrist. He grimaced, probably for Bishop's benefit. "Looks like they're waiting on me. Thanks again for what you did. It's good to see you're back where you belong, working protection detail, even if it's not for the Secret Service. See you around." He shook Bishop's hand again before following in Faulk's footsteps.

Bishop stood outside his car for several minutes after the agent left, surveying the area around him, the windows on the building overlooking the parking lot. Had Faulk and Thompson been watching from one of those windows? What was their real reason for hunting him down? They weren't Bishop's friends or coworkers. And neither had gone out of his way to speak to him during the planning leading up to Manning's visit. So why had they done so today?

Maybe he was being paranoid, especially since Thompson had seemed like such a stand-up guy just now. But he had reason to be paranoid. He had a son to worry about now. A son whose life was in danger. As far as he was concerned, everyone around the Mannings was a suspect until proved otherwise. And who better to pull off a kidnap-for-ransom scheme than someone who worked closely with the family, close enough to learn their secrets? Looking into those assigned to protect Earl and Julia Manning was already on Bishop's mental list of people to investigate. Faulk and Thompson had just moved to the top of that list.

He got into his Charger and sped out of the lot before anyone else could stop him. Once certain he wasn't being followed, he set his phone in the console and called his boss.

"Bishop," Mason's voice responded through the Bluetooth speaker overhead. "Where are you? I got stuck placating the former president after you turned down Harper's request. The next time I looked around, you were gone."

"I didn't turn her down. I just found out that she and I have a son. He's five years old."

After a long silence, Mason said, "Sounds like we have a lot to talk about."

"More than you know. But first, I could use some help from the Seekers. Is anyone available?"

"I'll make them available. What do you need?"

Chapter Eight

Harper was about to unlock her kitchen side door to go into her house, but hesitated. Clutching her keys like a weapon, she scanned the carport where she'd just parked her aging silver Camry after the long drive from Gatlinburg. The green rubber garbage can and yellow recycle bin sat side by side against the far wall as usual. Just a few feet farther down that wall, the door to the outside laundry room was closed to keep the occasional raccoon out. Everything looked the way it should. But something was off.

Smoke.

She wrinkled her nose at the unmistakable stench of cigarettes. Since she didn't smoke, the smell had her nervous, especially after Gage's comments about the kidnapper possibly watching her. Although rare, people did sometimes hike through the woods in this beautiful rural area without regard for the property they might be on. Had one of them dropped a cigarette?

Her closest neighbor, Blake Carter, lived fifty yards to the south of her east-facing home. His 1950's white-and-gray ranch house was barely visible through the trees and the sagging chain-link fence that separated their properties. Had he taken up smoking? Even if he had, would she be able to smell it from this far away?

There weren't any other homes close enough to be the culprits. Several acres of land separated most of these rural properties from each other. A deep, wide creek formed a meandering border to the west before eventually spilling into the French Broad River. And her gravel driveway was too long to allow cigarette smoke to drift up from the road if someone was passing by.

"Everything okay, Harper?"

She whirled around to see her next-door neighbor standing on the other side of her car.

Blake's eyes widened in dismay. He backed up several feet, holding his hands out in front of him as if to reassure her. "Didn't mean to startle you. I thought you saw me waving at the fence when you turned into your driveway."

"No. I didn't see you." Given his aggressive behavior over the past few weeks, she didn't temper her words or soften them with a smile. His surprising, sudden interest in her was annoying at best, harassing at worst. And she was in no mood to put up with him this afternoon.

She palmed the keys in her hand. "It's been a trying morning, Blake. Do you need something? I have a lot of work to catch up on." She shoved the key in the lock.

He stepped toward the front of the car, as if to round it to her side. "Is something wrong? You seem upset."

She quickly pushed open the door. "When someone sneaks up on me, I tend to get that way." He stopped; his crestfallen look had her feeling guilty. But in light of how handsy he'd been the last time he'd come over, the guilt was fleeting. "What do you want?"

He seemed to take her question as an invitation and moved closer. "If you're having a bad day, maybe I could bring you some iced tea. I just made a fresh pitcher and—"

"Blake, *enough*."

He blinked like an owl, a hurt look crossing his face as he backed up again.

She silently cursed her frayed nerves and lack of tact. She didn't want to encourage him. But she didn't want to make an enemy of the only person who lived within an acre of her, either. "Look, I'm sorry. I just… Like I said, it's been a trying morning. I appreciate your concern, but it's unwarranted. Okay?"

"Sure, sure. No worries. I'll check back later."

"No, no. I don't think that's a good…" She sighed as he headed across her side yard toward the fence between their properties, a fence that was falling down in many places and allowed him far too easy access to her house. Maybe he'd get the message if she hired someone to erect an eight-foot privacy fence on her side. It would cost a small fortune. But it might be worth the strain on her finances to do it.

She wrinkled her nose at another whiff of smoke and belatedly realized that she'd forgotten to ask Blake about it. Well, she wasn't going to go chasing after him, that was for sure. Instead, she hurried inside. After flipping the dead bolt, she dropped her purse onto the nearest counter then hesitated. There was a new smell in the air. Not smoke. Wait. Was that oleander?

"Please tell me that scrawny guy isn't who you've been dating," a woman's voice called out.

She whirled around, a scream lodged in her throat. Her sister stood in the doorway between the kitchen and the family room, a bottle of beer clutched in her right hand.

Harper cleared her throat. "You scared me half to death, Cynthia. What are you doing here? How did you even get inside?" She checked the relatively new alarm keypad on the wall. The light was green. It should have been red and beeping by now, threatening to go off if she didn't key in her code. Had she forgotten to set the alarm?

"I stole my mom's extra key out of her purse, the one you gave her in case of an emergency."

She turned around. "*Is* there an emergency?"

Her sister held up her beer. "This is the last brewski

in your refrigerator and I couldn't find any in the pantry. Does that count?"

"Hardly."

Cynthia waved to a potted plant on the counter that looked as if it had suffered a windstorm. One of the few remaining pink blossoms clinging to the stems told her it was the oleander she'd smelled earlier.

"It's that time of year. Mom's oleanders are in bloom. You know how nuts she is about those things. She's been pawning them off on everyone with a pulse. I figured maybe you could find a home for mine."

"Gee. Thanks. I'll add it to the dozen others she's given me in the past." She frowned. "That poor plant looks ready to keel over."

Cynthia shrugged. "Plants aren't my thing." She pulled a key out of her jeans' pocket and tossed it onto the counter. "You can give that back to my mom next time you're in Nashville visiting the homestead."

"The oleander or the key?"

"Either. Both. You didn't answer my question."

"About dating?"

She nodded.

"Blake Carter is the last man I'd date. I'm not dating *anyone* right now."

"But you *were*. Mom said so."

"Weeks ago, and only a few times. It didn't work out."

"That's a shame. You're really not bad to look at when you do your hair and makeup, like today. You'd probably smile more, too, if you *got* some." She winked.

Harper couldn't help smiling at her outrageous sister. "Why aren't you in Gatlinburg with the rest of the family?"

"I had things to do."

Meaning she'd probably gotten bored and had taken off even though her mom and Harper's dad had wanted both Cynthia and their little half brother, Tyler, to be with them this whole weekend. Harper would have, but with precious little time until the ransom deadline, she'd wanted to hurry back home.

"Where's your car?" Harper asked. "I didn't see it parked in the side yard when I pulled into the carport."

"Dean gave me a ride on his bike. It's around back. He's having a smoke. I told him you don't like people smelling up your house." She waved toward the sliding-glass door at the end of the family room, barely visible through the kitchen opening.

"Thanks for that. I was surprised to see you out the window in Gatlinburg this morning. I thought summer classes were still in session." At least she knew where the cigarette smoke was coming from. Harper opened the refrigerator and took out a bottle of wine she'd opened last night. If her sister could drink before five o'clock, she could, too.

"I'm taking this summer off. Life's too short to study all the time."

"I hardly think four years of college constitutes *all the time*." Once she had the filled glass in her hand, she took a deep appreciative sip. Then she moved past her sister into the family room, only to stop at the sight of a stack of envelopes and grocery store ads on the coffee table.

Cynthia strolled past her and dropped down onto the couch. "I checked your mail for you. Looks like you're due for your annual girly exam. The rest are bills. If you don't pay your utilities by next week, they're going to shut off your electricity. Are you having money problems?"

Harper's stomach dropped. Had the kidnapper sent another note? Had Cynthia seen it? "I'd prefer that you not open my mail." She sifted through the stack, both relieved and disappointed when there wasn't another letter. She checked the utility bill before tossing everything back on the table. "I'm not late paying my electric bill. Why would you say that?"

"Just trying to get a rise out of you, sis. Lighten up." She took a swig of beer and propped her legs on top of the table.

Harper gritted her teeth. "Would you please get your shoes off the furniture?"

"Why? That table's a piece of junk. Did you pick it up at a garage sale? You should get my mom to let go of one of those antiques she collects."

Harper shook her head. "I know the rules of the Manning household. No one touches your mom's garden, or her antiques."

"Oh, I wouldn't be so sure. I think she'd jump at the chance to part with some of her precious hoard for her favorite stepdaughter."

"I'm Julia's *only* stepdaughter. And I don't want another table. I want the one I've got. It may be cheap and falling apart, but it was *my* mother's. It's one of the few things I have left of hers."

Cynthia winced and gingerly lowered her feet to the floor. "Sorry, honestly. I had no idea that was your mom's."

Harper sighed. "How would you? It's been in my bedroom at the foot of my bed forever. I only recently brought it out here when I ordered a new chair for the other room. You don't visit often enough to know what I have or don't have."

"Not true. I noticed that ugly silver vase you used to carry around everywhere you lived. It was on your mantel last time I was here. Did you move it to the bedroom?"

"Vase?" She glanced at the mantel and realized Cynthia was referring to the urn. Shane's urn. "I, uh, threw it away. I was dusting one day and it fell, got dented. The top wouldn't stay on anymore, so I got rid of it."

"Well, if I'd known that's all it would have taken for you to throw that hideous thing away, I'd have accidentally dropped it years ago. It always reminded me of one of those things you put dead peoples' ashes in." She shuddered.

Harper's face heated. She put her hands on her hips, hoping her sister hadn't noticed. "Is there a reason you came all this way to break into my house other than to open my mail and criticize my decorating choices?"

"It's not breaking in if you have a key."

"A *stolen* key."

"Whatever. I was just curious about what's going on."

Harper kept her expression carefully blank. Had her sister overheard something? Had her father mentioned Shane, perhaps when talking to his lawyer about that nondisclosure agreement, and she overheard him? "What do you mean, you're curious about what's going on?"

She rolled her eyes. "Oh puhleeze. I'm twenty years old, not a naïve child. It's obvious you're stressed out about something. I saw you going into that conference room earlier, looking all worried. Then everyone left except you and that hot Secret Service guy who used to guard you when you lived in Nashville and I was stuck in DC with my mom and your dad. What was his name? Monk? Cardinal? One of those religious titles."

"Bishop. His first name is Gage."

Cynthia smirked. "*Gage.* Like the tool a mechanic uses? No wonder everyone calls him by his last name."

A flash of annoyance had Harper crossing her arms. "It's spelled differently. Is there a point to this conversation?"

"Are you dating him? Is that why you left Gatlinburg without even saying hi to my mom? So you could get naked with hot preacher guy and explore the Big O?"

"Good grief. And it's Bishop, not preacher guy."

"He *is* hot. You can't deny that."

Harper sighed. "I'm not denying it. But that doesn't mean that we're going to get naked and have *orgasms* together." At Cynthia's raised eyebrows, she said, "You thought I didn't know what the Big O was?"

"I was worried you didn't. Guess I figured that one day I'd have to sit you down and explain the facts of life. You don't get out much."

"We are *not* discussing my love life."

"What love life?"

"Cynthia—"

"Okay, okay."

Harper carefully lowered herself onto the couch so she wouldn't slosh her wine out of the glass, then rested her free arm across her eyes.

"Harper?"

"Hmm?"

"If you're not going to jump his bones, can I? I mean, have you seen his shoes? What are they, a size twelve? You know what that means. He must have a really big—"

"Enough!" She dropped her arm and shot her sister a reproachful glance.

Cynthia grinned. "Admit it. You've missed me."

Harper set her wineglass on the end table. "God help me, I have. Get over here you little devil."

They wrapped each other in a tight hug. Harper held on longer than her sister probably wanted, but she'd needed that hug far more than she'd realized. When she let go, she kept her arm around her sister's waist and they both leaned back against the cushions.

"I'm sorry I didn't see your mom before I left Gatlinburg," Harper said. "That was rude. I should have sought her out. Please tell her I'm sorry, that I'll visit her soon."

"To give her back her key?"

She smiled. "Is that why you took it? To force me to visit y'all in Nashville?"

"I would never be that devious." But the look on her sister's face told Harper that's exactly why'd she'd taken it.

"When you graduate college and get settled in your career—whatever that ends up being—I hope you find the love of your life. Then I hope you have lots and lots of babies." She rolled her head on the cushion to look at her sister. "And every single one of them is exactly like you."

Cynthia gave her a horrified look. "Now that's just downright mean."

They both laughed and, for the next few minutes, they were content to sit together in peace. A rarity with the two of them. Normally they were either fighting or Cynthia was playing some kind of practical joke on her.

"Don't worry about my mom," Cynthia finally said. "I don't think she even realized you were in town. She won't find out from me. And your dad is so busy lapping up all the media attention that he probably already forgot about your visit." She arched a brow. "Why *did* you meet with that Bishop guy? Isn't he the one who messed up and had to be replaced by Faulk?"

She frowned at her sister. "Who said he messed up?"

She shrugged. "I don't know. One of the agents, I suppose. Maybe Thompson. Yeah, I'm pretty sure he's said as much before."

"Well, he's wrong. Gage is one of the most honorable men I know. He did everything exactly right. What happened wasn't his fault. But he sure took the blame."

"What happened?"

"Ancient history. I'm not going to discuss it."

"Too bad you don't keep a diary. I'll bet there are a lot of really juicy secrets in that brainiac head of yours that no one would ever expect."

"What makes you think I *don't* keep a diary?"

Cynthia's eyes widened. She jumped up as if to hunt down the diary, but Harper grabbed her arm and yanked her back down. That was all she needed, for her sister to go rummaging through her room and find the baby book she kept under her mattress. It documented her pregnancy and had a memorial for Shane in the back. It was far more incriminating than a diary ever would be.

"Aw, come on, Harp. Let me read it. Out loud. It'll be fun."

"No. It wouldn't. Besides, I don't have a diary. I'm not dumb enough to write down anything that might incriminate or embarrass me later." She'd have to remember to put that baby book in her safe. She'd never thought about it being a liability before.

"Ouch. Remind me to never let you read mine." Cynthia tapped a tune against her thigh that only she could hear. "So, back to the guy with the really big—"

"Don't you dare say it!"

"—feet." Cynthia grinned.

"I'm not discussing Gage with you."

"Then what did you discuss with *him*? In the conference room?"

"Good grief, you're like a dog with a bone. Do you ever stop?"

She gave her a droll look. "Is that a real question?"

Harper rolled her eyes. "It's nothing juicy. Just a couple of…old acquaintances…catching up before dad's press conference. Gage was part of a private security company helping cover today's Fourth of July celebrations. He's the one who stopped that guy from shooting dad."

"Wow. Seriously?"

"Seriously. I don't know the details, but I overheard some of the agents chatting about it when I was leaving."

"Super cool."

Harper wasn't sure whether Cynthia meant someone shooting at her dad or Gage stopping him. Hopefully, it was the latter.

They talked a few more minutes then a tapping noise sounded on the back door. They both leaned forward to see past the opening to the dining room off the back of the house. Dean stood at the sliding-glass door, cigarette in hand, motioning to Cynthia.

"Looks like my future ex-boyfriend is ready to leave. I'd better get going."

"Future ex? I thought you really liked this one. You've been with him for several months now."

"His shoes are too small."

Harper burst out laughing.

They both stood and hugged each other.

Harper tucked her sister's straight black hair behind her ears. "You be careful on that bike. Wear your helmet."

"Yes, Mother." It was Cynthia's turn to roll her eyes. She jogged to the back door and gave Harper a parting wave before heading outside.

A few moments later, Harper stood at the front windows, watching her sister hang on to Dean as he sped down the driveway, shooting gravel up from beneath his tires. And, of course, she wasn't wearing a helmet.

She shook her head and turned around, letting out an embarrassing squeak of surprise a split second before recognizing the man standing in her family room.

Gage Bishop.

"Hello, Harper." He made a point of looking down at his shoes. "They're a size thirteen, not twelve."

Her face flushed so hot, she was amazed she didn't burst into flames. "I need a drink." She grabbed her half full wineglass and strode past him into the kitchen.

Chapter Nine

Harper tossed the wine into the sink and went on a hunt in the pantry for something stronger. When she stepped out with a can of soda and a bottle of Hennessey whiskey, she stopped, unable to tear her gaze from the insanely sexy Adonis lounging in her kitchen doorway. As furious as she was that he'd broken into her home and eavesdropped on her conversation, she was practically choking on her tongue at the way his crossed arms made his impressive biceps strain against his suit jacket. Her fingers itched to yank off that jacket and run across those delicious muscles. And she wouldn't stop there.

His slow, suggestive smile told her he knew exactly what she was thinking, and it had her belly doing somersaults.

He motioned at the whiskey. "Was it something I said?"

She narrowed her eyes in warning and crossed to the other side of the kitchen, purposely turning her back on him. After splashing some whiskey into a glass, she picked up the can of soda to mix with it. But after a moment of hesitation, she set the soda down and drained the whiskey in one single gulp.

The burn down her throat had her coughing, her eyes watering. She took several deep breaths, her hands braced against the sink. The Hennessey on an empty stomach, on top of the wine she'd already drank, probably wasn't the wisest choice she'd made today. Then again, between the ever-present fear for her son and her hopeless obsession with Gage, her nerves were tangled in knots. Maybe she should cut herself a break.

When she felt she could stand without wobbling, she turned around to confront the final straw that had brought her to this low point. "You're welcome to some Hennessey. But you'll have to make it yourself. I'm not feeling particularly hostessy at the moment."

"I don't drink."

She scoffed. "Since when, pool house boy?"

He arched a brow. "Since I found out I have a son and his life is in danger. I'm staying sober and in control."

Her face heated. Again. And now she was feeling guilty over the stupid whiskey. She crossed her arms and leaned back against the counter. "You were supposed to call me."

"I did. Three times."

She frowned and grabbed her purse from the counter where she'd set it when she'd come inside. After riffling through it for her phone, she sighed. There were three missed calls, from the same number.

"I had it on silent for the meeting and forgot to turn the ringer back on." She updated him as a contact then tossed the phone back in her purse. "What'd you do to get my address? Call in a favor with the Secret Service?"

"Something far easier than that. We used the internet."

"We?"

"The Justice Seekers."

"Right. Well, this property isn't listed under my name, for security reasons." She grimaced. "Not that it stopped the kidnapper from finding me. Still, I'll bet your Seekers had to do all kinds of searches and cross-checks to figure out where I live. How long did it take?"

"About thirty seconds."

She squeezed the bridge of her nose. "Of course it did.

What about getting inside my house? My sister had a key. What did you use? Some kind of fancy picklock set?"

"Credit card. Your locks couldn't keep a determined toddler out. You should upgrade all your windows and doors for something much more secure."

"On that we agree. And you need to learn better manners. Breaking into my house isn't a way to get on my good side."

"I'm not trying to get on your good side. I'm trying to keep you, and our son, alive. I purposely got here before you so I could make sure no one was waiting to harm you."

"I guess Cynthia's lucky you recognized her and didn't shoot, huh?" She rolled her eyes and grabbed a bottle of water from the refrigerator.

"Lucky for her *and* her boyfriend."

She froze and slowly turned around. "You're *serious*? That wasn't a joke?"

He lifted the edge of his suit jacket, revealing his holstered gun. "I don't carry this because it matches my outfit."

She stared at the gun a long moment and then grabbed a bottle of pain pills from another cabinet. After shaking out two, she hesitated before adding another. Nothing seemed strong enough for today's particular level of insanity.

"Is Cynthia having any money troubles that you know of?"

She clutched the pills in her hand. "Dad's paying her tuition and board like he did mine. He's frugal, but generally reasonable. He's not the type to lavish anyone with extras. Money's probably tighter than she'd like. But I doubt she's really hurting."

"What about her boyfriend? What's his story?"

"He's a student at Vanderbilt, like Cynthia. But that's about all I know."

"Full name?"

"Dean Everly. Want me to call Cynthia for his social and birthdate?" she teased.

He smiled. "Maybe later. Does your sister know about your pregnancy?"

She blinked then looked away. Her pregnancy—the long lonely months, the awfulness of losing Shane within moments of his birth—wasn't a topic she wanted to discuss, or even think about.

"Harper?"

She reluctantly met his gaze.

"I know that time in your life has to be an incredibly painful topic. I promise I wouldn't be asking if it wasn't important."

She pulled in a shaky breath, nodded. "I know."

"Could Cynthia have known about it?"

"I honestly don't see how. She's a lot younger than me and—"

"Six years. She would have been fourteen or fifteen when you were carrying Shane. Old enough to know what's going on when your body started changing."

"Did you remember that on your own? The difference in our ages? Or is that from one of those Justice Seeker internet searches?"

He shifted against the doorframe and crossed his long legs at the ankle. "I remember everything about you, Harper."

His declaration caught her off guard, especially since he didn't offer an explanation. She gave a nervous laugh. "I Imagine you remember pretty much everything about the people you've been assigned to protect over the years."

He slowly shook his head. "Only you."

Her mouth went dry; a legion of butterflies took flight in her stomach. The look in his eyes seemed almost… hungry. The answering hunger inside her took her completely by surprise. She tore her gaze from his, hoping he wouldn't realize just how out of sorts he was making her.

"I, um, I doubt Cynthia knew anything. About my pregnancy. She was in DC with my dad and her mom, living at the White House."

"What about weekends? Holidays? Didn't she see you then?"

"Early on, a few times, sure. We'd meet up at my father's house when he took some time off, as much as any president can really take time off. But once I started showing, that ended. I never left the rental house after that."

"What about your stepmom, Julia? Did she know?"

"Well, yes, but she wouldn't have told Cynthia. Can you imagine? A teenage girl, especially one as rebellious as my sister, having that kind of power over my father's reputation and career? No way. The only people who knew were my father and Julia."

"You said there was a midwife in the rental with you. Did you go see a doctor, too?"

"The midwife *was* my doctor. My turn. I understand Cynthia getting here before me. She probably hit the road while you and I were still in the conference room. But how did you get here before either of us? How long were you here before she arrived?"

"Twenty, thirty minutes. Give or take."

"Now I know you're exaggerating. That's impossible." She started to cross her arms and realized she still hadn't taken the pills. She tossed them back and washed them down with the water bottle.

"I took a shortcut," he said. "Headache?"

"Like you wouldn't believe. Its name is Gage Bishop." His mouth quirked in a wry grin.

Good grief, he was sexy when he did that. Who was she kidding? He was sexy no matter what he did.

She took another sip of water, using the time to compose

herself again. "There *aren't* any shortcuts to this place. You had to take I-40, which leads directly to the road out front. That's the same route I took, and Cynthia, too, I'm sure."

He shrugged noncommittally and moved past her to look through a slit in the blinds on the kitchen door. "Notice anything after you came in?"

"Other than a nosy neighbor, that my sister had broken into my house, her soon-to-be ex-boyfriend smoking on my back porch, and later, a six-foot-two-inch man hovering in my doorway?"

"Six foot three."

She arched a brow. "Funny how you keep correcting me to say everything is bigger than I thought it was. Is there anything else you want to clarify, size-wise?"

"Well, if we're being really honest here, my—"

"Don't you dare! Forget I asked." Her face was flaming hot.

Laughter rumbled in his chest.

She shoved her long hair back, belatedly wishing she'd braided it or put it in a ponytail. "I think you were about to tell me something else I should have noticed when I came inside. The G-rated version, please."

"But the R-rated one is so much more fun," he teased.

"Gage—"

He winked then tapped the alarm keypad beside the door. "This wasn't set when I came in."

That wink obliterated about fifty of her IQ points. No wonder she'd fallen for him back in college.

He was waiting for her reply. What had he said? The alarm. It wasn't set. "Right. I remember wondering about that. But I figured I forgot to set it this morning. It's fairly new, not exactly muscle memory yet."

He considered that. "Does anyone else have a key to this place? Maybe your neighbor, Blake Carter?"

"No way. How did you know his name?"

"You mentioned it when you were talking to your sister."

"Well, of course I did," she grumbled. She'd mentioned a lot of things. Embarrassing things. Like how hot he was. And the Big O. "Exactly, um, how much did you hear of our conversation?"

His eyes sparkled with amusement. "*All* of it."

Her face heated, again, which was really annoying considering she was twenty-six and should be well past the blushing stage in her life.

"Do you sometimes forget to lock your doors? Like you forgot the alarm?"

She was about to insist that she always locked her doors, but hesitated. "Honestly, I couldn't say. Living out here in the country, with only one neighbor close by, I never used to bother with the locks. But Blake's been so annoying lately I've started making a habit of it. Or trying to."

"Lately? This is new behavior on his part?"

"I hadn't thought about it like that, but yeah, I guess it is."

"How long has he lived next door?"

"Longer than I've been here. I bought this place two years ago."

Gage pulled out his phone and started typing a text. "You said you'd never dated him. What about sharing rides into town? Maybe grabbing a coffee together?"

"Okay, first of all, it's not fair that you know so much because of eavesdropping on my conversation with my sister. Second, give me some credit. He's definitely not my type."

"You're definitely *his* type. He was like a lap dog out there, panting at your heels."

"Jealous, *Bishop*?"

He frowned as he continued typing. "Don't call me Bishop."

"Why not? Everyone else does."

He put the phone away. "It doesn't sound right coming from you. How has your neighbor been bothering you? What's he done?"

She waved a hand in the air. "Stupid stuff. Doesn't matter."

He moved directly in front of her. "This Good Samaritan person hid our son for five years and is now trying to trade him for ransom. It's likely he's got someone keeping an eye on you, on this house. And you just told me your neighbor is acting differently than he has for the past two years. *It matters.*"

Her hand shook as she pushed her hair back again. "You think Blake's in league with the kidnapper?"

"I think it's a possibility. We haven't ruled anyone out yet. Mason has the whole team working on this, so things are going to move fast. They have to, with only a few days until the exchange. What's he done lately that's different than before?"

Her stomach did a little flip with him standing so close. Polite, nice, sweet Gage had been impossible to resist when she was a smitten nineteen or twenty year-old. This edgier, more confident, and oh so determined Gage was even more compelling. He had her selfishly wanting to step into his arms and lay all her worries on his broad shoulders. But she was afraid that if she ever did that, she'd never be able to let him go.

She'd built a life without him, had been forced to. And he'd built one without her. Going back to the way things used to be was impossible. Those people no longer existed. Did she even want to risk her heart with him? What if he rejected her? Again? She didn't want to go back to the broken woman she'd once been. And if there was anything she knew for sure, Gage Bishop, of all men, had the power to break her.

"Harper? What's changed with your neighbor?"

"It's just that… Well, aside from the small grassy areas right around the house, the rest is woods. And a navigable creek on the southern property line. But the previous owner built this house really close to Blake's. That means, every time I come up my driveway or turn on a light, he can see it, if he's watching. And lately it seems like he's been watching quite a bit. He's always underfoot, knocking on my door when I get home or wanting to visit."

She decided to leave out the parts about him brushing against her and swearing it was an accident. It had happened too many times not to be deliberate. Knowing Gage, if he thought Blake had touched her inappropriately, he'd stride over there and teach the man a lesson with his fists. "He's a pest, for sure, annoying. But he seems harmless."

She wasn't sure Gage believed her glossed-over version of events. But he didn't press the issue.

"I'm surprised you bought a place outside Knoxville. I expected you'd build a house on your family's Nashville estate. They certainly have the land for it. I remember your father offering it as an option."

"Don't get me wrong. I love my family. But living on the estate, even if it was at the back of their considerable acreage, would be too close for comfort. I want them far enough away so they're not visiting me all the time but not so far that I can't drive up and see them without having to drive forever to get there. What's this have to do with the kidnapper or figuring out who might be working with him?"

He shrugged. "Probably nothing. I was curious. You said you've lived here two years, but the alarm is new. How new?"

"It was installed two weeks ago, *before* I received the ransom note. The two aren't related, unless you really think Blake's involved somehow."

"If it makes you feel better, I think it's unlikely that he

is, given that he lived here before you bought your property. But I texted the team to do a background check on him, just in case. Was the ransom note mailed to you, or left at your door?"

"If I answer that, will I get a break? Or should I call my lawyer?"

"Sorry. I can be a bit intense when working a case."

"I think the word you're looking for is *relentless*. Yes, the ransom note came in the mail. Or…well, I think it did. It had a stamp on it and was in my mailbox. I'll answer exactly one more question before I cry uncle. After that, I'm either pouring myself another whiskey or breaking out a gallon of ice cream."

"What kind of ice cream?"

"Is that the final question you chose?"

He laughed. "Only if I get a follow-up."

"Mint chocolate chip."

"I'm not surprised. You always used to keep a pint in the freezer—for emergencies. I was never sure what constituted an emergency, though."

She smiled, remembering the few times she'd been able to entice him to watch a movie or to share a meal in the main house instead of retreating to the pool house. It hadn't happened often. But she'd treasured the times it had.

His gaze dropped to her mouth and his smile faded. His expression turned serious again. "Where's the original ransom note?"

"In the floor safe in my office."

He strode out of the kitchen.

She called to him as she pushed away from the counter to follow. "It's down the hall on the—"

He disappeared into her office.

"—left," she finished. Sighing, she hurried to catch up.

Chapter Ten

After retrieving the envelope and the original ransom note from the floor safe, Harper handed them to Gage, who was kneeling beside her. She was surprised to see he'd put on latex gloves. Even more surprising was that he put the note and envelope into two clear bags, like the kind law enforcement might use.

He gestured at a folder in the safe. "That looks like it came from a lab. Is it from the one your father hired to examine the ransom note?"

"It is." She reluctantly pulled it out then flipped open the folder to reveal the baggie she'd tucked inside.

His gaze shot to hers. "Is that Shane's hair?"

She swallowed against the lump that was suddenly in her throat. "I know it sounds crazy, but I couldn't bear to give it *all* away. I'd have nothing left of him."

His expression softened with sympathy. "It doesn't sound crazy to me. Hopefully soon you'll have Shane here instead of a hair sample." He gently took the baggie and held it up to examine it. "There isn't much here, but there are root tags. Might be enough for a new DNA test."

Her stomach dropped. "I don't... I don't see why it's necessary. The reports proved the mother-son relationship. Why run the same test again?"

"Labs make mistakes. It's better to be sure. Don't you think?"

She shrugged. "I guess so."

He moved to the desk, ransom note and envelope in hand, and sat in the chair.

"Where'd you get the gloves and evidence bags?" She sat across from him on the love seat.

He held the envelope up to the overhead light, studying it. "I always take a go-bag with me, no matter where I am. It has the bare minimum of supplies in case I have to leave in a hurry and can't go home first. Since you mentioned in Gatlinburg that you had the original ransom note here, I took some gloves and baggies out of it to bring inside."

"Gloves and baggies are the bare minimum of supplies?"

He gave her a shocked look. "You mean you don't carry evidence collection tools in your purse?"

"Ha. Ha. What else do you carry? A backup gun?"

"Of course. And a knife. Never leave home without a knife."

"That suit jacket must have all kinds of hidden pockets."

He smiled. "I use ankle holsters for the gun and knife." He ran his hand across the envelope. "I don't see any signs to indicate that someone checked this for prints, or took DNA samples from the glue flap and stamp."

"We weren't trying to gather evidence for a trial. We were determining whether the ransom demand was a hoax."

"Understood. But I'll have my team perform a deeper analysis, see what pops up. Has this Sam guy attempted to contact you since he sent the note?"

"No." She shifted on the love seat, impressed by his depth of knowledge, and his confidence. "In addition to providing security and performing investigations, the Justice Seekers are evidence technicians? They process crime scenes, too?"

"We do whatever it takes to get the job done. All of us

start with a common skill set. But we each have our own specialties, too, based on our previous occupations. That's the basis for our monikers. Mason calls us his Knights of the Round Table. His company is Camelot."

"Truly?"

"Truly. Our headquarters looks just like a castle." He shrugged. "It's mostly for fun. None of us takes it too seriously. But the monikers are fairly accurate."

Intrigued, she asked, "What's yours?"

"*The Bodyguard*, of course."

"Of course." She laughed.

He exchanged the envelope for the note.

"What's next? I mean, I don't see how analyzing this stuff can help us bring Shane home."

"My goal is to figure out who Sam is *before* the exchange. Information is power, and could be the key to ensuring we get our son back alive—especially if we can determine where Shane's being held and perform a rescue operation. That's my ultimate goal. It puts us in control of what happens. DNA, or a fingerprint, could give us a name, assuming he's got a criminal record and is in the FBI's databases."

"FBI? Let me guess, one of your Seekers is a former agent?"

"More than one, actually. And we don't go through official channels in a case like this, so don't worry about this staying low-key. It will."

"I appreciate that. What if he's not in the databases?"

"There are other things we can look for, like using the postmark to help us determine where the mail originated. If he mailed it at a post office, we might get lucky and have surveillance video of his license plate. Then again, he may have stuck it in some random person's home mailbox to mail it. It's a long shot, but there are other things we'll look for, too. Like the writing on the note itself."

"Writing? It looks typed to me, like on a computer. There's no handwriting to examine."

He set the note down. "You're right. *Printed* is a more accurate description. There are regulations on printers that require metadata to be embedded within the page, invisible to the naked eye. Metadata can tell us the manufacturer, model, sometimes even the serial number of the printer used. Depending on the types of records the company maintains, that could lead us to the person who purchased the printer."

"I never would have thought of that. This could be over really fast."

He gave her a look of caution. "Don't get your hopes up just yet. Someone demanding two million dollars isn't likely to be dumb enough to make it that easy. Sam probably printed the note on someone else's printer, like a library or a business center in a hotel. A fingerprint or DNA hit is our best bet right now."

She slumped back against the love seat. "Now I'm getting depressed."

"Don't be. We may only have a couple of days. But all twelve Justice Seekers are working on this. Plus, Mason's lining up a private lab to process anything we send him. Tests that normally take weeks, or months, can be done in a few hours in most cases—if you don't have to deal with the backlog and waiting in the queue to get processed. Mason has more than enough money to make that happen. He's already hired a linguistics expert who's examining the phrasing on the copy of the note I texted before I drove up here. They may be—"

"Drove. That reminds me. I didn't see any vehicles when I got home. Where did you park?"

"On the other side of the creek that runs behind your house. As I was saying, we might be able to get a basic profile of Sam, like the geographical region of the country where he lives, education level, age, sex, economic status—"

"Gage?"

"Hmm?"

"Why would you park on the other side of the creek? How exactly did you get here?"

He sighed heavily. "I took a canoe from the campground where I parked my car. Coming up to your property from the south, even with part of that trip being in a canoe, cut the commute considerably. I told you I'd taken a shortcut. You just didn't believe me."

"Yeah, well, if you'd mentioned a canoe, I might have. That took some ingenuity. I'm impressed. Sorry for the interruption. You were talking about economic status in this profile that can be created. You mean like whether Sam grew up in a wealthy family?"

"Exactly. People speak differently based on their up-bringing, their experiences. The slightest distinction in verb choice or even which adjectives are used can reveal a lot about them."

"The FBI has nothing on you Justice Seekers."

"Mason would take that as the ultimate compliment. Look, I know you're tired of my questions, but time is critical. I need to ask a few more. And if you don't mind, I'm going to record what you say so I can forward it to the Seekers. That way, they can immediately start investigating whatever you tell me."

She pulled her legs up beneath her and propped her head on her hand. "Whatever it takes. Fire at will, oh wise one."

His mouth quirked. "You're still feeling the effects of that whiskey, aren't you?"

"Only a little, unfortunately. I should have brought the bottle in here for the inquisition."

"I'll make this as painless as possible so you don't have to abuse the Hennessey." He shoved his gloves into his suit jacket pocket and crossed to the love seat. After setting the phone on the back of the couch between them, he sat beside her.

"The midwife, what was her name?"

"Colette Proust. And before you ask, yes, my father's lawyer hired an investigator to try to find her after the ransom note came. She doesn't live in the Nashville area anymore and neither does her brother, so—"

"Her brother?"

"Victor. The two of them shared an apartment in town until she came to live with me. The lawyer couldn't locate either of them."

"The same lawyer who was in the conference room today?"

"Yes. Mr. Roth."

"Was he working for your father when the midwife was hired? Is he the one who vetted her?"

"Let me guess. You suspect the lawyer of being involved, too?"

"It's a possibility."

"Do you suspect *everyone* of being involved in the kidnapping?"

"Did he vet the Prousts?"

She blew out an impatient breath. "I honestly don't know who looked into them or made the final hiring decision. Needless to say, it's not like I could run around interviewing potential midwives on my own and still keep my pregnancy a secret. My father arranged everything for me—and, yes, he likely used Mr. Roth for most of that. But I'm telling you, Colette was just as devastated as I was about Shane. Someone at the hospital must have stolen him and convinced her he'd died."

"Did you talk to anyone at the hospital?"

Her stomach did a nervous flip. "No, which sounds foolish now. But my whole life at that time was centered around keeping the pregnancy a secret. The plan was to put Colette's name on the birth certificate as the mother and then have Mr. Roth perform a private adoption to explain why I suddenly had a baby. But after the baby died—" She grimaced. "After I was *told* that he'd died, I didn't call the hospital and nullify all of my work keeping the pregnancy a secret. I trusted her."

Maybe she shouldn't have. Those words seemed to hang in the air between them, unspoken.

"You said the death certificate arrived a few weeks later. What can you tell me about it?"

She licked her suddenly dry lips. "It had Colette listed as the mother, just as we'd planned with the birth certificate. The, uh, father's name was left blank." She didn't look at him when she said that. It felt like a betrayal to not have listed him. But it would have destroyed the secrecy they'd worked so hard to maintain. "As to who in the hospital signed it, I don't remember. Some administrator or doctor."

Harper forced herself to meet his gaze. "The mistakes I made are like neon signs, in hindsight. I wish I'd done things differently." If she'd been open about the pregnancy, would Gage have heard about the baby, or seen his picture in news reports, and realized Shane was his son? Things might have been so different. If only.

"You were young, under a lot of stress, doing the best you could. Don't second-guess yourself now."

She nodded her thanks even though she didn't agree with him. She'd made such foolish decisions. "Anyway, at the time, I had no reason to suspect that she'd lied to me. Or that someone else had lied to her. We were like sisters, really close. I'm more inclined to believe that she wasn't in on the plot and that something bad happened to her."

"At the time of Shane's birth? Or recently?"

She blinked. "Good question. I guess I was thinking that someone stole Shane from her and…did something to her when he was a baby. But if she's the one who stole him, then maybe she's Sam. Or working with Sam."

"Or Sam took Shane from her later, after finding out whose child he was, thinking he could profit from that knowledge. Do you still have the death certificate?"

Her stomach twisted at the thought of Colette being hurt, or worse, by Sam. In spite of logic telling her Colette had likely been part of the kidnapping scheme all along, she couldn't quite picture the woman she'd thought of as her friend doing something so…insidious. "It's in the safe, near the bottom, with gold leaf around the edge."

He knelt by the safe, sorted through it, and took a picture of the certificate. Then he sent another text, probably to the legion of Seekers working the case. It dawned on her that she couldn't have chosen a more qualified man to help her. Shane had lucked out in the father department. She just hoped her son—their son—got a chance to know the Gage Bishop she'd gotten to know, before everything had gone so wrong between them.

"I need the combination to your safe."

"Should I bother asking why?" She went ahead and told him the combination, which he promptly typed into his phone.

"A Seeker's already on the way here to courier everything to the lab Mason hired. We'll be gone before he arrives."

She stared at him, a bad feeling starting in the pit of her stomach. "Why won't we be here when the courier gets here?"

"Because I'm taking you with me to my home in Gatlinburg. My alarm system is state-of-the-art and my locks will actually keep bad guys out."

She stiffened. "Um, no, *you're* not taking me to Gatlinburg. I can hitch a ride with the courier."

"No. You can't. The lab is in the opposite direction.

It would set back the lab tests by hours. Don't worry. I'll give you time to pack a bag before we leave. And we'll have someone keep an eye on your mail and notify us the minute the kidnapper sends another note."

"Stop ignoring the elephant in the room. You're talking about taking me with you...in a *canoe*. That's not happening."

He slid his phone into his pocket. "I've sent the recording of our conversation." He tossed the lab report and evidence bags into the safe and shut the lid before flipping the rug over the top. "You can go ahead and pack a bag to last you for the next couple of days."

"Gage, I'm not stepping foot in a canoe."

He sighed heavily. "You're still afraid of the water, aren't you?"

"Yes. I am. Nearly drowning as a child will do that. I'm terrified of water. You know that. Why would you even think I'd step foot near the creek? I never go back there."

"It wasn't my first plan. I'd assumed I'd stay here with you until the next ransom note showed up. But I had no idea your security was such a disaster." He held up his hands to stop her argument. "I get it. You win. I'll ask another Seeker to drive us both to my house. I can retrieve my car later. Will that work?"

She smiled with relief. "Yes. Thank you."

"No problem. I'll set everything up. You can go ahead and pack and—" His phone buzzed in his pocket. He pulled it out, looked at the screen and swore. "We have to get out of here. Now."

"What? You mean in the canoe? No. I told you. I won't do that. I *can't*."

He took her hand and hauled her to her feet. "I set up some perimeter alarms around your property when I got here. One of them just went off." His fingers fairly flew over the phone as he typed yet another text.

"It must be Blake, my neighbor. He mentioned coming back later, even though I told him not to. He—"

Gage turned the phone around. "Does Blake usually wear camouflage and walk through the woods carrying an M-16 rifle?"

She stared at the screen in horror.

"I didn't think so." He grabbed her hand. "Let's go."

Chapter Eleven

Bishop snatched one of the life vests from the bottom of the canoe and turned around to put it on Harper. She wasn't there. She was twenty feet away, moving at a fast clip through the woods back toward her house.

He swore and threw the vest in the canoe before taking off after her. When he reached her, he used his body to block her way. "Harper, we have to—"

"I can't," she whispered harshly. "Don't you get it? I've tried everything to overcome my fear of water. Nothing works. I would rather face that gunman with my bare hands than get into that stupid canoe. Why can't we just take my car and drive out of here?"

"Keep your voice down," he reminded her. "We *can't* take your car. The gunmen triggered alarms I'd set on your neighbor's property, which gave us the head start we needed to get out before they saw us. But I'm sure they've reached your house by now. Even if we managed to sneak around them without being seen, the moment we start the engine, they'll be on top of us. I'm wicked accurate with a pistol. But I can't outshoot an M-16."

Her eyes widened as his words sank in. "Gun*men*? Plural? Just how many did those cameras of yours pick up?"

His jaw tightened. "Five."

"Oh my God. What do they want? This doesn't make sense. They can't get their ransom if they kill me."

"This may not be about ransom. It could be a domestic terrorist group out to attack the former president's family, likely in league with the would-be assassin who tried to kill your father this morning. All I know for sure is that people sneaking around in camo with ski masks covering their faces and military-style rifles aren't interested in a civilized chat. I'm sorry to do this, Harper. I really am. But I don't have a choice." He grabbed her, tossed her on his shoulder and took off toward the creek.

Knowing time wasn't on their side, he didn't bother with the life jackets. After peeling Harper's hands from around his neck, he set her in the front of the canoe, the part that was already floating on the water rather than sitting on the bank. It did the job. It kept her from trying to hop out. But the heated glare she gave him as she gripped the sides of the canoe wasn't something he'd likely recover from any time soon.

He shoved the canoe fully into the water and hopped into the back. Using every ounce of his strength, he quickly paddled them into the middle of the creek to take advantage of the strong current. They had to get around that first curve and out of sight before the gunmen figured out where they'd gone. Every muscle in his body was tense, fully expecting a bullet to come slicing through him at any moment. But they rounded the curve without incident, allowing him to breathe a little easier. He set the paddle down and tore off his suit jacket so he could move his arms more freely. Then he grabbed one of the life jackets. "Harper?"

Her back was ramrod-straight, her arms shaking as she clung to both sides of the canoe.

"Harper, here." He pitched the jacket. It landed right behind her. "All you have to do is reach down and grab the life jacket. Put your arms through it, with the opening to the front. Click the buckles together and—"

"No." Her voice sounded strained. If anything, her death grip on the canoe tightened, as evidenced by the mottled look of her hands.

"I'm not even paddling right now. The canoe is floating with the current. I'll keep it nice and steady, okay? Just pick up the jacket and put it on." When she didn't say anything, he added, "I know you're scared. But if you put the vest on, you won't have to be afraid anymore."

"I thought your car was on the other side. Why are we in the middle of the river, parallel with the shoreline instead of heading straight for it?"

"We're still in the creek, not the river. The car's a little ways down. The road didn't quite reach your place."

"How far?" she snapped.

"Not far," he lied, and started paddling again.

His phone buzzed in his pocket. He yanked it out. When he saw Brielle's number on the screen, a feeling of dread shot through him. She knew he was trying to get Harper to safety. He'd texted her while shepherding Harper across her backyard and into the woods. She wouldn't call him unless there was a problem.

He put the phone in speaker mode and shoved it in his shirt pocket so he could talk and still paddle. "What's the sit rep? And keep your voice low." He didn't want Harper hearing something that might make her even more terrified.

"Where are you?" Brielle's voice was barely above a whisper.

Since his phone was encrypted with every bell and whistle Mason's money could buy, he didn't worry about someone intercepting the signal and hearing the conversation, so he spoke plainly, without using code words. "Just past the first bend in the creek. What's your ETA?"

"Dalton and I are already on the property. They were in and out of the house in under a minute. I only know that because of the cameras you set up. We haven't found an obvious trail yet."

"Five guys wearing military-style boots. There have to be some prints in the yard."

"There are, mostly partials, and not that many. They're keeping to harder ground, leaving as few prints as possible. These guys are really good. If I hadn't seen the video from your perimeter alarms, and the cameras you put in the house, I'd swear you were wrong about them even being here. There're no cars, no motorcycles, no four-wheelers. A group of heavily armed men in the middle of nowhere, with no obvious transportation. What's that tell you, Bishop?"

"They've got a boat. They came up the same way I did."

"That's our assumption. Dalton's hoofing it to the creek right now to see if he can spot them anywhere. I'm not far behind. Dang his long legs."

Gage eyed the woods, looking for signs of pursuit. Even though the current was strong, working with his strokes to move them forward, a sense of impending doom settled over him just as it had this morning when he'd followed the suspicious man through the crowd.

The canoe rounded another wide bend, the shore on each side slipping farther away. "We're getting close to the French Broad River. My car's not that much farther after that. Maybe you and Dalton should head back to the house. I don't like the odds if they stumble across you two alone out there."

"Don't worry. We've got the element of surprise. And no way are we leaving your six until we find these guys. Backup is on the way. Caleb and the new Seeker that Mason just hired, Eli Dupree, are bookin' it down the highway, not far behind us. You keep heading to the rendezvous point while we handle things from this end."

"Roger that. I'll call once we're on the road." He ended the call and kept paddling. His deep, long strokes pushed them quickly through the water, but also rocked the canoe from side to side.

Harper definitely noticed.

She was hunched down now, as if trying to lower her center of gravity out of fear that she was going to be tossed from the canoe.

"What's going on?" she called back to him without turning around. "You're paddling like you're trying to win an Olympic race."

He debated what to tell her. He didn't want to make her even more afraid.

"Bishop? Please. I may be terrified but I still want to know what's happening."

Her calling him Bishop again was like a punch in the gut. She'd always called him Gage. Always. The first day he'd introduced himself to her and told her everyone called him Bishop, she'd taken his hand in hers and said she never would. She liked the name Gage. And given she fully intended them to be friends, she wasn't about to call him by his last name. Since that moment, it had become a symbol of their bond and the deep friendship they'd eventually formed.

"Bishop?"

He winced. "Brielle and Dalton are trying to find the gunmen. Caleb and Eli will be at your house soon to help."

"Trying? They don't know where they are?"

"They'll find them. Don't worry."

She was silent for a long moment. "What's this rendezvous point you mentioned? Is it the campground where you parked your car?"

"You heard me say that?"

"Yes. What's the rendezvous point?"

"The campground. It's not much farther. Maybe ten minutes."

"Make it five."

He grinned, relieved that she was talking again, even if it was to give him orders. He maneuvered the canoe around a massive tree dipping down into the water, its roots sticking up like a giant land octopus waiting to snare anyone who got too close.

His phone buzzed, indicating a text coming through. He quickly checked the screen then clenched his jaw to keep a litany of curse words from tumbling out. It was from Caleb. He and Eli had checked Carter's place next door, in case any gunmen were hiding there. He hadn't found any gunmen. But they'd definitely been there.

Blake Carter was dead.

"Bishop? Is something else wrong?"

"You heard the phone buzz in my pocket?"

"Yes. Who was it?"

"You have superhuman hearing. It was Caleb, letting me know that he and Eli arrived to back up Dalton and Brielle." He kept his voice as light as possible, not wanting to alarm her any more than she already was. Carter's murder confirmed beyond a doubt that these men meant business. They were eliminating potential witnesses. It appeared even less likely that their presence could be related to the kidnapper.

The kind of men after them sounded like mercenaries, hired out to the highest bidder. Men like that had no morals, scruples, or loyalties other than to the almighty dollar. Two million dollars was a heck of a lot of money, but not if it was split between the kidnapper and five gunmen. Three-hundred, thirty-thousand a piece, give or take, was hardly enough incentive to justify risking the wrath of the federal government by killing a former president's daughter. Either the ransom was a diversion and not at all the goal, or the mercenaries were working for someone else entirely for a completely different reason.

Was it possible that a kidnapper was trying to ransom

Shane at the same time that someone else was trying to kill both the former president and Harper? It seemed so unlikely as to defy belief. So what the heck was going on?

"Bishop."

The new level of panic in her tone had him hyperalert. "What is it?"

"That noise. Do you hear it?"

He stopped paddling, letting the canoe drift as he tuned in to the sounds around them. The drip, drip of water off the paddle onto the surface of the creek. A bird of prey's throaty call as it searched for a late lunch. A rhythmic gritty noise off in the distance. Something man-made.

An engine.

He jerked around. Far off on the horizon, just rounding a curve in the creek, was a small silver boat. It was coming up fast, heading directly for them. The men in the boat wore matching camo. Each one held a rifle.

Gage swore and steered the canoe toward shore. He glanced back. A man in the front of the silver boat raised his rifle and looked through the scope. Bishop scrambled forward, grabbing Harper around the waist.

Her eyes widened with terror as she made a desperate grab for the canoe. "Don't, Bishop! No!"

A bullet pinged through the metal side, barely missing her.

"Take a deep breath, Harper! Hold your breath!"

She screamed as he yanked her over the side and into the water.

Chapter Twelve

Harper screamed in terror as the water closed over her head. She instinctively tried to gulp in air but Bishop's hand clamped down hard over her mouth. His fingers pinched her nose shut as he pulled her deeper into the murky void.

Her lungs burned. Dark spots clouded her vision. She twisted and kicked and fought his hold. She clawed and scratched at his hand on her face. But he held on with a grip so powerful she couldn't break it. Her body jerked back and forth as he kicked the water, propelling them forward with her locked in his deadly embrace.

Bubbles created by the force of his kicks and her flailing limbs rose to the surface, tangling with the long strands of her hair that reached for the blue sky barely visible above them. She tried to lift her hands again to push him away, but she no longer had the energy. Her lungs didn't even burn anymore. A strange calm settled over her. She stopped fighting. Her eyes drifted closed.

BISHOP LUNGED OUT of the water, gasping for breath as he sprinted into the cover of the trees with Harper's limp body draped over his shoulder. As soon as they were out of sight of the boat circling on the water, searching for them, he dropped to his knees behind a fallen log and laid Harper out on the ground. He knew she hadn't gotten any water in her lungs. He'd kept his hands over her mouth and nose. But she wasn't breathing. She was as limp as a rag doll.

He frantically checked for a pulse. Nothing. He'd held her under too long, desperately trying to shield her from the bullets pinging into the water all around them as he'd kicked toward shore. She hadn't taken a deep breath of air as he had when he'd pulled her over the side of the canoe.

He started CPR, performing chest compressions, desperately trying to start her heart again. "Come on, Harper," he urged. "Come on. Fight."

A shout sounded behind him. He jerked up his head, glancing back toward the water as he kept doing compressions. Sunlight glinted off the silver boat. It was crawling through the water, just past the shoreline as the men on board peered into the underbrush.

He ducked down, trying to stay hidden behind the log as he continued to pump Harper's heart. He couldn't stop now or she wouldn't have any chance at all. And yet, if the gunmen found them here, they'd kill her for sure.

He blew several quick breaths into her lungs then felt for a pulse. Nothing. *God help her. Please.* More compressions. More shouts. He glanced over the top of the log. They were tying the boat to a tree less than thirty yards away. The leader motioned to the others, barking instructions.

"Fight, Harper," he urged next to her ear as he pushed against her chest. "Fight. Fight for Shane. *Fight for me.* Come on. Breathe."

He glanced over the top of the log again. The boat was secured. Two men were heading away from them, guns drawn as they searched the woods. Two more were headed in their general direction. He didn't see the fifth man anywhere.

They'd be on them soon. It was now or never. He

slammed his fist down over her heart as he'd seen someone do on a TV show once. She gasped, her eyes flying open.

Yes! He knew he was probably grinning like a fool.

She blinked up at him in bewilderment. Then a look of pain flashed in her eyes. She moaned and started coughing.

He clamped a hand over her mouth then immediately snatched back his hand. He couldn't do that again. The very idea of cutting off her air had him nauseated. He rose, looking for the men. They weren't there.

"Bish—"

He turned back, pressing his finger against his lips, signaling her to be quiet. He wanted to pull her into his arms, to reassure her, to hold her tight and thank God she was alive. But he couldn't. He had to keep it together. They weren't out of danger by any stretch.

She slowly nodded, letting him know she understood, even as she pressed her hand against her chest and winced.

Guilt rode him. Hard. He'd done that to her, bruised her, possibly cracked some ribs. But he couldn't dwell on that right now. He had to focus. Figure out a way for one man with a pistol to defeat five men with assault rifles. Not exactly encouraging odds.

Glancing around, he pulled his gun from the holster. Still nothing, but that didn't mean the men weren't close by. He looked down at Harper and held up five fingers, then he pointed two fingers to their right, and two to their left. She held up one finger in question, obviously wondering where the fifth gunman was. He shrugged.

She looked past his shoulder, her eyes widening in alarm.

He whirled around, firing his pistol in that direction. The man behind him was dead before he even dropped to the ground.

Shouts sounded from either side of them. Bishop grabbed the dead man's rifle. He threaded the strap over his shoulder and shoved his pistol into his holster. He lifted Harper and threw her onto his back, then took off running toward the only place there didn't seem to be anyone crashing through the woods after them.

The creek.

When he reached the silver boat, he set Harper down and yanked out his knife. He cut the line tying the boat to a tree. Harper started to back away, staring at the water. He braced himself against the censure in her eyes and grabbed her, then lifted her over the side, shoving her down to shield her from sight. Then he hopped in and started the engine.

More shouts sounded from the trees. A bullet pinged into the water not far from the boat. Gage spun the wheel, bringing the boat around. Throttling up, he sent it racing toward the next bend in the river. Another bullet zinged past him, so close he could feel the puff of air beside his head.

He brought the rifle up and laid a line of fire into the woods even though he couldn't see any of the men. A guttural scream let him know he'd hit at least one of his targets. He turned around to see a tree hanging out of the water directly in front of them. Slamming the throttle back, he jerked the wheel, narrowly avoiding a collision.

"Bishop!"

He felt a tug against his side as he whirled around. Harper had snatched his pistol out of his holster and fired off two rounds toward a couple of men shooting at them from shore. He brought up the rifle and peppered the pair with gunfire. One of them fell forward, his body splashing into the water, floating facedown as the creek turned red around him.

"Go, go, go!" This time it was Harper yelling as she pulled the pistol's trigger over and over, making the men duck for cover.

He opened the throttle all the way and sent the boat speeding in the direction of the mouth of the French Broad River. They'd just rounded the second curve past where the gunmen had attacked them when the engine coughed, sputtered and died.

Immediately the boat began to drift toward shore. Unfortunately, it wasn't the side of the river where they needed to be.

Harper scrambled to him, clinging to seatbacks and railings so she wouldn't lose her balance. "Why did you turn it off?"

"I didn't." He tried to start the engine. Nothing happened. He rushed past her, rocking the small boat as he bent over the end to take a look. An oily smear on the water told him the story even before he saw the bullet hole.

"What is it? What's wrong?" She surprised him by joining him at the back of the boat. She was clutching the side but wasn't practically catatonic like she'd been in the canoe. She looked down at the water then surprised him yet again with some colorful curse words.

"My thoughts exactly." He rushed to the front and looked at the fancy equipment on the console. The engine might be dead but the equipment ran on battery power. He could see the coordinates of where they were in relation to the rendezvous point. Not far. Much closer if they could have used the boat. But they still might have a chance.

The boat was still drifting toward shore but it was moving far too slowly. If they waited for it to get there on its own, the gunmen would catch up to them before then. He glanced at Harper, who was holding on to one of the seats by the railing.

"Harper, there are still three gunmen left. You can bet they're booking it through the woods right now to catch up to us. And they will, if we stay on the boat. We're sitting ducks out here."

Her eyes widened. Then she shook her head. "No. I almost died! You can't ask me to go into the water again."
She rubbed her chest as if it still hurt.

He steeled himself against the sympathy and guilt that
nearly swamped him. "This time you'll have a life vest on
and I'll tow you ashore. I can probably get us there in less
than a minute and your head will never be under water."

Great plan. Too bad there weren't any life vests on
board. He checked every single possible hiding place, with
her watching him the whole time, her face turning paler
every time he opened a storage bin and found it empty.

Finally, he sighed and took the pistol from her to secure
it in his holster. After strapping the rifle over his shoulder,
he held out his hand. "We don't have a choice. We have to
get in the water, vest or no vest. Come on."

She held her hands out in front of her as if to stop him
and backed up. "I'll take my chances on the boat."

"It's not like last time. I won't throw you in. I'll get in
the water first. Just climb over the side, hold on to my back
and I'll swim us both to shore."

"I told you no." Her bottom lip trembled. "I can't." She
kept backing up, closer to the end of the boat.

He drew a sharp breath. "Harper, wait, you're going
to—"

Her legs slammed against the end of the boat. She
screamed as she toppled into the water.

"Fall." He hopped over the side after her.

Chapter Thirteen

Harper clung to Bishop's shoulders, floating on top of the water as he swam both of them toward the shore. He probably had bruises from how hard she was holding on. Goodness knows the awful, deep scratches on his hands were likely from her. But she was too scared to let go. The memory of her recent near-death experience was too fresh for her to risk that again.

At least the second time she'd gone into the creek, she'd only been under for a few seconds. Bishop had grabbed her and pulled her head up before she'd swallowed too much of the awful brackish water. As soon as he'd made sure she was okay, he'd placed her hands on his shoulders and carefully turned toward shore and began his powerful strokes.

She couldn't even be mad at him this time. It was her fault she'd fallen in. And, honestly, she couldn't really hold a grudge about the first time, either. He was doing everything he could to protect her. And in calmer moments, when not overcome with fear, she could admit to herself that what he'd done had been—as he'd said—the only choice. He'd saved her life, several times over. And that was just today.

Forcing herself to loosen her grip enough so that she wouldn't add more injuries to the ones she'd already caused, she dragged in a steadying breath and studied the trees to their left. There wasn't any sign of the men trying to kill them. But they hadn't seemed like the type of men to give up. No doubt, like Bishop had warned, they were hurrying toward them right now.

Bishop shifted, turning to her and taking her hands in his. She clutched them tightly before realizing they were in the shallows. She forced her feet down until she was standing. The water barely reached her hips. Smiling her thanks, she was careful not to talk or to make any noise that might give away their location.

When they reached the water's edge, he pointed to a group of rocks off to the side. She wasn't sure what he was trying to tell her, until he climbed up on the rocks and pointed at the mud close to her. He didn't want them to leave tracks, showing where they'd come on shore. She nodded and tried to climb up on the rocks. He ended up lifting her and setting her down beside him. He motioned for her to follow him, and they headed into the trees.

Once they were on harder ground, they picked up the pace. She noted he was careful about where he stepped and she was equally careful to follow his movements as much as possible. Gradually, the tension in her shoulders began to ease. They hadn't seen or heard anyone in at least ten minutes. Maybe the gunmen had given up after all.

He suddenly stopped. She would have run into him if he hadn't caught her against his side. Without looking at her, he stared at a stand of trees to their left. But there wasn't anything out of the ordinary there, not that she saw, at least. He looked to the right, as well, and again she saw nothing to explain his alarm.

But she did *hear* something.

Or rather, she heard *nothing*. Earlier, the sounds of the river had been all around them. The occasional chirp of a bird. Insects buzzing or whizzing past. An animal snuffling around in the bushes. But now? It was as if someone had pressed Pause on a noisy movie and the silence was nearly deafening.

He tugged her along behind him, his steps careful like before but fast, so fast she had to jog to keep up with his long strides. Then he was pulling her behind a hollowed-out oak tree and taking out his pistol. He surprised her by handing it to her and leaning down until his lips were next to her ear.

"From what I saw earlier, you're comfortable with a pistol, right?"

She whispered back, "Yes. Did you see someone?"

"No. But they're close. And we're still outgunned. I need to try to take them out one by one to give us a chance." He pressed her back into the hollowed-out section of the tree. "Can you hide here for me? Just for a few minutes? If you see anyone, shoot. Don't give them a second chance. They wouldn't give you one. Can you do that?"

She swallowed hard and nodded. She wasn't actually sure that she could shoot someone like that. But his urgency told her they were in deep trouble, so she'd have to try. Before she could even blink, he was gone, melting into the forest like a wraith.

Trying not to think about the other creatures and insects that might be sharing the tree with her, she clutched the gun in both hands, wincing when the movement made her chest hurt. Then she settled in to wait.

BISHOP ADJUSTED THE rifle over his shoulder to keep it from bumping against him as he crept through the bushes and trees. The rifle was a last resort. The sound would draw the others right to him. Surprise was his best element of defense right now. And his best weapons were ones that made no sound: his knife and his hands.

Crouching, he studied the ground where he'd seen some bushes move moments earlier. Sure enough, he found a set of boot prints. As Brielle had warned, his prey was careful, leaving only a hint of a trail to follow. But Bishop had done more than his share of tracking before, mostly while hunting with his father and brother. He was able to find a few bent blades of grass that told the story.

Moving to a more defensible position, with trees at his back, he watched, and waited. A few moments later, a whisper of fabric sounded off to his left. He dove to his right, rolling out of the way as a spurt of gunfire peppered the ground. He jerked back behind a tree as another gunman crashed through the brush up ahead, coming to help the first man.

Bishop moved with lightning speed, sprinting around the trees and launching himself at the first gunman. The man's shocked gaze met Bishop's a split second before Bishop violently twisted the man's neck. He slumped dead to the ground and Bishop was off and running before the other man even realized what was happening.

A guttural yell sounded from the second man. Bishop dove behind a tree as bullets strafed across the ground. The man was shooting indiscriminately, pumping bullets into the woods all around him, yelling his rage and making it easy for Bishop to pinpoint exactly where he was.

Bishop calmly tugged his rifle down from his back and waited behind a thick oak tree. Firing indiscriminately wasn't an option for him. His opponent was wearing body armor. He could shoot his legs to bring him down. But the kill shot had to be a head shot.

As soon as the shooting stopped, he lunged forward and strafed the man's legs with bullets. His body jerked like a marionette on a string as he screamed and fell to the earth. Bishop finished him off with a single, deadly shot, then dove for cover, fully expecting the last gunman to have followed all the noise and try to ambush him.

Several minutes passed in silence. Bishop listened intently, studying the woods around him. Nothing. The gunshots had practically been an invitation. Why wasn't the last gunman there, trying to end this?

Because he didn't care about Bishop. He was going after the main target. Harper.

His stomach dropped. He took off running.

When he reached the towering dead oak with the hollowed-out middle, he ran to the side, sweeping the rifle out in front of him. The gunman wasn't there. Relieved, he whispered, "Harper, it's Bishop. Lower the pistol. I'm going to step in front of the tree."

He lowered his rifle and swung around to face her. The tree was empty. Harper was gone.

He stared incredulously at the hollowed center of the tree. His pulse rushed in his ears. His hand shook as he felt the bark inside, fearing he'd find blood. When his hand came away dry, he let out a relieved breath. The gunman hadn't killed her, at least not here. There was still a chance. But he had to find her. Fast.

"Bishop?"

He whirled around.

Harper stood on the opposite side of the clearing.

Gage jerked his rifle to the side and ran to her, scanning the woods around them as he went. When he reached her, he yanked her behind a tree and then turned her around to face him.

"What happened?" he rasped. "I told you to wait in the protection of the tree."

"I did," she whispered back. "But I heard someone coming through the woods. Then I saw him, on the other side of the clearing, searching the bushes, looking for me."

"You should have shot him."

"He had body armor. I'm not confident enough that I could have…taken a…"

"Head shot?"

She nodded, her complexion turning slightly ashen at

his words. "I crept out of the hollow and hid behind a log a little deeper in the woods until he left."

He wanted to drag her against him and never let her go. She was so brave, and smart. He couldn't have been more proud of her. He had to clear his tight throat to be able to talk. "Which way did he go?"

"Upriver. Where we were going until the boat engine was destroyed."

"How long ago did he come through here?"

"Hard to stay. Not long after I heard gunshots sounding from the opposite direction. What happened? Did you find the other men?"

"I found them." He settled his rifle across his shoulder again. "They won't be bothering us anymore."

She wrapped her arms around her middle, looking a bit lost, overwhelmed.

"Let's head back toward your property. The Seekers are there. Let's hope the last gunman keeps going in the other direction." He took her hand to pull her with him. Instead, he pulled her toward him, unable to resist the impulse to hold her.

She wrapped her arms around his waist and buried her face against his chest. He heaved a shaky breath, not sure what he would have done if she'd rejected his touch. After the canoe, her nearly being shot a dozen times at least, then thinking he'd been too late, that the last gunman had gotten to her, he was nearly out of his mind with guilt, worry and grief. Now, just holding her like this, it was like taking the magic elixir. He was calming down, feeling centered, back in control.

"Thank God you're okay," he whispered against the top of her head.

Her hands tightened around him but she didn't say anything.

When he realized they'd been standing there for at least

a full minute, he forced himself to release her and step back. He stared down into her tremulous eyes and gently held her upper arms. "When I saw that empty tree hollow, I almost lost it. I thought I'd failed you again. That the gunman had you."

She gave him a sad smile. "You've never failed me, Bishop. Not once. Don't you get that? Nothing that happened in the past was your fault. Did it hurt that you didn't believe me about the pregnancy? Of course. But knowing what I know now, that you don't remember what happened between us that night, how could I expect you to have believed me?"

He took another step back, uncomfortable with her praise. "You should be angry with me, Harper. I don't deserve your forgiveness. I haven't earned it." Before she could argue with him, he took her hand. "Let's go. It's too dangerous to stand here any longer."

Without waiting for her reply, he tugged her along with him toward the river's edge so he could use it as a roadmap back to her property. A few minutes later, a sound downriver had him pulling her into the cover of trees.

"What's wrong?" she murmured. "Is it the gunman?"

He peered around a tree and then smiled his first real smile in a long time. "No. It's the Knights of the Round Table." He pointed downriver toward a small blue boat motoring around a curve, Dalton standing in the prow. There was no mistaking that black Stetson.

"The Justice Seekers are here."

Chapter Fourteen

Bishop looked past Brielle and Dalton, standing on the shore beside him. Harper was already in the boat, sitting on the floor so she was barely visible rather than up on a seat where she'd be too easy a target. Caleb was crouching in front of her, fastening her life jacket, while Eli stood guard, rifle hanging at his waist as he studied the shoreline with a pair of binoculars, searching for potential threats.

Harper wasn't panicking and had gotten onto the boat with surprisingly little fuss. But she was so pale, it was obvious she was scared. Considering the last two times she'd been on the water, he couldn't blame her one bit.

"She'll be okay," Brielle assured him. "Caleb and Eli won't let anything happen to her."

Dalton nodded. "The sooner you show us where the bodies are, the sooner we can mark the GPS coordinates for the cops and get back on the boat."

"Right." Bishop forced himself to turn away from Harper. He pointed to a gap in the trees upriver. "Dalton, dead guys three and four are in that direction. One was lying half in the water just past that next curve in the river, last I saw him. The other one is a good fifty yards in, perpendicular to his location."

"Got it. I'll let you know once I find them." He jogged just inside the tree line then began following the curve of the river in the opposite direction.

"Bad guys one and two are this way." He and Brielle headed into the trees.

Dalton texted Brielle's phone just a few minutes later that he'd found both guys, and tagged the GPS coordinates. It took a bit longer for Bishop and Brielle to find their two. Finally, with all four dead mercenaries accounted for, they headed back to the boat.

Some of the tension eased from Bishop's shoulders when he saw the boat still sitting where they'd left it, Eli and Caleb standing guard while Harper sat cross-legged in the bottom. He smiled at her when he climbed on board and sat on her far side so that he shielded her from the shoreline when the boat turned around and headed back in the direction of her home.

He didn't try to talk to her. He could tell she was struggling to hold back her panic. Instead, he scooted closer until his knees pressed against hers, trying without words to let her know that he was there and would watch over her. She glanced at him in surprise then gifted him with a smile.

Dalton sat beside him, lending his bulk as an additional shield. Brielle had taken up guard duty beside Eli, providing another layer between the shore and Harper while Caleb drove the boat.

Dalton motioned to the mouth of the creek as they left the river and steered into the more narrow waterway. "We'll be there in a few minutes. I've updated Mason. He's handling the police and contacting former president Manning to let him know what happened."

Harper's head shot up. "Police? We can't involve the police. The kidnapper might see the police and think I called them, that I told them about the ransom." She gave Bishop a pleading look. "He'll…he might hurt Shane."

Her fear was palpable. He wanted to tell her everything would be okay. But he couldn't. Truth was, he wasn't sure.

And he was scared, too, worried his son might pay the price for today's fiasco.

"We can't avoid telling the police," he told her. "There are four dead men in the woods. Someone is bound to stumble onto them at some point, either a camper or hunter or just someone out hiking. This isn't something we can ignore or cover up."

He exchanged a knowing glance with Dalton over the top of her head. There weren't just four deaths they had to worry about. There were five. But he hadn't told her about Blake Carter.

If it wasn't for Carter, the Seekers could and probably would have covered up the deaths of the mercenaries. But Carter's death had taken that option away. He wasn't an unknown, unnamed mercenary who no one would go looking for in a public forum. He had a job, presumably a family and friends who would notice his absence. The only way to ensure that none of the Seekers got caught up as suspects in his murder was to level with the police and answer their questions.

Harper looked from him to Dalton and back again. "What about Shane? The police presence will alert the kidnapper."

"It might. But I wouldn't worry just yet. Remember his incentive. Two million dollars. He's not going to throw that away without being absolutely sure that he has no chance to collect his windfall. When we talk to the police, we won't mention Shane or the ransom."

Dalton had been listening to their conversation with rapt attention. "We've got two completely different bad guys."

"Looks like it," Bishop agreed. He watched the shoreline slide past them. "We're not that far from your property, Harper. We need to get our stories straight."

She stared at him. "No mention of the kidnapper, or

Shane. But how do I explain you being at my home? And the Seekers getting involved?"

"That part's easy. The Seekers, including me, were part of your father's security detail for his trip to Gatlinburg. When I stopped the would-be assassin, your father asked for an audience with me, which I granted. From that point, we tweak a few things. You say that we had a private meeting after your father thanked me, so we could catch up on old times."

She slowly nodded. "Makes sense. I can do that. But what about you coming to my house? In a canoe?"

"Yeah, well. That's where we get creative. We capitalize on the truth—that your father and I aren't fans of each other, but without saying why. Just say that we never got along. To explain why I'd sneak onto your property instead of driving right up, we say that I did it so your father wouldn't find out."

She frowned. "And that would explain you coming there in a canoe how?"

Dalton stood. "I think this is my cue to check on Caleb to see if he needs my help docking this thing. We borrowed the boat from the neighbor on the far side of Carter's property. We'll have to let y'all off at Harper's property, then head down the creek to return the boat. My car's parked there as collateral. We'll drive to Harper's place as soon as we're done."

When he was at the front of the boat with Caleb, Harper gave Bishop a suspicious look. "I have a feeling I'm not going to like this. Otherwise your friend wouldn't have been so quick to escape."

"Yes, well… He knows what I'm about to say. It's a cover story that Mason suggested, one that he's going to tell your father, too, if he hasn't already."

"And what's this cover story?"

He cleared his throat. "That you and I are, uh, attracted

to each other. Always have been. And we kind of struck up that attraction in our meeting earlier. We decided to sneak and meet each other today. That explains why I hid when your sister was there, so we can keep the timeline straight."

She blinked a few times then finally said, "That's hardly necessary. Can't you just say I was inviting all of the Seekers to my place to thank them for saving my father? And for some reason you decided to come by canoe? I mean, it's eccentric, but it's closer to the truth."

"You're right. Except for one thing. Our goal isn't just to have a story for the police so we can cover up the ransom angle. It's also to ensure the kidnapper doesn't suspect that I was sneaking onto the property as your protector and that we're all trying to help you. It would be the same as you going to the police or FBI for help. By playing up the save-your-father aspect, as you said, which we'd planned to do already, that provides a reasonable cover for why the Seekers are here. But me sneaking you out back by canoe puts all of that into question. Playing up the lovers angle makes it more believable to the kidnapper."

She nodded but didn't look pleased with the idea. "You really think all of that works as a story? And explains why the other Seekers are here?"

"Absolutely. As long as you let me do most of the talking, I'll provide answers for all of their questions. Just go along with what I say. I don't like the hand we've been dealt. Me being here at all was supposed to be hush-hush so the kidnapper would never realize you'd asked me to help. But it's going public now, the part about those gunmen. All we can do is try to control how it's spun and hope the kidnapper sees it the same way."

The sound of the engine changed as Caleb slowed the boat. Dalton was pointing at a spit of land that jutted out into the creek at the back of Harper's land. It formed a natural dock of sorts. Caleb nodded and slowed even more, guiding the boat toward the outcrop.

"Don't worry," Bishop said. "I'll be with you the whole time we speak to the police. Just follow my lead." Without waiting for her reply, he got to his feet and joined Brielle a few feet away, still keeping watch. "Brielle, did you get a chance to get those things from the safe?"

She nodded, smiling past him at Harper. "I did. I gathered up all your perimeter alarms and cameras, too. Didn't figure you'd want anyone asking about those. They're hidden in the woods until we can retrieve them."

"Good thinking. Thanks, Brielle."

"Bishop?" Harper called out. "Are you worried the police will search my house?"

"There's no question they'll search it. They'll have to clear it and make sure no one is hiding inside. Ordinarily, we could stall them and demand a warrant. But not in exigent circumstances like this."

"Then there's something else you might want to get out of the house before they go inside." She cleared her throat. "I made a baby book for Shane. It documents my pregnancy and has a page at the back dedicated to the story of what happened to him, including his date of death."

Bishop exchanged a surprised look with Brielle. "Where's the baby book?"

"Under my mattress."

"Brielle—"

"No problem," she assured them. "I'll get the baby book, too. Mason's going to notify the police after he talks to your father, again, to keep our stories consistent. He's also going to make sure we have enough time to get back and take care of any loose ends before making the call to the police. We have time."

Harper gave her a grateful smile. "Thank you. I appreciate everything you're all doing to try to protect Shane."

"We'd do anything for Bishop," Brielle said. "We're a family. And right now, that extends to you and your son. I'll just pop inside and grab that book before the police search the house. No problem."

The boat bumped up against a sapling on the edge of the little peninsula. Dalton leaped across the few feet of water and tied the rope around the sapling, stabilizing it so the others could get off.

Bishop looked toward shore then cursed beneath his breath.

Harper stood, tightly gripping the chair beside her. "What's wrong?"

He said something to Brielle and turned around. "Seems the timing of Mason's call to the police was a little off." He waved a hand toward her property just as a group of four uniformed officers and a man in a suit who was nearly as big as Bishop emerged from the woods. "They're already here."

Harper followed his gaze, her eyes widening in alarm.

"Caleb," Bishop said, keeping his voice low, "looks like you and Dalton will have to return the boat later than planned. I could use your help creating a diversion so Brielle can get in and out of the house without the police realizing what she's doing."

"No worries," Caleb replied.

Bishop bent and lifted Harper in his arms.

She stared at him in shock. "What are you doing?"

"Did you hear me mention a diversion?"

"Picking me up is a diversion?"

He grinned. "It certainly is. But it will be an even better diversion, for the cops, when you faint."

"What?"

"Close your eyes, Harper. Don't open them until I tell you to."

"But I—"

"Do it. Now."

She closed her eyes and went limp in his arms.

He settled her higher against his chest and stepped over the side of the boat onto land.

The group of police officers stopped in front of him. The one in the suit held up his credentials. "I'm Detective Nick Radley. We're investigating a homicide." His eyes widened. "Is that who I think it is?"

"If you think it's former president Manning's daughter Harper, you're right. She nearly drowned and I had to revive her. I thought she was going to be okay but she just fainted. Call an ambulance." He brushed past them.

"Hey. Wait a minute," the detective called out.

Bishop ignored him and strode into the woods.

Chapter Fifteen

Harper sat in the back of the ambulance in her driveway, being examined by one of the EMTs while the other one sat in the cab. Bishop stood outside the double doors, having an often heated discussion with Detective Radley, who didn't seem the least bit intimidated by Bishop—probably because they were both almost the same height and equally broad-shouldered.

As they verbally sparred, Bishop kept a watchful eye on her. With the EMT asking questions and poking and prodding her, it was difficult for Harper to focus on Bishop's conversation or to hear what they were saying. But she did catch two words, spoken in disgust several times by the detective.

Brielle Walker.

Apparently, she was a former police officer, which made Radley even more livid that she'd disappeared rather than stick around to be interviewed. During the confusion of Bishop carrying Harper inside and laying her on the couch, with Eli, Caleb and Dalton all talking at once, distracting the cops, Brielle had slipped down the hallway. And she'd never come back. Radley had several cops looking for her right now. Harper prayed they didn't find her.

Beyond Bishop and Radley, she could see that the coroner's van was still parked in Blake's driveway, partially obscured by some of the oleander bushes her stepmom had insisted on planting when she'd bought the place. All that Radley would reveal was that a friend of Blake's had stopped by, then called 9-1-1 after discovering his body. Mason hadn't made a mistake and called the police too early after all. They were already on their way when he'd made his call, which just had Radley even more suspicious wondering why the call hadn't come in earlier if they'd left her house to get away from armed gunmen.

Clearly, Blake had been murdered, since that was the homicide Radley was investigating. But why had he been killed? And did it have anything to do with the gunmen who'd gone after her and Bishop? Those were the types of questions on everyone's mind, especially the extremely curious and determined Detective Radley.

Caleb and one of the uniformed policemen stepped past the ambulance and stood on the carport. Caleb gave her a subtle nod, as if to reassure her that everything was okay. Hopefully, that meant Brielle had successfully gotten away. Although how she'd managed it was a complete mystery. The place was swarming with police now. They were in her house, in Blake's house, grid-searching both properties, including the woods out back. And a handful had arrived by boat about forty minutes ago and had taken Dalton and Eli with them to locate the gunmen's bodies.

The sudden burn of tears in her eyes had her wiping her tears before they could fall. She ruthlessly tamped down her emotions. But it wasn't easy. She was so scared, terrified that the kidnapper was watching, that he saw all of this police activity and concluded that she'd broken his rules. She prayed he wouldn't give up on the ransom exchange, that he wouldn't hurt Shane. It was so frustrating not having a way to contact this Sam person, to make sure that her son was okay.

"Ms. Manning?" The EMT looked at her with concern. "Are you in pain?"

She wiped her eyes again. "No. I'm okay." She offered him a watery smile. "Thanks."

He didn't seem convinced. "Those are impressive contusions on your ribs. They're going to turn a rainbow of colors over the next few days." He sat back on the bench across from her. "Your vitals are good. And I didn't feel any breaks. But you could still have a cracked rib or two. It happens sometimes with CPR. I'd like to take you to the hospital for some X-rays."

Radley stepped closer to the doorway. "Are those contusions consistent with CPR or could they have been caused by some sort of a struggle?"

The EMT blinked, his eyes widening. "I, uh, I'm not—"

"Knock it off, Radley," Bishop interrupted. "Whatever happened to Blake has nothing to do with Ms. Manning."

Ignoring Bishop, Radley asked, "Was he a love interest? Did you two have a fight and you shot him?"

Harper gasped in shock.

Bishop narrowed his eyes at the detective. "Whatever happened to him isn't Harper's fault, or ours. If he's been shot, as you said, that's consistent with the gunmen who tried to shoot Harper and me. They likely killed him before going after her, to ensure there weren't any witnesses."

"Right." Skepticism practically dripped from Radley's voice. "And why would these armed killers go after her to begin with?"

"I'm sure you heard about the attempted assassination of former president Manning this morning in Gatlinburg. Is it really hard to believe that there may have been a coordinated attempt to go after his daughter, too? I'm sure the Secret Service will be crawling all over this soon. You might want to work on getting real evidence and real leads before then or you'll be left out in the cold. Hint, badgering the victim isn't the way to do that."

"Gentlemen," the EMT said, "I really think we should

get Ms. Manning to the hospital. She could have some cracked ribs. And since she ingested brackish water, it's likely she'll need to be put on antibiotics to fight any potential infection."

Harper pressed a hand to her chest and sucked in a breath when she touched one of the deep bruises. "Do you really think my ribs are cracked? It doesn't hurt that much as long as I don't press on them. I mean, I can breathe just fine."

"Didn't you faint earlier? That makes me think you weren't breathing deeply due to the pain and passed out from lack of oxygen."

"Um, yes. Or maybe I was just overwrought."

He gave her a doubtful look. "Take a deep breath."

She tried, but gasped at the sharp pain.

Bishop stepped closer to the back of the ambulance. "That's it. You're going to the hospital."

"I really don't think that's necessary. And I want to know what's going on. Have they caught the last gunman?"

"Good question. Radley, we gave you the GPS coordinates of the four bodies and Dalton and Eli took your guys upriver to show them in person. What's going on there now?"

"I received a text a little while ago that the bodies have been found. But there's no indication there was a fifth man. Are you sure you counted right?"

Bishop shot the detective a look that should have incinerated him. "We're done here." He hopped inside the back of the ambulance.

The EMT's brows shot up to his hairline but he scooted over to make room beside him.

"Let the driver know we're ready to go to the hospital. I want to make sure Ms. Manning gets those antibiotics on board and has her ribs x-rayed." Bishop leaned out and pulled the left door shut. But before he could shut the right door, the detective grabbed it.

"I'm not through asking questions," Radley said.

Bishop looked pointedly at the detective's hand. "Talk to Caleb. He's on the carport being interviewed by one of your officers. I'm going to close the other door. Whether you move your hand or not is up to you. We're taking Ms. Manning to the hospital right now." He shoved the detective's hand off the door.

Radley hopped up into the ambulance, standing in the tight space between Bishop's knees and the gurney where Harper was sitting. "I certainly wouldn't want to interfere with her care. I'll just ask my questions on the way to the hospital." He slammed the door closed.

Bishop leaned forward as if to toss Radley onto the gravel driveway.

Harper quickly slid over to the far end of the gurney and patted the space beside her. "Detective, won't you sit down?" She hadn't missed that Radley's right hand was hovering near his holstered gun.

Bishop's jaw tightened. "Harper, you don't have to put up with this. I can get rid of him."

Radley snorted.

Bishop started to rise.

Harper leaned over and grabbed his arm. "It's okay. *Please.* I don't mind answering his questions." She smiled at the EMT, who looked like *he* was about to faint.

After a long minute, Bishop finally gave her a crisp nod. "All right. But if he's a jerk to you, I'm throwing him onto the highway."

Instead of seeming angry, Radley looked amused, which had Bishop looking ready to kill him.

Harper rushed to prevent imminent bloodshed. "Let's go," she urged the EMT.

He nodded enthusiastically and rapped on the wall of the cab, signaling the driver.

Chapter Sixteen

Harper felt sorry for the EMT. He'd scrunched himself into the corner, as far from the other two men as he could get. She couldn't blame him. She didn't want to be there, either. And since she was obviously stable and this wasn't an emergency, they were running lights only, no sirens, and appeared to be doing the speed limit. That meant this was going to be a long, uncomfortable ride for all of them. And not just because it was so tight inside the back of a vehicle that didn't seem designed to hold more than two people.

The tension was palpable as the detective pulled out his phone. "I'm going to record our conversation so I don't forget anything."

"No." Bishop crossed his arms.

Radley gave him a disgusted look. "What's the problem now?"

"I don't trust you."

"I don't trust you, either. That is exactly why recording our conversation provides both of us with protection, proof of what was said or not said, if we need it later."

Bishop shook his head. "The point is that I don't trust you not to try to capitalize on the fact that you're interviewing the daughter of the former president of the United States."

"What? Oh good grief. You think I'm going to sell the recording to some gossip rag and try to make money off it?"

"It wouldn't be the first time someone's done that. Would it, Harper?"

She sighed. "No. It wouldn't. There were a few enterprising jerks in college who snapped pictures of me or recorded my private conversations and sold them."

The detective snorted. "I'm not some college kid trying to make a fast buck. But, fine. We'll do this the old-fashioned way." He put his phone away and pulled out a small notebook and pen. "Is this acceptable, Bishop?"

"Of course it is. Don't be an ass."

Harper stared at him in alarm. *Bishop.*

The detective surprised her by smiling. "It's okay." He slid the pen and notebook back into his suit jacket. "How about we take this down a couple of notches. No recordings, no notes. No one's under arrest—"

"No kidding," Bishop said. "Since Ms. Manning is the victim here."

"That may prove to be true. But take a minute to look at this from my point of view. I got a call from Dispatch to check out a murder scene. When I arrived, the scene had been secured, but there are a few remarkably hard-to-find shoe prints indicating the murderer went next door, to Ms. Manning's home.

"We manage to find a few more prints leading into the woods. So we head that way, guns out because we're expecting the murderer might be hiding close by. Once we arrive at the creek, we see a boat approaching with a woman sitting on the floor of that boat surrounded by heavily armed people. Then we're told five other armed men are the bad guys and tried to kill the woman, but that four of them have been killed and one is still on the loose." He held his hands out to his sides. "Can you see how it's just a tad confusing from my perspective? A bit hard to separate out the good guys and bad guys and what's really going on? Wouldn't you be suspicious if you were in my shoes?"

Harper exchanged a long look with Bishop. His mouth quirked before he surprised her by holding out his hand toward Radley. "My apologies, Detective. My concern for Ms. Manning has me a little cranky."

Radley's brows arched, but he readily shook Bishop's hand. "A *little* cranky?"

"Don't push it."

Radley grinned. "So noted. Let's back up and start with some basics. Maybe you can both help me pin down a time of death window for Mr. Carter. Ms. Manning, when's the last time you saw him?"

"Earlier today."

"What time was that? What were the circumstances?"

"I was in Gatlinburg this morning, to meet with my dad. There was the attempted shooting of my father—"

"That your former Secret Service agent foiled." He glanced at Bishop. "Your face is all over the news along with a little backstory. I recognized you the moment I saw you on that boat, which is the only reason we didn't come out of the woods shooting. And it's why I asked the uniforms not to arrest all of you while we sorted this thing out."

"The media actually helped for a change," Bishop said. "Guess there's a first time for everything."

Radley smiled. "You were saying, Ms. Manning?"

"I, uh, yes. Well, I met with my dad probably an hour after the attempted assassination."

"Close to ten o'clock then, if reports about the shooting were accurate."

"That sounds right. I met with Dad, then Bishop, then went straight home."

"What did you meet about?"

"What's that got to do with anything?" Bishop asked.

Radley shrugged. "Maybe nothing. Maybe everything. My job is to gather as much information as I can until I can form a picture that will help me figure out what's going on. Is there a reason you don't want Ms. Manning to tell me about those meetings?"

Bishop glanced at her. She realized this was it, where the lies had to start, so they could keep the ransom demand a secret. Time to become the actress she'd never wanted to be.

She gave him a shaky smile. "It's okay... *Gage*. He's not the paparazzi. And he's not recording anything."

Gage subtly nodded as if to reassure her. Then he motioned to the EMT. "Detective Radley might not be who we need to worry about."

The EMT's eyes widened and his face reddened like a child caught eavesdropping outside someone's door.

Two minutes later, they were back on the road, heading for Knoxville, both EMTs now in the cab.

"No more evasive answers," Radley said. "Unless the meeting was some kind of state secret—which doesn't make sense since Mr. Manning is the former president, not the current one—there's no reason you can't tell me what the meeting was about."

"It was just a photo op, a meeting with the press so my father could publicly thank Gage for saving his life."

"Then why the secrecy?"

"Because the meeting didn't turn out as planned. Gage doesn't have a great history with my father. They don't like each other. At all. Gage refused the photo op and wouldn't allow my father to thank him in front of reporters. Instead, my father and the others stepped out of the room so that Gage and I could meet for a few minutes."

The detective didn't seem surprised by her declaration, probably because she was making a point of using Bishop's first name, as someone intimately involved with him would. Now that she was calling him Gage again as part of the act for Radley, it felt as natural as breathing.

It felt…right…slipping into that old familiarity. He'd always been Gage to her. It was something special the two of them had shared. Calling him Bishop earlier today had been childish, her way of getting back at him because he'd made her mad. She wasn't proud of how she'd handled the stress and lashed out.

"What was discussed in the private meeting between you two?" Radley prodded.

Harper didn't have to work at looking uncomfortable. Her emotions from that meeting were still too raw. And she was afraid she might say something that could jeopardize Shane. She looked up at Gage, silently pleading for him to take over.

"It's okay," he told her. "Detective, as you've no doubt surmised, Harper and I have a…history. We didn't part on good terms and haven't seen each other in years. But when we saw each other this morning…well, we realized the attraction we'd always had was still there. She told her dad she wanted to thank me for saving his life and since I refused to even discuss it with the media present, he allowed us to have a private audience. We decided then and there that we wanted to see each other again."

"Romantically."

Harper's face heated.

"Yes," Gage said. "But her father doesn't approve of me, so we—"

"He doesn't approve of you because—what?—when you were the Secret Service agent protecting his daughter, you two hooked up?"

Harper gasped in surprise. "That's not what—"

"Yes," Gage said. "We were lovers, a very long time ago. That's why her father hates me."

Harper stared at him, stunned.

"And why you were fired as a Secret Service agent, I'm guessing?"

"I didn't know that was common knowledge. But, yes. You're correct."

Harper clutched her hands together to keep from reaching out to him. She hated that a man so honorable had to admit to being fired, for something that she didn't feel was his fault. His pride had to be hurting. And she wished she could somehow take away that hurt.

"Interesting. Go on. You were explaining, I think, that you and Ms. Manning were planning to see each other again."

Gage gave him a terse nod. "We came up with a plan for her to have a get-together for all of the Justice Seekers at her place to thank them for providing additional security at today's event." He hesitated. "I assume one of the others already explained about our company?"

Radley tapped his fingers against the gurney. "I know enough to fill up a few sentences in my notebook. But I'll work on fleshing that out later. You and your coworkers went to Ms. Manning's home and you were there when she saw her neighbor?"

"No." Harper cleared her throat. "I got home close to noon. I, uh, was hoping to spruce up the house before the Seekers arrived. But before I could get in the door, Blake came over." She explained about the brief visit, and then about her sister already being there with her boyfriend.

"Cynthia? Your middle sibling?"

"Yes."

"And you have a much younger brother, too, if I recall correctly?"

"Tyler. He's eleven."

Radley pulled out his notebook and pen, then hesitated. "Is it okay if I write some of this down? I'm going to mix it all up if I don't."

"It's fine," she said.

"Okay, let's see. I'm trying to keep the family dynamics straight. If I remember right, your mother died when you were little, then your father married his current wife?"

"How is this relevant?" Gage asked.

"Puzzle pieces. You never know which one you're missing."

"It's okay," she assured both of them. "I've been asked about my family a million times. Everyone seems to have trouble keeping it straight. My mom, Hope, died of breast cancer when I was nine. Dad had a really hard time moving on, so he went to group therapy. That's where he met Julia. She'd just lost her spouse, too. A couple of years later, they—my dad and Julia—got married. Cynthia was Julia's daughter from a previous marriage. But Tyler is both of theirs."

"Wait, okay. So Cynthia's not blood related to you? She's your stepsister? But Tyler's father is your dad, Earl Manning. So he's your half brother?"

"They're both my siblings. Blood-related or not."

He glanced up from the notes he was taking. "No offense intended. Again, I don't know that any of this matters. But if it does, I don't want to get it wrong. Sometimes there are issues in families, like jealousy, that might be important to know. You did say your sister Cynthia—no blood relation—broke into your home and was waiting for you. And not long after that you're running for your life from five armed men."

She blinked. "If you're saying my sister is trying to kill me, you're completely off base. She's a kid. And she didn't break in. She had a key."

"How old?"

"Excuse me?"

"How old is your *kid* sister?"

Harper hesitated, her face warming. "Twenty."

"Not a kid then."

She crossed her arms, winced when she pressed against her bruises, and dropped her arms to her sides.

The detective tapped the pen on his pad. "Sounds to me like there's someone else in your family who may have wanted to send those mercenaries after you. Except, I imagine if that's the case then the target would have been Bishop. Unless there's another reason your father might want you dead?"

She gasped. "My father? Now you're thinking he's the one who sent someone to kill me? Or Gage? That's—"

"Crazy," Gage supplied. "Completely out of character for the former president."

"Convince me."

"He loves me," Harper exclaimed. "He loves all his children. He would never do anything to hurt us."

Radley shrugged. "He's also a hard-nosed, unyielding narcissist, if the news reports from the past eight years are even a little bit accurate. And he's extremely tightfisted with his money even though he's a millionaire."

She clasped her hands together. It was either that or punch him. "He's far from perfect. But he's an excellent father. And if we truly need anything, he's more than happy to provide it. He just prefers that his children be independent and make their own way. I assure you, he wouldn't send gunmen after me."

"What about sending them after Bishop? You already admitted your father doesn't like him."

She shook her head. "He wouldn't. Not even against his worst enemy. He has a strong legacy of supporting law enforcement in his political career. He's an honorable man and wouldn't do something like that."

"Like I said. I need convincing. Bishop, you said it's out of character for him. Explain that."

"You already hit the nail on the head. He's a narcissist."

Harper sucked in a sharp breath.

Gage gave her an apologetic look. "You know it's true. Detective Radley, the most important thing in the world to Earl Manning is Earl Manning. Above all else, he wants to protect his reputation, his precious legacy as president. He'd never do anything to jeopardize that. I'll bet one of his own family members could be kidnapped and he wouldn't dare involve the FBI or anyone else to try to ransom them if there was any chance of it getting out into the media. It would destroy his reputation of being hard on crime and refusing to negotiate with criminals."

Harper's mouth fell open.

He quirked a brow, as if daring her to contradict him.

She couldn't believe he'd said those things. But if she tried to deny it, she'd be the hypocrite. He was, after all, right. Her father had done exactly what Gage had said. He'd offered money and Gage as his scapegoat to find his grandson. But he'd refused to involve anyone else for fear of harming his precious reputation.

The detective was writing notes in his little book and seemed to miss the nonverbal exchange between the two of them, which was probably a good thing. She didn't want to raise his suspicions any more than they already were about her family.

He stopped writing and eyed Gage. "I don't think you fleshed out that train of thought, but I think I followed it. You don't think the former president would hire thugs to kill either you or Harper for any reason because it could harm his reputation if things went bad. And that's more important to him than any grudge?"

"Absolutely."

"What about you, Ms. Manning? Do you agree with that assessment?"

She hesitated, still smarting over Gage's characterization of her father. But she couldn't ignore the truth, either. "Yes. I agree. My father isn't the one you're looking for."

"I think it's safe to assume your eleven-year-old half brother isn't part of this. That leaves your stepsister and stepmother as persons of interest."

Harper threw up her hands. "Enough. Okay? Leave my family out of this. They're good people." She glared at Gage, daring him to say otherwise. "My family's not perfect, my father least of all. But we love each other. We're very close. And, get real. It's not like we have mercenaries on speed dial. Who the heck hires five gunmen like that? I wouldn't know where to begin."

"It's easier than you think, Ms. Manning. Your father's anticrime platform means he's been heavily involved in investigations and cases against criminals. All he'd have to do is go through some old files he probably has in his home office right now and pull out names of some of the worst. He can afford any fee they'd charge. Wouldn't be hard to toss some money around to get the job done."

"I'm through talking with you about my family," she snapped.

"Fair enough." Radley didn't seem bothered by her anger and simply skimmed through his notes before continuing. "Moving on. We know Carter was alive around noon. As long as your sister corroborates that, and other people were with you from then on—which we'll need to establish, as well—you're in the clear for his murder."

"Well, thanks for that, I guess."

"But you're not, Bishop. Not until I get a timeline on you. Did you and the Seekers arrive together? Can they vouch for you?"

It was Gage's turn to cross his arms. "No. They can't. I took a shortcut, came up on the other side of the French Broad River in my car, parked at a campground and rented a canoe to take to Harper's place. I was already there when her sister arrived and I hid in a back room until she left. The Seekers arrived shortly after Cynthia and her boyfriend were gone. Since we established that Carter came over to see Harper while I was inside the house, obviously I'm not the killer."

The ambulance slowed then bumped and squeaked as it turned into the hospital drive that led to the emergency room entrance.

Radley's phone buzzed in his pocket. He read the message on the screen and tapped a reply before putting it away. He glanced from one to the other. "Why do I feel I'm being played here?"

Harper blinked and shot a glance at Bishop. But he didn't seem shaken at all.

"Just find the fifth gunman," Bishop told him. "Maybe you'll get lucky and he'll confess to killing Carter. Then he can tell you who hired him to kill Ms. Manning."

The ambulance parked and the cab's doors slammed shut as the EMTs got out. A few seconds later, the rear doors swung open to reveal the EMTs standing outside.

Detective Radley hopped out first. "Looks like I might get a chance to do exactly that—talk to the gunman. They captured him after a brief gunfight. They're bringing him here right now, to this hospital."

Chapter Seventeen

Harper blinked at the morning sun coming through the window blinds. The hospital was full so she'd been relegated to spend the entire night in the emergency ward, getting IV antibiotics and hoping the doctor would eventually agree to let her go home. Knowing she was the former president's daughter seemed to make everyone around her paranoid. They checked on her constantly and she suspected she was receiving far more care than she required.

Case in point, the day-shift nurse was hanging yet another IV bag on the pole beside her bed. How much fluid did one person need because they'd swallowed a thimbleful of brackish water?

The nurse set the call button on top of the blanket, next to Harper's hand, and smiled. "Need anything else? Perhaps another pillow?"

She had three already.

"No thank you. I'm good."

"Excellent. I'll check back in a bit."

"Take your time. Really."

The nurse's smile dimmed.

Harper immediately regretted her aggravated tone. "Sorry. I'm a bit stressed out. I really do appreciate everything you're all doing for me."

The nurse's smile kicked up to full wattage. "It's my pleasure to help in any way I can. As I said, I'll check back in a little while. In the meantime, there's an extremely handsome man waiting in the hall to see you. If you're not up for company, I'd be happy to keep him occupied." She grinned and fanned herself.

Harper couldn't help laughing in spite of the past few days being some of the most trying days ever. "Is his name Gage Bishop?"

"If I say no, do I get to keep him?"

Her annoyance with the nurse returned, tenfold. It was a struggle to keep her smile intact. "Thanks for the offer. But you can send him in."

"You got it." She held the curtain back and stepped out of the room.

A moment later, a knock sounded on the wall that separated Harper's room from the next one.

"Come in," Harper called out.

The curtain billowed to the side and Gage stepped in, looking just as mouthwatering as ever. He adjusted the curtain closed behind him before heading to the bed. He winced when he saw the IV taped to the top of her right hand and the tube running up the pole.

"Still hooked up to that thing, I see. Weren't the antibiotics supposed to be finished early this morning?"

"They were. That's saline solution, or something like that. I'll bet you slept a lot better than I did. You go home after you disappeared?"

"I've been up all night working on your case. I went to Camelot to brainstorm with the other Seekers, aside from the ones rotating in and out to guard your room."

"And here I am, being completely ungrateful with everyone this morning. I'm sorry."

"No worries." He pulled up the only chair in the tiny room, an orange plastic one with chrome legs. Before sitting, he tested it first with his hands as if to ensure it would hold him. Then he carefully sat and rested his arms across the top of the bed rail. "What did the doctor say? How bad did I mess you up?"

"Mess me up?"

"Your ribs. The CPR."

She automatically placed her hand against the bruises on her chest, and noticed him wince again as if in empathy. She lowered her hand. "You didn't mess me up, Gage. You saved my life—something I should have thanked you for long ago. Thank you. I mean it. I can't count how many times and how many ways you saved my life. I'd be dead right now if it wasn't for you."

He took her left hand in both of his. "Don't talk like that."

She swallowed, content to enjoy the rush of awareness that shot through her at his unexpected touch. He pulled his hands back, as if suddenly realizing what he was doing, and rested his arms on the rail again. The loss of his warmth was like an ache in her heart.

"You didn't answer my question," he said. "Does that mean I *did* crack some ribs?"

"No, no. The X-rays came back clean. I'm totally okay. Lying in this bed seems silly, honestly. But they won't let me go until the doctor gives the all-clear. He's supposed to make his rounds in an hour or so." She glanced at the curtain then lowered her voice. "What about the gunman? Is he talking? Who hired him? Was it Sam or someone else? When will—?"

He smiled and put his hand on hers again. "I think you lost me about three questions back."

"Sorry, I just… I'm worried. About Shane. We've only got one more day left. The kidnapper is supposed to make contact tomorrow."

His smile faded. "That's why we've all been up working the investigation. Mason's got Seekers looking into this from every angle." He scrubbed his jaw, then leaned on the railing again. "Let's see, the lab results should be back soon. That's taking a little longer than I expected, considering the money Mason's throwing their way. No luck with the post office surveillance, as I'd feared. The printer metadata is taking longer than expected, too. We're still waiting on the company to get back to us with customer purchase records. Mason's got a judge leaning on them for the information."

"A judge? Wow."

"Never underestimate what Mason can get done outside of the legal system."

"What about the linguist?" she asked.

"Her report wasn't as helpful as I'd hoped. It doesn't rule anyone in or out on our potential suspect list."

Harper gave him an aggravated look. "Let me guess. The profile matches everyone in my family."

"Bingo."

She rolled her eyes.

"As for the gunman," Gage continued, "we're in luck there. He was shot, but it was a through-and-through, a flesh wound on his side. They stitched him up right in the emergency room. Didn't require surgery. But he's been sick ever since, throwing up, running a fever. They're pumping him with fluids and keeping him sedated to try to calm his system down. He's still here, in the ER, down the hall. As soon as he's better and in a room upstairs, the Seekers will interrogate him and figure out who hired him."

"Interrogate him? How? I can't see Detective Radley allowing that."

"Radley won't even know about it." He winked.

She couldn't help smiling. "I guess there are perks to being a Seeker. Other team members to create diversions, things like that. You said the gunman's down the hall?"

His expression turned serious again. "Don't worry. You're safe. Dalton and Eli were with the police when they brought him in. Eli's standing guard outside your door right now and he's not going anywhere. And a policeman is watching the gunman's room. He's also handcuffed to his bed. He's not going anywhere."

Harper nodded, but it was hard not to worry. One of the men who'd tried to kill her and Gage was in the same emergency ward as she was. It felt surreal. And scary.

A knock sounded. Gage stiffened, his hand going to his side. It dawned on her he was wearing a clean suit again, with a jacket, and whoever had brought him the clothes had likely also brought him a gun. What shenanigans had he pulled to be able to wear it in the hospital she wondered?

"Who is it?" he called out.

"Eli." He leaned inside the curtain, nodding at Harper. "Your family's here again to see you. Is it okay to let them in?"

A woman's voice called out from the other side of the curtain. "Well, of course it's okay to let us in."

The curtain billowed and Julia breezed in, followed by Cynthia and her boyfriend, Dean.

Gage let his jacket close over his holster and joined Eli by the doorway. He whispered something and Eli disappeared.

"You poor thing." Julia hurried to Harper's bedside and kissed the top of her head before gently taking her hand in hers, careful not to touch where the IV tubing was taped on top. "I can't believe how bold burglars have gotten these days. To break into your home with guns and go after you—"

"Oh please," Cynthia said from the other side of the bed. "I told you last night they weren't burglars. Dad said Bishop told him over the phone that they were mercenaries or something like that. Someone paid them to kill her, just like that guy that went after Dad."

Julia rested her head against Harper's pillow as she

gave her a gentle hug. "Hired killers? What is this world coming to that a former president and his family are targets like this?"

Harper patted Julia's hand. "Please stop worrying. I'm okay. Gage saved my life and he's not going to let anything happen to me."

Cynthia grinned at Gage, who was leaning against the wall by the curtain silently watching them. Her gaze slid down to his shoes and she slyly glanced at Harper.

Don't you dare, Harper silently mouthed to her.

Her sister shrugged and pushed away from the wall. "Dean overheard some cops talking in the waiting room bathrooms before we left last night. They said some guy took out four gunmen all by himself. I'm guessing we all know who that was." She winked. "There was another one, though, right? He got away, but then the police caught him. Is he in the ER? Is that why there's a cop outside another curtained room a few down from this one?"

Julia's head shot up. "They caught one? And he's here?" She sounded horrified. "Bishop, what are you doing about that? He could come after Harper."

"I'm not in any danger," Harper assured her, trying to keep Gage from having to deal with her highly emotional stepmom. "Like Cynthia said, there's a policeman outside his room. Thanks to Gage, there's always a Seeker guarding my room, too. I'm perfectly safe. And I'll be leaving soon, once the doctor makes his rounds."

Julia looked up at the pole, frowning. "Why are you still getting an IV? I thought you were just having your ribs checked and you had to stay overnight for observation. Is something else wrong? Are you sick?" She pressed a hand against Harper's forehead.

Cynthia rolled her eyes. "The drama is only going to get worse once Dad gets here."

Harper's stomach jumped. "Please tell me you're kidding. He can't come here. This place will become a zoo with all those Secret Service agents milling around and stopping everyone."

"Welcome to my world," her sister said. "I'm living it every day. Can't wait for the fall semester to start up so I can escape back to campus."

Julia patted Harper's hand. "Cynthia's teasing you. Your father's still working with the FBI and Secret Service on the investigation into the assassination attempt. He couldn't get away, but he sends his love."

Harper let out a pent-up breath, relieved.

"Surprise, surprise," Cynthia mocked. "The king couldn't tear himself away from his admirers to check on his daughter who was nearly killed."

"Cynthia," Julia warned.

"Relax, mommy dearest." She scooted around the end of the bed and motioned for Dean to come with her. "Let's check out the vending machines and see if there are any chocolate doughnuts. I love those things. We'll grab a soda, too. Harper, you want us to bring you something back?"

"No thanks. With everything that's happened, I don't think I could eat right now." She'd had some hospital food last night. But after realizing this morning that they only really had one more day until the kidnapper was supposed to contact them, she'd lost any appetite she'd woken up with.

Gage must have been worrying about Shane, as well, from the grim look on his face as he held back the curtain for Cynthia and her boyfriend.

Harper wanted to ask him questions about strategy, what they should do in regard to the kidnapper and steering the message the media would take on all of this. But she was stuck consoling Julia and giving her a much watered-down version of what had happened.

Eli came in with two more orange plastic chairs and set

them against the wall. Harper smiled her thanks at him and Gage, knowing full well that must have been what Gage had whispered to Eli earlier. In spite of his sometimes gruff exterior and all the baggage between them, Gage was a gentleman at heart. Always had been.

A few minutes after Eli left the room to take up guard duty again, another knock sounded. Gage lifted the curtain back, revealing Dalton and Caleb, who both waved at Harper. She smiled in return, but couldn't wave. Julia was holding both her hands as she went on and on about how unsafe the world was.

The Seekers spoke in low tones to each other. At first, Gage shook his head no to whatever Dalton was telling him. But finally he nodded. The others stepped back and Gage let the curtain close. He strode to the other side of the bed and grasped the railing.

"Sorry to interrupt," he said, startling Julia, who apparently hadn't even realized he was standing across from her.

"Is something wrong?" she asked. "Oh my, has that bad man escaped?"

"No, ma'am. Harper, I've got both Eli and Caleb outside your room. Mason's here and needs to talk to me. He has some updates on…ah, a case we're working on. I need to step out for a few minutes."

Julia crossed her arms. "You're leaving? With that awful man just a few feet down the hall? Don't you care what happens to my daughter?"

Harper gasped. "Julia, don't—"

"It's okay," Gage said. "Ma'am, I assure you, I care *very much* about what happens to Harper. That's why there are two Seekers outside her room. And the gunman isn't a few feet away. He's around the corner, with a police guard."

Julia shook her head and looked away.

"Harper," Gage said. "Are you okay with this? If not, I'll tell Mason—"

"I'm more than okay with it," she assured him, still feeling surprisingly touched by his saying he cared *very much* about what happened to her. "I know you're working an important case, right?"

He gave her a subtle nod, confirming what she'd thought. Whatever Mason was about to tell him had something to do with Shane.

Chapter Eighteen

Bishop jogged across the ER parking lot and rounded the end of the building. Dalton and Mason were waiting for him by a retention pond dotted with ducks and geese, near a stand of thick oak trees.

He shook Mason's hand. "Thanks for everything you're doing, that all the Seekers are doing to help."

"We're family," Mason said. "When one of us is hurting, we're all hurting."

Dalton nodded. "I almost lost Hayley last year. I know what you're going through with Harper and Shane. You can count on me, no matter what."

Bishop gripped his shoulder in a show of solidarity. "Harper and I aren't a couple. But I appreciate what you're saying." He chose to ignore their disbelieving looks. Until this case was settled, he needed to stay focused. It was going to be hard enough to do that today without having slept. Letting loose the floodgates of his feelings for Harper right now would emotionally wreck him. He had to keep it professional, for both their sakes, at least until they got Shane home safely. Then, well, all bets were off.

"I want to get back as soon as I can. Harper's stepmother's crying all over her and I don't trust her sister's boyfriend. He's way too quiet. I can't figure out if he's an introvert or busy scheming."

"We'll be quick," Mason assured him. "I assigned

Bryson to try to locate the midwife. He couldn't find a Colette Proust anywhere around here, unsurprising since Earl Manning's lawyer couldn't, either. So, instead of starting with the present day and working backward, Bryson started with what was known about her six years ago. She lived in an apartment with her brother, Victor, until she moved in with Harper. A few weeks after she left Harper's place, she and Victor disappeared."

"Both of them?"

He nodded.

"Were they in on it together then? They moved to another town?"

"That was Bryson's assumption at first. But after conducting a thorough search of tax rolls in neighboring counties without any luck, he looked through surrounding states. Still nothing. He took a chance that someone in the apartment complex where the Prousts had lived might remember them. Sure enough, the property manager who was there during that time is still there, although just as a resident now. But she remembered them. Apparently, the brother was quite eccentric, which made them stand out in her mind. She said that at the end of their lease, which was right around the timeframe we're looking at, they planned on moving back home, to Paris."

"Paris?" Dalton and Bishop both said together.

"*The* Paris, as in France?" Bishop added.

"One and the same. Bryson couldn't get flight records going back that far, but he successfully located the brother, Victor, who is right now living in an apartment in the City of Lights."

"And Colette? Shane?" Bishop asked, hoping by some miracle Bryson had managed to find his son.

Mason shook his head. "Sorry. Bryson pulled some strings, used contacts he made while with the FBI, and had some constables do a wellness check on Victor. A very thorough one. They searched his entire home, top to bottom and even neighboring apartments. There are no signs of any children ever having lived with him. Interviews with his neighbors say he lives alone, rarely has any visitors. As for his sister, I'm afraid I don't have good news there, either. She became violently ill during the flight to France all those years ago. An ambulance was waiting for her when the plane landed. They rushed her to the hospital but couldn't save her. She had a massive heart attack."

Bishop swore. "Let me guess. Victor never heard of Shane or Harper."

"On the contrary. He knew his sister was staying with Harper. It was a lucrative arrangement and both of them were benefitting from it. But at the end of the pregnancy, Colette told him the same thing she told Harper, that Shane had died. The French authorities believed him, said there were no signs of subterfuge. Or, at least, no evidence that would justify them pursuing the matter any further."

Dalton crossed his arms. "Sounds like it's unlikely the Prousts were involved. So what are we looking at? Someone at the hospital stole Shane and said he'd died?"

"I don't buy it," Bishop said. "Colette just happens to bring a baby in distress to the emergency room and someone tells her he died? Then provides a death certificate, and yet she's not involved? You saw what it's like in the ER here. Tons of people all over the place going in and out of rooms. It would have to be a vast conspiracy. No, I think she was in on it but her brother didn't know.

"And even if I'm wrong, it makes sense to keep investigating that avenue to see where it leads. If she planned on using Shane to extort money, or even if she just wanted to raise him as her own, she'd have had to keep him with someone else for at least a little while so her brother wouldn't find out. Maybe she was going to come back for him later. But when she didn't return, why would whoever was watching Shane keep him for five years and then try to cash in on the opportunity? It doesn't make sense."

"Bryson pretty much said the same things you did when talking it through with me. And then he reminded me of what we all know but sometimes forget. When things start getting too complicated, they—"

"Probably aren't complicated at all," Bishop interjected, finishing his sentence. "We need to look at the simplest, most straightforward explanation."

"What would that be?" Dalton asked. "I'm not seeing anything simple about any of this."

Mason arched a brow and waited for Bishop.

"The simplest explanation is that Colette lied to Harper. The baby wasn't in distress. She used that as a ruse to take the baby wherever she'd planned to take him."

Dalton scratched his chin. "That eliminates the idea of a hospital conspiracy, which definitely simplifies things. But we still have a death certificate to explain. Where did that come from? You think Colette forged it?"

"Most likely," Mason said. "She probably had it ready the whole time. All she had to do was to fill in the date once the baby was born. And since Harper's father had gone to such lengths to hire Colette and keep everything a secret, there'd be no reason for Harper to doubt Colette or the validity of the document."

Bishop dragged a hand through his already disheveled hair. "If that's the case, then Colette planned this from day one, and never intended to take Shane with her to Paris. So what was her angle? An illegal private adoption to make a few bucks on the side? Then years later, whoever adopted him somehow figured out who his biological mother is and decided to cash in on it?"

Dalton shook his head. "That's really messed up. Who'd keep a kid for five years then offer him up for money?"

"Maybe they don't plan to make the exchange," Bishop

said. "Maybe they're hoping to keep Shane and disappear with the money."

"That's certainly a possibility," Mason concurred. "Bryson's working the money angle, looking for an electronic trail, interviewing anyone who used to know the Prousts, so he can see if one of her associates mysteriously disappeared around the time Colette left, perhaps with a newborn baby. If someone paid her, he'll find the transaction and figure out who's behind it."

Bishop fisted his hands at his sides. "We still don't have an explanation for the mercenaries. Who hired them? Why kill Harper before getting the ransom for Shane? Once again, it doesn't make sense."

Dalton shifted on his feet. "If the puzzle piece doesn't fit, maybe it's the wrong puzzle. I know we all agree it seems unlikely, but the gunman aspect may really have nothing to do with Shane and the ransom. Maybe for the time being we assume it's related to the assassination attempt on former president Manning and focus on the kidnapping, especially since the exchange is supposed to take place tomorrow."

"That's actually a good idea," Mason said. "Shane should be the primary focus right now."

"I wish we could keep all of this about the gunmen quiet," Bishop added. "But there are too many bodies, too many cops involved, to keep this fiasco out of the press. If, by some miracle, it's not related to the ransom scheme, I sure hope this Sam guy doesn't get too nervous and call the whole thing off."

Mason shook his head. "I don't think he will." He exchanged a quick glance with Dalton.

Bishop narrowed his eyes. "What? There's something else, isn't there? Another reason you wanted to meet with me?"

Mason gave him a curt nod. "There is one more thing.

The lab I hired is still rerunning the actual DNA tests. But they already did a quick paper-only review of the work the other lab did, a scientific walk-through of their methods, their analysis and conclusions. They reviewed the DNA profiles in the report and agreed that, based on those profiles, and the other tests that were done, the samples are mother and son, and the son's sample came from a live person."

When Mason didn't say anything else, Bishop pressed forward. "That confirms what we already believed to be true. Why do you look all gloom and doom? What's going on?"

Mason huffed out a long breath. "I want any testing the lab does for us to be as thorough and accurate as possible. They're retesting the sample of Shane's hair, as you asked. In the meantime, since a mother-son relationship was proved by the earlier testing, I felt it only made sense to make an additional comparison—to the alleged father."

Bishop stared at him incredulously. "You ran a paternity test? What'd you do, use my DNA profile on file with the Seekers, without my permission?"

"I did what I felt was necessary to protect my employee, and friend, from potentially being taken advantage of."

Bishop's stomach sank as he waited for the rest. "Just say it."

"I had the results double-checked, just to be certain. There is no mistake. Based on your DNA profile, there's no way that you can be Shane's father."

It felt like the air was being sucked from his lungs. He shook his head, his heart refusing to accept what Mason was telling him. But it made sense if he looked at the simplest explanation. He couldn't remember making love to Harper in the pool house because it never happened. She'd gotten pregnant with another man's child, just as he'd believed for years, until she'd convinced him otherwise in Gatlinburg. But why would she do that, drag him back into her life years later? Convince him he was her child's father? Was it just to ensure that he would help her get Shane back? So she could keep everything out of the media but have someone with the background, and incentive, to save Shane without telling anyone what had happened?

"No. I saw the picture. I texted you a copy. Shane has the same birthmark on his face that all of the men in my family have."

"Pictures can be faked," Mason said. "You know that."

He shook his head again. "You didn't see her in that conference room, the fear and grief in her eyes, in her voice. If she was lying, then she deserves an award. Because I bought every single line."

Dalton frowned. "I don't know, Mason. Harper didn't strike me as the kind of person who would do that."

Bishop closed his eyes, letting what he knew, what he didn't know, and what he suspected, flow through his mind. The clues bumped against each other until they all coalesced into one picture. He'd been such a fool. He opened his eyes. "It makes sense," he said quietly. "It simplifies everything."

"How so?" Dalton asked.

"Look at the simplest explanation for all of this," Bishop said. "There was no conspiracy between Colette and someone else. No fake adoption. Shane really was in distress. Colette really took him to the hospital where he…where he died. The ransom note is fake. There is no Sam. There's only Harper."

Dalton looked at him in disbelief. "No way. That can't be right. She's already wealthy. She wouldn't need to pull something like this to get money."

"She's not rich," Mason said, his voice subdued. "Her father is. And he's tight with the purse strings. He insists that his children make their own way in the world, like he did. But most of former president Manning's assets aren't liquid. We've been running financials on him as part of the investigation. He's struggling to raise the money to pay the ransom. Harper's very close to him. She'd likely know it would be difficult for him to come up with the money."

"That's why she involved me," Bishop said. "In theory, anyway. It also means she's kept tabs on me for years, found out I own a lucrative construction company on top of being a Seeker. She figured I'd be able to come up with the money. I already told her I'm paying the ransom."

Dalton held up his hands. "Hold it. Before you go off that deep end, there's one very big glaring hole in your theory. The lab said the hair samples are mother and son. And that the sample came from a living child. How do you explain that if Shane died at birth?"

Mason looked at Bishop. "If we assume the theory you just put forth is fact, then, again, the simplest explanation is that the child's hair samples weren't from Shane. And the mother's weren't from Harper. They're from some other mother and son."

"Which means your theory that I'm not the father could be wrong, as well. Apples and oranges."

Mason nodded reluctantly. "Agreed. We don't have Harper's DNA profile to compare. But it wouldn't be difficult to get a blood sample while she's in the hospital. She wouldn't know it was for a DNA test. I can make it happen. If you're okay with it."

Bishop stared at the pond for a long moment before giving him a curt nod. "Go ahead. But tell Bryson to keep digging. Tell *all* the Seekers to keep digging. I have to know for sure what's really going on and I'm too tired right now to know what to believe." He met Dalton's gaze. "I agree with you about Harper. She's a good person. It's hard to believe she'd try to pull a stunt like this. That she'd purposely hurt me, or anyone else. Until or unless I have incontrovertible proof to the contrary, I choose to believe that she's not trying to rip my heart out, that Shane is still alive, and that he's my son."

He turned to leave then froze. A man had just stepped out from behind one of the oak trees.

Detective Radley.

"Hello, gentlemen. Nice weather out here, isn't it?" He motioned to the pond. "And a gorgeous place to take a break from all the craziness going on inside."

A feeling of dread settled in Bishop's gut as he exchanged a quick glance with Mason and Dalton.

"Don't worry. There's no one else out here, just me, standing behind the trees when you three came out to have your little huddle. I was going to announce my presence but once you started talking, I was too stunned to stop you." Radley smiled. "Let me see if I have this right. Harper was single and pregnant and tried to hide it. I assume to keep from embarrassing a sitting president. A little old-fashioned if you ask me, but whatever. She was secluded somewhere with a midwife, this Colette Proust you spoke about. Then she thought the baby, Shane, died. But years later, someone is trying to say Shane is alive and wants to trade him for ransom. Or, in your alternate theory, the baby did die and Harper's just some money-grubbing treasure hunter out for a quick buck."

Bishop winced.

"Oh, wait," Radley added. "I forgot the part where Shane may or may not be your son. Does that pretty much sum it up?"

Bishop took a menacing step forward, but Dalton stepped between them.

Radley held up his hands in a placating gesture. "In spite of what it probably looks like to you, I'm not your enemy. I'm not the media or some paparazzi trying to sell a story. I'm just here to solve a murder. Blake Carter's murder. And of course, I need some kind of explanation for why I have four dead gunmen in the morgue and another guy in the ER.

"If you cooperate with me," he asserted, "you'd be surprised what kind of damage control and manipulation of the press that I can do. But I can't help you if you don't help me. I need information. If you're dealing with extortion and kidnapping, that's exactly the kind of thing that might explain a bunch of mercenaries being involved, and it could explain Mr. Carter's murder if he saw something he shouldn't have. Or maybe he was part of the kidnapping plot. Did that theory occur to any of you?"

None of them said anything.

"Okay. How about this?" Radley tried again. "How much money are we talking about here? Would it be enough incentive for daddy dearest to hire gunmen to kill his daughter so he wouldn't have to pay? Or maybe he was more concerned with protecting his crime-fighting legacy in the court of public opinion than trying to ransom a grandson he never acknowledged he had. Please tell me one of you Seekers has thought of those possibilities." He glanced at each of them. "Anyone? Bueller?" He chuckled at his reference to the movie from the eighties. The rest of them weren't laughing.

"There's another theory that comes to mind," he continued, as if they were all best friends chatting on a golf course about which club to use for the next hole. "What if the hair samples are indeed fake, as you've theorized, but Harper doesn't know that? What if, instead of her playing you, someone else is playing her?"

Bishop was about to tell Radley where he could go with all his theories when his phone buzzed in his pocket.

All of their phones were buzzing.

They pulled them out and read the messages on their screens. Then, as one, they took off running for the emergency room.

Chapter Nineteen

The curtains billowed in the doorway of Harper's room as more people ran down the hallway outside it. Eli stood by the curtain, his back to the wall, pistol in his right hand pointing down at the floor as he peered out the crack. Caleb had shoved Harper's bed against the wall on the left, as far from the curtained doorway as he could get it. And he, too, stood guard, at the foot of her bed, gun in hand as he kept himself between her and the doorway.

Her frustration mounted as she clutched the bed rail, keeping quiet as they'd ordered her the moment code blue was called on Room 14. Was that the gunman's room? Even if it was, why were Caleb and Eli acting as if they thought a battalion was about to lay siege to her room?

The curtain billowed again. She leaned to the side to look around Caleb and saw Gage standing just inside the room. He cast a quick glance her way then spoke in low tones to Eli. Before she could ask him what was going on, he slipped back out and Eli jerked the curtain almost all the way shut again, leaving only a slit for him to keep an eye on what was happening outside her room.

Just when Harper was ready to hop off the bed and try to make a jail break, Gage entered the room again. This time, when he spoke to Eli, Eli holstered his gun and stepped outside the curtain. Gage strode to the bed and sent Caleb out, as well. He eyed the wonky way the bed was pressed up against the wall and gave her what seemed to be a reluctant smile.

"Want me to straighten out your bed?"

"I want you to tell me what's going on."

He rolled the bed back into position and slid the three orange guest chairs all on the far side of the bed, closest to the door, before taking up a stance on the other side, his back to the wall. "Our gunman had a medical emergency. Caleb and Eli guarded you in case it was a diversion so someone could slip inside your room."

She stared at him in surprise. "Was it? A diversion?"

"Not as far as I can tell. No one tried to get past Eli."

"And?"

"And what?"

She sighed. "You're being awfully tight-lipped. What happened? Is the gunman okay?"

"They couldn't revive him."

She pressed her hand against her chest. "What happened? Were his injuries worse than the doctors realized?"

"No one's sure at this point. But it looks like a heart attack."

"Looks like?"

Before he could respond, a knock sounded. Eli moved the curtain to let her stepmother and Secret Service agent Faulk into the room. Her mother was smiling and holding two cups of coffee, but stopped when she saw them, her smile fading.

"Is something wrong?" she asked. "You both look like someone kicked your favorite dog."

Harper started to reassure her but Gage spoke first.

"Faulk, I heard you were assigned to protect Mrs. Manning these days. Where were you earlier this morning when she was here alone?"

The agent stopped, his eyes widening. "I was told she

was being looked after by your team, so I went to the cafeteria. Was there a problem?"

"Leave him alone, Bishop." Julia headed to the bed and set the coffee cups on the tray beside it. "You're not a Secret Service agent anymore, so it's none of your concern."

"Julia," Harper chastised, "don't speak that way to Gage."

"It's okay," Gage assured her. "Where have you been, Mrs. Manning? You missed the excitement."

She frowned and gestured at the coffee cups. "I think it's obvious where I've been. I wanted to get my daughter a decent cup of coffee. That stuff at the nurse's station is awful. The cafeteria's not much better. I threw some cream and sugar in to hopefully make it drinkable. Why? What did I miss?"

Another knock sounded and this time Cynthia and Dean entered the room, each of them carrying a soda and a small bag, presumably of snacks. Cynthia had been smiling at her boyfriend but her smile disappeared when she stopped at the end of the bed, looking at each of them. "Who died?"

"Interesting you should ask," Gage said. "The gunman just passed away. I'll ask you and Dean the same question I just asked your mother. Where did you two disappear to for so long? You both left before me and I've been gone far longer than I expected. The vending machines aren't that far away."

Cynthia rolled her eyes, unfazed, and crossed to the other side of the bed. "I think your boyfriend is accusing us of having something to do with that slimeball's death."

Julia gasped. "Bishop, how dare you—"

"Julia," Harper interrupted. "Cynthia, everyone, would you please give me and Gage a few moments alone?"

Her stepmother sputtered in outrage. Cynthia grabbed her arm and hauled her toward the doorway, with Faulk and Dean following behind.

"Come on, Mom. Harper's had enough of your drama for one morning." She winked at Harper, earning a glare from her mom.

When they were gone, and the sound of their bickering faded down the hall, Harper threw the covers off and wrestled the railing down so she could sit on the side of the bed. "My sister got that part right, for sure. I'm tired of drama. Of all the drama. Tired of being told to be quiet and treated like a child who can't handle the truth. And I don't appreciate you practically accusing my family of murder. Even if they were cold, bloodthirsty killers, how would they have gotten into the gunman's room, much less caused him to have a heart attack?"

"He was sedated and handcuffed to the bed. Apparently, that was enough for the cop guarding his room to leave his post and flirt with the nurses at the nursing station farther down the hall. Anyone could have slipped inside his room."

"Check the cameras," she snapped. "Those little surveillance bubbles on the ceiling are all over this place. Then once you see my mom and sister haven't gone near that man's room, you can come back and apologize. To all of us."

His jaw tightened. "Actually, checking the cameras was the first thing we did. But they're pointed at the main entrance to the ER corridor, not the entrances to each room."

"Okay. Then I'm sure you can clearly see when my mom and sister left and when they came back. Which was obviously after the code blue."

"Funny thing about that, too. There's a good ten-minute gap I can't account for in their movements around the hospital."

She blinked. "Good grief. You're serious, aren't you? You really think they could be involved."

He sighed and straightened. "As I've said before, everyone's a suspect. Anything is possible."

"Well, how about this as an explanation for that ten-minute gap. Knowing my mother and sister, they probably stopped at the waiting room inside the ER to argue about something stupid, as usual, before coming into my room."

"I'll be sure to ask them about it."

"Good grief."

The curtain slid back a few feet and a tech stepped into the room carrying vials of blood in a plastic tray. Behind him, Eli pulled the curtain closed again.

"Hello there." He smiled at both of them and set his tray on the end of the bed. "I'm here to take a blood sample. Need to check your ID bracelet first." He scanned the bar code on her wrist. "Let's see who we have. Harper Manning?"

She nodded and confirmed her birth date. As the tech drew the sample, she asked, "Why are you drawing blood when I'm supposed to get out of here soon? Where's the doctor anyway? He should have been here by now."

He shrugged. "I just follow the orders the doctors write up. Sorry, ma'am. Maybe the nurses can answer your questions."

"Thanks. I'll be sure to ask them."

Gage stood on the other side of the bed, watching in silence.

The tech printed a label from the scanner and attached it to the blood vial, then gathered up his trash and put it in the medical waste container attached to the wall. "Thank you, Ms. Manning. I hope you feel better soon."

She smiled her thanks. When he left, she pinned Gage with a glare, ready to tear into him. But he was already pushing away from the wall and heading for the doorway.

"Gage, wait. We need to talk."

"I need to take care of a few things first." He whipped the curtain back and left.

"Oh no you don't," she muttered. She slid to the edge of the bed and yanked the tape off her IV.

Eli took a step forward as if to stop her. She narrowed her eyes in warning. He immediately retreated to the curtain.

Biting her lip, she slowly pulled the plastic needle out, then laid it with the tubing over the IV pump. After locating her clothes in the closet, she tossed them on the bed and aimed a taunting look at Eli. He promptly stepped outside the room. Once dressed, she headed off into battle.

The battle lasted all of five seconds, the time it took for Eli to grab her arm in the hallway and pull her back into the room.

"Ms. Manning, I'm sorry. But I'm under strict orders to keep an eye on you."

She shoved his hand off her arm. "Keep an eye on me? Do you mean make sure I don't go into another patient's room and kill them?"

His eyes widened. "Um, no, ma'am. My orders are to protect you, to keep you safe."

"It's Eli, right?"

"Yes, ma'am."

She gritted her teeth. "Eli, I'm pretty sure you're older than me. Can we drop the ma'am?"

"Yes, ah, Ms. Manning."

She crossed her arms. "Where's Gage?"

"In a meeting."

"Another meeting? I'm sure it has to do with me. I'd like to join that meeting. Where is it?"

"I can't tell you that. But I assure you that he'll be back soon and—"

"Eli?"

"Yes?"

"If you don't take me to Gage right now, I'm going to open every door in this hospital until I find him. And if you grab my arm again or try to stop me in any way, my father's lawyers will slam you with an assault charge that will have you tied up in court for the next decade and drain all your assets. Pick a side, but do it fast. Because I'm leaving, Right now."

Chapter Twenty

After Eli led Harper down several hallways in the hospital, she was beginning to think he was calling her bluff about getting lawyers involved. In spite of her threat, she certainly had no intention to create legal problems for him. He and the other Seekers were risking their lives to help her. But it had been the only threat she could think of to get her back in the game instead of sitting—or in this case, lying—on the sidelines.

Just as she was ready to tell him he'd won this charade and to take her back to her room, he stopped. The door in front of them boasted a bright orange-and-white nameplate. The VOLS Conference Room was obviously a nod to Knoxville's University of Tennessee.

"I'll go in first," he said, "and give everyone a heads-up that you're here."

"No need. Thanks." She swept past him, entered the room, and stopped in surprise. The usual suspects were there. Mason, Caleb, Dalton and, of course, Gage, who was frowning at her from his seat directly across from the door. What she hadn't expected was the man sitting at the far right end of the long table—Detective Radley.

Gage stared at Eli. "Do you need my assistance in escorting Ms. Manning back to her room?"

Eli's face reddened. But before he could say anything, Harper pulled out the nearest chair and sat. "I'm not going anywhere. You don't get to practically accuse my step-mother and sister of murdering that gunman and then leave me out of a meeting about it. I want to know what's going on."

"Excellent," Detective Radley chimed in, much to Gage's obvious displeasure. "We were just discussing our John Doe gunman and the fact that we have a name for him now—Jerry Wallace. His fingerprints returned a match in the FBI's AFIS system. Wallace is an ex-con whose brother is still in prison, in large part because of strict mandatory sentencing laws championed by none other than your father, Earl Manning."

Harper stared at him in shock. "Then the men who tried to kill Gage and me…it was revenge, because of my father's policies? Wait, that means the attack at my house is related to the assassination attempt in Gatlinburg?"

Gage crossed his arms on top of the table. "We don't know yet. The Secret Service is looking into a possible connection and they're still investigating the man who tried to kill your father. Detective Radley is just throwing out potential links." He shot Radley a decidedly cool look. "Even though we've said repeatedly that we need to focus on other things right now, because of the tight deadline."

"The Secret Service is looking into the gunmen now? Good grief. This is much bigger than I'd realized." She swallowed hard. "Or hoped."

Gage tapped the table. "There are no secrets in this room, Harper. Radley knows about Shane."

She shot the detective another shocked glance. When he nodded, she tightened her fists beneath the table. "I don't understand. Why would you tell him that? You're jeopardizing our child's life."

"He didn't tell him." Mason, sitting to Gage's left, gave her an apologetic look. "I'm afraid in my eagerness to bring Bishop up to speed on some findings regarding your case,

I didn't realize the detective was nearby—within hearing distance. He heard enough to guess the rest, so we're working together from here on out.

"Radley understands the need for discretion, that it's potentially a matter of life or death for…your son. The hope is that he can spin the information provided to the media to ensure that nothing about Shane and the ransom demand is revealed. For now, at least until we know all the facts of what's going on and who's behind it, the attack on you will be reported as part of a plot against the entire Manning family."

"Ms. Manning?"

She looked down the table at Radley.

"I promise you that I'll do everything in my power to keep the plot against your son quiet. No one wants to do anything that could jeopardize his life. On the other hand, as Bishop has emphatically pointed out, knowledge is power. You have a much better chance of a desirable outcome if we can figure out who the kidnapper is and rescue Shane before the appointed exchange. And that's exactly what we hope to do. We were just discussing what we know about the gunman since we still don't know for sure whether it's related to the ransom demand or not."

She rubbed her hands up and down her arms. "If you're trying to reassure me, you're doing a lousy job."

"We're trying to get to the facts," Gage said.

His demeanor was less hostile than when she'd first come into the room. But now it bordered on chilly. What had happened to the man who'd been so overcome with emotion over the knowledge that he had a son that his voice had sounded close to breaking? What had happened to the man who'd done everything he could to reassure her, and promised to keep her and Shane safe? She wanted that version of Gage back, wanted him to hold her, to make her feel safe again, and to fill her with hope. Something must have happened that had him angry with her. What was it?

Mason tapped the table this time, drawing everyone's attention. "Let's get back to the discussion at hand. Radley was filling us in about Wallace."

"There's not much more to tell," Radley said, "other than that he's a career criminal with an ax to grind against former president Manning. What's important is that the last physical he had during his most recent stint in jail showed he was quite healthy with no history, and no family history, of any kind of heart trouble. That is why I've instructed the medical examiner to cast a wide net of toxin testing on his blood. If someone gave him something to cause his heart attack, we want to know what it was." He paused briefly before adding, "I've also put the medical waste disposal container from his room into evidence. The state lab is backed up too much to help us with the tight window we have. So Mason's contacts at a private lab will process the evidence, examine any syringes inside the container and test those for toxins, too. If any are found, they'll swab for DNA to see if someone without gloves touched the syringe. No guarantees, but it's a solid place to start."

Harper looked at Gage. "Then you really do think someone poisoned him, gave him something to cause his heart attack?"

He shrugged. "It's the first thing that occurred to me, given his athletic build and the fact that he seemed in good health other than a fairly insignificant gunshot wound. It also seems suspicious that he's not the first person associated with you to have died of a heart attack. Colette Proust had a heart attack and passed away a few weeks after Shane's alleged death."

"Colette's dead?"

He nodded.

She stared at him a long moment, ruthlessly pushing

back the shock and grief over Colette's death. She'd deal with those feelings later. "And you think—what?—that I'm somehow involved in her death, and this Wallace guy's death years later, because I'm *associated* with them?"

He frowned then shook his head. "I wasn't saying that. No one suspects you of being involved in their deaths."

Mason, Caleb, Dalton, even Eli, who'd taken a chair at the far left end of the table well away from her, all shook their heads, agreeing with Gage.

Radley, however, remained silent.

When she speared him with a questioning look, he held his hands up. "I'm just following the facts. I don't have any suspects yet. But I'm also not willing to rule anyone out."

She shoved her hair back from her face. "Can someone please tell me more about what happened to Colette?"

Gage brought her up to speed. "We don't have records from a doctor to state that she was healthy or what kind of cardiac history she might have had. But her brother doesn't recall any heart problems in the family. So Radley pulled some strings. And Bryson—another Justice Seeker with some international contacts—called in some favors and put some pressure on Victor, Colette's brother."

"Victor was more than willing to allow an exhumation after I wired an obscene amount of money to his account," Mason said. "It was much faster than obtaining a court order."

She gave him a weak smile. "Thank you. I don't know that I'll ever have an obscene amount of money to be able to repay you, though."

"It's not a loan, Ms. Manning. I don't expect repayment."

She knew it was because of his friend and employee, Gage. But she still appreciated that he'd gone all-in to help save Shane. "Thank you."

He nodded.

Gage took over the narrative again. "Colette's body will be tested for signs of poisoning, with particular emphasis on things that can mimic or cause a heart attack. If we find that poison played a role in her death, and Wallace's, and the same kind of poison was used, it will be hard to argue that their deaths are unrelated. As it is, given our severe time constraint with the ransom date looming, we're moving forward with the assumption that they were both killed by the same person. We're looking into who could have interacted with both of them. And before you ask, yes, we're looking hard at your immediate family."

Harper started to argue, but he held up a hand to stop her.

"We're also looking at everyone who had access to your family during the time that you were pregnant. If your family isn't responsible for what happened to Colette, then someone close to them likely is—someone who overheard one of them talking about your situation."

She considered how cold he'd been to Faulk in her room earlier. "The Secret Service. You suspect them?"

"Faulk and Thompson are both high on my list of people we're looking into, especially Faulk since he was around during your pregnancy and recently popped back into your family's lives after being reassigned. The reason for his reassignment seems fuzzy at best, as if it's a cover to get him back at the Manning estate. I'm trying to get more information on that."

She sat in silence, letting it all sink in. The idea that people who'd sworn their own lives to keep her and her family safe could be the same people trying to kill her was sobering, to say the least.

A knock sounded on the door.

Caleb, to Harper's left, opened the door a crack then swung it wide to let the person in.

A tech in a white lab coat and green scrubs stepped inside carrying a familiar-looking tray with vials of blood and supplies. "I'm looking for Mr. Bishop?"

Gage held up his hand.

Harper watched in confusion as the tech rounded the table and prepped Gage for a blood draw. She glanced around the table, but no one would even look at her. Except Gage. He kept his gaze locked on hers the whole time the tech worked on him.

As soon as the tech left, Harper asked, "Why did he take your blood? My blood was drawn before I came here, even though I'm supposed to be discharged soon. I can't help but wonder if that's not a coincidence. What's going on?"

Mason stood and motioned to the other Seekers, who immediately exited the room. "Detective? If you have more questions, I'll address them. And Bishop has some suggestions he told me about before you joined us. I'll run those by you. Let's step outside."

Radley readily agreed and soon Harper was once again sitting alone in a conference room across from Gage. But this time, she wasn't there to plead her case or to ask for his help. This time he held all the cards. And she didn't even know what game they were playing.

"Gage?"

He started to say something, but seemed to think better of it. Instead, he rose, rounded the table and sat in the chair beside hers, swiveling it to face her.

"I don't know an easy way to tell you this, so I'll just say it. The Justice Seekers keep records of each employees' DNA profile, in case the worst happens and they need to identify…well, remains. Mason had a private lab compare my profile to the one from the lab your father hired. According to Mason's lab, Shane can't be my son."

She waited for him to say something more. Like, that he knew there'd been a mistake so he'd asked the lab to double-check the results. Or that he'd been with her nearly

24/7 for over two years and had reconciled his knowledge of her character with what she'd told him in Gatlinburg, and he realized how wrong he'd been all these years. She waited for him to assure her that it didn't matter what the lab said. Shane was his son. Their son. Forget the faulty lab. But he said nothing, and once again her heart fractured along one of those poorly healed cracks.

"You think I lied about that night in the pool house?"

He hesitated.

She pushed out of her chair and threw open the door.

He grabbed her arm, stopping her.

"Let me go." She desperately struggled to keep the threatening tears from falling.

"I will, but be warned. You're not leaving here without me by your side. Five armed men tried to kill you, and nearly did. Whatever threat you used on Eli won't work with me."

Her face heated. "I'm leaving. Tag along if you want, but don't expect me to talk to you. We're done."

He sighed heavily yet didn't let go of her arm. "You can't go home. It's a crime scene, and it's not safe there anyway."

"Then I'll go to a hotel."

He shook his head. "You'd be far too vulnerable. I have somewhere else in mind. The Manning family estate."

Her mouth dropped open and she looked up at him in spite of the tears she knew were shining in her eyes.

He frowned. "Harper? I should have been more diplomatic in how I said all that. I didn't mean to—"

"It doesn't matter. What matters is what you said about taking me to my father's home. It doesn't make sense. After saying you suspect my family, and the Secret Service agents assigned to guard them, you're going to take me right into the middle of all that?" To her horror, a tear slid down her cheek.

He winced and reached out as if to wipe it away.

She ducked back from his hand.

He grasped her shoulders. "We're running out of time to figure out who has Shane before we're completely at the kidnapper's mercy. I can't think of a better way to flush out whoever is behind this than to offer you as bait."

Her heart cracked even more at his declaration. "Why am I not surprised? Of course you'd offer me as bait. Now *that* goes along with the opinion you've always held of me. Because I don't matter."

"The hell you don't." He slammed the door shut and swung her around so that her back was against the conference room wall. She only had a second to register what was happening before he swooped down and captured her mouth with his.

She wanted to bite him, to hit him, to yell at him. No, she wanted to *want* to do those things. Instead, what she really wanted to do was to pull him close and drink him in. Her traitorous body did exactly that, melting against him and returning his fevered kiss with all the heat and passion banked inside her for the last six years.

Ever since that one night they'd shared in the pool house, she'd lived with the memory of how incredible they'd been together. Of how perfectly their bodies fit, like two pieces of the same puzzle, two halves of the same soul. And she'd craved recapturing that elusive magic again. She'd grieved his loss in her life and had longed for him after he'd left. But her memories had faded. They'd become a pale copy of what could be. Until now. All the emotions and lust and longing inside her was reawakened, and she couldn't get enough of him.

He groaned low in his throat, his tongue tangling with hers, his hands spearing through her hair as he moved his lips to her neck. When he lightly sucked, she had to bite down on her lip to keep from crying out at the sheer ecstasy of his touch. His hands slid down her back, caressing, stroking, learning her body all over again.

Then he swept her up in an even hotter kiss, making her practically weep with wanting him. He shuddered against her and pressed the entire length of his body into hers, pushing her hard against the wall.

A sharp pain shot through her ribs. She arched away from him, turning her head to the side.

He immediately stepped back, a look of chagrin on his face. "Did I hurt you? I'm so sorry. I forgot. Your ribs—"

"Are fine." She took a shallow breath and then another, riding through the pain.

He grabbed a chair, scooted it beside her and carefully helped her sit. He crouched in front of her, his face lined with concern. "Do you want me to call for a doctor?"

"No, no. Just…" She drew another shallow breath. "Just give me a moment. Apparently, the drugs they gave me are wearing off. Super bummer. Really *really* bad timing." She laughed and immediately grimaced at the protest her ribs made.

His hand shook as he gently feathered her hair back from her face. "I'd never intentionally hurt you, Harper. I hope you believe that."

"I'm fine. Really. The pain's almost gone."

He took her hands in his. "It's not just the ribs I'm talking about. Mason is running fresh lab tests to validate the original ones. That's why the tech drew blood. Mason insisted and I'm way too tired to think straight. I was a fool to agree to it. But it doesn't matter. I don't care what those lab results say. Shane matters to me because he's yours. Whether I'm his father or not, I'm going to do everything in my power to rescue him and to keep you safe. I won't let any harm come to you."

She blinked, shock and hurt warring against each other as the euphoria of everything they'd just shared began to evaporate. He still didn't believe her. He thought she was lying, that Shane wasn't his. And he thought by saying he'd accept Shane as his own, even though he didn't believe he was, that it made everything okay between them.

He searched her gaze. "Are you sure you don't want me to get a doctor? You still seem to be in pain."

A doctor couldn't do anything for the type of pain she was feeling right now. She forced a smile and steeled herself against the urge to break down and weep for that tiny glimpse of a future between the two of them she'd foolishly pictured while in his arms.

"I'm okay. I'll just…head to my room and demand some discharge papers so I can get out of here."

He helped her stand. But before opening the door, he said, "I care about you, Harper. God help me, I always have. And I wouldn't do anything to put you in danger. Taking you to the Manning estate makes sense. I'll explain why on our way. But I need you to trust me. Can you do that?"

Not with her heart. Never again. He'd proved he couldn't be trusted with that. She nodded, letting him make of it what he would.

He pulled open the door.

Chapter Twenty-One

As Gage performed a security check on all of the rooms throughout the Nashville Manning family home, Harper waited in the two-story foyer in front of the massive stair-case, surrounded by gold-framed ancestral paintings dating back to the Revolutionary War. It was surreal being here again, even if for only a few days. The last time she was here, she'd wavered between the euphoric high of discovering that Shane might still be alive to a bottomless well of despair fearing that the whole thing was a hoax.

It was no hoax. The first lab had proved that. Or at least, she'd thought it had. But Mason's lab claimed that Gage wasn't Shane's father. She'd immediately assumed his lab was mistaken. After all, she knew for a fact that Gage was the father. But it was hard to believe that with the full resources of the Justice Seekers behind the lab, and so much riding on the results of the tests, that they'd be careless enough to make that kind of mistake. Other possibilities had crept insidiously through her mind, sinking the talons of doubt deep into her soul.

What if Mason's lab *hadn't* made a mistake?

The only way for that to be possible was if the hair sample from the ransom note wasn't Shane's.

She closed her eyes for a moment, trying to reason it all out. The first lab had done two tests, one on the hair sample from the note, and one from her. The conclusion

was a mother-son relationship. That was what had proved
to her that her son was still alive. That's what had given
her hope. But Shane was the only child she'd had. If the
hair wasn't from Shane, then the lab had to have made a
mistake when testing *her* hair. Was it even possible for a
lab to find a mother-son link between two DNA profiles
if they weren't related? Was it possible for another lab *not*
to find a father-son link between two DNA profiles if they
were related?

It was all so confusing. She couldn't reconcile any of
it, no matter how she looked at it. And nothing explained
what had happened at her home, the attack by five gunmen
who'd clearly been trying to kill her. Was that completely
unrelated to the ransom demand? Or was it something far
worse, something so sinister that goose bumps rose on
her arms as she tested and weighed suspicions seeded by
Gage's comments at the hospital?

Could someone in her own family want her dead?

As if against her will, her gaze was drawn to the right
of the massive staircase to the open double door that led
into her father's office. Not long ago, she'd gone into that
cavernous room with her father and stepmother. They'd sat
in the U-shaped grouping of couches in front of the fireplace and she'd showed them the ransom note, the dark
hair in the baggie. Her father had seemed overjoyed at the
prospect that Shane might still be alive.

But did he really feel that way? Or had it all been for
show?

He was the one who'd suggested they involve Gage.
She'd understood his desire to keep things quiet, to protect his legacy and to protect future leaders by not setting
a dangerous precedent for making deals with criminals.
But had he taken it a step further? Had he hired someone
to eliminate her and Gage to ensure the ransom was never
paid? So that nothing about the ransom ever made it into

the media? Would he really trade his own daughter's life for his legacy?

Opulence surrounded her, enormous sums of money spent by a frugal man solely because appearances mattered. Appearances truly were everything to Earl Manning. And he, more than anyone, knew the public would look much more favorably on a grieving father than on a hypocritical former president who'd broken the rules and policies he'd touted his entire political career to ransom his grandson. Would he go so far as to hire someone for a bogus assassination attempt so he could later pin his daughter's death on similar zealots, out to hurt him by hurting his family?

She shivered and reflexively rubbed her arms.

"Harper?" Gage asked.

"Sorry. Did you say something?"

He smiled. "The past few weeks have to feel like the longest weeks of your life. You're exhausted, aren't you?"

Exhaustion didn't come close to covering how she felt. And she really didn't want to deal with her family once they got home. She was barely holding herself together right now.

"I guess I am. I could use a nap. So could you. At least I got some sleep last night. You didn't. There are guest rooms in the back hallway beneath the stairs." She rolled her eyes at herself. "Why am I telling you? You know this house as well as I do."

"Thanks for worrying about me. I'll go to bed soon. But first, I'll escort you to your room."

"I grew up here. I think I can find it on my own."

His smile dimmed as he picked up her overnight bag, which he'd left in the foyer while he'd made sure there was no one waiting for them inside the house. "I'm sure you can. But with your sore ribs, I'd like to carry this up for you."

"Oh." Harper's face heated. "Sorry." What else could she say? Things were...awkward between them now. While he seemed to think he'd cleared the air, her heart had been shattered.

Gage followed her up the stairs, stopping at the open railing that ran about thirty feet across the gallery that looked down into the foyer. "You remember the plan I explained on the way here?"

"I remember. It's all set?"

"It is. I didn't want you to be surprised."

She headed down the hallway, stopping in front of the next-to-last door on the right.

Gage opened the door and set her bag just inside. "I hear cars outside. Your stepmom and siblings are probably here with the pizza they said they'd bring. I know it's closer to bedtime than dinner at this point. But you have to be hungry. I don't think you ate anything at the hospital today with everything going on."

"I really couldn't eat if I tried. Everything hinges on tomorrow, on the kidnapper making contact. And yet, nothing seems to have been resolved. What are we going to do when he sends the note with instructions for the exchange?"

"I think we're closer than you think to having the answers we need. Come morning, we'll have a plan in place."

"I hope you're right." She headed into the room and locked the door behind her.

BISHOP LISTENED TO the click of the lock then leaned against the wall outside Harper's door. Everything was set for tonight's plan. All the parts were in place. But he wished more than anything that he could undo so much of what had happened today.

He'd hurt her.

That was the last thing he'd ever wanted to do. Even

when he'd thought she was the reason his career had imploded at the Secret Service, even with the resentments he'd carried for so long, he'd never wanted her hurt.

There was a time, when he was still assigned as the agent to protect her, that he'd considered quitting his job and exploring the attraction between them. His whole life he'd wanted to be a Secret Service agent. And yet the thought of a future without Harper in it had had him second-guessing whether his career mattered like it once had. But then things had gone horribly wrong and he'd turned bitter and resented her, blaming her for everything that had happened.

Yesterday, after seeing the picture of a little boy with a familiar birthmark, hope had flared inside him. A picture of a little family, the three of them, had taken root in his chest and expanded his heart. Everything he'd done since then had been with that picture in mind. Then Mason's comment about him not being Shane's father had destroyed that dream. It had filled him with pain, and resentment that Harper had lied to him.

But she *hadn't* lied.

He didn't need a lab test to tell him the truth that he'd seen in her eyes when she'd told him about Shane. Even though he still couldn't remember that night in the pool house, he absolutely believed her about it. Because it was the missing piece of information he'd searched for all this time. It was the one fact that made what had happened all fit together. It explained how she could have been carrying his child even though he had no memory of sleeping with her. It also spoke to another question he'd never been able to answer—how she could have been seeing someone else without his knowledge as her protector.

Because of all the incidents back then where people had harassed her or threatened her over her father's political views, Bishop had stuck to her like glue. He knew who her friends were, who she'd associated with, and where she'd been at all times. He'd racked his brain over the years trying to think of who could have fathered her child and had come up empty. That was why he'd believed she'd lied about the pregnancy.

Now he knew differently.

He'd seen the pain in her eyes, heard the grief warring with hope in her voice as she'd pleaded with him to help her get her son back safely. Out of everything that had happened, that was the one constant, the one thing he knew to be true. She'd had a son. She'd named him Shane. And he was *their* son. His son. He never should have let the hurt and shock of Mason's announcement about the lab results sink in for even a moment. He never should have hesitated when Harper had asked him whether he believed her about the pool house. That one lapse had destroyed any hope left inside him that the picture of his future, a future with her, could be realized.

"Bishop? Harper? Are you up there? We've got the pizza." Julia's voice carried up the staircase from the foyer.

Bishop straightened away from the wall and headed for the stairs. He'd just reached them when Julia crested the top with her eleven-year-old son, Tyler, in tow. From the way he was yawning and rubbing his eyes, there was no question where they were going.

Bishop got down on one knee so he could look the little boy in the eye. "Hi, Tyler. My name is Bishop. I worked here a long time ago. You were only five. You might not remember."

Tyler stared at Bishop and cocked his head, as if studying him. "You took us to fly kites, me and Harper."

"Yes. Yes, I did. A few times." He smiled. "I'd forgotten about that. It's good to see you again."

Tyler let out a huge yawn.

Bishop laughed.

Julia tousled Tyler's hair and gave Bishop a wary look, no doubt remembering their unpleasant encounter in Harper's hospital room. "The nanny had already fed him but this little guy heard we were getting pizza and insisted that we stop and get him some chicken nuggets on the way. He's full, and sleepy, and about to pass out." She glanced down the hallway behind him. "Where's Harper?"

"Just as tired as your little guy there. She's not coming down for dinner." He stood, but kept his smile, not wanting his size to intimidate the dark-haired little boy who looked so much like his father. Tyler's wide-eyed stare seemed to indicate he wasn't sure about the big man standing in his house, even if he did remember flying kites with him.

Julia tugged on Tyler's hand. "Come on, kiddo. I'll see you downstairs, Bishop." She turned left and the two of them disappeared into one of the bedrooms that faced the backyard.

Bishop headed downstairs. He wasn't particularly hungry. But other than Dean, who'd claimed at the hospital that he needed to go back to the dorm for something, the rest of the people on Bishop's short list of suspects were all here. He might as well keep an eye on them to see if any of them slipped up and gave anything away.

When he entered the dining room, the sideboard had been set up with drinks, three different pizzas to choose from, and an array of real plates and silverware. The Mannings were probably the only people he knew who ate takeout pizza in a formal dining room on fancy china instead of on paper plates and with their hands.

Bishop kept silent for the most part as he ate a slice of pizza. He knew his earlier actions had everyone feeling unsure around him, not just Julia. But they seemed to gradually relax around him and the talk began to flow freely once Julia returned.

It was interesting to see the camaraderie between Faulk

and the two women. Their relationships seemed far more casual than Bishop had allowed his to be with Harper when he was guarding her. In addition to trying to maintain his professionalism, he'd been struggling with his wild attraction to her. So he'd made a point of not joining her for meals very often in spite of her constant invitations. Most of the time he patrolled the property. And he'd slept in the pool house, relying on the security gate and alarms to alert him if anything happened at the main house.

Faulk seemed more like a friend than a bodyguard. And he'd chosen to stay in one of the guest rooms downstairs in the hallway beneath the stairs rather than the fully equipped pool house. That only made Bishop more suspicious of him. He could easily picture him and Julia, or maybe him and Cynthia, trying to make money off the ransom scheme, especially since Faulk and Harper didn't seem to share a close relationship.

Harper barely glanced at Faulk other than polite greetings whenever they saw each other. She'd been much warmer and more outgoing with Bishop than she ever was with Faulk.

When the leftover food was put away and the women headed up to their rooms, Faulk went outside to patrol the perimeter. Bishop headed into his guest room under the stairs. Much later, after Faulk had gone to his room and the house had settled down for the night, Bishop snuck out of his room and headed up the stairs.

A BARELY AUDIBLE click sounded from the direction of the bedroom door. Seconds later, a faint puff of air indicated the door had opened and then closed behind whoever had just snuck inside. It was too dark to see anything, but a whisper of fabric indicated the intruder was heading deeper into the room.

Heading toward Harper's bed.

Another second passed. Two. Three. The light flicked on overhead.

The man whirled toward the door then stopped and slowly raised his hands in the air.

Bishop stepped out of the open closet doorway, aiming his pistol at the man's chest. "The only reason I haven't shot you yet is because Harper isn't here."

Faulk's brows rose in surprise. He half turned to see the empty bed. "Where is she?"

"In a guest room, with a bodyguard. I took her usual bedroom to see if the person who was trying to kill her would take the bait. Looks like he did."

The blood rushed from his face, leaving him pale and gaunt-looking. "Kill her? I'm not trying to kill her. I swear it."

"Says the man who snuck into her room, in the dark, with a gun."

"The gun's in my holster. Part of my job, as you well know."

"Maybe I'll go ahead and shoot you anyway. Just be done with it."

"No, no, no." A bead of sweat popped out on Faulk's forehead and began to roll down the side of his face. "Let me explain."

"I'm waiting."

Faulk swallowed hard. "I needed to talk to Harper in private, away from her family. I wanted to warn her. And I couldn't do that in front of anyone else. I'd lose my job."

"Start making sense, fast. I'm losing patience. And this pistol's getting heavy."

"All right, all right. I was here a few months ago protecting the current president when he came for a visit. The whole family was here, all of the Mannings, including Harper. As you can imagine, there was a lot of security. Too many for all of us to be inside without being underfoot. So I went outside, patrolled the perimeter. On the way back, I heard a couple of people talking near the back kitchen doorway. I didn't want to intrude, so I ducked behind some shrubs to wait. I heard some things that…well, alarmed me. I mean, there wasn't a specific threat. Nothing I could really act on. But there was frustration, and anger."

"Directed at who?"

"Earl Manning."

"What's that got to do with Harper?"

"Everything. They were talking about using her to get back at him. But they went inside before saying anything else. I knew if I told Mr. Manning, he wouldn't take it seriously. He'd laugh it off. But the anger in their voices…" Faulk shook his head. "I felt it was a credible threat. But I had no proof. I didn't even know what they were planning, or when. So I did the only thing I could do. I asked for temporary reassignment to the Manning home so I could figure out what was going on."

"Thompson said you were reassigned because you screwed up."

"Yeah, well. That's Thompson for you. When has he ever not been a jerk? He's just ticked that I wouldn't tell him why I asked for the change in assignment. He's the last person I'd trust with my career."

"I'm with you on that. So why did you sneak in here tonight?"

"To tell Harper what little I know. I didn't tell her before because, quite honestly, I began to doubt myself. Nothing else had happened since then. But after hearing about those gunmen who went after you two, I'm convinced that I know who's behind it."

Bishop slowly lowered his gun. "Tell me exactly what you heard that night. And who you heard."

Twenty minutes later, Bishop carefully lowered himself into a wing chair in one of the guest rooms downstairs.

Across from him, sitting at the small desk by the window with his laptop open, Mason poured a glass of whiskey and offered it to him.

"No, thanks. I'm running on empty right now. It's going to be hard enough getting up in a few hours without alcohol in the mix."

"I should probably take the same advice, but I'm going to drink a glass anyway. Brielle's with Harper?"

"She is. Harper's not thrilled to have Brielle camped out on the floor by her bed while I took Harper's usual suite. But once she hears what happened, I have a feeling she'll be far more accepting of the inconvenience."

Mason took a sip from his whiskey and sat back. "So our would-be killer took the bait, only he wasn't our guy."

"I'm not marking Faulk off the short list just yet. But it seemed like he might be telling the truth."

"What about Thompson? He hasn't been sniffing around the Mannings since this started. But he was here a lot over the years for inspections and assessments while Faulk was assigned here. Could he be our guy?"

Bishop shook his head. "I wish I could say yes. Being arrested couldn't happen to a nicer person. But I called in some favors with some Secret Service agents I still know. Thompson's schedule has taken him a lot of places and his movements are pretty well accounted for. I don't see him having the opportunity to set all this up. Or, frankly, the motivation. His finances are healthy. His investments are solid. He won't be hurting once he retires. I think we can safely cross him off the list."

"That leaves us with the family."

Bishop sighed heavily. "Yes, it does. But even given what Faulk said, we don't have anything to tie a bow on this and offer it to Radley. He heard frustrations, generalities. Nothing concrete. I think they were in the early planning stages and hadn't really come up with a strategy when Faulk overheard them." He checked the time on the new phone he'd bought to replace the one that had been destroyed in the creek. "It's really late, or really early, depending on how you look at it. I don't suppose the discarded soda cans we collected at the hospital have already been tested? And that the fancy lab you hired has results this fast?"

"For what I paid them, they should have had everyone on staff working all day and evening on our stuff. If nothing else, I'd expect them to at least have blood types by now, even if full-blown DNA takes several more hours." He pulled out his cell phone and made a call.

It took another hour to get preliminary results, with final results promised by morning to be one-hundred-percent conclusive. Still, the preliminary ones had a high rate of confidence. When Mason clicked the emailed report and displayed it on the screen, he and Bishop both stared at it a long, solemn moment.

Mason finally shook his head in disgust. "You were right to ask the Seekers to follow the family and get those discarded sodas for DNA testing. And I'm equally glad we got those additional blood tests." He shot Bishop a concerned glance. "You realize what this means?"

Bishop straightened away from the computer. "I do."

"I'm really sorry, Bishop."

He gave him a curt nod. "I hope Radley hasn't already gone to bed. If he has, he's about to be woken up."

Chapter Twenty-Two

Harper sat beside Brielle in front of the makeup mirror, but she couldn't seem to concentrate on whatever Brielle was saying. All she could seem to think about: this was the day the kidnapper was supposed to contact her. This was the day she was supposed to get Shane. She should have been home, *with Shane's father*, waiting for the mail. Instead, here she was at her father's home, feeling more alone and confused than ever, even though she was surrounded by other people. Everything was mixed up, and wrong, and—

"Earth to Harper. Are you even listening?"

Her gaze flashed to Brielle's in the mirror. "I'm so sorry. What?"

Brielle gave her a playful shove. "Girl, you missed my best analysis about the advantages of selecting just the right shade of blush. My talents are truly going to waste here."

She eyed her reflection in the mirror and shook her head. "Honestly, it doesn't matter how much makeup you goad me into putting on. I'm still going to be ridiculously pale."

"Yeah, well. Not everyone is blessed with my gorgeous brown skin." Brielle winked. "And I didn't goad you. I encouraged you. After all, if you want to catch a man like Bishop, you need the right kind of lure."

"I'm not trying to catch him."

Brielle grinned and gestured at Harper's face. "Now there's the right color of blush. Do that every time he smiles at you and you'll have him wrapped around your... well, whatever you want him wrapped around. Know what I mean?"

Her eyes widened in shock.

Brielle laughed. "Oh, come on. I've seen how you two look at each other when neither of you think the other's noticing. And I saw how dejected you were last night when you shut the bedroom door, with him on the wrong side of it. You're pining after him, whether you realize it or not. The heart wants what the heart wants."

Harper stood and washed her hands at the sink. "We're not having this conversation."

"Suit yourself. We can talk or not talk. Up to you. But breakfast is nonnegotiable. I'm starving. And until we catch the guy trying to hurt you, my existence in this guest room is our little secret. So I'm at your mercy. Go get me some food, Harper. Heavy on the carbs. The greasier, the better."

On impulse, Harper gave her a hug.

Brielle's eyes widened. "Not that I mind, but what was that for?"

"You're putting your life on the line for me. All of the Seekers are. 'Thank you' seems pretty lame. But I really do appreciate your help. Maybe I can sneak a cot in here tonight to make you more comfortable."

"It's all good, Harper. Thank me with breakfast. Don't dawdle." She winked as if to soften her words.

"I'll tell my stepmom I'm really tired and want to bring my food back to my room and rest some more after I eat. Give me ten minutes. Tops."

"That's my girl. Extra bacon. I can smell that bit of heaven from here."

"You got it." Harper smoothed her hands down her navy blue slacks then headed to the door.

Suddenly Brielle was in front of her, blocking the way. "Hold it. Bishop just sent me a 9-1-1 text. Give me a second." Her fingers fairly flew across her phone as she exchanged messages with Gage. Finally, she shoved her phone in her jeans' pocket and checked the small pistol hidden in her other one.

"What's going on?" Harper asked.

"Unfortunately, it looks like breakfast is on hold. And me being here is no longer a secret. There's a meeting about to happen downstairs in your father's home office."

When Harper and Brielle began to descend the stairs, Gage was waiting at the bottom, watching them. Dressed in a fresh charcoal-gray suit, he was so handsome, her heart hurt to look at him. But as she drew closer, her steps slowed. He seemed so tired, his face drawn, his brow creased with worry as he watched her. She stopped two steps above him, clutching the railing as she met his eyes on even ground for a change.

"What is it? Did the kidnapper cancel the exchange?" She pressed her hand to her throat. "Shane. Is he okay? What's happened?"

Brielle stepped past her. "Is Mason in the office already?"

"He is. Just buy us a few minutes, all right?" He never took his gaze off Harper.

"Take as long as you need." Brielle hurried into the office and closed the double door behind her.

Harper twisted her hands together. "Mason's here? Why is your boss here, Gage?"

"Let's go into the family room. We need to talk privately before meeting with everyone else."

She glanced at the closed doors. "Everyone?"

"Your family, including your father. Dean, a few others."

"My father? He's here?"

"I contacted him late last night. He arrived a few minutes ago. Detective Radley's here, too. Don't be surprised if you see some uniformed officers through the windows. They're out front and a few out back. Along with some Secret Service agents, of course."

"Good grief. Why are all those people here? How are we supposed to make the exchange today and keep it quiet?"

"I'm about to lay everything out on the line, walk through what we've discovered. Get a few remaining answers I need to tie up the loose ends."

She tightened her hand on the railing. "You know who tried to kill us?"

He nodded.

"And...and Shane? What about him?"

He held out his hand. She grabbed it instinctively, her knees nearly giving out as he led her down the last two steps and into the family room on the opposite side of the foyer from the office.

As soon as he closed the door behind them, she turned to face him, her fingers splayed across his chest. The sight of unshed tears shining in his eyes as he looked down at her told her far more than any words ever could. But she still had to hear it out loud.

"Say it," she whispered, her voice tight and raspy.

"The plan to have me use your usual suite to draw out the killer worked, except it wasn't the killer who came into your room. It was Faulk."

"Faulk. But...if he's not the one who hired those gunmen, why would he sneak into my room?"

"He had suspicions and wanted to warn you. He witnessed things here last summer that had him worried, but with no provable facts. That's why he got reassigned. He asked to be reassigned, so he could find out what was going on."

"And you believe him?"

"The parts I could verify, yes. I was finally able to get someone to validate the facts about the reassignment. Everything else he said seems to fit with other things we've discovered. It paints a solid picture of what was happening. There are just a few questions remaining. This meeting brings everyone together so we can try to get those answers. But one thing is clear." He gently cupped her face in his hands. "I'm so sorry to have to say this, Harper. But the ransom demand was a hoax. There is no kidnapper."

She grabbed his wrists, holding on to him like a lifeline. "But... Shane. The ashes in the urn, they weren't real. Where—?"

"I don't know where he is, what Colette did with his remains. But there's no evidence that he's alive, that anyone has kept him all these years. We have to accept the facts. Our son died the same day that he was born. I wish with all my heart that I was wrong, that I could tell you he's alive. But I can't."

Harper squeezed her eyes shut. Her world tilted as he lifted her in his arms and carried her across the room. She buried her face against his chest and clasped her arms tightly around his neck as he held her, whispering sweet, reassuring words as he gently stroked her back. She wanted to cry, wanted to scream her grief and rage to the heavens. But the tears wouldn't come. Instead, a strange calmness settled over her. The grief was there, deep inside, battering at her wounded heart. But she realized she couldn't let it out, not yet. If she started crying, she might never stop.

She eased back in his arms to look at him. "I think that was my deepest fear this whole time, but I didn't want to admit it."

"That Shane was gone?"

She squeezed her eyes shut. "Yes. I wanted him back

so desperately that I shied away from anything that didn't fit with making that happen."

Harper opened her eyes and stared up into his deep blue ones, looking at her with such concern. "I need to know everything you know. I need to know who did this, who hates me so much that they twisted the most precious thing I've ever had into a weapon to use against me." She pushed out of his arms and straightened. "Let's end this charade, right now. For Shane. For what could have been but never was. Let's do this for our son."

His Adam's apple bobbed in his throat as he searched her gaze. "Are you sure? I can take care of the meeting, and tell you everything later. You don't have to do this."

"I want to. Need to. Please."

He pressed a whisper-soft kiss against her forehead. "Then that's what we'll do."

WITH BRIELLE STANDING guard just inside the office doors to prevent anyone from leaving, Bishop stood shoulder to shoulder with Detective Radley and Mason, their backs to the fireplace. Facing them from the U-shaped collection of couches and love seats were Earl, Julia, Cynthia and Dean.

Bishop glanced at Harper. He was so proud of her for being so strong, but he wished she didn't have to be. She'd chosen to sit in a chair off to the side in spite of her father's and stepmother's attempts to get her to sit with them. She'd simply shaken her head, her back ramrod-straight as she'd kept her gaze focused on one person. Him, Bishop.

He gave her a nod of encouragement then addressed the others. "As you're all aware, the Justice Seekers, in conjunction with Detective Radley, have been working together to find out who hired the gunmen who went after Harper."

"And you," she said, her voice quiet. "They tried to kill you, too."

Cynthia piped up. "Why do you assume someone hired them? I thought they were some radical group out to hurt my father by hurting his family. The media said they were likely tied to the guy who tried to assassinate my dad."

Her father reached past Julia to pat Cynthia's hand. "Let Bishop explain why he brought us here for this meeting."

She huffed an impatient breath and crossed her arms. Beside her, Dean looked positively bored.

"That may well prove to be true," Bishop said. "The Secret Service is looking into that angle. The Seekers have been focusing more on the ransom demand."

Cynthia exchanged a confused look with Dean. "Uh, ransom? Hello? What are you talking about?"

"A couple of weeks ago, Harper received a letter, along with some hair samples, demanding ransom for her son, Shane."

At Cynthia's shocked look, he quickly summarized the events surrounding Shane's conception, the stint where Harper was in seclusion with the midwife, and the fact that Shane had died at birth. He pulled no punches, taking the blame for everything. And when Harper tried to interject a defense of him, he politely cut her off. No way would he let her blame herself for anything that had happened.

"Holy Hannah," Cynthia exclaimed. "So that's why you used to keep that urn everywhere you went. You told me it got dented and you got rid of it."

"I had to explain it being gone somehow. But when the ransom demand came, we needed to have the ashes examined."

Again, Bishop took over, bringing everyone up to date. "A lot of things have happened in the past few days to help us see a more clear picture of what's truly going on. That's why you're all here. Radley, Mason and I have a few more questions we need answered, and we're hoping you can help us." He motioned to Mason to take up the explanation.

"The first lab ran tests on the hair sample sent with the ransom note, as well as a hair sample that Harper gave the night she came here to tell her stepmother and father about the ransom demand. The lab concluded a mother-son relationship. They also tested the ashes in the urn and discovered they were likely fireplace ash, not cremation ashes. Based on that, it was reasonable to believe the ransom demand was legitimate. Former president Manning has been working since that time to liquidate assets to be able to pay the ransom on the designated date."

Julia smiled at her husband and rested her head on his shoulder. He took her hand in his and held it between them.

Cynthia looked at Harper. "Okay. So, apparently, I have a nephew I never knew about. And what? You guys are the ones in charge of paying the kidnapper?"

"That was the original intention," Bishop confirmed. "Things changed once the gunmen entered the picture. There was no way to keep this off either law enforcement's or the public's radar. But we've been trying to keep it out of the media as much as possible to give us the best chance at not spooking the kidnapper."

"You're still going to pay the ransom and get Shane?" Cynthia asked.

"No."

She exchanged a startled look with Dean.

Mason glanced at Harper and then explained. "I paid a private lab to conduct several tests on Harper's behalf. We provided a DNA sample from Harper and Bishop, as well as the hair sample allegedly from Shane that wasn't consumed in the first lab's tests. And since we had a short list of those who might possibly have found out about the pregnancy, about Shane, I had several of my Justice Seekers follow the three of you around yesterday to collect drink containers you discarded." He looked at each of them before continuing.

"The only person whose DNA we didn't collect was former president Manning's. But it turns out, we didn't need it. The lab's tests were rushed last night to provide preliminary results. We also had another lab analyzing the ransom note for DNA. Unfortunately, there wasn't any in a detectible amount. The person who sealed the envelope and put the stamp on it used a wet paper towel or something like that rather than saliva. But we did retrieve metadata from the ransom note."

Dean straightened in his chair. "What are you talking about? Metadata? In your earlier summary, you said it was printed, not emailed."

Bishop's jaw tightened. "Yes. It was. And the printer embedded data onto the page, providing the serial number and model number. We were able to trace the ransom note to the exact printer used to produce it. A printer in the library at Vanderbilt University."

Cynthia stared at him in surprise.

Dean swore and crossed his arms. "You're accusing me or Cynthia of printing it because we go to school there. You might as well accuse Mrs. Manning, too. She volunteers in the library." He gave Bishop a smug look.

"Well I sure didn't create a ransom note." Cynthia slowly turned her head to look at her mother. "Mom?"

Julia's eyes widened. "I had nothing to do with any ransom note."

Harper was watching her family, her face now pale, a haunted look in her eyes. But still she said nothing.

Earl's face was red but it wasn't clear whether he was angry or upset on Harper's behalf. "Mr. Ford, Bishop, Detective Radley, I hope you have something more than a piece of paper that supposedly came from a printer used by the community, not just students at the university, before accusing any of my family of being involved in this heinous crime against my daughter."

"Yes, sir," Bishop said. "We do. Quite a bit more, actually. But first, I need to ask Harper some questions. Harper, the night you came here with the ransom note and hair sample, can you walk me through the timeline? And who was with you, up until your hair sample and Shane's were given to the courier to take to the lab?"

She shifted in her chair and clasped her hands tightly together, looking at the floor as she spoke. "I called Daddy as soon as I got the note. He was here to visit Cynthia because it was her first weekend home. She'd moved out of the dorm for the summer semester. I drove straight here— I think it was about five. I know it was before dinner, because we ate together later and Julia always serves dinner at six."

Earl patted Julia's hand. "Yes, she does. Shortly after five sounds right. We went into my office to look at the note together."

Detective Radley pulled out his pocket notebook and pen. "Who is *we*?"

Earl's brows raised. "The three of us—Harper, Julia, me."

"Where was Cynthia? And Dean?"

Cynthia crossed her arms. "That's right. Try to blame whatever's going on, on the least favorite daughter and her boyfriend. Here we go."

Her father gave her a warning look. "I love all my children equally."

Cynthia rolled her eyes.

"Where were Cynthia and Dean?" Radley asked again.

Dean held his hands up as if in defense. "Don't look at me. I wasn't here. I still had a paper to finish that weekend. I was at my dorm."

Cynthia frowned at him. "Nice."

"What?" He blinked.

She shook her head. "I was upstairs, unpacking. I never

heard anything about all this until today. I wasn't with them in the office when Harper came over. I only saw her once we went to dinner."

"That's true," her father said. "It was just the three of us in here, with the door closed. Julia got a plastic baggie from the kitchen and then used a pair of tweezers to pull out some of Harper's hair to make sure the root tags came with it. I'd called a lab I've used before and they said for a DNA test using hair we needed roots."

Radley jotted some notes. "And that same lab sent a courier to collect the samples?"

"Yes. He arrived about halfway through dinner. I'd put the samples in my desk drawer and came and got them, then gave them to the courier. That's it. Why does any of this matter?"

"Was your office door locked?"

"Of course not. I never lock it. There's no need. Again, why all these questions? What's it matter?"

"When Cynthia came down for dinner, where were the three of you?" Radley asked.

Harper stared at Radley then slowly looked at her sister. "The three of us were together in the office, then went to the family room. From there we helped each other serve dinner in the dining room. That's where we were when the courier came. We were together, the whole time."

Cynthia glanced back and forth from Harper to the detective. "Why does that matter?"

"It matters," Bishop said, "because of all the DNA testing I mentioned earlier. Yes, the samples sent to your father's lab had a mother-son relationship. But the mother in question is your mother, Julia. And the son...is Tyler."

She blinked. "What? I don't understand. What are you saying?"

Her father's face had gone pale. He stared at Cynthia in horror. "I saw Julia take Harper's hair samples. For the lab

to say the hair wasn't Harper's can only mean one thing—
someone switched the samples."

"How could you do this to us, Cynthia?" Harper whispered brokenly. "You knew I would come to Daddy when I
got the note. And you made sure you were here. You must
have been watching from the gallery when we went into
the study. When you saw Julia get the baggie and tweezers, you realized what she was doing. Or you listened
outside the doors and heard us talk about it. You knew if
they tested my hair against…" She briefly closed her eyes.
"They would know it was a hoax if they tested my DNA
and found no mother-son relationship. You did the only
thing you could to salvage your plan. You got samples of
Tyler's and your mom's hair from their hairbrushes and
switched them."

Cynthia frantically shook her head. "No way you tested
Tyler's DNA. I don't believe you."

"We didn't have to," Bishop said. "When the lab retested
Shane's hair sample and Harper's blood, they confirmed a
relationship. A *sibling* relationship. We knew that Shane's
hair was really from her brother—which means it wasn't
Shane's. It was Tyler's.

"There's no way anyone else could have switched the
samples for the first lab. It was you, Cynthia," he charged.
"By your own admission, by everyone's admission, the
only people in the house that night were you, your father,
your mother and Harper. Even Tyler was out. We verified
that with the nanny this morning over the phone. Julia
took him there so he wouldn't be here for the meeting with
Harper. It's you, Cynthia. You're the one who set up the
ransom hoax. And we believe Dean helped you."

"Me?" Dean squeaked. "You're crazy. It's all her. I'm
not involved in this."

"You liar!" Cynthia yelled at him. "You're the graphics
major. I'm not the one who Photoshopped that birthmark

onto a picture. It was your idea! You talked me into it."
She punched his shoulder.

"Why?" Harper's grief-stricken voice cut through the
noise. The room fell silent and everyone looked at her.
"Why would you give me false hope that my son was alive?
How could you be so cruel?"

Cynthia's face turned red. "I wasn't trying to be cruel,
Harper. I love you. I would never hurt you—"

"Stop lying. Just answer my question. Why?"

Cynthia stiffened. "You don't know what it's like being
the stepdaughter, the only child in the family not related
to the great 'President Earl Manning.' His blood is in your
veins, in Tyler's, but not mine." She pounded her chest in
emphasis. "Nothing I do is ever good enough for him. And
while he spends thousands of dollars buying rare books
to sit on the stupid shelves in this office to impress total
strangers, and donates hundreds of thousands of dollars to
charities, he leaves the rest of us to scrap for every penny
we have. Do you know how embarrassing it is to have to
turn down your friends to go to the movies or a concert because you don't have enough money to buy a stupid ticket?
When your father is the former freaking president? Correc-
tion. Stepfather. No relation. And certainly never wanted."

She glared at Earl, who'd gone white as a sheet.

"I didn't want to hurt Harper," she continued. "God
knows she's the only one around here who ever really
cared about me."

"Cynthia!" her mother exclaimed.

"Oh stop it, Mom. All you care about is your stupid
antiques and that ridiculous garden out back. How many
freaking plants does one person need?"

Her mother blinked, her chin wobbling.

"Spare me the crocodile tears, Mom."

Cynthia turned back to face Harper, her own tears
freely flowing now. "I'm not the stupid kid you thought I

was when you told me that urn was a vase. I knew it was an urn. But I never understood why you hauled that thing around with you until I snooped in your room one day and found that baby book you keep."

Harper sucked in a breath.

"I'm sorry, Harper. I truly am. But, I mean, Shane died the day he was born. It's not like you had him for years and then he died. I didn't think it would hurt you that much by pretending he was alive. All I wanted was to make Daddy suffer. And get enough money that I could disappear, have a fresh start, and never have to see the disappointment in your father's eyes again whenever he looked at me."

"I loved Shane," Harper said. "I carried him for nine months, talking to him, singing to him, planning our future together. He was all I had of the only man I've ever loved. And it destroyed me when he died. How could you be so callous?"

Bishop stared at Harper, stunned. Her face had turned red and she refused to look at him, as if only just realizing what she'd admitted.

"What about the gunmen?" Radley asked. "Where do they fit in all this? Did you want to hurt your father by having his daughter murdered?"

"What? No. Of course not. We had nothing to do with that."

"I'm sure the search history on both your laptops will back that up."

"Whatever." She gave him a mutinous glare and looked away.

Radley shrugged. "The truth will come out soon enough. The hospital lab is running tests on the gunman who supposedly had a heart attack. And did I mention we're exhuming the midwife's body? Collette Proust? We're testing her to see if a poison could have caused her heart attack. My theory is that someone poisoned both of them to cause their heart attacks. We'll be able to prove who that person is once all the hypodermic needles from the medical waste container in the gunman's hospital room are tested and examined for any DNA."

Cynthia shook her head. "You're delusional. I was a teenager when Harper had Shane. I couldn't have killed some midwife woman. Why would I?"

"Teenagers kill all the time. It's a sad fact of our times." She rolled her eyes.

"What about your boyfriend, Dean?" Radley asked, switching gears. "Is he the one who printed the ransom note?"

While Cynthia and Dean fell all over themselves to rat each other out, Bishop gave Mason a questioning glance.

Mason nodded, understanding what he was asking—whether Mason would work with Radley to try to get the details ironed out, and try to get a confession regarding the gunmen. Bishop had something far more important to take care of. Or someone. Harper.

He crossed to her chair and crouched until she looked at him. "Harper, there are a few more loose ends to take care of. Would you mind coming with me?"

She frowned, looking confused. But she nodded, let him take her hand and pull her to standing. They crossed to the door and Brielle silently opened it and then locked it behind them.

Chapter Twenty-Three

Of all the places that Gage could have taken Harper to tell her whatever last remaining devastating piece of information he thought she had to know, she felt this was probably the worst choice he could have made.

The pool house.

But as he shut the door behind them, cocooning them in together, an unexpected feeling of peace settled over her. The ups and downs, the fears, the horrific discoveries revealed in her father's study, all of it faded away.

Harper was transported back in time, almost six years, to this exact spot. This was where it had all begun. This was where she and Gage had created life. This was where Shane had been conceived. Her wonderful, precious little boy. And for some unknown, miraculous reason, she felt closer to her son at this very moment, in this place, than she had since the day he was born. It was as if he was here with them, trying to let her know that everything was going to be okay. That he was at peace. That he loved her.

"What other loose ends did you want to talk about?" she asked without turning around.

"Honestly? Nothing. I didn't want you to have to witness what was happening next. You were upset enough already."

She twisted her hands together. "Thanks for that. What *is* happening next?"

"Radley's going to arrest your sister and her boyfriend. Mason's working with him to wrap up the details. Cynthia…she did searches on her computer about hiring a hitman. It appears that she and Dean were behind both the Gatlinburg assassination attempt, and hiring those men to attack you."

She let out a shuddering breath. "I can't…wow. I knew she had issues with my dad. But I never thought she'd take it this far. And I never… I thought we were okay. The age gap made it hard sometimes. And she always felt I got more attention. But we were…friends." She shook her head. "All this time she wanted me dead? It's hard to fathom."

He gently clasped her shoulders. "It appears your dad refused to pay her tuition for next term unless she got her GPA up. Her grades came in and…well, she was going to be on her own. She was furious and desperate for money. Killing him, then deflecting attention by making it appear someone was after the entire family, was her real plan. I don't know that she really wanted you killed. She might have hired them to make it look like they were trying to kill you but she was in over her head, hired the wrong kind of guys. It went too far."

"You really believe that? She didn't want me dead?"

"Honestly? I'm not sure. Just playing devil's advocate."

"To make me feel better?"

He slowly pulled her back against his chest, giving her plenty of opportunity to stop him. She didn't. He slid his arms around her waist and rested his cheek on the top of her head. "I'd take it all away if I could, to make you feel better."

She shuddered against him then put her arms on top of his. Closing her eyes, she tried to forget the bad and remember the good. In this place, with him here, holding her, she could almost picture the future she'd once hoped for. The three of them, a family.

"What are you thinking about?" His voice was hesitant, cautious.

"The day he was born. Our son."

"Tell me," he whispered.

She smiled. Remembering. "He had blond hair, a head full of hair."

"My hair was blond when I was born."

"Mine, too. I wonder if his would have turned dark like ours. I always assumed it would. That's why Tyler's dark hair in the baggie never phased me."

He kissed the top of her head. "Was he tiny? I always assumed he came early, because he was in distress when he was born."

She frowned and slowly turned around, tilting her head back to meet his gaze. "He never seemed like he was in distress to me. He seemed...perfect. He was full-term. A bit thin perhaps, but a healthy pink color. Long, lanky. He would have been tall. Like his father. Colette laid him on my belly while she cut the cord. He...he opened his eyes. And I swear he smiled at me, though anyone else would say I'm crazy to believe that."

Gage smiled, surprising her again with the unshed tears sparkling in his eyes. "I believe you. What color were his eyes?"

"Blue. Deep blue, like yours. I made him a baby blanket, with his initials embroidered on the corner. I tried to match the blanket to the color of your eyes. Silly, right?"

Ever so slowly, he threaded her hair back from her face, letting his hand linger against her neck when she didn't pull away. "That was sweet of you. If I had my preference, I would have wanted them to be a lighter blue, like his mother's eyes."

She smiled again, surprised that she could after everything that had happened. But the cruel, awful world beyond their door didn't matter at this very minute. All that mattered right now was him, her, and the little boy they'd created.

"Tell me more," he urged.

She reached up and lightly ran her finger over the small birthmark on his right cheek. "This. He had the same mark on his face, just a little higher than yours. I…made a sketch in the baby book." She swallowed. "My sister must have seen that and gotten the idea to Photoshop the picture."

He tilted her chin up. "Don't let her in. This is our memory, our moment with our son."

She stepped closer to him. He folded his arms around her, wrapping her in his embrace. It felt so natural, so… right, to be held like this. Because this was Gage. This was the gentle, kind, protective, wonderful man she'd fallen in love with years ago. The man she'd wanted for so long that she ached for him at night lying in her bed. A man who'd turned to her in his grief and let her soothe him, or so she'd thought at the time. She knew better now. But even though that memory, of them making love, was hers alone, she would always cherish it.

"How long did you get to hold him before Colette took him to the hospital?"

She tightened her arms around his waist. "Not long. Maybe ten minutes. He coughed, and started crying. Colette immediately grabbed him up and suctioned out his mouth. But he coughed again. I thought it was normal." She frowned. "I never realized he was in any kind of trouble. But she said he was having a hard time breathing, that she needed to get him to the hospital immediately. I kissed the top of his head. And then…he was gone. Just like that. She took him. And I never saw him again."

He rubbed a hand up and down her back in a soothing gesture. "I'm sorry, Harper. I didn't want to make you sad."

She shook her head. "It's okay. It was good to see him in my mind again, to share that with you."

He kissed the top of her head then pulled back. "Is it okay that I brought you out here? Everyone else should be gone by now. We can go back to the main house if you want while we wait for an update from Radley."

"It's okay. Honestly, I haven't been here since…since that night. I thought it would be a bad memory. Instead, it feels good to be here again. With you."

He looked around the large room that was part bedroom, part kitchen, part living room, just like it was all those years ago. "I don't understand why it's such a blank spot in my mind. I wish I could remember. I can promise you one thing, though. I'll never forget Shane, the memory you just gave me."

A single tear slid down her cheek. She wiped it away. "What happens now?"

"With your sister?"

"No. I don't want to talk about her. Not yet. I still love her, and I'll eventually forgive her, as crazy as that sounds. It will eat me alive if I can't figure out how to do that. But I'm not ready for that yet. I meant what happens now…in regard to Shane? I'm not naïve enough to think that he's alive. But why would Colette give me an urn full of fireplace ashes?"

"The Seekers are working on that. Tracing Colette's movements, interviewing anyone she may have interacted with back then, trying to figure that out. I promise I won't stop searching until I have all of the answers, until we can lay him to rest, together."

She tilted her head again. "I'm so sorry, Gage. About everything. I wish I could go back in time and—"

"Shh." He pressed a finger against her lips. "Don't agonize over what might have been, what could have been. It will make you a bitter person, and give you nothing but regrets. Believe me. I'm the champion at that."

She blinked. "You? What regrets do you have?"

He framed her face with his hands. "Don't you know, Harper? Haven't you figured it all out? I'm in love with you, have been probably since the day I was assigned to watch over you, when you were in college. It killed me that I couldn't act on that, ask you out, pursue you the way I wanted to. It's haunted me all these years that I didn't realize the truth, that you were far more important than a career.

"If I had realized that earlier, then maybe we'd have spent the past few years together, raising our son, instead of wasting all that time apart. I had myself convinced that you were the villain in my life, until I walked into that conference room in Gatlinburg. It took all of two seconds for me to realize I was still in love with you. But I was still holding on to my pride, my grievances. Well, I'm not going to do that anymore. I'm not going to waste another second." He lowered his mouth to hers in a whisper-soft caress, gently testing, tasting, teasing.

She'd wanted this, craved it, for so long. To have him here, telling her he loved her, wanting her as much as she wanted him. It was like a piece of a dream she'd barely glimpsed a very long time ago. But now the whole dream was within her reach. All she had to do was take it.

Harper slid her hands up his chest to the back of his neck and stood on her tiptoes, pressing her mouth to his. He groaned and suddenly she was in his arms, her legs wrapped around his waist. With one arm supporting her bottom, the other at her back, he turned, half stumbling as he carried her to the bed without breaking the kiss. His tongue tangled with hers, fanning the flames inside her.

This, this was what she remembered. This inferno of heat and passion that exploded between them the moment his lips met hers. She nearly wept from the beauty of it, the joy, the knowledge that her craving for him was about to be assuaged. Finally.

He sat on the edge of the bed, her body still wrapped around him as his hot mouth moved to her neck. He seemed to know exactly where to touch, where to press, where to taste. When his mouth moved to a sensitive spot just below her ear, she shivered. He kissed her hypersensitive skin then sucked. She almost fell out of his arms then and there.

Laughing, he stood, turned with her in his arms and then slowly lowered her to the bed. His blue eyes had darkened to the color of midnight. And all signs of amusement fled as he slowly covered her with his body, propping himself on his elbows to keep from crushing her. The feel of him, there, pressing her down, even with their clothes on, was almost more than she could bear. It was exquisite, magical, perfect.

He feathered his fingers through her hair, sweeping it back from her face, his gaze never leaving hers. "I've wanted this forever, wanted you, in my arms."

"That makes two of us," she said. "Don't stop now."

He grinned. "I have no intention of—" His phone buzzed in his pocket, startling both of them. His smile faded. "Don't go anywhere."

"You, either."

He pulled out his phone. But when he saw the screen, he bit off a curse. "Perfect timing."

"Ignore it, whoever it is."

He gave her a look of regret. "I'm sorry, Harper. It's Mason. He's says it's urgent. I can't ignore this."

She sighed as he rolled off her and stood. "I know, I know. It's just…like you said. Really bad timing."

He glanced up from the screen where he was typing a text, and winked.

Her stomach did a delighted little flip.

He shoved the phone back in his pocket then leaned down and pressed a quick kiss against her lips. "He's at the police station and needs me to look at some file on his laptop in the guest room, then call him. Hopefully, this will be quick. Wait for me?"

"I've waited for you all my life. A few more minutes won't kill me."

His hands shook as he cupped her face. "I think I've waited for you my whole life, too. I was just too stupid to realize it before." He gently stroked her cheeks and stared down into her eyes. "You are so beautiful." He gave her another kiss that ended far too quickly. Then he was gone.

Harper fisted her hands against the mattress in frustration, but she couldn't quit smiling. Things hadn't gone the way she'd expected, not at all. And there were going to be some really rough times ahead with her family. But she knew she wouldn't have to face it alone. Gage would be with her. Settling more comfortably against the pillows, she closed her eyes and waited for his return.

Thump. Thump. Thump.

Her eyes flew open and she sat up. What was that noise? She heard it again, a rhythmic sound, coming from outside. Crossing to the bank of windows that looked across the pool to the back of the house, she didn't see anything to explain the noise. The thumping sounded again, and she realized it was coming from the side of the pool house. She headed past the living room area to the windows there, looking out over the maze of oleanders her stepmother had planted over the years. It was a sea of green with white and pink blooms that had Julia blushing with pride every summer.

It took a moment for Harper's eyes to adjust to the bright sunlight, and then she saw her. Julia. Sitting in the dirt about twenty feet from the house, wearing the same dress slacks and blouse she'd had on earlier. She was digging around the base of one of her precious plants with a foot-long hand shovel. Weeding, or maybe thinning out overgrowth. Harper had never been much of a plant person, so she wasn't sure.

Puzzled that her stepmother wasn't at the police station with her daughter, it dawned on her that Julia was crying. Tears tracked down her cheeks, glinting in the sun. She wiped at her streaming eyes after every two or three stabs of the shovel in the dirt. Apparently, she was doing what she always did when the stress of the world was more than she could bear. She turned to her gardening.

With a heavy heart, and more than a little guilt, Harper moved to the side door and stepped onto the concrete path that circled the pool house. Not wanting to startle her step-mother, she quietly made her way between the rows of six-foot-tall plants, stopping several yards away. But her intended greeting went unsaid when Julia had a sneezing fit then cursed her allergies and wiped at her eyes again. She wasn't crying. And she wasn't weeding or thinning out the plants. She was digging something up.

A large metal box.

Where her movements had been methodical and measured before, now she was viciously stabbing at the dirt, hacking at the roots of her beloved oleanders, then frantically tugging at the box.

It jerked free, slamming against her face. She let out a small cry and fell back. The box fell to the ground.

Harper rushed forward. "Julia? Are you okay?"

Julia whirled around on her knees, her eyes wide with surprise. "Harper? What are you doing here?"

"I needed some time alone before heading downtown to see Cynthia." She frowned. "You're bleeding. Your cheek is…" She stared at the box. It had come open and a delicate blue blanket spilled from the corner, satin initials embroidered on its edge: S.B.

Shane Bishop.

Harper's hand shook as she reached out and lightly

traced her fingers across the monogram. "That's…that's the blanket I made for my son, for Gage's and my son. Colette wrapped it around him to take him to the hospital." Tears spilled down her cheeks as she stared at the blanket. Then she looked at the box again, horror making her shake as she mentally measured it.

Two feet long.

One foot wide.

One foot deep.

She started to reach for the box, but snatched back her hand. Her entire body was shaking. "My God. What have you done? Please tell me my son isn't in that box."

"I'm so sorry, Harper. It wasn't supposed to be like this."

A sob escaped Harper's clenched teeth. She dragged in several more agonizing breaths, desperately trying to make sense of what was happening. "What did you do, Julia? What in God's name did you do?"

"I'm sorry," Julia said again.

A tinny sound had Harper glancing up to see a metallic flash in the sunlight. She threw up her arms to try to block the blow from Julia's shovel. It slammed against her forearm, making her cry out and fall to the side. She desperately scrambled back. The next blow slammed against the side of her head. White-hot pain burst through her skull.

Everything went dark.

Chapter Twenty-Four

Bishop sat at the desk in the guest room, scrolling through the report while Mason and Radley spoke to him through the speaker on his phone.

"You're both right," Bishop said. "It's all too neat. Too perfect. Both computers with internet searches on hiring hitmen and assassins—and how to get away with it? I don't buy it.

"Cynthia's smart, always has been," he conceded. "The only reason she gets bad grades is that she's rebellious and doesn't want to do the work. And that boyfriend of hers is a computer graphics major. Why would they go to the trouble of printing the ransom note in the library so it didn't come back as having been printed on their own printers, then leave search histories in their computers that make it look like they're killers? If you ask me, someone else did those searches, hoping we'd find them. It's as if they knew what kind of evidence we'd need to tie everything up in a nice neat bow and handed it to us for an open-shut case."

"Agreed," Mason said. "That's why Radley and I are on our way back with some computer forensics guys and a warrant. We're going to look at any other computers in the house to see what else we can find. We think there's way more to this."

"I still think Cynthia's guilty," Radley said. "And her boyfriend. Of the ransom gimmick. But everything else?

My gut tells me they've been set up to take the fall for the rest of it. The more I've seen them, talked to them, read reports from interviews with their friends and professors, they just don't seem organized enough or methodical enough to set up the assassination attempt or to hire those mercenaries."

Bishop sat back, steepling his fingers. "Cynthia was in high school when Shane died. I know Radley said teenagers kill—it's not unheard of. But I have a hard time picturing her doing it. I knew her back then. She was focused on weed and boys, period. Not to mention, there's just no motive."

"Someone else hired the assassin and the mercenaries," Mason said. "I think we agree on that."

"We do. The question is who, and why. Radley, have you gotten the results from the tests on the syringes from the hospital?"

"No, and it's not looking good. I don't think we can count on that to be our smoking gun."

"So all we really have at this point is a gut feeling, and a belief that a killer may have injected two people with something to cause a heart attack," Bishop said. "The labs haven't come back with any conclusions there, either?"

"In spite of our bluffing in the meeting at the Manning estate," Radley said, "that's not looking promising. Typical toxicology screens look for hundreds of drugs. Nothing popped up. I'm going to ask a professor at one of the local universities for suggestions of other things to look for, something that doesn't show up on normal tests unless you know to specifically test for it. We could very well be looking at real heart attacks. Seems oddly coincidental, but it happens."

Bishop had been staring out the window as he'd listened to them. The tall plants on the left side of the pool house seemed to go on forever. The same plants he'd seen at

Harper's yard. He remembered her saying her stepmother had given them to her... Something was niggling at the back of his mind about those plants, something he'd seen on some forensics show on TV. He pulled the keyboard to him and typed a string into the search engine. "Hey, Radley. Can you tell me how Julia Manning's first husband died? I've got a hunch."

"I've probably got that right on my phone. I have a brief background on all our potential suspects. Hang on." A moment later he said, "Here it is. Well, what do you know. Heart attack. I think that coincidence theory is out the window at this point."

"I'm with you on that." Bishop pressed Enter and his screen filled with pictures of plants. He scrolled down to the bottom of the page. "Bingo! That's it. There's a plant that's highly poisonous and if ingested in large enough quantities can mimic the reaction of a drug that saves lives if someone has a heart attack. But if they don't have heart trouble, it will give them a heart attack."

"You're talking about digitalis?" Radley said.

"I am. Guess what plant mimics digitalis?"

"No clue."

"Oleander." His gaze shifted out the window. "And I'm looking at hundreds of them right now."

"Where?"

"The Manning's backyard. Julia Manning's garden is full of them."

"Great work, Bishop," Radley said. "If we can use Mason's lab for quick results, maybe they can look specifically for oleander poisoning with the gunman?"

"Of course," Mason said. "I can get Bryson to call his Paris contacts, too, and make sure they also test Colette's remains for oleander."

"If those both come back positive," Radley chimed in, "I'll see about exhuming Julia Manning's first husband.

What about motive? Juries always need a motive and I'm stumped on this one."

"I'm blank on that one, as well," Bishop said. "But if she killed her first husband, what's to stop her from killing the second one? Maybe she got tired of him, who knows? But with Earl being so high-profile, and having a physical every year by the same doctor who gives the sitting president his physicals, I imagine she didn't think she could get rid of him by faking a heart attack."

"Divorce by assassin," Mason said. "And make it look like the whole family was at risk by having them go after Harper, too? To draw attention away from Mrs. Manning?"

Bishop unclenched his hands. "It's a theory. And it makes sense she'd go after her stepdaughter instead of her biological children. If you lay it all out, think it through, it's a macabre kind of logic. Cynthia creates the ransom hoax to get money. Julia decides that's the perfect diversion to allow her to get rid of Earl and frame her daughter."

"If that's the case, what about Shane? And Colette Proust?" Radley asked.

"The one thing that Harper and everyone else drove into us this whole time is how important the Manning reputation is to Earl," Bishop said. "When Shane was born, he was still in the White House, seeking a second term. What if Julia's the one who safeguarded his reputation? In her own sick way, maybe she thought if she eliminated Shane, and the midwife, then there was no chance of the truth ever getting out and potentially harming her husband's career. To a sane, normal person, it makes zero sense. But if she's a sociopath, with no conscience, who'd already killed at least once—"

"Her first husband," Radley said.

"Exactly. Killing again after that was considered a reasonable way to take care of a problem—in her mind. Killing an innocent baby, and the midwife, no big deal for her. It was a means to an end. Later, when she grew tired of Earl, killing him would be quick and easy and she'd still get his millions. Except that because of who he was, there'd be investigations. Cynthia's scheme gave her the perfect opportunity."

Mason swore. "And framing her own daughter didn't bother her at all. She truly is a nut job."

"If our theory is true," Bishop added. "It's still just that, a theory. We need proof, preferably before Cynthia is railroaded for murder."

"I'll get the lab on this right away," Mason told them. "Exhuming the first husband is the key. And I'll text Eli and Caleb to go to the hospital to hang in the hallway outside Mrs. Manning's room. The Secret Service agent assigned to watch over her is there to protect her, not to keep her from escaping."

"The hospital? I thought she was at the police station."

Radley answered. "She was so distraught on the way to the station that Secret Service took her to the hospital. She's been sedated."

Bishop straightened in his chair. "Who's the agent guarding her?"

"I think it's Faulk," Radley said. "Why?"

Bishop shoved back from his desk and hurried through the main house. "If we assume that Julia injected the gunman at the hospital to make sure he wouldn't tell anyone that she'd hired him, how would she have known he was there so she could bring the poison with her? I didn't mention the gunman when I called the Mannings."

"Maybe she's crazy enough to carry the poison with her all the time," Radley said. "Or, what are you thinking? Someone else poisoned him?"

"No. I think someone else called her and told her about the gunman so she could mix up a batch of poison and bring it with her. He was sick that first day in the ER. She probably poisoned him the very first time she came to the hospital to visit Harper…

"For her to have come that first day, with the poison, she had to have been given advance notice that the gunman was there. She has to be working with someone else. I'm betting it's the same person who's been with her since he requested reassignment. He sounded believable about over-hearing Cynthia and Dean talking about wanting to hurt Earl in some way, because he really did hear that conversation. But he used that information to try to frame Cynthia for murder, not the ransom route they eventually chose."

"You're talking about Faulk."

"Yes. I think he's in this just as deep as Julia. Mason, did you text Eli and Caleb already?" He yanked open one of the French doors off the back and jogged past the pool, heading to the pool house.

"I did. The hospital's not too far from the station. They were— Wait, Eli's texting me back now. Hang on."

Bishop shoved the door open and ran inside the pool house. The big bed to the left of the door was empty. So was the couch, and the kitchenette. He hurried to the bathroom. The door was standing wide open. "She's not here."

"Who?"

"Harper. She was supposed to be in the pool house." He ran to the front windows and looked out. Then he ran to the side windows.

"Bishop, Eli said they called the hospital. Faulk and Mrs. Manning never arrived."

"Why wasn't I told?" Radley swore. "I'll get my team looking for her right now. I'll get a BOLO out on her car. She didn't go back home?"

"That's what I'm worried about," Bishop said. "If she did, I didn't hear or see her." He spotted some broken plants in the otherwise pristine garden. He yanked open the door and ran outside.

"Bishop?" Mason asked. "What's going on?"

"I'm trying to find Harper. Mason—"

"We're almost there. I'll get the Seekers out there. I just texted Eli and Caleb. They're turning around now and heading your way."

Gage stopped in the middle of a row of oleanders, the blood draining from his face, leaving him cold as he looked at the ground that had been destroyed.

His hand shook as he spoke into the phone. "Radley, get your cops out here. Get the Secret Service. Get *everyone*."

"What's wrong?" Radley asked. "What have you found?"

"In the garden, beside the pool house. Evidence of a struggle. Broken plants. Footprints. I think they're Harper's. And someone else's. They're small. Probably Julia's." His heart seemed to squeeze in his chest. "There's blood. A lot of blood."

"Hold on," Radley said. "We're just down the street now. I can see the house."

"Harper. I can't…she can't—"

"Don't lose hope, Bishop," Mason said, his voice tight.

Bishop bent, studying the dirt. "There's a blood trail. It's faint. A few drops here and there. And, thank God, two sets of footprints. I think Harper's still alive." He hurried along the row of plants. Good grief, did this garden never end? He stopped every few yards, searching until he found another drop.

Finally, he reached the end of the row. The drops were long with a slight tail, indicating the direction the person was heading as the blood dripped from them. He continued off to the right, deeper into the estate, toward a stand of trees about thirty yards away.

"What's going on, Bishop? Sit rep!" Mason demanded.

Gage jogged to the trees then slowed to check the ground again to make sure he was going in the right direction.

"Bishop?"

"Give me a second." He turned in a slow circle, widening his search radius. Then he spotted it. Another drop, with an elongated tail, proving he was headed the same way as the injured person, presumably Harper.

"They haven't left the estate. Mason, the trail leads deeper into the property, toward the woods on the south side of the property." He shaded his eyes, scanning the trees and bushes a hundred yards away. Two figures moved in the shade, the one in front slightly hunched over, holding some kind of box in her hands. *Harper.* Behind her, Julia shoved her forward. The two of them disappeared into the woods.

Bishop took off running.

Chapter Twenty-Five

Harper shook her head, desperately trying to clear her vision. Her ears were ringing from the blow with the shovel. She'd thrown up twice already and was having an awful time just trying to keep from falling over.

Julia nudged her from behind, pushing her deeper into the woods. Harper stumbled, catching herself against a tree with one hand while keeping the precious box clutched against her chest with the other.

"I'm sorry, Harper," Julia said. "I shouldn't have hit you so hard. I never meant for you to suffer." She reached for her arm, but Harper jerked away.

"You never meant for me to suffer? You *murdered my son.*"

Julia dropped her hand, but kept the lethal shovel in the other hand at the ready. "You didn't give me a choice."

Harper stared at her incredulously. "What are you talking about?"

"The pregnancy. Your father's reelection was coming up and he was slipping in the polls. His entire platform relied on a show of strength and integrity. One little mistake could have cost him everything.

"I couldn't risk anyone finding out about you having a child out of wedlock. So I bribed Colette to give me the baby as soon as it was born. I told her I would give him to a family in a private adoption. But of course I couldn't risk that, either. Someone was bound to figure it out eventually, especially with that birthmark on his face, like his father's."

She gave Harper a plaintive look, as if expecting sympathy. "He didn't suffer. I held my hand over his nose and mouth. It was over in just a few minutes. But Colette grew a conscience. She didn't trust me and demanded to see the baby. I had no choice. I went to her apartment right before she left for the airport, and made up a story about the baby being with a nanny. We talked over tea and I spiked hers with stewed oleander leaves. She agreed to be quiet if I sent her baby pictures soon. As far as I know, no one in Paris ever suspected anything when she died. It was a perfect plan."

Harper stared at her in horror. "Would you listen to yourself? You murdered my child. Then you murdered Colette. And you justify it because of a political campaign?" She pressed a hand to her throat. "Did my…did my father know about this?"

"What? Earl? Of course not. He's weak, always has been. He never would have gotten reelected if it wasn't for me." She prodded Harper with the shovel. "Hurry up. Head that way."

Harper wove her way between the trees, grateful they were close together so she could brace herself against them to keep from falling. She glanced over her shoulder. "Was the ransom your idea?"

Julia snorted. "That stupid plan? Of course not. My idiot daughter and her equally stupid boyfriend thought that one up all by themselves. I realized what was going on, of course, since I knew there was no child to ransom. I figured I'd take it as an opportunity.

"Earl's been talking to a divorce lawyer and doesn't think I know about it. I knew this day would come, so I've been stashing money away. A *lot* of money. But if I could have him killed, and you, too, I could blame it all on Cynthia when her ridiculous ransom plan fell through. I'd have gotten everything. But you ruined it by bringing your ex-lover into the picture. You and your father would both be dead by now if it wasn't for his interference. Now I have to go with plan B."

A familiar thumping noise sounded up ahead. Harper stumbled to a halt when she saw someone with a much larger shovel than Julia's, digging a hole in the ground.

He turned around, his eyes widening in shock when he saw her. "Harper?"

"Faulk. I should have known you were helping Julia. You've been her constant shadow for months."

He climbed out of the hole and tossed two large plastic bags onto the ground. Neat stacks of bills filled each one. Harper's fuzzy vision was useless for figuring out the denominations. But even if they were only twenties, or fifties, it was an enormous amount of money in those bags. Probably hundreds of thousands of dollars.

"It always comes down to money, doesn't it?" she accused. "My family trusted you. How could you help my stepmother kill my baby? Then hire those thugs to kill my father and me?"

"What? No, no, no. I didn't do any of that. I've been trying to talk her out of her crazy plans from day one."

Julia shoved her forward until she was just a few feet away from him.

"Day one?" Harper accused. "Was that before or after she murdered Shane?"

His face reddened. Then his gaze fell to the box in her hands and he wrinkled his nose. "Is that where you disappeared to, Julia? I told you to leave it. All we had to do was get our money and get out of Dodge."

"I was going to plant evidence in the box to make it look like Cynthia's the one who killed the kid."

"What good would that have done?"

"If she gets charged with our crimes—"

"Your crimes."

Julia narrowed her eyes at Faulk. "If she gets charged, I'm in the clear."

"Did you miss the part about them doing lab tests on the syringes from the hospital?"

She waved her hand in the air. "Anyone could have put a syringe in one of those medical waste things. Any lawyer could get that tossed out."

"If you're so sure you could beat this thing, why bring Harper here? Now you have a witness. There's no way out for either of us except to run at this point."

"Yeah, well. Like I said. I didn't expect her to catch me digging up the stupid box. I brought her with me to buy some time. We can keep her as a hostage."

He shook his head. "No way. She'll slow us down."

"Fine. What do you propose we do about her then?"

Faulk swore and drew his gun.

Harper gasped and stumbled back.

He gave her an apologetic look. "I'm sorry about this. I really am." He raised the pistol.

Bam! A gunshot echoed through the woods.

A red dot appeared on Faulk's forehead. His eyes rolled up in his head and he slowly crumpled to the ground.

Julia shouted with rage and dove for the gun he'd dropped.

"Harper, move!"

Gage's voice galvanized her into action. She threw herself into the gaping hole that Faulk had dug and covered her head with the metal box.

Gunshots seemed to ring out all around her. Loud pings echoed in her ears. She squeezed her eyes shut, making herself as small as possible as she pulled her knees to her chest beneath Shane's box.

The deafening sounds suddenly stopped. An eerie silence fell over the glade.

A moment later, a puff of dirt rained down on her. She jerked back and opened her eyes.

Gage was beside her in the hole, his face pale. "My God. I thought you were..." He shook his head, gently tugged the box from her arms and set it aside.

"Is she okay?" Mason's face appeared above them, just past Gage's shoulder. Another familiar face joined his. Detective Radley.

"I think so." Gage ran his hands over her arms, along her torso, down her legs. They were shaking when he gently probed her scalp.

She winced and ducked away.

"Sorry, sweetheart. I'm going to get you out of here now, okay?" He scooped her into his arms and climbed out of the hole with Mason and Radley helping him up.

"Wait," she said, her voice groggy even to her own ears. It was so hard to stay awake. "The box. It's—"

"I know," he said, his voice hoarse. "Don't worry. Mason will get it for us. Won't you, Mason?"

"Of course." He hopped down into the hole. A moment later, he was back in front of them, his face pale. "I don't understand it. The bullets. There are holes all over the top. Nothing on the bottom."

"Shane protected me," Harper said, resting her head against Gage's chest. "He saved me. You both did. Father and son."

Gage exchanged a startled glance with his boss then turned and strode back toward the house.

Chapter Twenty-Six

Bishop helped Harper out of the wheelchair beside the last pew in the aisle. She wobbled and grabbed his arm to keep from falling.

He frowned as he steadied her. "You shouldn't have worn those dangerous high heels. Kick them off. The preacher isn't going to mind if you're barefoot. And if he does, who cares? There's no one else here to notice, and I'm fine with it."

She gave him a reproachful look and leaned past him to smile at the preacher waiting at the front of the little mountain church just a few miles from Bishop's home in Gatlinburg the two of them now shared. She looked up. "I care. I'm not going barefoot to my son's funeral."

"Our son."

She straightened his tie and smoothed his suit jacket. "Our son. Come on, Gage. Let's say our final goodbyes to Shane."

He tucked her hand in the crook of his arm. "Are you sure you're ready for this? It's only been two weeks. A brain bleed is nothing to sneeze at."

"No. It's not. But you ordered everyone around at the hospital like a general, so they took excellent care of me." She rolled her eyes. "I'm fine, *Bishop*."

"Are you always going to call me Bishop when you get aggravated with me?"

"Maybe."

"I prefer my fiancée to call me by my God-given first name."

To his horror, she blinked back threatening tears.

"Okay, okay," he said. "Call me whatever you like. I just want you to be happy."

"They're happy tears, future husband. But sad, too. I'm happy we're finally together, after all this time. And I'm happy to be able to put Shane to rest. But I'm sad, too. I wish my mom had lived long enough to know I had a son. And I wish my dad could have been here."

"We can postpone this if you want, wait until he's come to terms with everything that's happened and feels he can face the memorial service."

She shook her head. "No. He'll never feel right being here, not after what Julia did. He feels guilty that he didn't realize how unbalanced she was. Not to mention how much Cynthia was hurting, without him even realizing it. He's doing a lot of soul-searching right now, and he's focusing on helping Cynthia."

"That doesn't bother you?"

"Surprisingly, no. Not really. She's young, immature. She didn't realize how much she was hurting anyone with her scheme. I think it got away from her, became bigger than she expected. She admitted she never thought she'd really get the money. She was hurting, and wanted to hurt my father. At least she's finally getting what she really needed all along."

"What's that?"

"His attention. And love."

"You're an amazing woman, Harper Manning."

"No. I'm a blessed woman. I had a son I cherished. I spoke to him, sang to him, read to him, while I carried him for those nine months. And I got to look into his beautiful blue eyes and tell him I loved him when he was born."

She reached up and cupped his face with her hand. "I'm also blessed to love one of the most decent, strong, smart, handsome, and honorable men I've ever known. I love you, Gage. With all my heart and soul."

He cleared his throat, twice, before trusting himself to speak. "I love you, Harper. More than you can possibly know. I thank God every single day that I got a second chance. And I plan on spending the rest of my life doing everything I can to make you happy."

She dabbed at her eyes then gasped in dismay at the makeup smeared on her fingertips.

He smiled and gently wiped the dark smudges from beneath her eyes. "Brielle wouldn't appreciate you messing up her hard work putting makeup on you this morning." He winked to let her know he was teasing. "You're beautiful, with or without makeup."

"Oh stop it. You're going to make me cry even worse."

He kissed her again, this time on the lips. "Come on. Let's head up the aisle before the preacher gets tired of waiting."

HARPER STOOD BENEATH the tent in the church graveyard, her hand on top of the casket as she whispered her final goodbyes to Shane. Gage stood off to the side, thanking the preacher and the altar boys who'd served as pallbearers during the private ceremony.

Once the others left, he returned to her with the wheelchair. "Come on, sweetheart. This is the longest you've stood at any one time since you woke up in the ICU. You have to be exhausted."

She gave him a tentative smile and sent up a silent prayer that she'd made the right decision. He wheeled her around to face the parking lot and stopped. She didn't have to ask why. She knew why.

An older man with white hair and faded blue eyes stood

about twenty feet away from them, leaning on a cane. He, too, was dressed in a suit, his tie slightly askew.

His mouth drooped slightly at one corner, as if he'd suffered from a stroke sometime in the past. But he stood straight and tall, a proud-looking man in spite of the anxious look on his face, the uncertainty in his gaze that was locked on his son like a laser.

As Gage's father limped forward, Harper turned in the chair. Gage's jaw was set, lines of tension crinkling around his eyes as he looked at her.

"Why?" His voice was a harsh whisper.

She winced then put her hand on top of his on the chair handle, relieved and hopeful when he didn't pull away from her touch.

"Because I've learned how precious and short life can be. I've also learned how special love is, and that it should be cherished, and nurtured, and never taken for granted. He loves you. And you love him. It's my fault what happened between you two. I don't know if this can be fixed. But I know I owe it to you to at least try."

Bishop looked down at the woman who meant more to him than breathing. He ignored his father who'd stopped just a few feet away. His annoyance that Harper had contacted his father had evaporated the moment she'd looked up at him with those gorgeous light blue eyes of hers. She had a pure, true heart.

Even though he didn't want this, he knew she'd set up the meeting because she cared, because she loved him. And he didn't want her to ever feel guilt again about anything in his past. He squeezed her hand and tried to reassure her. "It's not your fault, Harper. It never was. It's his."

"Listen to what he has to say. That's all I ask."

"I already did. Years ago." He finally met his father's

gaze. "He made his feelings perfectly clear. And he told me he never wanted to see me again."

His father's chin wobbled as he drew a bracing breath. "What I said that day was foolish and wrong. I've regretted it every day since. But by the time I got over my stupid pride and pushed past the grief that was still eating me alive, I couldn't find you. I tried. I went everywhere, called your phone. But your number was out of service. You were gone. Vanished."

Bishop frowned. "You went looking for me?"

"Two weeks after our fight. And for months after that. No one I talked to knew where you were."

He'd left Tennessee within days of the fight with his father. He'd sold his expensive smartphone, opting for a much cheaper one that wouldn't drain his savings while he tried to find a new way to make a living. If his father had tried to find him, unless he'd hired a private investigator, there really hadn't been any way to track him down.

"Fair enough," he grudgingly allowed. "But you being here now, as if you actually care, means nothing."

Harper gasped.

Bishop threaded his fingers through hers. More than anything, he didn't want to hurt her, or even to disappoint her. That was the only reason he hadn't walked away from his dad, that he was still standing there. He was doing this for her. But, as she'd said, he didn't know that this could be fixed.

"You're only here now," Bishop continued, being brutally honest, "because Harper told you the full story. She told you that I was drunk with grief over Shane the night we made love. That even to this day, I have no memory of the night we conceived our son, which is why I refused to stand up as his father when I learned she was pregnant. Not because I had no honor, as you accused me that day. I didn't have all the facts. And I was foolish enough not to trust her." He waved his hand dismissively. "Doesn't matter. Harper and I have made our peace. It's not for you to forgive or not to forgive."

His father's brow wrinkled in confusion. "Son, I'm not even sure what you're talking about. Harper didn't tell me about you being drunk, or anything else. She just told me about…about your child, my grandson, that he'd died at birth. And that you were holding a memorial service. I understood it was private, but I asked if I could be at the graveside afterward, to pay my respects—to him, and his parents."

It was Bishop's turn to be confused. "Then, you're not here to forgive me?"

The elder Bishop stepped forward and clasped his son on the shoulder. "It was never my place to forgive or not to forgive. My job, as your father, was to love you unconditionally. And I completely failed in my duty to you. I said some awful things that day. But I didn't mean any of it. I do love you, always have, no matter what.

"I'm here, as I said, to pay respects to my grandson. But I'm also here to beg *you* to forgive an old man who has nothing but regrets for what he did to you. I love you, son. What can I do to try to make it up to you?"

Bishop slowly shook his head in wonder. "Just love me, Pop. That's all I ever wanted." He stepped forward and clasped his father in a tight embrace.

Harper was crying like a watering hose when the two men finally stepped back.

Bishop grinned and motioned toward her. "Dad, meet my weeping soon-to-be bride, the love of my life, Harper Manning."

She gave Bishop a playful shove and wiped at her tears.

His father wiped at his own tears before offering a hand to Harper.

She motioned for him to come closer and she hugged him instead.

When his father stepped back, Bishop gave Harper a soft kiss on the lips and whispered in her ear. "Thank you for giving me back my family, for *being* my family. You're my everything."

She gave him a tremulous smile. "I love you, Gage Bishop."

"I *adore* you, Harper soon-to-be Bishop." He moved behind the chair and grabbed the handles. He smiled down at her as he spoke to his father. "Come on, Dad. You can ride with us to our home. We'll come back later for your car. We have a lot of catching up to do. To start, Harper and I will tell you all about your grandson. And how he saved his mother's life."

* * * * *

SUMMER
STALKER

NICOLE HELM

To back roads and the strange places you find on them
that inspire whole books.

Prologue

Two years ago

Reece Montgomery had seen many a man injured. Shootings. Explosions. He'd watched men die before he'd grown into a man himself.

But there was something particularly poignant about Granger Macmillan—the man who'd taught Reece how to be a good one—being confined to a wheelchair and looking gaunt and weak.

Granger sat in said wheelchair in front of the entire body of North Star, a secret group set up for the sole purpose of taking down the Sons of the Badlands, a powerful gang who'd caused destruction and death across the whole of South Dakota.

Reece would know. His parents had been Sons groupies for several years before the state had permanently taken him away from them. They were probably both dead now, though Reece refused to look into the matter.

They'd been dead to him too many years to count.

Reece wouldn't say he blamed the Sons of the Badlands for his unfortunate childhood, or for being bounced from foster home to foster home, but he was determined to take them down all the same.

The fact that they, in collaboration with another organization of morally bankrupt men, had set a bomb off in the heart of the North Star headquarters ate away at Reece. Also, the fact that Granger had been shot in the midst of said explosion, leaving him weak even all these weeks later, felt like a particular failure.

Reece didn't know what exactly he'd failed. He'd been hurt in the blast himself, but was mostly healed now. He just knew…this wasn't right. Nothing that had gone down the day of the explosion was right.

Never mind the fact that, with some help, North Star had won—catching the man who'd left the bomb. Winning was so much less satisfying when he was in a room filled with the collateral damage from that victory.

"As you can see," Granger continued, "I'm not going to be physically capable of taking the reins back for quite some time." Even his voice sounded tired. Still, he was here and clearly determined to give the speech, and the room of about fifty field operatives, IT people and medical staff stayed very quiet in order to hear him.

"Shay will be my replacement until I'm able to return."

No one spoke a word. If there were concerns or doubts, no one voiced them. No one would dare. Even in a wheelchair, recovering from both a bullet wound and the injuries due to the blast, Granger Macmillan was their leader.

Shay could take over for a while—Reece figured she'd do well enough. She too had been hurt in the explosion—burns, mostly. She was recovering quickly, much like Reece and the others who'd been in the building and injured, but not shot like Granger had been.

Shay was a rarity in North Star. She'd lasted more than the prescribed four years. She had experience in each of North Star's many areas of expertise. No one could *replace* Granger, to Reece's way of thinking, but Shay could certainly step in and hold things together while he got his strength back.

If Reece had been thinking about it over the past year, he might have noticed Granger was grooming her to be his replacement. She was given missions in every aspect of North Star's operations. Granger sometimes asked her advice. Despite multiple instances where she hadn't followed orders, or even some where she'd gone directly against them, Shay was always a part of North Star. In retrospect, it was clear she was Granger's second-in-command, ready to take over at a moment's notice.

Reece had just never considered Granger bowing out or getting injured, or anyone *needing* to step in.

Shay took the floor next to Granger.

"You all know me well enough. I've been here longer than any person here except Granger himself. I hope you know, no matter what it may look like on the outside, I've always been dedicated to eradicating the Sons. Like most of you, they are responsible for the deaths of loved ones of my own. As acting temporary head of North Star, I can assure you we won't slow down or stop until our mission is done."

She looked down at Granger in his chair, something odd passing over her expression. Reece didn't know her well enough to figure it out.

"We won't quit now. Not when we've made real progress. I know some of you will balk at a new leader, but I hope you'll do me and Granger the courtesy of bringing it to me and letting us try to work it out. North Star will go on as it always has while Granger recovers. That I promise you."

Reece watched Granger's face. It was impassive. Something about that lack of expression or emotion, no matter how common for Granger, made Reece wonder if there really was a recovery expected—at least one that would bring him back to lead an elite group dedicated to taking down a gang as dangerous as the Sons.

"Our fight doesn't stop with one setback. As we all heal, we're going to keep working, keep fighting, and we'll make sure the Sons are wiped out forever."

There was some applause, some shouts of assent and encouragement. No one looked particularly defeated or upset about the change in leadership.

Because North Star had always been about one thing, and one thing only.

Wiping out the Sons.

Reece wouldn't stop until he'd helped bring that eventuality to fruition.

Chapter One

Present day

Reece was not a fan of meetings. He preferred for his duties to be communicated through one-on-one briefings or, even better, the written word. Still, with the Sons of the Badlands essentially decimated in every way that mattered to the North Star Group, Reece figured a meeting was necessary.

He arrived at the sprawling ranch house in eastern Wyoming that now acted as the headquarters of North Star. Though they had been moved in for well over a year, Reece still wasn't used to the change.

North Star was, in fact, his north star, orienting him and giving purpose to his life. He'd long ago given up hope of any kind of stability, but his work at North Star headquarters under the guidance of his mentor had started to get past the wall he'd built around himself, until the explosion two years ago. The blast had taken both from him—the headquarters, as well as the leader who had recruited him.

Granger Macmillan had retired. Reece still didn't know how to fully accept that a man he'd so respected had given up the fight for good and right and opted for…domesticity.

However, Shay was a fine enough leader. She was smart and firm like Granger, but she had her own ideas, and she implemented them as she saw fit. Reece didn't always agree, but he'd honed himself into a soldier long ago. He knew how to take an order.

And his mostly solo missions out in the field gave him the chance to go by his own internal sense of right and wrong.

Missions. They'd be over now, with the Sons of the Badlands completely and utterly annihilated. What little factions remained were of absolutely no consequence.

Now what will you do?

Reece didn't much want to figure that out, so he'd decided to go to this meeting and hope it wasn't about what he'd been dreading.

You're free to go, Reece Montgomery.

No one stayed in North Star for long. Even with Shay allowing people to stay beyond Granger's four-year rule, the explosion had cost them some good people who'd decided to move on. Since then, some others had left for law enforcement or other careers where they thought they could do more than grind the Sons of the Badlands into the South Dakota dust.

Now the Sons *were* dust, and what did that leave for North Star to do?

Holden Parker and Sabrina Killian were already sitting in Shay's office when Reece stepped in. They greeted each other with brief nods, and Reece took the lone empty seat.

Apparently, it would just be the four of them.

Shay didn't waste any time. She closed the door and stood in front of them, her expression grim and assessing.

"There isn't much left for us to do in our fight against the Sons of the Badlands," she said with no preamble, explaining what they all already knew. "There are still some very small, very ineffectual factions, but local law enforcement will be able to see to those without help from us."

"You disbanding us?" Holden Parker asked, legs thrust out and crossed at the ankles. He had his arms crossed casually behind his head, as though he didn't care.

But there wasn't anyone fooled in this room.

Everyone cared.

"Not as such," Shay replied evenly. "There are other groups. Other missions. If your personal mission ends with the Sons of the Badlands being reduced to rubble, then you're free to go. No questions asked."

"What's our other option?" Sabrina asked. She made no effort to appear casual. She leaned forward, fingers clasped tightly together, expression intense. As always.

Shay held up a small folder. "I've been approached by a small, secret group looking for help with a particularly difficult and sensitive mission. You three are here because I think you'd be the best options for the initial research and fieldwork. But it's only if you want to stay."

"What the hell else would we do?" Holden replied, his grin doing nothing to soften the bite in his voice.

Shay's gaze turned to Reece. He hadn't said a word—didn't make any effort to be casual or intense. If he allowed himself to consider it, he supposed the feeling that coursed through him was relief.

But he'd long ago given up *feeling*.

When Shay looked at him and simply *waited*, he gave a nod.

"I'm in," he said.

"Good, because you're up first. We have next to nothing to go on. A man was killed early last year, presumably via an unknown hit man. Because of this man's contacts and jobs, they believe there will be more targets. This organization doesn't know why. They don't know who. They barely know what."

"Don't make it so easy," Holden muttered.

But Reece was happy for complicated. For nearly impossible. It meant his life hadn't lost all purpose and meaning with the Sons eradicated.

He still had a mission to complete, and the more difficult the better.

"What we do have to go on is the widow. The government agency thinks she knows something, but she's been wholly unwilling to talk to them. Presumably, she blames her husband's death on his work, whoever his employers were. At this point, they're hoping a stranger and an uninvolved group like ours can get through to her."

"You going to tell us this agency's name?" Sabrina demanded.

Shay shook her head. "No. They've made it very clear everything is on a need-to-know basis, and knowing who *they* are isn't necessary."

"Then how do we know they're the good guys?" Reece asked.

"We don't," Shay said. "But they didn't ask me to get through to this widow via any means necessary. They didn't act as though they'd used any scare tactics. It could be for any reason, but it makes me more prone to want to look into this. They're not hurting or threatening an innocent woman, when they probably could be."

Her honesty was one of the things that Reece figured made her an excellent successor to Granger. Like Granger, she didn't let anyone labor under false pretenses. It was what had always made North Star work: knowing that a mission wasn't safe or easy. An agent was risking a lot.

"But we don't know for sure, obviously. That's part of what I want you to find out, Reece. I want you to pose as a guest at the widow's bed-and-breakfast. Find out what you can about what she might know, and the organization her husband was working for. We don't move forward with the rest of it until we get a better picture of who we're dealing with. I'll continue to research on my end, but I think the widow is the key to figuring out if we want to be involved. You'll do your best to befriend the widow and get whatever information you can."

Sabrina laughed. "Reece? *Befriend* someone? You've got to be kidding me."

Shay gave him what passed for a smile. "I'm sure he can handle it."

All Reece did was take the folder and nod.

HE COULD INDEED handle it. Truth be told, he knew how to turn on the charm when needed. Most especially when he wasn't himself. When he checked into the inn, he would be Reece Conrad, traveling nature photographer.

Reece knew how to play a role.

The Bluebird Bed & Breakfast was situated in eastern Wyoming, in the small town of Echo. As far as Reece could see, there was nothing special about the town except that it was nestled near the borders of both Montana and South Dakota.

It was a picturesque enough area. There were slight rolling hills as he drove along, with pretty ranches tucked away just off the two-lane highway. He passed the occasional rock formation—though nothing as grand as Devil's Tower a ways to the southwest.

Reece turned off the highway onto the paved but poorly maintained road mentioned in the directions on the Bluebird Bed & Breakfast's website.

It was a good half mile before he rounded a curve around a small pond and the house came into view. Reece slowed without fully realizing he was doing so.

The house and yard that came into view was like something out of a Norman Rockwell painting. The pretty little farmhouse looked just like the picture he'd seen on the website, with its gleaming white-and-blue shutters and an expansive porch with colorful chairs. Trees closed in around the house on three sides, but the front yard was sprawling and well kept.

It was like some stupid childhood dream he'd had of the perfect life. A family, a house like that and space to run.

He shook his head. He had to leave Reece Montgomery behind. He was Reece Conrad. A married man, two kids. He traveled from national park to national park via back roads, photographing landscapes and the various nature he found. He stayed at places off the beaten path, hoping for great pictures along the way. He was a man who'd had a normal childhood, gone to college and built a life.

He stopped the car next to a compact sedan. It was an older model, but it looked like it was kept in meticulous shape. Still, when he glanced inside the car, there was the debris of children in the back seat.

Though it looked to be the mess of more than one child, this was the make and model of Lianna Kade's car, according to the file he'd been given.

The proprietress, the widow, had one child. A son. Seven years old. That Reece knew from what Shay had been able to dig up on her. Mrs. Kade didn't have anything remarkable in her background. The house had been in her family since it was built, but it was her great-grandmother who'd turned it into a bed-and-breakfast in the late 1940s, after her husband had died in World War II.

The current innkeeper had married Todd Kade when she was just twenty. Todd Kade wasn't his real name, but it was interesting that the widow had kept the last name for herself and her son.

Shay was still trying to track down the man's real name.

If the agency wanting more information on his death knew, they weren't telling.

Reece hefted his duffel bag over one shoulder, and the camera bag meant to keep up pretenses over the other. He walked across the green yard. There were gardens…everywhere. Along the tree line, huge beds—protected by chicken wire—boasted what appeared to be local grasses. There were artful groupings of red and orange tulips and yellow daffodils. Bracketing the house and porch were more beds, pots and planters, full of flowers he was more familiar with. Pansies and impatiens and the like.

Reece made his way up to the porch. Hanging from the railing on one side was a cheerfully painted sign that said *Welcome to the Bluebird Bed & Breakfast*. There were little bluebirds painted around the words. Underneath was a tab that said *Vacancies*.

He took the stairs onto the porch. There was a welcome mat, more bluebirds. The door itself was painted a bright blue. The knob was an ornate metal that had been fashioned to look like a bird, as well.

He was fairly certain that if someone looked up *domestic bliss* in the dictionary, they'd find a picture of the Bluebird Bed & Breakfast.

Not that he knew *anything* about domestic bliss.

The directions he'd been given upon reserving a room had been to let himself into the house. Not very safe for a woman whose husband had been murdered just last year.

Still, Reece pushed the door open and stepped into what appeared to be a living room. A bell on the door tinkled, and he heard footsteps from somewhere deeper in the house.

A woman, blond hair pulled back in a swinging ponytail, entered the room. Her smile was warm and welcoming, though her blue eyes didn't quite match the expression. There was nothing particularly remarkable about her—she was medium height, medium build. She wore well-worn jeans and a T-shirt that had the name of the bed-and-breakfast emblazoned across the pocket.

Reece felt a bit like he'd had the wind knocked out of him, and couldn't begin to imagine why.

"You must be Mr. Conrad," she said, her voice polite and husky. "Welcome."

Okay, maybe Reece Conrad *wasn't* married with two kids. Maybe he was a very single man and—

He cleared his throat, not sure where all that…response came from. Or why he was oddly uncomfortable with the fake part of his name. "Please call me Reece."

"Of course. You can set your bags down if you like, and we'll get you checked in." She moved behind a desk, set up in a little alcove surrounded by windows that looked out over the front yard.

She carried the scent of lemons as she passed him.

"You're the…owner."

He noticed the infinitesimal stiffening of her spine, but her expression was perfectly friendly. "Yes, I am." She jiggled the mouse of her computer, the monitor coming to life. She typed in a few things, then unlocked a drawer and pulled out a large envelope.

"You booked our attic room. You can follow me and I'll show you up, giving you a bit of a tour along the way."

"Sure."

She made a move to take his bags, but he grabbed them first. She didn't comment or slide him a look. She just started…talking.

"This is our common area. Cold nights—and we can have those well into June—we have a fire in the hearth.

Through that entryway, you'll find the dining room and kitchen. On this side of the house you'll find the TV room. There's also a public computer you're free to use."

She led him to a staircase and Reece found himself unduly mesmerized by the swing of her ponytail.

Get a hold of yourself, Montgomery.

"This is the second floor. It's all guest rooms. You're the only guest here for right now, but this weekend we'll have an almost full house. Obviously we ask that you stick to your own room or the common areas downstairs."

"Of course."

She led him to a door and pulled a keychain out of her pocket. She fiddled through the keys until she found an antique-looking metal one. She fitted it into the keyhole and unlocked the door.

It pushed open with a creak. "You have a key in here," she said, shaking the envelope in her hand. "The staircase leads straight into the room, so I advise locking it when you want complete privacy. Cleaning hours are outlined in the packet in the envelope, and most guests are incredibly polite, but you just never know when someone might want to poke around."

She led him up a rickety staircase. He followed, half expecting the attic room to be, in fact, very attic-like.

"I read the history on your website," he offered, testing the friendliness waters. "It's always been in your family?"

"Yes, since it was built in 1900 by my great-great-grandfather. But it wasn't turned into a bed-and-breakfast until the 1940s by my great-grandmother. Nevertheless, much of the history you'll find here is related to my family."

"But your name is Kade, not Young."

She stopped somewhat abruptly on the stairs, then

turned to face him. "It is. Did you have a personal question you wanted to ask about that?"

She reminded him of a very stern schoolteacher. "No, ma'am."

She nodded firmly and turned on a heel, and then finished the ascent up the stairs. He followed, giving her a respectable distance.

The room was the complete opposite of the narrow, creaky staircase. It was A-framed, with low ceilings on either side, but the bed was situated right in the middle of the room against the far wall. There were large stained glass windows on either side of the bed, big picture windows on the other walls that let in streams of light so that the whole room seemed to glow.

There was a desk on one side of the room, and a door on the other.

"The door leads to a small bathroom, but it's all yours. There's also a bathroom on the main level available to any guests. Breakfast is served from eight to nine in the dining room. We offer a small selection for a help-yourself lunch at noon. Dinner is from five to six. If you need to eat earlier or later, you can make arrangements."

"This is amazing."

"I'm glad you think so." She handed him the envelope and Reece noted the careful way she made sure her hands were nowhere near his when he took it. "Please enjoy your stay, and don't hesitate to ask for anything you might need. I'll do my best to accommodate."

"Thank you, Mrs. Kade."

She clasped her hands together and offered him a smile that, if he wasn't totally off base, had chilled considerably. "Please call me Lianna." She pointed to a phone on the desk. "Dial one if you need assistance."

With that, she turned and left the room. He heard the

subtle *click* of the lock being engaged once she'd reached the bottom of the stairs.

Reece shook out the contents of the envelope she'd handed him. A pamphlet of information about the inn, a printout of events around town for the month and the key to his room door.

The top of the key was in the shape of a bluebird. Reece had never considered himself a fan of whimsy, but something about it made him smile.

But that smile only lasted a few seconds before he got to work.

In less than five minutes, he'd unpacked his clothes, found a secure place for his weapons and unearthed a listening device on the smoke detector.

Now the question was—who had put it there? Lianna Kade? The group who'd hired North Star?

Or someone else altogether?

Chapter Two

Lianna Kade was not one to make a mountain out of a molehill. She'd survived six years married to a man who'd shown himself to be a monster more and more over time. Then, once he'd been killed, she'd found out he was some kind of spy. All of that had given her the space to learn to handle what came, without getting too worked up about it.

But Reece Conrad was *something*. He made her…itchy, she thought as she walked down the attic stairs. She locked the door, making sure not to give one last look up the stairs.

It wasn't nerves so much. Though he was a quietly intense man, he didn't give off any kind of threatening vibe. She might have been very stupid and naive at twenty, but she'd honed those instincts she'd lacked then.

Reece Conrad wasn't a threat exactly, but she was tempted to call Sheriff Reynolds and see if he could run some kind of background check.

But that would only start the whole *thing* over.

Grandma had retired and handed over the bed-and-breakfast to Lianna to give her and Henry a fresh start. Away from everything that had happened.

Lianna had taken it because her grandparents and parents didn't know the half of what had *actually* happened, and she wanted to always keep it that way. They could stay off in Denver, and she could raise and support her son in one of her favorite places in the world.

The alarm on her phone went off. Time to walk up to pick Henry up at the bus stop. Time to get her head back into the important parts of her routine.

She went out the front door, telling herself to enjoy the walk on a pretty, late-spring day. So pretty that once she reached the parking lot, she glanced back at the house.

Perfect. A dream come to life, and she got to run it. Inn-keeping wasn't some perfect dream job, but living here... It was exactly what she wanted.

She happened to look up at the attic windows. Her stomach swooped in a jolt of surprise and embarrassment. Reece was standing there. Looking at her.

She turned quickly, striding for the road. She didn't look back. If he was watching her, well, so be it. She'd probably watch *him* if the situations were reversed.

She didn't usually have to worry about men in a suitable age range showing up at her B and B looking like...that.

Yes, situations reversed, she would look and she would indeed watch him walk away.

"You're hopeless, Lianna," she muttered to herself, for-getting her usual routine. Her walk up to the bus stop was supposed to be a meditative time. Resetting. Her therapist back in Denver had given her a lot of strategies for coping with her newfound anxiety.

He had *not* been supportive of the move to middle-of-nowhere Wyoming, even if it was home. But Lianna had needed this fresh start. For her. For Henry. She'd needed home, and a place to find her confidence.

She would have never done that in San Francisco, with all the lies Todd had told. All the lies that had ended up with him murdered. Not that anyone knew *why*. No, the story the papers had told had been a burglary gone wrong.

Lianna knew better. Six years too late, but she knew better. And no matter the horror those years with Todd had been, she'd gotten Henry out of them. She couldn't wish them away. Not when Henry was her whole world.

She'd moved here for him, too. Getting out of San Francisco and to Denver had been the first step. Her parents had gotten their lives together—after letting Lianna's grandparents raise her—and in the first months after the murder, they, along with her grandparents, had been rocks, standing solidly behind her. They had been everything she needed.

But now she needed space. She needed to do some things for herself without being afraid of her own shadow. Besides, when she ran an inn, no one cared how often she checked the locks.

Henry had been able to go to first grade in the same elementary school she'd gone to. He would grow up in the same town, in the same place she had. That was important. It was *right*.

She'd been afraid Todd's cronies at his little spy group would follow her here, forever harassing her for information. Forever so sure she knew more than she'd let on.

But she knew *nothing* about Todd, it turned out. She'd have to live with that for the rest of her life.

Once she'd moved out of Denver, they'd let her be. Thank God. She could relax. Enjoy her life. Far away from the lies and wrongdoings of her late husband.

Lianna stopped at the edge of the road where the bus would stop and let Henry off. She shaded her eyes against the sun as the bus rumbled around the curve. The door opened and Henry bounded off, already talking a mile a minute.

"Mom! Mom! Joey is getting a dog! Can we get a dog? Wouldn't it be great to have a dog?"

Lianna waved at the bus driver before turning to follow Henry back down to the house. "You're allergic to dogs."

Henry sighed heavily. "That's so stupid."

"I know. Terribly stupid. We could always try getting the shots."

Henry pulled a face. "I *hate* shots."

"I know." She slid her hand over his shoulder, giving her seven-year-old a squeeze. Truth be told, she was secretly relieved there was an excuse not to get a dog. Between Henry and the Bluebird, she didn't have the time or energy to take care of another living thing.

Not that it stopped her from feeling guilty over Henry's lack of pets.

"Can we get a bird?"

Lianna had to suppress the shudder that ran through her. "Well, maybe we can look into it." She might lean into the bluebird part of her bed-and-breakfast's name, but that didn't mean she actually wanted a bird in her *house*. Birds were best kept as artistic decoration.

"Or a lizard? Or a hamster? Maybe a ferret."

"We can talk it over more tonight. We have a guest today." *Never a ferret. Never.*

"It's not another old lady, is it?"

"Henry Patrick Kade."

"Well! They always smell like a bathroom. And that one pinched my cheek *every* time she saw me."

"The horror," Lianna replied dryly.

Henry raced ahead, then back to her, pretending to be an airplane. He made explosion sounds and at one point even somersaulted over the soft grass.

She should admonish him, since he'd forgotten to zip his backpack and a few papers and pencils fluttered out, as well as his water bottle jostling out of its side pocket. But it was almost summer and her baby was happy.

How could she scold that?

She picked up after him as he continued to expend the pent-up energy of a first grader who'd been stuck in school on a sunny day.

They began to cross the yard. Lianna had almost forgotten about Reece and the churning of...too many feelings at the sight of him. But he was standing on her porch, still as a statue, and she came to an abrupt halt.

He looked imposing. She felt the brief need to shield Henry from him, but that was silly. She knew how to take care of herself these days. Keep both her and Henry safe from anyone who might wish them harm.

Which was no one. She'd made it clear she knew nothing about Todd's death, understood nothing about whatever he'd been secretly involved in. She'd worked with the police and FBI and in the end had moved to a different state. She'd moved *home* to hunker down into the B and B.

Henry darted around her, clearly intrigued by the impressive-looking stranger. They didn't get a lot of guests under the age of seventy. "Hi, mister. Do you like birds?"

Reece's blank expression scrunched into something closer to befuddlement. "Uh."

"We're discussing the merits of different pets," Lianna offered, forcing herself to move forward. To act casually. She and Henry were safe. The police had assured her.

"Oh, well, I'd prefer a dog, I suppose."

"Ugh," Henry groaned. "Everything is stupid." He stomped up the stairs and slammed inside.

Reece gave a puzzled glance at the front door and then back at Lianna. "I'm sorry."

She forced a kind smile. "Don't apologize. He's having a bit of a crisis over being allergic to dogs."

"Ah."

Lianna pressed her lips together. Reece still seemed

utterly confused. "You don't have any kids of your own, do you?"

"No. Can't say I know much about kids."

"Everything being stupid is par for the course. In the next moment, he'll be happy as a clam thinking about something else."

"Well. Good. I just wanted to walk around and take some pictures, if you don't mind." He held up his camera.

"Of course. Be careful in the woods. It's easy to get turned around and you don't want to get lost."

"I think I'll be all right. Thanks." He walked off toward her gardens and snapped a few pictures as she watched.

There was something…*something*. But she had homework to oversee and dinner to make, and she didn't have time for *something*.

BEING THE LONE guest in an inn run by an attractive woman and her precocious son was… Reece really didn't know what it was.

He usually had no problems pretending to be someone else. He was in no hurry to be himself. But there was something so domestic about eating breakfasts and dinners with her and the kid. Watching Lianna walk Henry to the bus stop and back.

It was fascinating. He'd never witnessed that level of care or affection.

Which was not what he was here for.

He'd found five more listening devices scattered around Bluebird's common areas. At night, he'd sneaked into the other guest rooms and found one in each of those. He had yet to figure out how to get into Lianna and Henry's private area of the house without detection. Lianna struck him as the type of woman who'd know if the order of things had been disrupted. Besides, he'd seen a serious-looking security camera bolted above the door to her private quarters.

That being said, she didn't appear to be particularly nervous or careful. She was certainly somewhat suspicious of him, but every day he went out and took pictures, sometimes even showing the better ones to Lianna or Henry. Henry liked the pictures of animals he'd found, and Lianna asked him more technical questions about the camera.

He was never sure if she was interested or if it was a test.

More guests would be coming tomorrow, and he was no closer to having a clue how to unearth the necessary information than he had been when he'd arrived.

He took his usual afternoon walk, deep into the woods and away from sight or hearing distance to the house. Once he felt he was far enough away, he set up his computer and phone so he could make the phone call to headquarters.

He attached everything, connected to the secure server and dialed. Shay didn't bother with greetings.

"Anything?" she asked.

"Not really. I found a listening device in every room— not just the common areas, but all the guest rooms, as well."

"What about hers?"

Reece bit back a sigh. "I haven't had a chance to get into her private living space yet, but it's not her."

There was a pause. "Have you been *trying* to get into her rooms?"

"She's on the premises all the time. If I'm keeping my cover, I can't sneak into her room unless there's zero chance of being caught. She's clean, Shay."

"If you sent off one of the devices, we could run the diagnostics, maybe get a clue where it came from."

"Taking one of the devices poses a problem since we

don't know who's placed them in the first place. If they know someone is on to them, it could escalate something. She and the kid shouldn't be caught in the cross fire of that."

"You have to get into her room and see if she's got them there, too. It's the only way to know for sure she's not involved."

Reece sighed. "She really takes care of this place—it's a family business. These kinds of listening devices in guest rooms would violate all sorts of privacy laws, not to mention they're way more high-tech than the cameras she has guarding her private quarters. I can't see her doing it. None of it would add up."

"But you don't know for sure she's not involved with the people doing it until you check her rooms. I trust your instincts, Reece, but we can't be too careful. We just don't know enough, and that's why I sent you. To *find out*. Now, I can ask this group hiring us if they're the ones who put the devices in."

Reece could read the hesitation in Shay's tone. "No, I'd like to figure it out as much as I can on my own. We want to keep the widow and the kid out of it, don't we? That's a priority for me. Kids don't get caught in the cross fire."

"That's a priority for me, too," Shay returned.

"Do we have a time limit on this?"

"They haven't prescribed one, and I figure as long as nothing pressing is going on, you've got the time to earn the widow's trust."

Reece glanced back at the house. Earning Lianna's confidence was getting complicated. He figured it was the kid. He'd follow orders to complete a mission as long as it didn't interfere with his one simple moral tenet. *Don't get kids caught in the middle.*

He'd never had a mission—in the military or with North

Star—where he'd had to deal with kids. This was a first, and he didn't like it.

"Reece?"

"It seems pretty peaceful here. Maybe it's the wrong line to tug to get the information."

"I might agree with you if you hadn't found listening devices."

Shay was right. The devices could mean Lianna and Henry were in danger and Lianna didn't have a clue. But despite a few days of being underfoot, Reece still didn't know how to bring up the subject of the dead husband and who he'd worked for. With no direct threat to her, it felt like bringing unnecessary trouble to her doorstep.

"Get into her rooms, Reece. Whether she knows what's going on or not, she might have something in her private quarters to point us in the right direction. We have to explore every possibility until we have more to go on."

Reece grimaced. He wasn't sure how he was going to accomplish that task, let alone how he'd live with the guilt of poking around in her private belongings when he did.

"All right, I—"

"Hey, Reece! Whatcha doing way out here?" Reece whirled on Henry, who was bounding through the trees.

Reece swore inwardly and slapped the phone and laptop shut. "Hey there, Hank," he said, trying to use his body to block the kid's view of the equipment.

Henry laughed like he always did when Reece called him Hank. Something shifted deep inside Reece, but he ignored it and shoved his laptop into his bag. There'd be no way of hiding it completely, but he could pretend it had something to do with the camera.

"I thought you weren't supposed to come out this far," Reece said as Henry came up on his side.

"I'm not, but I heard your voice." Henry peered at the bag. "Who you talking to?"

"Oh, I...got a call from my boss."

"Mom said her cell phone doesn't work all the way out here. Who's your boss?"

"Uh. The person who pays me to take pictures."

"That's cool. I think I want to be a firefighter when I grow up. My friend Joey's dad is a cop and he said firemen get to play video games all day."

"Huh. Well..."

Henry jumped up and down, trying to grab a tree branch, presumably to hang off, but it was just out of reach. "But Mom says it's a dangerous job."

"That's..."

"I could help Mom with the inn, but it gets kinda boring way out here."

Reece smiled against his will. "Well, you probably have some time to figure it out."

Henry shrugged, giving up his attempt to jump and grab the branch. "Did you see any animals today?"

"No, not today."

"My other friend Avery has a dad who's in the army. It sounds pretty cool, but sometimes he goes away for a long time."

Reece was surprised at the viscerally negative reaction he had to that. Even more surprised when words tumbled out of his mouth. "I was in the military for a little while. It's not bad, but... Well, I think your mom would miss you. You have to travel a lot. Work and live overseas." *See things you can't unsee.*

"Have you been to foreign countries?"

"Yeah."

"Which one's the best?"

"Too many...to name."

"Did you ever get hurt?"

"A little."

Henry hopped again, though this time it seemed to be to some inner rhythm rather than trying to grab the branch. "How? Why? Where?"

"That's probably more of a bedtime story," Reece offered, hoping that would get him off this line of questioning.

"Will you tell it to me at bedtime, then? Mom usually makes me read." Henry rolled his eyes. "But sometimes she'll read to me. Maybe you could tell me the story instead."

"Well… I guess that would be up to her." It'd give Reece a reason to be in Henry's room. He doubted very much Lianna would leave them alone, but he could get an idea of the layout, maybe a way to sneak in when Lianna was busy with guests this weekend.

If she'd let him. "We should get you back. Your mom might worry."

"Can I carry your camera?"

"Sure. Sure." Reece handed it over.

And felt like slime.

Chapter Three

"You know we don't allow guests in our rooms, Henry," Lianna said, trying to add groceries to her online cart and give Henry her full attention. But he was going on and on about Reece, and she had dinner to start and groceries to order for the weekend. "It's a very important rule."

Henry's groan could have been heard in Montana. "He's my friend."

Pain cracked through Lianna's chest. Friend. A guest couldn't be a friend. Still, it was no mystery why he was fascinated with Reece. The man was the embodiment of adult male attention that Henry didn't get. That he'd never gotten, because Todd had not been a good father. He'd considered children the domain of the wife.

A complication.

Lianna had gone out of her way to shield Henry from that, but she couldn't make up for the lack. She knew… She knew what it was like to grow up without parents. No matter how much she'd loved her grandparents, knowing her parents couldn't take care of her had been… It was a scar. Even having them in her life now didn't change the fact that they hadn't been then.

Now Henry had his own scar and wanted some random stranger to tell him a bedtime story.

"It isn't fair," Henry said, turning a furious shade of red.

Lianna turned away from the computer. She'd found one person in town who would pick up and deliver for her, and the extra money was worth the time she saved. But Freya could only deliver on Saturday mornings, which *wasn't* convenient.

Neither was this. She forced a smile for her son. She would never let him know his feelings came at an inconvenient time. He would never ever feel like an inconvenience to her. "I'm sure he can tell you the same story in the common areas."

"I hate the common areas and this stupid place. I want to live in town like Joey. I want…"

He didn't say it, but she knew what he wanted. A father. She knew because everything in him wilted, the anger fizzling out. He could want a father with everything he was, but it couldn't make his father alive.

"I want to show him my map," Henry said, speaking of the wallpaper on one wall of his room—a map of the whole world. "He's been to foreign countries," Henry said loftily. Some of his anger had faded, but he hadn't given up the fight.

Lianna's chest still hurt, but she figured the hardest part of Henry's outburst was over. She turned her attention back to groceries. "Oh, has he?"

"Yeah, when he was in the military. He even got hurt."

Lianna's body went cold. Military. Todd hadn't been military, and neither had the group he'd been involved with, as far as she knew. Still, military was a far cry from unassuming nature photographer.

Military meant…guns. It meant knowing how to do things. Bad things. Scary things. It meant he wasn't so unassuming. It meant he wasn't safe. They weren't safe.

"Excuse me, Henry." She pushed away from the kitchen table and marched through the dining room, panic beating through her chest. She knew she had to control it before she talked to Reece. She had to—

But he was walking in the front door, carrying that backpack that was abnormally large for a camera. Wasn't it? Wasn't everything about him just a shade wrong?

You're being paranoid. This is what Dr. Winston warned you about. Being alone. Spiraling out of control.

"You were in the military." She blurted it out like an accusation and then winced at how off-balanced she sounded.

Reece didn't move a muscle. He simply stood in the entryway, eyebrows raised. "Yes," he agreed very calmly.

"I… I don't like people lying to me. To my son." Her throat felt too tight, anxiety cutting off the oxygen.

It's just in your head. Breathe.

"Lianna, I haven't been active duty for over five years."

And he wasn't *her* friend, or anyone but a guest in her inn. It wasn't his fault Henry was getting attached. It wasn't *a lie…* "If you want to stay longer, I'm going to have to run a background check on you."

He didn't pause or hesitate. "Okay."

She wanted to cry, and she didn't have the slightest clue as to why. Except she still wasn't right. She still wasn't herself. "I'm sorry."

"For what?" He didn't step toward her. He didn't do a thing but stand there. But his next words were so gentle it felt like he put a warm hand on her shoulder like her grandmother used to do when Lianna was unreasonably upset.

"You should always trust your gut, and you should always be careful to protect your son. Run whatever checks you need to feel safe. You should feel safe."

It was all she wanted. For her and Henry. "My husband was killed. Murdered." The words had fallen out. Words she hadn't spoken since they'd moved to Echo. Oh, she knew some people knew. Especially those who had been friends of her grandparents, but she hadn't had to say it.

Why had she said it now?

Reece blinked. "I'm sorry."

He didn't sound shocked or dismayed. His sorry was… kind, but not particularly effusive. She appreciated that. She hadn't wanted his gasp of horror or praise of her bravery. She only wanted him to understand.

"My husband wasn't who he said he was." She swallowed and glanced back at the kitchen. Henry hadn't followed her. He was likely sneaking chocolate chips in the kitchen.

Thank God.

"Henry likes you. He's never had someone… Even when his father was alive, he didn't spend much time with Henry. He's desperate for… He likes you, and I…"

"I like him, too."

"You're just a guest. You…" She stepped forward. She couldn't explain it to Henry. He was only seven. But maybe if she explained it to this man, he could understand. He could…do something. "He can't get attached like that. I'm sorry. It isn't healthy. You won't stay forever."

"People generally don't."

Sadness dripped from those words. A sadness she recognized, because she'd been lost in it herself once. Henry had saved her, though. She'd had to take care of him, protect him, love him, and in doing all of those things for her precious boy, she'd learned to do the same for herself.

She wasn't perfect. Clearly this little meltdown wasn't at all mentally healthy. But Reece was just a person. With his own story. His own sadness and hang-ups. And he'd been here a few days and nothing out of the ordinary had happened. No questions about Todd. Nothing out of place. It wasn't like Denver.

She had to get a hold of herself. "I'm perfectly happy

to let him hear your stories. A friendship is certainly acceptable, but you cannot come into our private quarters. I have to maintain that boundary."

The sadness didn't lift. If anything, he looked sadder. But he nodded. "Whatever you want, Lianna. He's your son." He held up his camera. "If you'll excuse me."

Then he left again, as if he hadn't come inside for anything at all. Somehow, despite him being a stranger, Lianna felt guilty about his feelings. Feelings she didn't understand.

And are none of your business.

But she stood, staring at the door much longer than a busy woman had any right to.

"You've got a fake background ready for Reece Conrad?" Reece demanded when Shay answered his phone call.

Shay didn't hesitate at his sudden phone call or the demand. "More or less."

"Make it airtight."

"Will do. She's suspicious?"

"Not exactly, but the kid… He likes me. God knows why. She's more worried about that sort of thing. She told me her husband wasn't who he said he was."

"So she knew he was shady."

Reece sighed. "Found out, anyway. Which isn't surprising. He *was* murdered."

"All the reports on it say it was a burglary gone wrong. And use the fake name. I bet she knows the real one. Did you—"

"I don't have any other updates," Reece bit out. "I just want to make sure the background is in place."

"It is, but we'll flesh a few things out if we know she's running a check. Got a preferred wife name that you'll remember?"

"No wife."

"I thought…"

"She's seen me with the kid—she already called it that I don't have one of those. I haven't been wearing a ring, and I haven't mentioned a wife waiting for me. It doesn't make sense. Especially if I'm going to stay longer."

There was a long silence. "She's pretty," Shay said at length.

Reece didn't speak. No answer was better than anything he could have responded with.

Shay sighed. "All right. You'll look good for a background check—Elsie will make sure of it. If your innkeeper found out her husband wasn't who he said he was, she knows *something*." Shay's voice changed. Got hard and authoritative. "Get in her room, Montgomery. No more excuses."

"We got a time limit?" Reece returned, bristling at the order even knowing he shouldn't. This was what he came for—not making Lianna feel safe or to be a friend to Henry, but to get information.

"I'm giving you one. You give me something to go on by Monday night or I yank you and send Sabrina."

"Sabrina has all the subtlety of a horse."

"Your subtlety is costing us time and money. Maybe a heavier hand will do the trick."

Reece ran his free hand over his face. "Fine. Monday," he muttered, and ended the call before Shay could say anything else.

He looked through the woods. He couldn't see the house this far in the trees, but he could see it in his mind's eye. Easily. Not just from a tactical standpoint but from a…a…

He *liked* the inn. Liked being here. Hell, he even liked taking pictures. Not so much the pictures themselves, but the long walks and the paying attention to something other than what he had to do.

But he had things to do. And now he had a deadline.

It was clear he was looking at this all wrong. Yeah, he felt guilty, but a conscience didn't keep Lianna and Henry safe. He had to get to the bottom of those listening devices, even if it violated her trust to do it.

He'd known her for only a few days. Guilt was misplaced. Where had this *softness* come from? Too much time between missions? Too little to go on for this assignment?

Too much time alone?

He shook away that thought and marched deeper into the woods. He couldn't go back to the inn until he had a hold of himself. Until he had a plan. He had to know if she had listening devices in her quarters by the end of the day Monday.

How would he do it? Lianna never seemed to leave the inn. The first step would be to find a time she did. She had to leave *sometimes*. He'd prefer it if Henry were gone, too. Anyway, Lianna wasn't likely to leave Henry behind.

He could probably convince Henry to let him into the personal quarters when Lianna was busy, but even *thinking* about using the kid that way made him feel ill. No, he couldn't use Henry. It wasn't right.

He went over plans, potentials, dismissing almost all of them as he trudged around the woods. The sun sank lower and lower, until it was nearly pitch-black. He didn't have a choice. He had to head back to the inn and figure... something out.

It was quiet when he made it back to the yard, but all the lights glowed warmly. Welcoming. It made him feel like he could belong here.

Which was the stupidest thought he'd possibly *ever* had. Even when he'd been a kid who'd thought a foster home could be permanent, that someone besides his parents could love him. At least he'd been a dumb kid then.

Now he was a grown adult.

You have a mission, Montgomery. Stop dancing around it.

The stars shone brilliantly above—he'd always had that, even as a kid. Starshine and endless space—and the hope there was something beyond the hell he'd lived in when he was still with his parents.

Now he was independent, doing what he was meant to do and helping people. It was stupid to beat himself up over a little guilt. If Lianna was the good person she seemed to be, then he was protecting her. He was doing his job by going through her personal things.

He closed his eyes and accepted a few things right here and now—so he could move on and deal with what had to be done.

He liked this place. He liked Lianna and Henry. He wanted them to be okay.

However, for them to be okay and safe, he had to accept that he didn't belong here. He had to do his duty and get out.

He opened his eyes, gave himself a nod as if it was the physical shake he needed and headed inside. It was nearing eight o'clock, which meant Henry was likely in his room.

Reece had missed dinner, and though he didn't find himself particularly hungry, he knew that fuel was necessary no matter how a man felt. He moved for the kitchen, aware that he'd likely find Lianna there doing the dishes.

He wasn't disappointed. She hummed some nameless tune to herself as she rinsed off a dish and put it in the dishwasher.

She was beautiful. It was time to stop dancing around the truth. He liked her and was attracted to her, and that was what was holding him up. Now that he'd admitted it, if only to himself, he could move past it.

He retraced his steps, went all the way back to the front door, then made sure he made noise as he closed the door and walked heavier than necessary through the common areas, dining room and to the kitchen.

She looked over her shoulder as he came to a stop at the entrance to the kitchen. "There you are," she offered.

"Sorry I missed dinner. Stellar sunset."

She returned to loading the dishwasher. "You're a guest, Reece. No need to apologize. There's a plate of leftovers in the fridge. If you can wait about ten, I can serve you in the dining room. Or—"

"I could grab it myself. I don't want to get in your way. I *was* the one who missed the dining room hours."

"Well. I suppose that would be okay. Let me heat them up for you—" She made a move for the fridge, but he shook his head and made it there first.

"No need."

She held her wet, soapy hands in front of her, looking wholly perplexed. "But it won't be any good cold."

He smiled and took the plate from the fridge. "It's a very rare occasion I get a home-cooked meal. Hot or cold, it's still a treat."

She frowned at him, then let out a gusty sigh. "Well, if you're going to do that, you might as well eat at the kitchen table and not dirty up my dining room." She gestured to the small table he knew she and Henry often ate at, rather than joining guests in the dining room.

She gave Henry a life separate from the inn. Clearly on purpose. He wondered if it was to protect Henry, or for some other reason. One more in line with why he was here.

"You do an awful lot on your own," he said casually,

settling himself at the table. "Don't most places have a cook and a maid and a handyman?"

She waved that away and went back to the dishes. "I have an on-call handyman, a maid service that comes in once a month to do a deep clean. But I usually don't have more than four or five guests. It isn't all that different than keeping house. Except I actually make some money off it."

"Do you ever leave?"

She huffed out a laugh. He wouldn't say she seemed *comfortable*, but she'd put her genial innkeeper persona back in place. "Do parent-teacher conferences count? Sometimes I don't have guests, and those are usually the days for personal shopping or haircuts and taking Henry to the park. But I love this place. I like being close to home. Free days and errands are more than enough for me." She pushed a few buttons and then closed the dishwasher.

"So, if I wasn't here on Monday, and Henry was at school, you'd go into town and do errands?"

"Oh, maybe. Depends." She turned to face him. He watched her school her relief into something more casual. "Are you checking out?"

She wanted him to go, and that should not…hurt. "No. Not permanently, anyway. The park I want to go to is a bit of a drive. I thought I'd stay over, then drive back Tuesday. It might give you a chance to do that background check."

"Don't you have…? It's none of my business, of course, and I'm not trying to push you out. You've got our most expensive room, so your staying is good for my bottom line." She smiled. "Don't you have a home to get back to?"

"I like it here. It's…" He had to think and speak like a photographer, not like a man who'd never had a home. He looked at the plate in front of him. Pot roast, mashed potatoes and cooked carrots. It was delicious regardless of temperature. It was a dream.

He could hardly tell her he was having stupid home fantasies. "It's inspiring. I travel for my work. Sometimes I find a place I like and stay awhile. If it's resulting in photos, that's all that really matters."

She nodded.

"If you ever don't want me here, you only have to say it."

"And have you leave me a bad review?"

"I wouldn't. I understand. You have to look out for yourself and your son. I've never…" He shook his head. This wasn't the way to assuage his guilt over needing to rifle through her things. He should be keeping his distance and getting the job done.

But she studied him, and there was something in her blue eyes that… It felt a bit like this place. Somewhere to be. Home.

Which convinced him he'd lost his mind. His objectivity. *Something.* He needed to get back to what he knew. Completing assignments and missions.

"You've never what?" she pressed.

"You're a good mother. You care about your son and want to protect him. I haven't really seen that." He shoved a bite of pot roast into his mouth and hoped to God it'd remind him to stop talking.

Her eyebrows drew together. "Your parents…"

He gave a shrug, trying to play it all off as casual. Unimportant. "Didn't care much about me. Enough neglect that the state took me away. I bounced around in fosters till I aged out."

"I'm sorry."

He shook his head, uncomfortable. But she was talking to him, studying him. Maybe she'd share some of her own past. Something about her dead husband. It was for the mission. A give-and-get.

Not his own soul.

"My parents couldn't take care of me, either, but my grandparents took me. I... They were great. But it's hard having parents who weren't. It always made me want to be better. And then Todd..." She sucked in a breath and then made a sound he thought was supposed to be a laugh. "Well, I have to go get Henry away from the screens and ready for bed. I allow him thirty minutes of playtime before he has to go to sleep."

She started walking out of the kitchen, and he should let her. Let her get back to her normal life, knowing on Monday he'd find the answer he was looking for, and hopefully be able to wrap this up in just a few more days.

But words came out anyway.

"If he still wants that story, I'd be happy to tell it. Wherever you're comfortable."

Chapter Four

Lianna stopped midstride. Not only had Reece remembered, but he was also casually offering to tell her baby a story. Something she knew Henry desperately wanted.

It was more care than the boy's own father had ever shown him. Which was saying next to nothing, but it still made Lianna's heart hurt. It made her...soft, when she had to stay strong for Henry.

Reece might like it here, he might be *inspired*, but he would leave. And Henry would be heartbroken to lose a companion, wouldn't he?

Or is that just what you tell yourself to keep you both safe?

She looked at Reece. He continued to eat, as if his offer was casual and any response she gave would be fine enough, but she saw something underneath that. Especially now that he'd mentioned his parents and foster homes. The military.

The man had no home. No family. He was lonely, and didn't she know that feeling? Intimately at that. This place had always been a balm to that loneliness, even when her grandparents weren't here. Why should she be surprised it reached out to someone else? It was what she counted on—people to view her inn as a charming home away from home.

Maybe he made her a little nervous, and caused those anxious thoughts to spiral, but the only way to deal with those reactions was to confront them. To *deal*.

"I'm sure he'd like that."

Reece gave a nod.

Lianna walked out of the kitchen but stopped just outside the door. Why would she get Henry ready for bed, then have him come back out to the common area? It made more sense to just have Reece come to Henry's room. What harm could a ten-minute story do?

Don't do it. You don't know him. The background check could come back and he could be a murderer. A rapist. He could be a con artist who wheedled his way into people's rooms and lives and...

She shook away the destructive thoughts. She wouldn't let Todd take her trust away from her. She wouldn't think the worst of everyone she came into contact with. Reece had been nothing but kind and good with Henry. He was just a lonely man.

And if he's some serial killer?

No. Not everyone was Todd. Echo and the Bluebird were supposed to be real life. She didn't want her real life to be full of silly suspicion and over-the-top fear.

"Why don't you come on back to his room?" Lianna heard herself say, or screech. She wouldn't leave him alone with Henry. She had a gun and pepper spray. She had a camera system and locks and... She would not be paranoid. She was prepared.

When she turned to look back into the kitchen, Reece had an arrested look on his face, fork halfway to his mouth.

He set the fork down at length. "You sure?"

Lianna kept her clenched fists behind her back where he couldn't see them. "Of course. Just for tonight. He wants to show you his room. He needs a bath first, and you need to finish your dinner. I'll come get you in fifteen. There's ice cream in the freezer."

With that, she turned on a heel.

And fled.

She was breathing heavily, heart beating in overtime as she reached the door to her private quarters. She had a special lock installed, a security camera fastened to the ceiling that watched the door to see who came and went.

She took precautions to keep herself and her child safe.

And now you've invited a stranger into your safe space.

She did some of the breathing exercises Dr. Winston had taught her. Calmed her ragged breathing. They would still be safe. If she couldn't do this, if she couldn't run her inn and have the occasional connection to a guest, then they might as well move back to Denver.

She eased into Henry's room, where he lay, head hanging upside down off his bed, playing with his handheld video game.

"I play even better upside down, Mom."

"Uh-huh. Time's up."

"Let me finish my level."

"Henry, we've talked about—"

"I can't save until I finish!" he yelled, as he did every night, furiously punching the keys as he raced her inevitable countdown.

"If you want Reece to come tell you his story in your room, the games better be off in five, four, three—"

Henry tossed the device onto his pillow and popped up on his knees. "You're going to let him come see my map?"

Lianna nodded, ignoring the way her chest clutched in fear.

"Really? Really!" Henry did a little dance.

Lianna blew out a breath. It was the right thing to do. Such a small thing, and it made Henry happy.

Once Reece told his story and left, she would be convinced she was fine, and they could live here forever.

And she'd never let this happen again.

She started Henry's bath and then left him to it, folding laundry just outside the bathroom so that she could listen for excessive splashing or anything out of the ordinary.

He chattered about Reece, about the map wall and the military and how jealous Joey would be that he'd be hearing *real* war stories.

Lianna cringed at that, but once she had Henry in his pajamas and ushered him into his room, she told him she'd return with Reece in a few minutes.

A kindness. For Henry. For a lonely man. Being kind to strangers was supposed to be a rewarding experience.

Lord, she was terrified. But Dr. Winston had told her she'd fall into this spiral. He'd warned her against taking on so much responsibility alone. He'd told her she wasn't ready.

Her hands clenched into fists as she walked back to the kitchen. He'd been wrong. She'd felt it deep in her bones. No matter how scarred she'd been by Todd's lies and death, she'd been determined to face the challenges head-on. At first for Henry, but then for herself, too.

She stepped into the kitchen, where Reece stood at her sink, drying off the dishes he'd used. He'd washed them, by hand.

It was kind of him to take care of it himself, but it was her job. *Her* job to attend to. Because she was the innkeeper and he was the guest and things were getting muddied.

But this weekend they'd have more guests and everything would…right itself.

For tonight she would prove to herself she could do

a kindness for a stranger and not be punished for it. She forced a smile.

"Henry's all ready. And possibly too excited to sleep after."

"Military stories aren't that exciting," Reece said, carefully placing the cleaned dishes on the dish towel on the counter.

"Good," she said emphatically.

He turned, a rare smile flirting with the corners of his mouth. He smiled at Henry a lot, but there was a gravity about Reece in general. A seriousness.

"I'm not sure where to put—"

She waved the dishes away. "Leave them there. I'll take care of it. You *are* the guest." She motioned for him to follow her.

She took him back through the hallway, then to the left, where her personal wing was blocked off from the rest of the house by a door. She pulled her key out of her pocket, watching out of the corner of her eye as Reece glanced at the security camera, at the lock. But he didn't comment on the precautions. He simply waited patiently.

So she let him into her private rooms and prayed to God she hadn't just made the biggest mistake of her life.

LIANNA DIDN'T WASTE TIME. She immediately walked down the narrow hall to the door farthest from the one they'd walked through. She opened the door and motioned Reece inside.

He stepped into a small room that screamed *little boy*. Action figures and video game posters, sports knickknacks and the faint smell of *sweat* under the lemon scent that permeated most of the inn. There was a baby monitor receiver on the windowsill—Reece knew Lianna clipped the main device to her belt when she did her early-morning or evening chores so she could hear Henry was safe and sound as he slept in his room. Just like she had the camera outside their private area. Lianna did everything she could to protect her son.

But as he'd mentioned to Shay, these were low-tech options a woman chose to make sure no guests took advantage of her and her son. Not someone trying to do any spying of her own.

Reece glanced up at the ceiling, and in less than five seconds, he saw it. This listening device was in the same place as it had been in his and the other guest rooms. A small unnoticeable sticker on the side of the smoke or carbon monoxide detectors in each room.

That was not from Lianna, and she definitely didn't know they were there. Someone was listening to her every move.

He didn't know how to react to that in the moment, so he could only look at Henry, who bounced on his bed in video game–themed pajamas, his blond hair a haphazard, damp mess.

Something inside of Reece's chest clutched. "Ready for a story?" he asked, his voice rusty as he lowered himself onto the too-small desk chair.

Lianna settled herself on Henry's bed, leaning against the wall, while Henry wiggled in the middle of the mattress.

He looked at the two of them. Henry a ball of energy, Lianna… He might have called her calm or serene if he couldn't sense all the tension tightening underneath the surface.

His presence in the room made her nervous, but she was powering through. So he'd tell his story quickly, make it just interesting enough to entertain Henry, and then…

He had no idea how he was going to tell her she was

being listened to. That she was still in danger. That he'd been lying to her about who he was. Because he was going to have to—whether Shay gave him the okay or not.

"I was stationed here for a while," he said, pointing to Afghanistan on Henry's map wall. "We were trying to…" Reece trailed off. He'd figured he'd throw out some story of something that had happened, not realizing how complicated it was when faced with the excited blue eyes.

"Protect people," Lianna supplied for him. "That's the job of the military, right?"

"Right. Right. Protect people." He wished it had been that simple. So distinctly black-and-white. He liked to think what he did now for North Star was clearer in terms of right and wrong, but the "bad guys" in any situation almost always thought they were the good ones.

"Did you drive a tank?" Henry asked.

"Not so much. It was more foot patrol. Walking around. Talking to people. Finding out who did what wrong and trying to…stop bad things from happening."

"Did you shoot people?" Henry asked earnestly, the wriggling slowing. The excitement dimming into something more like captivation. Not just about hurting the bad guys, but about what Reece himself had done.

"There were times we shot back at people shooting at us." There were no doubt things he'd done to end people's lives. But how did he explain that to a seven-year-old?

Luckily, Henry just kept right on asking questions. "Was it scary?"

"Very."

"What did you do when you were scared?"

"I depended on my training, but mostly my team. My fellow soldiers. I knew they had my back and I had theirs. You're all in it together."

"Like a family," Henry said softly.

Reece couldn't respond right away. His throat got too tight and the pain in his chest was almost unbearable. He stared hard at his shoes.

He had no family, but the army and then North Star had been as close as he'd ever gotten to almost feeling like he had one. "Yeah, I suppose."

In the end, he told no stories at all, just answered Henry's endless questions until the boy's eyes began to droop and Lianna insisted it was bedtime.

"Good night, Henry."

"Night, Reece. Thanks for the story." The boy yawned, long and loud. "You're the best."

Reece didn't have anything to say to that, though it was easy to tell Lianna wasn't pleased as she pulled back the covers and instructed Henry to crawl under them. She whispered a few words to Henry as Reece moved for the door.

He knew he should walk out of the room. Go up to his room to get his stuff and then right out the front door— away forever. Let Shay and the group hiring them handle the rest of this.

But instead he watched as Lianna smoothed the hair off Henry's forehead, gave him a kiss good-night, whispered, *"I love you."*

You're all in it together.

Like a family.

Lianna met his gaze, something like sympathy in her eyes, as if she could see every untimely, unnecessary emotion on his face.

He turned abruptly and moved into the hallway. He looked back toward the door he'd entered. No doubt Lianna's bedroom was the door closest to that one. No doubt she kept herself as some kind of barrier to shield Henry from the outside world.

He'd never had anyone in his life shield him from anything. He'd learned to get over that—or thought he had. Army. North Star. He'd depended on himself and that had been good and right.

Lianna stepped into the hallway and closed Henry's door behind her. She looked at him enigmatically. "It was very kind of you," she said quietly. She had her innkeeper voice on. Courteous but firm. "But I don't think we'll be having a repeat performance."

Reece nodded stiffly. No. No repeat performances. No more letting himself get walloped by a ship that had sailed a long time ago.

He belonged to no one and no one belonged to him, and that was the way of his world. Nothing could change it. Wishing he could was useless. Pointless.

He reminded himself to move, to walk toward the door out. He glanced once more at her room door. He could barge in and show her exactly what he knew. But the listening device would hear.

And you don't want to hurt her.

She followed him to the door back to the main areas of the inn. He knew she still had chores to do out there, but she'd wait until Henry was asleep.

He had to tell her she was in danger. Surely someone listening to her every move meant she was in danger.

Or she's perfectly safe, because she knows nothing, and people have likely been listening for months without acting on it.

Regardless, he couldn't tell her here. He'd have to tell her outside. A note would be too long and complicated. This had to be done face-to-face and away from the bugs. Maybe he could catch her while she was gardening or walking to get Henry at the bus stop. He'd tell her and...

And what?

He knew she was waiting to close the door behind him. To lock him out. Where he belonged.

He knew he should *go*, but words tumbled out instead. "For what it's worth... I know I shouldn't be attached, or care. I'm nobody. But I am and I do. So I'll keep my distance." He stepped out, headed for his room, without even a glance behind him.

He'd pack up and leave. Let Shay send in Sabrina to get the rest of the information. He'd gotten the first step figured out—Lianna didn't know she was being listened to.

Sabrina could do the rest. This was one assignment that was too... It was beyond him. He wasn't right for it. They could send him into danger, into the wilderness. Something remote and challenging. Not a widow and her cute kid.

This was too much. He couldn't do it. He just couldn't.

Chapter Five

Lianna went through her usual routine feeling like spun glass. As though one thing might shatter her into a million pieces.

She waited until she heard Henry's snores on the monitor. Would he ever be old enough for her not to need to hear his heavy breathing to know he was okay? It was just the house was so big, and she had so much to do.

She had to know he was safe. If that was paranoia, so be it. She'd let a stranger into their private quarters today. A stranger.

She leaned against the back door she'd been locking, squeezing her eyes against the lance of pain. Reece had sat there and answered Henry's questions with a patience and…a thoughtfulness Henry's own father had never given him.

He'd looked so wrong. His big frame taking up that small desk chair meant for a little boy. But the way he'd seemed so *arrested* and then devastated when Henry had said, *Like a family…* Lianna had wanted to be able to give Reece something. Anything to ease that heartbreaking look.

So you told him he couldn't do it again.

Yes, she'd had to.

Reece and his loneliness and lack of family were *not*

her problems. Who knew? It could be all fabricated. Made up to make her sympathetic so he could do any number of terrible things.

She was being smart and safe. It wasn't anxiety, paranoia or fear. It was just common sense.

She walked through her evening responsibilities—making sure everything was in its place. She ended in the kitchen and stared at the dishes Reece had used and washed.

She didn't like this conflict inside of her. This inability to stick to a course of action. It reminded her too much of what she'd been in those last years with Todd. Someone who knew what she had to do, but had been too afraid to do it. Not because of any real threat, but because it required courage.

Lianna marched into the kitchen, put Reece's dishes and the clean ones from the dishwasher away. She would check to make sure the doors were locked, go to sleep and wake up with a clear head.

There'd be other guests here this weekend. Maybe that would help her work through all her conflicting feelings about Reece.

And maybe you should know better than to indulge in conflicting feelings about another man.

She stopped at the back door. It was locked, but instead of moving on to the front door, she turned the dead bolt. She stepped outside onto the much smaller back porch. She took a deep breath of the night air. The spring peepers were chirping and night rustled around her. Summer was trying to push through, but it hadn't arrived this far north yet. The moon and stars shone and everything was...

She'd felt so settled, and then Reece Conrad had walked into her inn and sent her into some kind of spiral.

It wasn't his fault. Whether he was a good man or an

evil one, she was the only one who could control her life. Blaming paranoia on Todd didn't get her anywhere. Todd was dead. She was alive, and she had Henry.

It had been a rough year, with a lot of change, but Henry was thriving.

And what about you?

She wasn't there yet, no, but she could get there. She just had to work through what she was feeling. Not be afraid of it. Not hide it away.

So, here in the dark, she let herself cry. Racking sobs. She'd never let herself cry when she was married to Todd. Never let herself feel. She'd blocked it off and away deep inside to get through the day.

She had to keep a certain kind of control on the worst of her negative emotions around Henry, so as not to scare him, but that didn't mean she couldn't indulge when she was alone.

"Lianna."

She whirled around at Reece's voice, her heart beating too hard in her chest. And it wasn't just fear. It was something else. Something she hadn't allowed herself to feel in a long time.

"What is it? What's wrong?" he asked. It was dark, but in the moonlight it looked like he was scanning the woods around them. That was when she noticed he hadn't come out the back door; he was standing at the bottom of the porch stairs. Why would he have come around the front? Why…was he here? Asking her what was wrong when she was trying to have a good private cry?

She immediately wiped at her cheeks, hoping to…avoid *this*, whatever it was. "I thought you'd gone to bed."

"What's wrong?" he asked again, undeterred by her attempt at deflection.

"Nothing," she said, a little too shrilly. Or like a guilty

child. "I just needed a moment to myself. The moon is pretty tonight. Excuse me, I have to—"

But he stepped in front of the door, stopping her from darting inside. Alarm spread through her and she tried to think of how she would fight this man who was so much bigger than her and... And carrying a bag.

"What are you doing?" she asked, sidetracked by the fact that he was carrying not just his camera bag in the middle of the night—which would have been strange enough—but the big duffel he'd shown up with, too.

He cleared his throat. "I heard you crying. I wanted to make sure you're okay."

"Are you leaving?"

"I..." He blew out a breath, and though he'd stopped her progress back inside, he kept his distance. A very careful distance. "I thought it would be best."

"Why?" And why was she asking why? He should go. Disappear. Then she could go back to feeling settled.

But where would he go? How alone would he be? It made her heart pinch to think of him just going off with nowhere to go and no one to go home to.

He is not your responsibility.

"I thought you'd be more comfortable if I left."

She would be. It would be good, and yet... The thought of him leaving didn't settle her at all. "And quite a bit poorer."

"I'll pay for the full week."

How did he make her feel guilty? She had every right not to want a strange man to forge some bond with her child. To make her heart flutter and remind her of all the things she couldn't trust ever again.

But she felt a sinking sensation in her stomach and she couldn't... She couldn't just let him disappear into the night. "I think you misunderstand me. It's not that I don't… I have to worry. I'm a single woman in an isolated bed-and-breakfast. I have to worry. I have to be careful, but I was upset… It's hard. Watching Henry… He should have that kind of thing. A man to look up to, to answer his questions."

"He has you."

"Yes. I try to make it enough, but… When you're a mother, you want to give your child everything. I couldn't give him a decent father. I couldn't—"

"It's not your fault your husband was killed."

"Todd was no father before he was killed," Lianna said, the words as heavy as her heart. "I should have known… I should have gotten out. I should have done so many things. And it's not me dealing with the consequences—it's my child. I promised myself that wouldn't happen. Henry wouldn't pay for my mistakes with Todd. I failed there, and I can only hope to God he never knows what his father really was."

"What was he?"

"A very bad man." She shook her head. This wasn't Reece's problem. "I'd hate for you to sneak out on my account. I can't promise open doors or a lack of suspicion, but if I think you need to leave, I'll tell you."

Something crossed his face. Pain or guilt or something she was making up entirely. And he didn't agree with her or disagree. He didn't go inside. He only looked at her, something heartbreaking in his gaze.

"Lianna, do you know what a bug looks like?"

WHEN LIANNA ONLY looked at him in confusion, he knew she didn't have a clue.

"What kind of bug?" she asked, eyebrows drawn together, frown wrinkling her brow. "We have lots of them. I…"

Reece stood on her porch in the quiet, peaceful eve-ning and knew he was about to ruin everything for her. He hated himself for it, but there were no other choices. Not now. "A listening device. Would you know how to iden-tify a listening device?"

She stiffened. Immediately. Any confusion in her gaze turned cold. He could tell from the way her eyes widened and darted toward the house—as if his mentioning them would make them suddenly visible to her—that she didn't know about them. And his mentioning any kind of listen-ing device made her immediately afraid. Of him.

Good. It was time she understood who she was dealing with. No more guilt. Just the cold, hard truth.

She edged away from him, but then seemed to realize her son was inside the building he was blocking her from. Her hands curled into fists, as if she was ready to fight him tooth and nail.

He'd win. Easily. But he didn't want to fight her.

He moved to the side, so that if she wanted to dart for the door, she could. But he spoke as he did it. "There is a listening device fastened to the smoke or carbon monox-ide detector in each of the rooms in your house. I haven't checked your room, but I can only assume you have one, as well."

"What are you even talking about?" she said, her voice strangled.

"I saw the one in my room first. Then I searched the rest of the inn. Someone wants to know what you know, Lianna."

"How do I know *you* didn't put them there?" she de-manded.

"I guess you don't. But I haven't been in your room. I'm sure your camera could prove that."

She inched closer and closer to the door. "What are you...? *Who* are you?"

He blew out a breath. How to answer that? If he was smart, he'd lie. A man who'd done what he'd done for as long as he'd done it knew better than to be *honest*.

"You know what? Don't bother answering, since it will clearly be a lie. Go. And don't ever come back. If this is about Todd... I don't know anything about him. I never did. I just want you to leave me alone. All of you."

"What do you mean *all*?"

"All the men who bothered me in San Francisco, and then again in Denver. I told the FBI and whoever else everything I knew. If they thought I was going to change my mind because...because..."

The FBI. That was something North Star could check into. Reece didn't get the impression they were the ones asking North Star for help, but Todd Kade could have had ties to the FBI or an FBI case under his real name.

"You were going. Please don't let me stop you," she said, now standing in the door. He could see she had a death grip on the knob. She'd slam the door in his face, try to fight him off with everything she had.

He'd made a mess of things. And there was no one to blame that on but himself. He'd gone soft, or lost an edge somewhere along the way. He'd failed...everything.

So, yes, he should go. Drive back to North Star. Give his report on everything he knew. If they needed more from Lianna, they could send Sabrina. Leave him out of it.

And what? Prove to Lianna she can't trust anyone even with her husband dead?

Lianna couldn't be his problem, but Shay wasn't going to keep him around if he failed this very simple mission. There was no reason for her to, and North Star was everything.

Reece scrubbed a hand over his face. "We only wanted to help."

"We?" she all but screeched. "Who is we?"

Before he could explain that he *couldn't* explain, she held up a hand.

"No. I don't want to hear another lie. Just…go." And with that, she stepped fully inside and closed the door. The lock clicked into place, and no doubt she'd set the alarms, as well.

Reece stood there in the dark. He knew she was watching, waiting to make sure he left. Then she'd likely go check on Henry. She wouldn't sleep tonight. She'd be too worried.

He blew out a breath. She'd been crying over everything she couldn't give Henry because he'd had a father who didn't care. But Lianna didn't seem to understand that having a mother who cared like she did would give any kid the chance at a really good life.

Unless whoever put those listening devices comes for them.

Reece had to get to the bottom of it. He couldn't just leave her to the wolves. He'd messed it all up, but he could hardly leave that mess and not clean it up. Not when she and Henry could be in potential danger.

Sabrina wasn't the answer. He hadn't been able to lie to Lianna and Henry any longer. His failing, sure, but that didn't mean the whole mission had to be a failure.

He glanced at his watch. Late, but not too late, hopefully. As he walked toward his car, bags still strapped to his back, he slid his phone out of his pocket.

"Hello," a woman's voice grumbled into the receiver.

"Elsie? I need your computer expertise."

"Reece, do you know what time it is?" Elsie Rogers said over a yawn. She was a newer member of North Star, but her computer skills were unparalleled. She also didn't go into the field, which meant Reece could tell a few half-truths to keep her from reporting everything to Shay.

"Sorry, this can't wait. I need you to hack into the computer and security systems here, and I figure that will take a while."

"That bed-and-breakfast where you're staying? They're not even on a server. I'll have it cracked in fifteen minutes."

"Great. I'll call you back in fifteen." He hung up before she could protest or ask for more information. He threw his bags into his car and turned on the ignition. He could see the shadow of Lianna in the attic window—she'd likely gone up there to make sure he hadn't left anything sinister behind.

Nothing sinister. Just a note for her, and one for Henry.

She stood there in the window, clearly watching and waiting to make sure he left. He wasn't going anywhere.

But Lianna didn't need to know that.

Chapter Six

So Reece Conrad was a liar in a long line of liars. Lianna shouldn't be surprised and she really shouldn't be hurt. He was a stranger. If the man she'd been married to for six years could lie to her, day after day, year after year, why wouldn't some stranger posing as a guest at her inn be able to?

She frowned. Sheriff Reynolds had said Reece's background was clear, and that it existed. Surely he hadn't given her his real name. Was he as deceitful as Todd? Going around taking on other identities. Or had he stolen someone's identity? Or…

It didn't matter. It did *not* matter. He was a liar—no matter how he did it.

She looked at the letters he'd left on the desk in his room. She wouldn't read them. She certainly wouldn't give one to Henry. They'd known each other a few days. It was hardly worth…letters.

Once he'd pulled away in his car, she'd left his room, armful of bedding and those letters in hand. She dumped the bedding in the laundry room, checked the locks three times, checked on Henry even though the sound that came through the baby monitor hooked to her belt was still nothing more than the soft snuffling of his snores.

She stood in the doorway of his dark room, watching

the lump of blankets that was her son. Her safe, sleeping son. Reece had been here in his room. Lianna had let that happen, and Reece had talked to Henry and answered his questions and looked as though...

Well, if he was a smarter bad guy he would have used Henry to get information out of her. So he was either very stupid or...

He is the bad guy. He is. Don't you dare be this foolish over a man ever again.

She turned away from Henry and forced herself to go to her bedroom. The locks were locked. The security measures were in place. And it turned out she should definitely listen to her gut, because it had told her Reece was bad news.

Well, no. Her gut had told her the opposite. Her *brain* had told her Reece was bad news. So from here on out, she'd listen to her brain and her paranoia, because clearly they were right.

Except Reece left of his own accord. Some bad guy.

So maybe he wasn't all bad. Maybe, unlike Todd, he had some kind of conscience. He still wasn't who he'd said he was. He was still a *liar* who knew about listening devices and had been sneaking around her inn, either finding them or placing them.

Lianna flipped on the light in her room. There'd be no sleeping tonight. Should she even bother trying?

She glanced up at the smoke detector above her doorway. It was the same innocuous device she had in every room. The little green light was on as it always was, showing that the batteries were still good. She had a note in her ledgers of when to change the batteries so guests were never woken up by that annoying beeping reminder.

Still, she stared at it. She didn't see anything out of

the ordinary. Anything attached. Certainly nothing Reece would have been able to see just by looking.

She marched over to her desk, dropped the letters she would definitely throw away and pulled her chair over to place it under the smoke detector. Maybe he was lying about the listening devices, too. Maybe this was some kind of mind game.

She found herself thinking Reece would never do that, but she had to remember she didn't really know him. That wasn't even his real name. Who even knew *what* he was.

He probably worked for the same people Todd had. Or was with the FBI. Maybe some elite military group. Maybe all three. God knew Todd liked to spread his "talents" around.

Whatever it was, it had *nothing* to do with her. She only wished the ghost of Todd Kade would stop haunting her.

She got up on the chair. She inspected the smoke detector. She didn't really see anything. Well, a little piece of plastic that looked like a stray piece of tape, maybe? Of course, she wouldn't have put any tape on her smoke detector.

She reached up and touched it, then pulled the edge. There was *something*. She pulled it harder. Slowly a thin piece of adhesive came off, revealing a small circle that looked almost like a coin with holes in it.

She didn't fully understand how something so small and flimsy could be a listening device, but this was something she definitely hadn't put there, and it most certainly didn't belong on a smoke detector. Whatever it was, someone had been in her house and put something foreign on her smoke detector.

Reece could have put it there. Yes, she had cameras, and she always zipped through the videos when they had guests just to make sure nothing was amiss. She hadn't seen Reece.

But he could probably hack computers. He could probably...

She curled her fingers around the device. He'd told her the truth. In this, he'd told her the truth. Which could be a trick, but had Todd ever told her even a tiny bit of the truth? Even to mess with her?

She wouldn't go chase him down, of course. But maybe she should take his warning at face value. Maybe she should call Sheriff Reynolds tomorrow and have him take a look at the listening devices.

She looked at the one in her palm. She thought about saying something inflammatory. Like "Screw you and leave me alone." It would be satisfying.

And stupid.

She got down from the chair and placed the listening device on her desk. Was someone actively listening? Or were they just recording her? What would they be after?

No one could possibly know what she knew about Todd. Not Henry, not the FBI, not her parents or grandparents or the stray acquaintance. No one knew what she'd seen in that file.

She thought about the way the FBI agent had brought her into his office in San Francisco. How nervous she'd been. They'd said, "Sorry for your loss," and she hadn't known what to say.

Todd being dead had been a relief, which had made her feel terrible at the time. No one should be relieved that their own husband and child's father was dead. But she had been.

Then...it had gotten so complicated she didn't even feel guilty about her relief anymore. Questions from the FBI, and a couple of other men in suits who'd claimed to be

Todd's associates. The move to Denver, where they'd all followed her. With constant questions.

None of them had threatened her. If anything, they treated her like Todd had treated her. Like a stupid liability.

And if she was honest with herself, as it had gone on and on, she'd played up that role. Convincing them of her stupidity and ignorance. So much so that she'd been able to see Todd's real name in that file, and the name of two of the groups the FBI thought he was working with.

She'd never uttered Todd's real name, never so much as even googled the group names. She'd packed up Henry, moved home to Echo and convinced herself she could keep Henry safe by resolutely *not* knowing what she knew.

Lianna sank onto her bed. Who was listening to her? The FBI? One of the other groups? Did it matter when she'd never given them any reason to believe she knew what she knew?

She blew out a breath and had to reconcile the fact that in comparison to everyone who had come before, Reece had never asked her anything. Not one question about what she knew or who Todd was. Oh, she'd offered up a few things, but nothing people wouldn't be able to find out.

Especially people who know how to recognize a listening device as small as that at a glance.

Maybe she'd been too hasty. Maybe Reece could have helped her.

She shook her head. That was stupid. No one could help her. Just like always, she had to help herself.

And she would. She'd do whatever she could to keep her and her son safe. Destroy those letters, forget Reece Conrad had ever existed, and…and…

She would figure it out. She had to.

REECE HAD BEEN conditioned from birth to survive on little sleep. His parents hadn't kept normal hours, and had never allowed him a full night, from what he could remember. There hadn't been a foster home he'd been able to relax in enough to fully sleep. Then he'd put those habits and skills to good use in the military and his work with North Star.

Including right now. He'd camped the past three nights in the woods a good two miles from the Bluebird. He kept watch, harassed Elsie about what she could find through Lianna's computer files, and he did not mention to Shay or anyone else that he'd had a little blip of conscience and was no longer precisely *at* the Bluebird.

He slept in short patches of time in order to keep his mind sharp and his response times quick, but mostly it was like being on patrol in Afghanistan again. Watching. Waiting. Without fully knowing what for.

He dialed Elsie, knowing she wouldn't appreciate the early-morning call. Still, he couldn't help himself.

"I told you I'd call if I found anything," she said by way of greeting. She sounded grumpy and aggrieved. He didn't blame her one bit, but that didn't mean he was going to back off.

"I just wanted to check in."

"Whoever put in those listening devices did it a long time ago, and my guess is they knew enough about computers to bypass the inn's remedial security measures." She paused and audibly yawned. "I don't think we're going to catch the guys on tape. I've been through it until my eyes are dead, and no one aside from the woman and the boy go into her or his room."

"How remedial are the security measures?" Reece demanded. He was close and he'd been watching, but...that sounded worse than he'd assumed.

"It'd keep a common criminal out, but I don't think we're dealing with the common criminal."

No, they weren't. "What about files?"

"Reece, I only have two hands."

"And I've got all day."

"I've already told you it'd take all day to download anything on your hot spot. Unless you plan on getting closer to civilization and a better signal, you're out. I could walk you through hacking into her computer and you could go through that yourself, but again, bad internet means slow hacking."

It would have been tricky to find that kind of time even if he was still a guest at the Bluebird. But he was not, and he wasn't ready for North Star to know he'd messed up yet. And hopefully wasn't ever going to be honest about that part.

"So whoever planted the devices got around the cameras," he said.

"Or she deleted the older footage, though usually I can dig that up, too."

"She wouldn't have deleted it."

"Getting to know her, then?"

Reece didn't say anything to that. He needed more to go on. He needed *something*. "What about reservations? Can you look into those?"

"Of course, but to what end?"

"I doubt someone broke in when they could easily be a guest and plant things. Find someone with a fishy background."

"You want me to go back through almost a year's worth of reservations and look at everyone's background?"

"Why not?"

Elsie sighed. "Oh, no reason at all," she muttered.

"Start at the beginning." Reece thought of his conversation with Lianna on the porch. He hadn't seen any listening devices outside, and he'd definitely looked. Still, it didn't hurt to be cautious. "But check this weekend, too. Any new reservations this weekend I want to know about ASAP."

"Anything else, sir?" Elsie asked dryly.

"I promise to keep you drowning in those disgusting sour candies you love so much when this is all over."

She made a slight huffing noise. "You're starting to act like Holden, you know that?"

"Well, there's no need to be insulting."

She chuckled. "All right. I'll see what I can dig up. But I'm holding you to the candy."

"Got it. Thanks, Elsie." He hung up the phone and shoved it into his pocket, then went about cleaning up his camp.

Though he planned on sleeping here every night until… well, until there was no reason to, he didn't leave any trace of him behind on the off chance someone came out hiking this way during the day.

Once everything was packed into his backpack, he walked up to the road, where he kept out of sight but made sure Lianna got Henry safely on the bus. He watched the area to make sure no one else was paying too close attention to the woman and her child.

Then, as the bus rumbled away and Lianna walked back to the inn, he got in his car and drove the bus route, a plan he'd worked on all weekend. Everything went according to plan, including pulling into the subdivision next to the school where he could see through the backyards of houses and to the bus drop-off.

Once Henry was safely inside the school, Reece could convince himself all was well and return to be closer to the Bluebird.

He returned to his hiding spot near the Bluebird, parking his car in a wooded area he'd found that kept the car out of sight of any passerby. It was a good two miles direct from the Bluebird, and a five-mile drive since no roads went through the woods. Besides, as far as he knew, only Lianna was aware of the kind of car he was driving, and he'd never seen her drive anywhere. If she did, she'd be heading into town, he had to assume, and this was the opposite direction.

He was surprised when his phone went off and Elsie's number was on the screen. She'd found something. God, he hoped she'd found something, to be calling back so soon.

"Got something?" Reece demanded, getting out of the car.

"I started with this weekend's reservations," she said with no preamble. "One reservation Friday night. Made late at night, which is kind of weird, though not unheard of. Still, I looked into the guy. His background is fake."

"How do you know?"

"What do you mean, how do I know? I make up fake backgrounds for you guys myself. I know what to look for when it comes to fake records. He's fake."

"Who is he?"

"That I don't know, and won't be able to find out without a picture or a fingerprint or something more tangible. He's checking in this afternoon, according to the reservation. Get me something I can use, and I'll figure out who he is."

Reece rubbed his free hand over his jaw. Late at night. Someone had overheard his argument with Lianna. Which meant she was in danger.

And it was all his fault.

Chapter Seven

Lianna prepared the attic room for her new guest, erasing every last shred of evidence Reece—or whatever his name was—had ever been here.

Why should a man who'd spent less than a week at her inn leave such a…void? It didn't make any sense, and it made her hate him even more than she already did. She'd been safe and happy, for the most part, before he ruined everything with his listening devices and heartbroken eyes.

He probably had a family. A big one. He probably had three wives and twenty kids and great parents.

If she kept telling herself that, maybe she could erase the memory of his expression when Henry had said, *Like a family.*

The alarm on her phone went off, signaling it was time to walk up to the bus stop to pick up Henry. He'd been sullen all weekend, with Reece gone and two older women exclaiming over how cute he was.

The cruelest of all comments, in Henry's estimation. Still, he'd bounded off to school with his normal restless energy, eager to spend time with Joey and other kids his age. Even if reading was *stupid*.

She really needed to plan another playdate for Henry and Joey, but her schedule was so packed, and she hated feeling like she was making the Hendersons' lives difficult by always needing them to handle transportation.

It was weirdly nice to have the normal worries in her mind as she began her walk to the bus stop. She'd much rather worry about mom stuff than…danger.

Hopefully her new reservation wouldn't arrive early, but if he came in before she got Henry home, she'd be able to wave him down from the road. No one came down her road unless they were looking for the Bluebird.

As if on cue, she heard the pop and rumble of tires on gravel. A sleek black car with tinted windows appeared around the curve. It looked like a very…*official* car. But it was the make and model the man had given her on his reservation form.

She waved and the car slowed, coming to a stop next to her. The window rolled down and the driver leaned toward her. He wore big aviator sunglasses and he made no move to take them off, despite the gloomy weather.

"Hello," Lianna offered. "Are you Mr. Adams?"

The man smiled. "Yes, ma'am."

She had to ignore the jitter of nerves. Reece couldn't make her distrust every single man who came to her inn. She forced a smile in return. "I'm Lianna Kade and I run the Bluebird. I'm just picking up my son at the bus stop. You go on ahead and let yourself inside. I'll be there in just a moment to check you in. There's coffee in the common area. Make yourself comfortable."

"Thanks."

She gave a little nod, then continued walking up to the main road. She looked back once at the car. It was just a car. He was just a guest. Just a man.

But she was beginning to wonder how she'd sleep at night every time a lone man came to stay at the inn. How was she going to ever let Henry out of her sight? How was life *ever* going to be normal?

"Thanks a lot, Reece Conrad, or whoever you are."

She reached the road and glanced at her watch. Just another minute or two and the bus should show up.

She took a deep breath. She'd be extra cautious when it came to having strange men stay at her inn, but that didn't mean she had to ban them entirely. She'd just protect herself. And keep Henry completely separate.

She didn't like the way he'd looked at her. It had been... cold. A very fake friendliness. Reece had—

Good God, Lianna, you cannot live in fear.

Sheriff Reynolds had always been kind enough to offer a deputy or even himself if she ever felt uncomfortable. She knew in part because he'd been good friends with her grandparents and they'd asked him to watch after her, but also because he was a nice man. Always had been.

She wouldn't be too proud to ask for help. In fact, maybe she'd offer a free room to the sheriff and his wife for tonight. Or Joey and his parents. Yes, she'd fill up the inn with friends. Make it a party.

And drag them into what Todd started and Reece brought up all over again?

No. She wouldn't think like that. She'd— She whirled around at a noise—a crack, a footstep, something.

And there he was.

Reece held up his hands as if she had a weapon trained on him. She certainly wished. But all she had were too ineffectual fists. "What are you doing here?"

He dropped his hands and stepped closer. When she jumped back, he paused his approach. "Lianna, I'm going to need you and Henry to come with me."

Go with him? She forced a caustic laugh out of her mouth even though she felt shaky with fear. What was he doing here? What was he playing at? "I'm not going anywhere with you."

"Your new guest isn't safe."

It sent a bolt of icy fear down her spine, but she refused to show it. "And you are?"

"I know you don't believe me, but yes. I am."

"I told you to go, Reece. If that's your name."

"It's my name."

"Sure."

"Lianna… The man who made this reservation… There's too much of a coincidence to the timing. I didn't find any listening devices outside, but maybe he overheard our conversation."

Lianna stilled. She had taken the listening device off the smoke alarm and shoved it into her desk drawer. Would whoever was listening know she'd tampered with it? Obviously. It would have changed what they could hear.

"Wait. How do you know about this man's reservation?"

Reece's expression didn't change, but she thought she saw a flash of something like guilt in his eyes as the bus rumbled around the corner.

"You and Henry. Come with me. It's for your own good. I promise."

"You're insane to think I'd do that. To think I'd leave my business. When you admitted to lying to me."

"Yes, admitted, and I'll gladly admit a lot more. But you have to come with me."

"Neither Henry nor I will be going *anywhere* with you, and if you keep pestering me, I will call the police."

"You can go back to the inn. Fine," Reece said, and impatience was snapping at the edges of his calm, controlled voice. "You're an adult and you have free will to put yourself in danger, but you can't put Henry in danger."

"*I* am Henry's mother."

"You're right. And, honestly, I'm not letting you go, either."

"Not letting me? What are you going to do? Force me?"

"If I have to."

"You are out of your mind." The bus door opened and Henry bolted out, already yelling Reece's name and rushing toward him.

"Reece, you're back!"

"I am. And you know what, Hank? We're going to play a game."

"We are?"

Lianna moved to step in between them. "No." She should be afraid, but she couldn't seem to access fear over the hot sputter of fury. "We are not going to—"

In a move she didn't anticipate, Reece was behind her and then effectively throwing her over his shoulder. It was all very smooth and sudden and even gentle.

So much so that she didn't even protest immediately. She could only blink at the grass bumping along underneath her head.

"That's funny," Henry was saying, and she could see his tennis shoes happily prancing next to Reece's steady strides. She didn't even bump against him as he walked with her over his shoulder.

His *shoulder*. She managed to break through the shock and confusion and twisted in his grasp.

"Put me down! This isn't funny. I'm going to…" She didn't know what. Kick him? Scream?

Henry was prancing beside them, laughing hysterically. They were being kidnapped, essentially, and her child was laughing.

And you're allowing it.

REECE KNEW IT wasn't a laughing matter, but Henry's sheer joy at Reece lugging around his mother had his own mouth curving into a smile.

"You're going to be in *so* much trouble when you put her down." Henry giggled as Reece led them into the woods.

He didn't know how much time they had, but Sabrina would arrive shortly to take care of the man at the inn.

Ideally the man poked around a little bit first, giving Elsie a chance to fully ID him. Then Sabrina could swoop in and take care of him. If things didn't go ideally? Well, they'd roll with the punches.

Lianna twisted in his grip. He could feel her tense her body as if she was going to punch or kick, but she never did anything. Except demand he put her down as he carried her into the woods.

"What are we doing? Where are we going?" Henry asked.

"We're going to take a secret trip."

"We are not. We are absolutely not taking a trip. Henry…" She trailed off, and Reece realized she didn't know how to yell at him without scaring Henry, and Henry was her first priority.

He couldn't even imagine what it would have been like to have a mother or any foster parent who cared that much if he was afraid. How different his life would have been.

Didn't matter. His life was the way it was, and he'd made some mistakes here, but he would not allow Lianna and Henry to pay for them. Even if Lianna ended up hating him.

"I promise. Once we get to my car, Lianna, you'll have as many answers and reassurances as I can give you."

"Yes, that's known advice," she muttered into his ear. "Go with the crazy man to a second location and let him explain everything to you."

He chuckled in spite of himself and all the danger he was in. *She* was in. Maybe Elsie couldn't prove the new reservation was after Lianna yet, but the timing was too suspect. Reece was sure that once Elsie ID'd him, they'd be able to pin him to the group that North Star's client was after.

Lianna didn't say anything else, and she didn't fight him. Oh, he could practically hear the wheels turning in her head. She was probably paying attention to the surroundings and planning her escape once he let her down.

Reece could hardly blame her.

He reached the car and gently put her down on her feet, knowing she'd grab Henry and try to bolt. Except, maybe she wouldn't, because that would scare Henry.

"I've got a computer in the car," he said, before she could grab Henry and run. "It has all my files. Who I am. Missions I've been on, both in the military and for the group I currently work for, including this one. The only thing that's been redacted is the name of my group and the people I work with—which is for your safety as much as theirs. You can listen to phone calls I made while I was staying here. They're all recorded. I know... I get it. You can't trust me. You shouldn't, but I want to help, and I want you to understand that... I'm here to help you."

"Why do we need help?" Henry asked, blinking up at Reece. His face clouded. "Is this about my father?"

As someone who was adequately familiar with that acidic feeling toward one's father, Reece still felt his heart pinch. He wanted to assure Henry he was safe, and Reece would make sure everything was taken care of, but...

Reece glanced at Lianna. He didn't want to step on any toes. He didn't want to hurt Henry *or* Lianna.

Lianna slid her arm around Henry. "Yes, sweetheart. But it's going to be okay."

"You're going to make it okay. Right, Reece?" Henry asked, smiling up at him, hope and something like adoration lighting up his features.

Reece wished he'd turn into primordial ooze right then and there. "I'm going to do everything I can. I just need you both to trust me, and you know, that's rough, because you shouldn't trust people you just meet. Trust should be earned, and I haven't earned it."

"That's okay," Henry said, with a seven-year-old shrug.

Reece looked at Lianna again, knowing it was very much not okay. "The computer is in the back of the car."

"Why would I get in the back of your car?"

Reece sighed and pulled the computer out of the back seat. He handed it to her, along with some headphones. "Sit wherever you like. Look at whatever you like."

"You could have made all this up. It could be fake," she said, not taking either device.

"You're absolutely right," he agreed. He stepped close enough he could lower his voice so Henry wouldn't hear. "But it's an awful lot of work to convince you I'm a good guy when I could just as easily throw you and Henry in that car and drive you where I want to take you."

Her scowl was so deep, her blue eyes practically a flame of rage, and yet she said nothing. He stepped back and waited for her response.

"What about the man who I'm supposed to be checking in?"

"We're getting a clear ID on him. Then, if he's who we think he is, we'll handle it."

"Who's we?"

"My associates. Once they handle it, your inn will be locked up while we try to figure out the rest. You don't have any reservations for the week, so that shouldn't eat into business. If we can't get you back by Saturday, we'll figure something out."

"How do you know my reservations?" she demanded.

Reece sighed. "Do you really want to know?"

"Yes, I…" Then she closed her eyes and shook her head. "No. No."

"So can we speed this along?"

She took the computer and the headphones with a jerk and stomped over to the hood of the car. She settled herself against it, put the headphones in her ears and kept her eagle gaze split between the screen and Henry.

Henry shed his backpack and chased a butterfly for a few seconds. Reece knew he should keep his mouth shut, but the kid entertaining himself… Yeah, he'd been there. Henry had Lianna, of course, but there was still likely to be some loneliness, given the somewhat isolated life he lived, without a father figure.

Reece swallowed at the rust in his throat and moved to the trunk. Lianna looked like she was about to charge him, as if she was afraid he was going to toss Henry in the trunk. He knew he deserved her suspicion, but that didn't make it easy.

He popped it quickly and grabbed a baseball glove and held it up before she could dive at Henry.

"Hey, Hank, you want to play catch?"

Henry perked up, looking at the glove in Reece's hand. "Here?"

"Your mom has some reading to do before we can go on our trip. Not much room with the trees, and I've only got one glove, but it might pass the time."

"Yeah, cool."

Reece tossed the glove at Henry, who caught it with a fumbling grab. "I played T-ball last year, and this year we're actually going to pitch."

"That's cool. You got a team?"

"Giants."

"Giants? You can't be serious."

Henry giggled. "They're awesome."

Reece scoffed. "West Coast teams," he said with mock indignation. "Don't have any heart." He tossed the ball at Henry, with an eye on Lianna. She was watching them, but not with that same suspicious gaze. It was something that made his lungs squeeze.

Henry tossed the ball back and Reece caught it bare-handed, fumbling with the catch when usually he was as sure-handed as they came.

"Who's your favorite team?"

"Huh?" Reece focused back on Henry and playing catch. He cleared his throat. "Twins all the way."

"The American League! DH is cheating!" Then Henry erupted into a fit of giggles, clearly a fight he enjoyed having with someone in his life. Not his father, maybe the grandfather or the great-grandfather.

Because the boy wasn't alone like Reece had been. He had love and a family, and Reece would do good to remember to keep his distance.

Somehow.

Chapter Eight

The first thing Lianna did was pull up the file marked
REECE CONRAD MONTGOMERY. She was absolutely
certain it was fake, since it mirrored everything he'd told
her almost exactly.

Born in South Dakota, became a ward of the state at
age ten, where he spent the next eight years jumping from
group home to foster home and back again. Enlisted in the
army at eighteen, served for twelve years, including two
tours of Afghanistan. There were all sorts of cross-refer-
ences to missions.

Everything looked…real. There were enlistment records
and school records. There was even a birth certificate.

He was right. It was an awful lot of effort to convince
her he was the good guy when he could have just…kid-
napped them.

Though he *had* grabbed her. So. He wasn't…perfect.
Even if it had been careful and gentle and…

She couldn't believe this was happening. She couldn't
believe she was considering going with him. This had to
be lies. It had to be.

She opened a folder labeled PHONE CALLS. Each file
was named with a date and time, and each date was one
of the dates he'd spent at her inn.

The first one was his conversation with a woman. She

seemed like a boss, or at the very least a coworker. They talked about the listening devices and getting into her room.

Lianna almost turned it off. It felt like an invasion of privacy to listen to him like this, even though it was his idea. Even though he was discussing invading *her* privacy. It felt wrong to hear him *plan* to get into her room.

We want to keep the widow and the kid out of it, don't we? That's a priority for me. Kids don't get caught in the cross fire.

She didn't hear what came next. That echoed in her ears instead. He said it so…fervently. Like he really meant it.

She glanced up at him. He wasn't smiling anymore. That look from the other night was on his face as he caught the ball Henry lobbed at him.

Loneliness.

She shook her head. She couldn't be fooled again. But everything on this computer…well, it pointed to a good man whose job it was to help people.

He'd helped take down a murderer by posing as a gang member. He'd saved a young girl from being kidnapped into the same gang. He'd done all sorts of things to protect people from this Sons of the Badlands group. All while working for some mysterious, nameless group.

A group who'd been approached to find out more about Todd's death. And what she knew.

Lianna chewed on her lip. Reece obviously wanted what she knew. But he didn't know she knew much of anything. And he hadn't been pushy like all the men who'd come before. He hadn't demanded answers or made her feel stupid.

No, he played you.

Lianna blew out a breath, listened to another phone call where he reiterated keeping Henry out of it. He sounded frustrated and…

She didn't know because she didn't know *him*, and she

was fooling herself if she thought she could just tell. Hadn't life taught her she was a terrible judge of character?

She opened another folder, labeled LETTERS, hoping to find some clarification. Some…sign to point her in the right direction. A flat-out lie. *Something* she could use to convince her she should walk away.

Instead, she found the letters Reece had left for her and Henry. Letters she'd shoved in her drawer with the listening device and hadn't read.

Oh, she'd come close a few times, but she'd known that if she read them, she might feel some misplaced sense of grief, and she had enough real grief in her life. But now…

She opened the first one and read the short letter.

> *Dear Lianna,*
> *Thank you for letting me into your home. Not just the bed-and-breakfast, but your life and Henry's. I'm sorry I couldn't stay and enjoy it longer. If you should ever need anything, please don't hesitate to contact me.*
> *Reece*

It didn't say much. It didn't say anything, except the offer to be in touch. To help. How did a lonely man, clearly in desperate need of a family, get into the business of helping strangers?

She opened Henry's letter, and it was more of the same.

> *Hank,*
> *Sorry I had to rush out without saying goodbye. I had an emergency to take care of. If you'd like to contact me, your mom has my information. Hope to see you again someday. Keep asking questions.*
> *Reece*

Neither said anything particularly groundbreaking or poignant. So why did she feel like crying? Like he was the only one she could trust, when it could be an act.

It's some act.

She looked up at Henry and Reece. Reece made an impressive one-handed grab that had Henry hooting with delight and Reece grinning.

Yes, he could be acting. She'd learned just how good at acting people could be. But this was all so unnecessary. So over-the-top. Unless he was who he said he was. Unless he really wanted to help them.

If he was the bad guy in this scenario, there were a million horrible ways he could have tried to get information out of her or Henry.

She couldn't discount the fact he might be a bad guy with some kind of conscience, but she'd been interrogated before. By men with less…everything. Even the FBI agents, who she had to believe were trying to do the right thing, had been cold and off-putting. Dismissive at times.

Reece was none of those things.

You're really going to trust the guy who carried you away from the bus stop like a sack of mulch? Leave your inn to whoever? Run away? Again?

A phone rang. Reece pulled his mobile out of his pants pocket. "Montgomery," he answered, tossing the ball to Henry and then holding up a hand to pause their game.

Henry busied himself by throwing the ball high in the air and then darting around in an attempt to catch it. Reece's expression was grim and serious as he gave terse responses to whoever was on the other end.

When he shoved the phone back in his pocket, his gaze met hers. It was direct, and something shivered through her that wasn't fear. It was something she couldn't possibly allow herself to name.

He walked over to her, digging something else out of his pocket.

"Our operative at the Bluebird needs backup." He handed her the keys to his car. "If you want to drive away, that's fine. Just go. Don't come back until someone gets in touch with you with the all clear."

Lianna blinked. "Wh-what?"

But Reece had dropped the keys and was already backing into the trees. "If you want to stay, I'll be back soon."

"But—" He was already gone, though. As if he'd simply disappeared like some kind of magical creature.

Henry stood next to her. "Is Reece in trouble?"

"No." Lianna looked down at the keys he'd handed her. She could run away with Henry. They could disappear. He'd given her the means to escape. "I think he's trying to help us."

Henry's hand slipped into hers. "I think so, too. We should probably wait for him."

Lianna took a deep breath. Reece had given her a choice. Stay or go. Trust him or not. Knowing she had no real reason to trust him, probably knowing she didn't trust herself.

"Maybe we should."

REECE WAS SURE Sabrina wouldn't appreciate backup, but Elsie's call about what she was seeing on the cameras had made Reece nervous enough to want to make sure.

Besides, it gave Lianna a chance to make her decision without him there to muddy the Henry waters. Once they dealt with this threat, he'd find her one way or another and make sure she stayed safe.

He ran through the woods to the Bluebird, the path well enough known to him now that he didn't even stumble over the stray log or slip in the muddy earth beneath his feet.

He slowed as he reached the tree line, assessing the situation as he approached. He didn't hear anything or see anything, so whatever was progressing must be going on inside the house. Which likely meant whoever had sent their man could hear every word.

Reece edged into the yard, scanning the area around him. Had the man really come alone? Well, why not? He likely thought he was only dealing with a woman and her child.

Unless they'd figured out who Reece was. Depending on what they'd overheard the night he'd left, it was possible they could make some assumptions. They'd have to have quite the computer guru to get to the bottom of who he was and who he worked for—but if they simply knew he wasn't who he said he was, and worked for *someone*, it was enough to potentially go in guns blazing. Depending on what they were looking for.

Reece moved forward, but stopped short when a man came sailing out of the door, crashing into the porch. The bannister held, but the man didn't. He tumbled over and fell with a thud on the damp earth below.

Sabrina followed him. She glared at Reece and flipped her dark braid over her shoulder. "I can handle one guy," she said dismissively.

Her lip was bleeding, but other than that, she'd definitely handled him. "Blame Elsie. She called me and said you might be in trouble."

Sabrina rolled her eyes. "That one. She doesn't understand a tactical display of weakness."

The man between them on the ground groaned, slowly coming to.

"What's the plan with the muscle?" Reece asked.

"I'll tie him up. Get Els on the phone and see if she got a real ID. Where's your quarry?"

"Left them with the car."

"Did you *want* them to run off?"

Reece didn't respond to Sabrina's question. As far as he was concerned, this mission might be North Star business, but Lianna and Henry were *his* assignment.

Sabrina hopped off the porch over the bannister, grinning down at the man she'd beaten. "You picked the wrong lady to screw with, you son of a—"

She was securing his hands and wrists with zip ties before the man had a chance to even attempt to roll away.

Reece dialed Elsie, who answered without a hello. "I'm working on an ID. Getting there."

"So what do we do with him?"

"Leave him. Once I get the ID, I'll send the appropriate cleanup crew. You two need to get out of there. I'm pretty sure the guy sent an SOS to his cronies. They'll be swarming the place soon as they can. Get back to headquarters. By the time you get here, I'll have more information to go on."

"Got it." Reece ended the connection. He headed for the door.

"What are you doing?" Sabrina demanded. "My bike is right there. We'll ride over to your friend."

"Locking up the place."

"You can't be serious."

"It's her home."

Sabrina rolled her eyes. "It looks so sweet and peaceful. Makes my skin crawl."

"You're a strange woman, Sabrina."

She grinned.

Reece did a quick walk-through, turning off lights and unplugging things. He grabbed a few things for Henry and Lianna—his video games, her purse.

"Ticktock," Sabrina called from outside.

Reece sighed. He dead-bolted all but the back door, but used the inside lock to secure it. It wasn't *secure*, if someone wanted to break in, but at least he'd be able to tell Lianna he'd done his best. And whatever happened, Elsie had eyes on the inn now.

He rounded the house and walked back to the front, where Sabrina was waiting on her bike. "You done playing maid?"

"Yeah, yeah," he muttered. "You really going to make me hop on the back of that thing?"

"Climb on, Montgomery. Don't be a wuss."

Frowning at the bike between her legs, Reece sighed. He'd look like an overlarge oaf on the back, but he supposed that was close enough to what he was.

He climbed on, then held on for dear life as Sabrina flew out of the yard. He had to clamp his teeth together to keep from lecturing her on safety.

She flew down the road, then over bumpy grass, cutting through a field to bypass the highway, without getting caught in the woods. As they approached where his car had been parked, Reece's stomach tensed.

Lianna had probably taken off and they'd have to track her. Well, he wasn't going to do that on the back of Sabrina's motorcycle, that was for sure.

"Looks like your friend stayed," Sabrina said over the roar of the engine.

Not my friend, he wanted to say, but he didn't. Because that wasn't the way Sabrina meant it, and it had too many uncomfortable sensations tangling with the needs of the moment.

He could see the sun glinting off the metal of his car and, as they got closer, Lianna standing in almost the exact position he'd left her. Henry still tossing the ball.

Reece felt an indescribable pressure inside him. One he

couldn't deal with because they had to get to safety. They had to get to the bottom of this.

Sabrina pulled to a screeching halt in front of Lianna and Henry.

"Whoa," Henry said with clear awe as he stared at Sabrina and her motorcycle. "Are you a Valkyrie?" At Sabrina's confused stare, Henry smiled. "You know. Like in *Thor.*"

Sabrina laughed. "Something like that, kid." She turned to Reece, who'd gotten off Sabrina's death trap at the first opportunity. "Well, I like him."

"Yeah, he's all right," Reece said roughly, offering Henry a smile. "Meet you at headquarters?"

Sabrina nodded. Then she glanced at Lianna. "No worries. Prince Charming over here locked up your inn. Can't promise more goons won't come, but we've got cameras on the place. He can fill you in."

Then Sabrina took off, as loudly and dangerously as she'd come.

Lianna stood stock-still, as if she'd been shocked into some kind of vegetative state. It only broke when Reece approached and spoke.

"You didn't leave," he said, his words rougher than necessary.

She blinked, then swallowed, looking down at the keys in her hand. "No, I didn't." She held the keys out to him, met his gaze. He could see trepidation in the blue depths of her eyes, but she straightened her shoulders with purpose. "I guess you should drive us to this headquarters of yours."

He blew out a breath. He didn't know what had won her over, or if it would last, but it was a step in the right direction. In the direction that would allow him to put all his effort into keeping her safe.

He took the keys, but instead of letting her drop them

into his palm, he closed his hand over hers. "I'm going to do everything in my power to keep you and Henry safe. *Everything.* Whether you believe that or not, I want you to hear me say it."

She stared at him, arrested, but she didn't tug her hand away. It was small and capable in his large one.

Reece knew he was letting himself get in too deep. Even if no one else knew it, he was drowning in something he didn't understand. Didn't know how to fight, when he'd always known how to fight.

The fight was all he'd ever had.

She pulled her hand away, blinked and turned to her son. "Come on, Henry. We're going on a road trip."

Chapter Nine

Lianna dozed off as they drove, unable to keep her eyes open. She supposed it was the adrenaline wearing off.

And you clearly trust Reece way too much.

He'd locked up her inn. He worked with some…amazon woman who roared around on a motorcycle with a split lip and smoky laugh. He promised to protect her and Henry with a fierceness she didn't know how to convince herself was made up.

Every time the rough drive bumped her awake, she'd glance back at Henry. Reece had offered him his video game device, which he'd apparently swiped for Henry when he'd been locking up.

Sleep was a lot less complicated than all…that. So she let it overtake her again. The next time she woke up, the sun was setting in a riot of oranges and bright pinks in front of her. They were pulling up on some sort of circular driveway to a…

House was too subtle a word. It was more like a compound. Rustic decor, but like some high-end hunting resort rather than…

Well, whatever she assumed it actually was. "This is something else."

Reece smiled wryly.

She glanced back at Henry. His head was bent over the

game, that glazed-over look in his eyes when he'd spent too much time playing. "All right. Hand it over."

"Mooooo*om*."

It was comforting that even in the midst of all *this*, Henry could maintain his epic whining skills.

"Right now."

He groaned and moaned for a few extra seconds, likely trying to finish some battle before he finally logged off the device and handed it over. He looked up grumpily, but then the frustration on his face melted away.

He flung himself forward in the car, squinting at the big house in front of them. "Whoa! You live here?"

"Not really," Reece replied. "This is where I work."

"And the Valkyrie?"

"Yeah, her too."

"Cool. Can we get out?"

Reece nodded, pushing his door open. Henry scrambled out of the car, and Lianna knew she should, too, but for a moment she was so overwhelmed by *everything* that she felt like nothing more than dead weight.

But Henry was bounding toward this strange place, and she couldn't let him be out there alone. She couldn't…

There were so many things she couldn't do, no matter how she felt. She pushed out of the car and forced her heavy legs to move.

"There's plenty of space. You and Henry will have a room. You can rest up for a while before we go over everything."

She shook her head at Reece. She'd grabbed Henry's backpack and she held the straps in a tight grip as if it would keep her centered in this strange new world. "No. I want to…" She didn't know how to complete that sentence, but Reece nodded as if he understood anyway.

He led them to the door. There were a series of security

hoops to jump through. Some sort of fingerprint scan, hidden behind a slab in the wooden planks of the panel next to the door. Then there was a code on the door to punch in. Henry watched it all with wide eyes, and Lianna imagined she had a similar expression on her face.

What had she gotten herself into?

Eventually, Reece put a normal-looking key in the door and the lock clicked. He pushed open the door and ushered her and Henry inside. There was a petite woman waiting for them.

"Betty," Reece greeted her.

"Hey, Reece. Shay sent me to grab bags, show room assignments."

"We want to get the important stuff out of the way first."

Betty nodded, then turned to Lianna with a smile. "I can take your bags if you'd like and put them in your room. We should be able to supply you with whatever you don't have."

"I don't have…anything. Not my purse. No clothes or… I just have my phone."

"I got your purse. And Henry's inhaler. The rest I'm sure we'll be able to supply for you temporarily," Reece said.

Lianna blinked. How would he even know to…? Where had he put…?

Betty held out her hands, and it took Lianna too long to realize she meant to take Henry's backpack. After a few more seconds of utter confusion, and the utmost patience on Betty and Reece's part, Lianna handed over the bag. Reece also handed her a backpack she hadn't realized he'd been carrying.

"You can take them to the meeting room, Reece. Shay will be available shortly," the woman said, then bustled away purposefully.

Lianna watched her go, then looked at Reece. "You all just use your real names?"

"For the most part. We don't really exist for the years we're with the group, and I didn't have much of a profile before that. It's easy to be erased, which allows us to be who we are here."

The group. Erased. It sounded ominous, but the woman who'd taken their stuff had seemed so…normal.

Reece led them down a hallway and then into a big room. It looked like some sort of meeting room with a large table and lots of chairs around it. There was a computer and monitors lining one wall. Lots of speakers and absolutely no windows.

The woman from the motorcycle earlier was already there, kicked back in a chair as if she was relaxing. She straightened when they entered. "Hey, kid." She grinned at Henry, to his clear delight.

"Hi, Valkyrie," Henry said.

"Call me Sabrina. And if it's okay with your mom, I'm going to go show you our game room."

"Like video games?"

"Yup. You ever been to an arcade?"

"You have an arcade?" Lianna asked under her breath.

Reece shrugged. "Sometimes you gotta pass the time as mindlessly as possible."

"Can I go? Can I go?" Henry demanded, clearly not at all concerned about all the strangers around them. Or the strange place and danger and…

Lianna looked up imploringly at Reece. "I'd really prefer it if he stayed with me."

"I might be able to help with that." Another woman entered the room. She looked more like the first one than Sabrina. Normal. Just an average young woman dressed in jeans and a T-shirt. But she went to a computer, tapped a few keys and then pointed to one of the many monitors along the wall.

On one monitor was the view of a room filled with arcade games. "You'll be able to keep your eyes on him. I can even turn on audio if you want."

"I…"

"Come on, Mom. Please. Please. *Please.*"

Well, she certainly didn't want him hearing anything she had to say to Reece or his…coworkers. And this provided her no excuse. She'd be able to see and hear Henry.

And what if they do something to him? They could…

"You remember the red door we passed?" Reece asked. "In the first hallway."

"Well, yes."

"That's the arcade room."

Apparently, he could read her thoughts. Or she was *that* transparent. "Fine. All right. Just…be good, Henry. Polite." She had no idea why she was warning her son to be polite when they were in the midst of all this. Just…habit. Ridiculous, mindless habit.

"Awesome!" Henry bounced, turning his attention to Sabrina. "Can I play whatever games I want?"

"Sure thing, kid." She led him out of the room and Lianna had to curl her hands into fists to keep from panicking and running after them. She glanced at the monitor. It only took a few seconds, and then Henry raced into the room. Sabrina kicked back in the corner, giving him the run of the place.

Lianna could see everything. Hear everything.

"I'll tell Shay you're ready for her," the woman who'd brought up the room on the monitor said. She smiled at Lianna, then waited for Reece's nod before she left the room.

"Are you in charge?" Lianna asked.

"Hardly. Elsie is tech, which means she'll answer to whatever operative is handling the assignment."

"And you're handling the assignment of me."

"Yes."

"Why?"

REECE HAD NO idea how to answer that question, especially when she asked it with that baffled horror. He knew she was struggling with the decision to come with him, struggling with trusting them. Who could blame her?

She kept her eyes glued to the monitor, so Reece figured he'd give her all the truths he could.

"I'm a field operative. When an…assignment comes up, Shay determines who's going to handle it."

"Shay is your boss. The one you were talking to when you…" She trailed off but finally took her eyes off Henry on the monitor. "You said you wouldn't let a kid get caught in the cross fire. I'm holding you to that, Reece. For whatever it's worth, I'm *depending* on you and yours to keep Henry safe."

"I will."

She nodded, though he knew she didn't fully believe him. She didn't *not* believe him. She was just conflicted, and rightfully so. "Shay is in charge here. She manages the rest of us, a combination of field operatives, tech gurus and medical staff."

"You have medical staff?"

"Yes, though most of them are on call. But Betty is our head doctor. She's headquartered here and takes care of, well, anything that pops up."

"Like someone getting hurt."

"If the mission is dangerous enough. But it's not just that. We're normal people who need physicals and to be told to get some rest or eat better if we're run-down."

Lianna took some time to think over that, watching Henry's every move again.

"I'm sorry we had to bring you here. I should have… handled this better. I know Henry missing school isn't ideal, and you have an inn to run, and I promise we'll do everything to get you back home and safe as soon as possible."

Lianna nodded. "What…what happens next?"

"Elsie should have an ID on the guy at your inn today. Hopefully she can trace him to whoever placed those listening devices. From there, ideally, we can neutralize any threat against you and Henry."

Lianna looked perplexed. It wasn't fear, exactly, but still he wanted to soothe her. Assure her that North Star was the best of the best and she'd be safe. Everything would be taken care of. If he had to lay down his life to make it so.

But Shay strode in, Elsie following behind.

"Reece," Shay greeted him. "Mrs. Kade, I want to thank you for coming with us. It makes it a lot easier to keep you and your son safe with you here under our protection. At least until we understand the threat against you." Shay settled herself in her normal seat at the head of the table. Elsie sat next to her.

Normally, Reece stood for these interactions, but he thought Lianna needed to sit. She wasn't used to…any of this.

So he pulled a chair back for her and she hesitantly slid into it. He took the seat next to her.

Shay's gaze remained on Lianna. "Do you?"

"Do I what?"

"Understand the threat against you?"

"Oh, well." She slid a glance at Reece. "Reece said they must have overheard our conversation. About the listen-

ing devices. I don't understand why they'd be listening. I
don't understand…any of it."

"You don't know who would put listening devices in
your home?" Shay asked. Her voice was casual rather than
demanding, but Reece still had to hold himself back from
telling Shay to cool it.

"Not specifically," Lianna said. Her gaze darted from
Shay to Elsie to Reece to the monitor. She couldn't seem
to settle on any one place to look. She twisted her fingers
in her lap. "Any one of the men who wanted more information about my late husband."

"Right. You understand that at this point we're concerned not just about the threat against you, minor though
it's been, but what they might have overheard about *us*."

This time the look Shay gave Reece was not casual.
Apparently, Shay had deduced a little bit more about his
slipup than he'd hoped.

"It's just…" Lianna looked at Henry on the screen, then
down at her folded hands. "I don't think they overheard
things, exactly. At least, not… It's just…" Lianna blew out
a breath and Reece was…confused.

This was not the woman he had come to know, however
superficially. There was a timidity to her and an almost
stream-of-consciousness way of speaking that wasn't Lianna at all. Even when she'd agreed to go with him, she
hadn't led him to think she was lost and confused and
didn't know what to say. It had been a resigned best-of-
two-rotten-situations attitude.

This was different. *An act.*

"Reece mentioned the devices during a conversation,
yes, and a little bit about his work. But I didn't believe him,
exactly, and I told him to go. So when I went to my room
that night, I… Well, I pulled the one in my room off the

smoke detector. And instead of putting it back, I threw it in my desk drawer."

Reece leaned back in his chair. Well, he hadn't expected *that*. No wonder she was acting fishy. She'd tampered with the listening device.

"I suppose that was all the tip-off they needed," Shay muttered.

"Except I don't understand. For months right after Todd was killed they asked me questions. I didn't have answers. Then someone set these listening devices up, and I haven't talked about Todd beyond saying that he was killed and that I didn't know anything. Why do they think I know something?"

Shay's expression was as grim as Reece's felt. They didn't have the answers for that question. And that grated.

"Here's what we can offer, Mrs. Kade. A place to stay while we identify the man who came to your inn this afternoon."

"We're close," Elsie offered, tapping away on her computer. "I've dug through the first two fake identities. I think the real one is just within reach."

"All we need from you is your cooperation in telling us what you know about your late husband."

"I don't know anything," Lianna said, a trembling note to her voice that…

Reece had to wonder what was wrong with him. It sounded fake, and didn't inspire any of his usual sympathy or protective instincts when it came to Lianna. Instead, it made him suspicious.

You're losing it, Montgomery.

"Maybe something we find will jog a memory or two. All we're asking is that you're honest with us, and answer any of our questions to the best of your ability. It's our top priority to keep you and your son safe, but we can't promise that for good until we know who and what we're dealing with."

"How did I come to be an assignment if you don't know who or what you're dealing with?"

And *that* reminded him more of the real Lianna. A smart question, delivered in a strong voice. Determination, even if fear and worry were at the edges.

Shay leaned back in her chair, eyes narrowing as she studied Lianna. Immediately Lianna dropped her eyes and started fiddling with her hands again. "This is just so hard and I don't know… It's overwhelming." She dabbed at her eyes. Eyes that, as far as Reece could tell, were dry.

She *was* playing a part. She had to be.

"What do you know, Lianna?" he demanded, maybe a little too harshly.

Her gaze whipped up to his, and the look in her eyes did not match the fumbling, scared mask she was putting on for Shay. "What do you mean?"

"You're hiding something. You're putting on this scared, grieving widow act, but it doesn't work. I've been around you. I know this isn't you."

"A few days' stay at my inn hardly gives you leave to *know* me, Reece," she said, but it was that sharp, strong voice again. Her real backbone showing through.

Reece saw Shay and Elsie exchange a glance. They were seeing it, too. Whether they knew her or not, they'd realized she was playing the hapless widow.

"I know you're scared that whatever Todd did might touch you and Henry. I understand that. And I promise you, we all promise you, we will do everything we can to keep you and Henry safe. No matter what you know or don't. But that only works if we know what you know. You're putting us at a disadvantage if you're hiding things. We won't be able to protect you as effectively. I know you don't trust me, but you have to trust that we're working toward keeping you safe, or you wouldn't be here with Henry."

"You kidnapped me."

"You waited for me, Lianna. Please, tell us what is it you know."

Her gaze went back to Henry on the monitor. She was quiet for a few humming seconds. She wasn't twisting her fingers anymore; she had them clasped in her lap. Tightly. When she finally spoke, it was with a gravity befitting the situation and with none of the melodrama. "Everything I've done since Todd died is for my son. To keep him safe. To keep us both safe."

"You won't be in any trouble, Mrs. Kade, if that's what you're worried about. No matter what you might have done—"

"Oh, please, I haven't *done* anything," Lianna snapped. "But I do…" She trailed off and looked at Reece, and he could read every doubt, every worry, every fear of hers in her blue eyes.

She looked for the longest time, so he held her gaze. Willing her to believe. To understand. To lay some of this burden on him instead of keeping it solely on her own shoulders.

"I do know a few things," she finally said. "Things I shouldn't."

Chapter Ten

Lianna's heart was hammering in her chest. The act that had worked so well when she'd talked to the FBI and whatever other men had come to interrogate her after Todd's death hadn't worked at all on Reece. If she wasn't totally misreading the room, Shay and Elsie hadn't bought it, either.

How had she gotten so bad at pretending? How had they seen through her?

Why are you going to tell them?

The truth was… She didn't know how to keep Henry safe now. Not with listening devices and strange men in her inn. She thought she'd won, but she hadn't. Not fully.

And despite all the ways her brain told her not to ever trust anyone again, she couldn't help believing Reece and his "group" would keep her safe. They'd been too kind. They'd bent over backward to make her feel comfortable, to give Henry something fun to do. To give her the space to make her own choices, such as they were.

Reece had played *catch* with Henry. Sabrina was currently battling him in some arcade game and they were both laughing. Shay, Elsie and Reece were all looking at her expectantly, but they weren't demanding immediate answers.

She had no other choice now. She'd thought maybe

she could get the protection without the cooperation, and maybe if it had just been Reece, she would have been able to do it. Maybe. But Shay was not going to be swayed by fake tears.

Reece didn't buy your fake tears, either.

"Todd's real name," she croaked, telling them what she'd never told another living soul. "I know it."

The entire room was silent except for the crackling audio of Sabrina and Henry laughing over a game.

"All right," Shay said very carefully. "That information will go a long way in helping us sort out our next steps."

But she didn't ask, and she didn't demand. She waited.

Lianna didn't know why it felt as though that cracked her wide open. She didn't know why it made her want to confess everything right there. Or maybe grab on to Reece and cry into his very broad shoulders. She wanted, desperately, to fall apart in the way she hadn't allowed herself to this whole hellish year.

Instead, she swallowed down all those wants, all that pain and all that fear. It took her longer than she would have liked to fight back the tide. But she did it.

Then Reece's hand slid over her clasped ones in her lap. Big, rough, warm and gentle. There was no pressure here. This was support, because the table between them and Shay hid the action.

Though Lianna wasn't convinced Shay didn't see it or sense it or *something*. The woman was unnervingly perceptive.

Did it matter what she saw? It didn't mean anything. Nice as Reece was, sort-of kidnapping aside, she was his mission. His assignment.

Which reminded her she had her own mission. Keeping her child safe. She believed these people could help her. She had to believe that.

If they didn't, if they turned out to be bad, she'd find a way to get Henry out and to safety. She just would. This was a calculated risk, and she could mitigate it, even in telling them, if she never relaxed, never fully believed. If she was always waiting for the other shoe to fall.

Do you want to live that way?

No, of course she didn't. But Todd hadn't left her a choice in that matter.

"Charles Jackson. That's his real name, or the name the FBI think is his real one. Todd Kade was the identity I knew. He may have had more, but… I don't think he did."

"Why not?"

There was no way to lie about this and expect help. Not this deep. She had to be completely honest. "I didn't know Todd's real name, or that he even had a real name, while we were married. I was fooled, completely. I never suspected…whatever this is. It was only after he died, the way people kept asking about him, that I began to realize something wasn't right. And the more I was questioned, the more I started to piece together Todd's lies."

"So how did you find out his real name if he didn't tell you while he was alive?"

It was Shay asking the questions, but it was Reece with his hand on hers. He hadn't pulled it away, and for some reason that settled her, helped her call upon the inner strength she'd had to build since Todd's death.

So when she spoke, she spoke to Reece. "At first, when the police came and told me Todd had been killed, their questions were… It didn't make it sound like a burglary. They asked if I knew anyone who might have hurt him or had been threatening him. They thought it was a purpose-ful, specific-to-him murder in those early hours."

She didn't want to relive those awful hours. That spurt

of relief, even as the questions had left her more confused than anything. Then telling Henry…

She wanted to remember none of what had happened in San Francisco.

"She gave us the name," Reece said to Shay. "Isn't that enough for now? It's been a long day for her."

Lianna straightened and shook her head. "No, I want to get it all out. It's hard to… I've never told anyone this. Not anyone. Not Henry, not my parents or grandparents. I kept it all to myself. Always. So it's hard to…undo that. Keeping it locked down has kept us safe."

"I understand," Shay said. "Take your time, Mrs. Kade."

Lianna winced. "Please stop calling me that. Just Lianna is fine. And *I'm* fine," she said to Reece. She took a deep breath and slowly let it out. "Then the FBI got involved. They mentioned that Todd might be involved in something. They asked me questions and I was legitimately in the dark. They seemed to believe me. But day after day, week after week, more men came. At first I thought they were all FBI, but then…" She told herself she'd kept this secret because it had kept her safe, but as an embarrassed flush worked its way up her neck, she realized part of her was trying to save face. Trying to hide how utterly stupid she'd been.

Because it hadn't just been Todd lying to her. She'd believed every man in a suit who'd come to her door with questions. She'd answered them all, never suspecting anything. Until…

"I moved to Denver, to my parents' house. My grandparents came to stay with us, too. I thought that would be the end of it. Here I am home. Surrounded by family. Then an FBI agent there wanted to talk to me. Tie up loose ends, he said." She looked up at Shay. "He wanted me to meet him at a coffee shop, and it took me all that time to realize some of these men—the ones *not* meeting me at their FBI offices—clearly weren't FBI. That's when I knew I couldn't just say I didn't know. I had to act as stupid and inept as possible so they'd *believe* it."

"Let me guess," Elsie muttered. "The men fell for it hook, line and sinker."

Lianna chuckled, though it felt bitter in her throat. "Yeah, the stupider I acted, the less they bothered me. But I thought… I thought the FBI should know that other men were questioning me. I knew Todd was… Well, that he wasn't involved in good things. I thought maybe the FBI would be able to figure it out and what I told them might help. But I'd been playing stupid for so long, they didn't really believe me. Oh, they took the meeting, asked a few perfunctory questions, but that was it. Except they had gotten out Todd's file."

"Like a paper file?" Shay asked.

Lianna nodded. "It was sitting there between us. Labeled 'Charles Jackson.' And I didn't have a clue who Charles Jackson was at that point. I just figured he grabbed the wrong file because he was that bored. Then he opens it, and there's Todd's picture. That's when it dawned on me."

"Did you say anything?" Reece asked.

Lianna shook her head. "I kept waiting for him to…say something about it. Or act weird. Or anything. But he was bored. Flipped through a few pages. I didn't react. I tried not to look once I figured it out. I didn't want to know. Or knew I shouldn't know, but I saw some things."

"Like?"

"His real birth date, three years before he'd told me his was. That he was born in Michigan, not Wyoming."

Elsie was already tapping away on her computer. "That's a lot to go on, Mrs.—er, Lianna. A *lot*."

Shay nodded, clearly surprised that Lianna had been

able to give them so much. Lianna knew she could leave it at that. With a name and a birth date they could maybe figure some things out.

But she knew more. More that might point them in the right direction. She'd decided to be honest. No point in holding back now. "I'm not...finished."

"You know *more*?" Shay asked, the unflappable woman seeming a little bit...flapped.

"There was a list of groups they'd connected Todd to. I didn't see the full list, but I saw two of the names. And I remember them."

REECE PULLED HIS hand away. Clearly Lianna didn't need his support. Hell, she'd have been better off if he'd never crashed into her life.

She knew all this. But had never told a soul.

Reece slid a look at Shay. *Flabbergasted* was the only word he could use to describe it. Then her eyes narrowed and met his.

Still, her voice was mild when she spoke. "What were the groups' names?"

"One was Ripe for Execution."

"Oh, brother," Elsie muttered under her breath.

"The other was a series of letters and numbers. I can't be sure I remembered them in the right order, but the letters were definitely *T* and *K*, and the numbers were 29. I only remember because it was his initials and his birthday—at least the ones he told me. Not his real ones."

"That's excellent," Shay said, leaning back in her chair. "Much more than I expected. Thank you. Is there anything else?"

Lianna shook her head. "No. Not that I can think of."

"We'll likely have some questions for you once we investigate on our end, but for now, why don't you go get some rest?"

"Oh. Well. I... Henry's probably starving. We usually have a snack after the bus, and dinner by—"

"We'll get that all sorted out." Shay stood and walked over to the door, opening it to reveal Betty. "Can you show Mrs.—Lianna to the kitchen? Give her a tour, see if she has any special requests?"

"Sure," Betty said, giving Lianna a friendly smile.

Reece stood. No need to push all that off onto Betty just because there weren't any medical concerns right now. "We've got a whole gym set up in the basement if Henry gets restless. Why don't I—"

"Sit, Montgomery. We have a lot of things to discuss," Shay said sharply.

Lianna looked back at him, eyes wide. So, despite his sense of impending doom, he smiled. "A few formalities. I'll catch up with you and Henry soon."

Lianna looked at Shay, then back to him, then Betty. She sighed, clearly understanding there was nothing she could do here. She followed Betty into the hallway.

Shay closed the door behind them. Reece didn't sit. Maybe it was petty, but he wouldn't sit for the dressing-down he was about to get.

"What I'd like to know is why this woman has a good chunk of the answers we're looking for and you spent a week with her and didn't have a clue." Shay crossed her arms over her chest and leaned against the door behind her.

Reece stood, posture rigid, feeling a bit like he was back in the military, without the salute. "She told you. She didn't share that with anyone."

"Yeah, your job is to be better than *anyone*. That's why we sent you to her inn, Reece. I don't like knowing you kept things from us."

"I didn't…" No point lying. He'd done what he'd done because he thought it was the right way to handle things. "Look, I had a little slipup. I was fixing things."

"Hardly." Shay pushed off the door. "You're off this one."

"What?" Reece demanded, stepping forward without fully realizing he was doing it. "You can't do that."

Shay opened the door and was already stepping out of the room. "I can and I will. Sabrina and Holden will handle her from here on out. You stay out of it. I'll get you a new assignment." She started to leave, muttering about how she'd like to send him to Alaska.

Reece had been a member of North Star for over six years now. He had never once ignored or argued with an order. He'd certainly never outright refused one. "No," he said firmly, and perhaps with a little too much volume.

He could feel Elsie's eyes on him rather than on the computer like they were supposed to be.

Shay stood stock-still, her back to him. She took a very slow, deep breath before she stepped back in the room and calmly closed the door and turned to face him. Her expression was *not* calm, but her voice was controlled, if icy. "You took an oath when you signed on to North Star, and part of that oath was following orders."

"To Granger Macmillan."

She blinked, the only clue that the statement had hit its mark. "Two years, Reece. Don't try to play this off as some sort of misplaced loyalty to Macmillan. I've been in charge for two years, and you haven't disobeyed an order the entire time."

"I haven't felt the need."

"You shouldn't feel the need now. Your loyalty is to North Star, not a woman you just met. If this is some sort of…"

"Let's not pretend you, of all people, can lecture me on following orders to the letter regardless of personal feelings."

Shay cocked her head, and this time her surprise was written all over her face. That he'd dare mention the fact she'd gone her own way, against Granger's clear orders, and more than once.

"You're right. When I was in your position, I stayed true to what I knew was right when Granger had lost track of it. What was *right*, Montgomery. Not my own personal feelings."

"Yeah, well, this is *my* right." But he wasn't handling it very well, and that grated. He'd never...*not* handled things. He'd never been out of control or made decisions because of *emotion*. He wished he could back down having realized that. But he couldn't.

"Lianna and Henry are my responsibility. You won't take me off this mission."

Shay's eyebrows drew together as she studied him. "Is there something you're not telling me?"

"No."

She sighed and then rubbed her hand over her face. Exhaustion seemed to line her expression and Reece felt... guilty. He'd always believed in the party line. In following orders. In letting the leaders lead.

But he didn't know how to sit back and let Sabrina and Holden handle this when he...when he... "I just care, okay? About them specifically."

"After a few days?" Shay asked skeptically.

Warranted skepticism. Understandable skepticism. A skepticism he wished he could access. But all he had were these feelings inside of him he couldn't reason away. "Yeah, after a few days."

"Caring about someone can be a dangerous liability on an assignment. Trust me."

"Dangerous liability or not, would you ever let someone else handle something that involved people you cared about?"

Shay didn't answer that question, but the twisted expression on her face was all the answer Reece needed.

"Fine," Shay said at last. "You're still lead. But you *have* to keep us in the loop. Slipups or no. Anything she tells you, you have to tell us. It's the only way it works. It's the only way we end this for them."

"Even if this group who's hired us turns out to want to hurt them?"

"*Especially* then. North Star won't be used to hurt people," she said vehemently. "Not as long as I'm in charge."

"All right. I'm going to go help them with dinner." He turned to Elsie. "I want whatever you find, whenever you find it. Everything on him, on those groups, no matter how inconsequential."

Elsie's lips twitched. "Sure thing, boss."

"I'm not the boss," he muttered, stalking away from her and past Shay.

"Remember that, huh?" Shay called after him, but she smiled at him, making it clear she was sort of joking.

Which was a nice way to end things that had been tense there for a minute. But he'd said things he maybe shouldn't have, or at least shouldn't have used as weapons. He didn't want to let that sit on his conscience. "For what it's worth, you've done a hell of a job since Granger. I haven't doubted you once, and I doubted him a time or two."

Shay stood completely still, as if shocked by his words. Hell, she probably was. He wasn't one for compliments or any sort of heart-to-hearts. Admitting he cared about Lianna and Henry and then telling her she was a good leader

were two very un-Reece-like things to do in a short period of time.

But eventually she nodded. "Thanks. Now let's wrap
this up so your friends can go home."

It was Reece's turn to nod and walk away, and try not
to think too deeply about this being over, with Lianna and
Henry back home and Reece...

Here. Alone.

Just like you were meant to be.

Chapter Eleven

The kitchen was overwhelming. About three times the size of her kitchen at the inn, and twice as stocked.

Betty was a kind, quiet soul. Lianna couldn't figure out how she fit in around here, but she was grateful for her calming presence as she showed them their options for food.

"Why is everything so healthy?" Henry whined.

Betty chuckled even as Lianna was embarrassed Henry would complain about free food and free safety.

"We do keep it pretty healthy around here, but I have the makings for a PB and J or a grilled cheese."

"You really don't have to. I can make food for us. It doesn't feel right having you fuss over us when…" Lianna trailed off, not sure how to put to words what this whole situation was.

"I know it must feel awkward, especially since you've been pulled into something against your will, but the whole purpose of this place is to help. That's why we're here. Whether that means out in the field or making a grilled cheese."

Reece appeared in the kitchen, so quietly Lianna nearly jumped. Her heart thumped against her chest and she told herself it was nerves. Now he knew everything. Now what would happen?

But there was a flutter in her chest, underneath all that thumping, which spoke of a completely different feeling than nerves and worry.

"I can take it from here, Bet."

Betty nodded at Reece. "I'm around for the next few days. Let me know if you need anything."

"Thank you. Really. I…"

Betty waved her off, then slid out of the kitchen almost as quietly as Reece had entered.

"Are you gonna have grilled cheese, too, Reece?" Henry asked, trying to peek into the pantry without Lianna noticing.

"That sounds good. Why don't I handle dinner?"

"But…" Lianna didn't know how to argue when she didn't know where anything in the kitchen was, but she was the innkeeper. Even without the inn, she was just used to being the one who made the dinners and handled things.

Reece ushered her over to a large table. "Sit. Relax. Much as you can, anyway." He patted her shoulder in a casual manner, then went about gathering tools and ingredients.

Henry sat, but then immediately popped out of his chair to hover around Reece. Lianna didn't have the energy to scold him, and Reece handled it all deftly anyway, melting butter in a pan and taking out slices of cheese to put on pieces of bread.

"How come you don't live here? I'd love to live in a place with an arcade. I'd play *Street Fighter* every day. I'd have all the high scores."

"Lofty goals," Reece replied. "But video games get a little boring after a while, don't they?"

Henry made a scoffing noise, then wiggled his way back to her at the table. "How come we're at Reece's work, Mom?"

Lianna looked at her son and found herself completely and utterly at a loss for words, when usually she had a plan in place. Words to say to assure Henry everything was fine and she was handling it.

"Is it about Dad?" he asked, looking at his shoe as he kicked it against the table leg. *Tap. Tap. Tap.*

She didn't want to lie to Henry. Omission was one thing. Lying… She looked up at Reece. He was watching her, and as much as she would love for someone else to swoop in and lie to her son for her, she could tell he wasn't going to do that.

"Yes, it is." She'd never flat-out told Henry that his father was not a good man. What would be the point? Henry hadn't seen much of Todd—Todd had made sure of that—and Lianna figured Henry knew enough to know Todd hadn't been, well, *there*.

But it didn't feel right to say, *Hey, your dad was a bad man involved with bad things, and now we're paying the price.* Not to a child who was seven. So she had to choose her words very, very carefully.

"There are some men who want to know some things about your father. They think I know. So Reece is just helping us explain to them that I don't know anything."

Henry's eyebrows drew together and his gaze didn't leave his kicking foot. "Are they bad men?"

"We can't control what other people are," Lianna said sternly. "We have to focus on who we are and how we can be good people. And if we…need some help, we can't be afraid to ask for it."

Reece moved over, sliding a plate in front of Henry and then her. Grilled cheese, some grapes and some baby carrots.

After everything today, somehow *that* was the thing that put her closest to tears.

But Reece wasn't done. He crouched next to Henry's chair and looked the boy right in the eye. "Do you trust me?"

Henry nodded.

"I know you have a lot of questions, and you should. You're a smart kid. But it's a lot of complicated adult stuff. The bottom line is I'm going to keep you and your mom safe here until we can convince these men to leave your mom alone. So there's nothing to be afraid of. Because your mom and I are handling it."

Henry stared at Reece for a few more seconds, seemingly searching the man's rugged face for...something. Lianna felt herself searching for something, too, and she was just as in the dark about what she wanted to find as Henry seemed to be.

Eventually Henry nodded. "Okay," he said. Then he smiled crookedly. "It'd probably help me to play more *Street Fighter*."

Henry had always been a give-him-an-inch-he'll-take-a-mile type. But he was so dang cute it was hard to be stern about it. Reece laughed and glanced at Lianna, who couldn't help smiling in return. Their eyes met and...

Her stomach swooped, and there was no pretending that the flutter wasn't all those things she'd promised herself she would never allow in her life again.

But she would not listen to attraction. She would not indulge in conspiratorial smiles. For Henry, she would just shut that feminine side of her off.

Apparently, around Reece Conrad—no, Reece Montgomery—her feminine side wasn't listening to her brain... because it was too busy noticing Reece. The way his eyes crinkled when he smiled, the warmth in those dark eyes, the easy way he rested his very large hand on the back of Henry's chair.

After having made grilled cheese for all of them.

Henry dived into his dinner. Lianna picked at hers. She knew she should eat, but her stomach wasn't cooperating. Too much fear, too much worry, and sadly, not just over the current predicament. Reece was turning into his own predicament. Especially when he took a seat at the table with them with his own plate—a turkey sandwich rather than grilled cheese. He talked baseball with Henry as if this was…

Well, all the things it could never be.

After dinner, and a little bit more *Street Fighter*, Reece showed Lianna to the room she would share with Henry.

"I figured you wouldn't want separate rooms."

She smiled at him, trying to strike the right balance between polite and grateful and not give away any of that… inappropriate, untimely *fluttering*. "You figured right."

Something beeped and he pulled out his phone, frowning at it. "Looks like Elsie got a hit on some things. Do you want to meet me in the conference room once Henry's asleep, or do you want to wait?"

"I'll meet you there. I assume there's some way I can watch him from anywhere in this place?"

Reece's mouth curved wryly. "*You* assume right. Take your time. I promise I'll fill you in once he's in bed."

Lianna nodded and then Reece disappeared. He was much…quieter here. She figured it was instinct or habit. One he'd purposefully broken when he was staying with her. Whether to put her at ease or to act more like your average civilian, she had no idea, but his footsteps had been heavy. She'd mostly known when he was about. Here it was all…appearing and disappearing and… Well, she supposed what he was. An *operative*.

She went into the bathroom, found the toiletries Reece had said would be available to them and made Henry brush his teeth. They'd even thought to provide clothes. An oversize T-shirt for Henry, and what looked like women's sweats for her.

She didn't change, but she had Henry change and brush his teeth. He crawled into the bed without much argument, which was how she knew he was beyond exhausted. She sat on the edge of the bed and ran her hand over his hair. "Get a good night's sleep, baby. Lots of fighting games await you in the morning."

Henry smiled, but his eyes were already drooping. "When can we go home?" he asked around a yawn.

Lianna closed her eyes against a wave of pain and guilt. "I'm not sure, sweetheart." She wondered if she'd ever be sure about anything ever again.

"WE'VE GOT TROUBLE," Elsie said with no preamble when Reece strode through the door. "Major trouble."

"How?"

"I started digging into Charles Jackson, right? Well, everyone and their brother has a flag on the guy's record. Got around the FBI and a few other groups I didn't take the time to identify yet, no problem, but one group had their flag hidden."

Reece didn't know much about computers, but he knew that meant… "So someone knows we're looking for Charles Jackson."

"They don't know who or where we are. I have protections against that. But they know someone is looking, and it doesn't take a leap of reason to realize that if someone just happened to start looking into him today…"

"They know Lianna told us his name."

"Or they're at least going to make that assumption," Elsie confirmed.

Reece swore. Instead of getting her out of trouble, they'd

put her smack down into the middle of it. They'd made her a target, not just a questionable liability.

He swore again.

"I take full responsibility," Elsie said, her voice quavering just a hair. "It's completely my fault. I didn't see the flag. I've never seen one like that. This is my fail."

"Or they're that good. Sometimes the wrong people get the best of us, Els," Reece said with more calm and graciousness than he felt. Elsie was young. She wasn't an operative. Tech geniuses couldn't be expected to handle everything. "Now we just have to make sure we take the next step first and best."

"I'm not handing any of this off to my other tech people. I'm going to take extra precautions before I look into the names of the groups she gave us. But it'll take longer."

"Then it'll take longer. We don't want to rush into anything."

Shay strode into the room. "I agree. No targets on anyone's head. Unfortunately, you're going to have to break it to Mrs. Kade so she understands how important it is for her and her son to stay here for the time being."

"I don't think she's under the illusion she'd be safer at the inn," Reece returned stiffly. Better stiff than furious. Better closed off than let go of all the anger building inside of him.

"You never know," Shay replied with a shrug that grated on Reece's frayed temper.

"We should send an operative to each group," he said through gritted teeth. "Including the FBI. Who knows how they're involved?"

Shay shook her head and Reece had to curl his fingers into fists to keep from demanding to know why.

"I just spoke to my contact, the one who brought this little assignment to our doorstep. I told him we'd found some information, but that I needed more on his end to share it. Eventually, he gave me a little more to go on."

"FBI?" Elsie asked.

"No. A group called T2K9."

Elsie frowned at her computer screen. "That was one of the groups Lianna told us about that was on the FBI file. So they're bad?"

"Not exactly. After some circular arguments, and calling in a favor from Granger, I was given enough information to believe they actually are one of the good guys."

"You talked to Granger?" Elsie asked, wide-eyed. "I thought he wouldn't talk to anyone."

"He makes the occasional exception. Mostly when I threaten him with all of us invading his little ranch or whatever he's calling it these days. Besides, it was just information. Information he had."

"Did they plant the devices?" Reece demanded. Much as he cared about his former boss and his recluse act, now was not the time to dwell on it. Reece needed to know more before he agreed with Shay's assessment that the group that had approached them wasn't going to hurt Lianna— whether on purpose or collaterally.

"No. They didn't. Apparently Todd Kade was a member, under the name Jack Charles, so Lianna was wrong about him not having any other names. T2K9 discovered he was playing them shortly before he died. They made the connection to the Todd Kade identity, and knew they needed more information. They couldn't find it, so they came to us. You won't be surprised to know the head guy over there knew Granger and enough about us to think we'd be able to find what they couldn't."

"I don't understand. How was this one guy involved in so much?" Reece demanded.

"Charles Jackson liked to spread his talents around.

He's got links to more than just the groups Mrs. Kade gave us. Good, bad, questionable. It's not clear why or how."

"Jack Charles was an FBI informant," Elsie said, typing away at her computer. "There aren't any flags, hidden or otherwise, on that name. I can dig up all sorts of things on him."

"That explains the FBI's involvement," Shay said, leaning over Elsie's shoulder to look at the monitor.

"So which of these groups put out the listening devices?" Reece demanded, irritated that the two women seemed more interested in what one man had done than what certain men were *currently* doing. "Who sent the man?"

"We're still working on those answers."

"Damn it, Shay, that's not good enough," Reece said, and though he kept his voice controlled, it was an outburst all the same.

One he immediately regretted when he turned and saw Lianna standing in the doorway, hands clasped together. Her expression was carefully neutral, but she held herself so very still.

He wished he could reason out the emotion that slammed through him every time he looked at her, and that it was never quite the same, but always...deep, immediate. Troubling.

He didn't know what it was, and he couldn't fight it. He could only stand there while she looked at him with wide, scared eyes.

"It seems things are a little more tense than they were an hour ago," she finally said when no one spoke. And there was no stutter, no tremor of fear. Her voice was perfectly calm and steady.

Because for a year now, she'd faced down this uncertainty and had to put on a brave face for Henry. She was a strong woman, made stronger by a circumstance beyond her control.

And Reece had to stop worrying about stupid feelings plaguing him and focus on giving her what she really needed—safety and peace of mind. This problem erased so she and Henry could have a normal life.

"We've got a few leads," Shay said. "Unfortunately, the people who want information from you are a little more... underhanded than we might have anticipated. It's very possible they know you've given us a name."

Lianna's face paled, but she raised her chin. "How would that have happened?"

"My fault," Elsie said, and her tone was both professional and apologetic. A fine line somewhere between a human courtesy and maybe some real guilt. But Reece could also detect confidence that she could still handle the mission in front of her. "In layman's terms, they hid what amounted to a tracking device on the name Charles Jackson."

"Which means *they* know his real name," Lianna said. "Whoever these people targeting me are."

Shay nodded. "Yes. It appears Todd had a few aliases, worked for a number of groups. He couldn't have been home much."

Lianna's shoulders straightened almost imperceptibly, as if she'd taken Shay's observation as a personal insult. "He told me he was a salesman who traveled a lot. We had a baby ten months after we were married and Todd made it clear he wasn't interested in fatherhood. His trips increasing in frequency and length made sense in how much he didn't want to be around to be a father."

"No one's saying you could have known what he was," Reece offered, understanding what she considered to be an insult now.

"Aren't they?" Lianna returned with an arch look at Shay.

Shay's mouth curved. Not a patronizing smile. More of respect at a point earned. "It's not my job to make insinuations or interpret what you should have known or not, Lianna. I'm collecting observations."

Lianna made a scoffing sound. "Observations you have to weave together to form some kind of hypothesis. Some kind of mission. I didn't know what he was. I've told you everything I know, and you know what? I regret it. Because I'm apparently now in even more danger."

Shay's expression didn't change, but Reece knew her well enough to know Lianna had landed her blow. Shay nodded almost imperceptibly.

"You'll be safe here. For as long as it takes. I promise you that."

Lianna shook her head. "We can't stay here forever." She wrapped her arms around herself, eyebrows drawing together. "If we don't know who's after me. If we don't know why. If we don't know anything, that means we—"

"It means *I* will handle it," Reece said firmly. "We'll send an operative to each group we've got. We'll get what we can out of the FBI—surely they know more than they're letting on. We'll—"

"We'll remember that *I'm* in charge here," Shay interrupted.

"With all due respect, and the understanding I'm just a civilian with no understanding of all…this," Lianna said calmly, but her nerves finally betrayed her as her hands shook before she shoved them into the pockets of her jeans. "The only way to find out who's after me is to let them come after me."

"Not a chance," Reece said, unaware those words had come out of his mouth until he realized all three women's surprised gazes were on him. Still, he didn't back down.

"We're not letting an untrained civilian act as *bait* to a group we know nothing about. End of story."

"No, it's not 'end of story,'" Lianna retorted with a barely leashed fury that surprised him. "You are not in charge of me, Reece. None of you are in charge of me. I have run or hid for a year now, and I'm not any closer to safety. Henry's life is disrupted once again. It has to stop, and if I have to be the one to stop it, so be it."

Chapter Twelve

"Lianna." Shay's voice, kind and patient, made Lianna want to haul off and punch something. Particularly Reece's handsome face.

"I understand you're frustrated," Shay continued. "But like you said, you're just a civilian. You can't—"

"So train me. Help me. I don't care what you have to do. This has to end. And we all know, thanks to Todd or Charles or whatever the hell his name really was, I'm at the center. I'm the thing they're worried about or... I don't even know what they want from me, and neither do you. We won't find out without *me*."

Lianna tried to pretend that didn't scare her. Tried to brave her way through this like she'd braved her way through the past year. She liked to think she succeeded. Oh, inside she was a petrified mess, but on the outside she appeared certain. Impassioned.

She hoped.

"I'm sorry. No. We're not considering this," Reece said, more to Shay and Elsie than to her.

She couldn't say she was surprised Reece didn't like the idea, but she was surprised at the...immensity of his conviction. Vehemence pumped off him, barely restrained. He'd begun to pace, something she'd never seen him do.

He'd always been kind and gentle and contained. Even

when he'd picked her up and carried her to his car. He'd been certain and determined but not...

Impassioned.

"Lianna." Reece's entire demeanor changed. He took a deep breath and then spoke to her in a calm, authoritative manner. "You've had a long day. You should rest. We'll handle all this, since it's our fault you're a target in the first place."

Maybe he'd transferred his fury to her, because it leaped up, hot and reckless. "You will not dismiss me."

"That's not—"

"That's exactly what you're trying to do. And sure, if you want to point fingers, your little group holds some of the blame, but my home was *bugged*. Clearly whatever Todd was involved in wasn't done with me yet, even if they'd let me be. That isn't your fault. It's Todd's."

"How do you know they wouldn't have given up after enough time of not getting any information they wanted?"

"How do you know they would?"

His jaw tightened, and he adopted that preternaturally still posture that might have poked some holes in her determination if she wasn't so mad.

"I've protected myself and my son for a year. Without you," she said to Reece. "Without you," she said, pointing to Shay and Elsie. "I need help, yes, but I don't need some mysterious group sweeping in and blowing up my life, no matter how nice you all might be. You can't take away my free will. You can't tell me what to do. You are *not* in charge of me."

The room went silent. She would have categorized Reece's silence as *tense*, at best, but Shay and Elsie weren't tense so much as...curious. They both gazed at Reece as if they'd never seen him before.

Lianna didn't know how to read into that. She supposed

it was beside the point anyway. "They now know I know Todd's real name. But they knew it to begin with, so they want more than that from me."

"Elsie is working on finding the real ID for the man who came to your inn this afternoon," Reece said. Through clenched teeth. He didn't have his fists bunched, but she felt that kind of tension from him anyway. As if he was ready to physically fight his way through this but was holding himself back.

"That's good," Lianna said, finding the more she observed the bubbling ferocity beneath Reece's controlled facade, the more controlled she felt. Sort of like when Henry was throwing a tantrum. She wanted to laugh at the comparison, but unlike a child's tantrum, she didn't think Reece would handle her laughing in a petulant or dismissive way.

"There are definitely some blocks. Someone doesn't want us to know who he really is or who he's connected to. I'll be able to unearth it," Elsie said, with a kind of quiet confidence that helped ease some of Lianna's fears. "It just might take more time than I'd like."

"What happens when you unearth it?" Lianna asked, with none of the snap or demand she'd had earlier. No, she was too tired for that. She was too…fed up with half answers that didn't actually *end* what Todd had brought to her doorstep. "You know the name of the group who Todd was potentially working for. But you don't know what they want from me. We won't know what they're after unless we give them some access."

"They will get *no* access to you, and that's it," Reece said. His voice was controlled, but nothing else about him was. He shocked her completely when he said no more and just stormed out of the room.

"Well, *that* was interesting," Shay murmured.

"I was laboring under the assumption Reece was a robot," Elsie said, sounding awed. "*That* was not robotic."

Both women turned their gazes to her. As if she understood…any of what they were saying or getting at.

"I…wouldn't know. I've only just met him."

"And made quite an impression. Reece has dealt with a lot more complicated, dangerous missions than this," Shay said.

"Seriously. He single-handedly saved all those guys in Afghanistan," Elsie said, though she'd turned back to her computer and was tapping away again. Trying to find the man who'd wanted to check in to her inn.

"And came out with barely a scratch when he saved that girl from, what was it, ten Sons members?"

Elsie nodded. "Then he came back and shrugged it off as nothing and asked for the next mission." Elsie slid a look at Lianna. "And did *not* storm out of any rooms."

"Ever. I've been here longer than him. I have *never* seen him act even a little bit like that."

"I don't know what either of you are getting at," Lianna said, trying to ignore the odd flutter of…something in her chest.

"Just observations." There was some humor in Shay's expression, but it slowly melted away. "Putting yourself in harm's way is a dangerous proposition, Lianna. Even with our help. You're risking your life."

Lianna rubbed at her chest, where that nice, if alarming, flutter had turned into a jerky, beating panic. "I don't want to risk my life. But I don't want to live in fear. Henry is missing school. If this goes on much longer, he'll miss baseball. If we have to move again…" She shook her head. "He deserves a childhood. In one place. He deserves more than this. I don't know how else to give it to him."

Shay nodded. "Can you give us some time? We can plan something. Use a team. Protect you, as much as we can."

Lianna didn't understand these people. What they were getting out of it. Why they'd swooped into her life and upended everything. And worse, why she trusted them. "Why? You don't know me from Adam. I can't pay you. Why would you help me?"

"It's what we do. Protect innocent people."

She thought of Reece's story about his parents, and how his records had backed all that up. Being taken away by the state. No one had protected him growing up. Were they all like that? "Because you were once innocent people who weren't protected?"

Shay shared a look with Elsie, then turned back to Lianna. "That's exactly why," she said, firmly. Vehemently. Like it wasn't just the truth, but an oath she'd taken.

"I'll take whatever help you can give me," Lianna said in return. "Whatever protection you can give me. I don't have a death wish here. I only want it over so I can give my son the life he deserves. I think I have to put myself in a little danger to do that, but I'll absolutely wait for you guys to mitigate the level of danger I have to step into."

Shay's mouth curved. "Reece's reaction is starting to make more sense."

Lianna blinked, irritated at the heat rushing into her cheeks. She couldn't think of a thing to say.

"It's late," Shay said, with a gentleness Lianna hadn't seen from her this whole time. "Why don't you get some rest? We'll reconvene in the morning and brainstorm how this is going to work."

Lianna didn't know how she was going to sleep in this strange place, with so much worry and anxiety filling up her mind. How could anyone sleep knowing their life could be in danger? Or even just completely upended—again?

And if she worried about that, she didn't have to think about how she felt toward Reece. A stranger. Someone she barely knew but… She'd been foolish once. She'd fallen for Todd, let her heart sweep her away, because she'd chased a stupid emotion that had turned out to be fake. Fabricated.

She wouldn't do that again. Not to Henry and not to herself. Maybe she'd come to trust Reece when it came to helping her, but that didn't mean she could trust this…flutter inside of her. She *couldn't* trust it. Wouldn't.

But as she walked back to the room she'd be sleeping in, she stopped short at the entrance to the hallway. Reece was pacing agitatedly in the hallway outside the door where Henry slept. He looked a little wild, and that should put her off. It should scare her.

But it didn't. She wanted to soothe him. She wanted… him. She just needed to work on convincing herself she couldn't trust those feelings. Not so quickly. Not when her own judgment had already failed her.

Reece was nothing like Todd, but that didn't change who *she* was. The mistakes *she'd* made. In the end, the only thing that could matter was making sure Henry was safe.

Forever.

REECE PACED THE hallway outside the room where Henry was fast asleep. He knew he had to get control of his emotions before he spoke to Lianna, but he also knew he had to speak to her tonight before Shay and Elsie ran with any ideas of using Lianna as bait.

He couldn't stand the thought of it. It made his insides feel like rock, and like he wanted to punch his way through…well, the wall.

He hadn't felt this way in a very long time, and he didn't

revel in the return of that raging storm. In fact, it only made him *more* unsettled. Which wasn't productive. At all.

He sensed movement at the end of the hall and looked up to see Lianna standing there. She stared at him the longest time, some internal conflict going on behind her eyes, before she started toward him.

He didn't say anything as she approached. The words just…left him, and he knew he didn't have the handle on his inner turmoil or his worry to keep a lid on things that needed to stay completely buried.

"We came to an agreement," Lianna said coolly. "If you'd stayed, you might have heard it."

"If I'd stayed, I would have punched a hole in a wall," he muttered.

If she seemed surprised by that response, she didn't show it. "That's hardly constructive," she said, and she sounded like she did when she was scolding Henry.

It didn't do a lot for his temper. "I don't find myself feeling particularly constructive. I don't find myself…" He sucked in a breath, calling on all his training—as a soldier, as an operative, hell, as a foster kid who couldn't make trouble without severe consequences—and pushed down his turmoil.

Unfortunately, that left room for all those *other* feelings to take hold. Her standing there looking so…put-together, even as he could see the worry around the edges. The way her blue eyes regarded him with a wariness she *should* have, but he didn't want.

Her honey-blond hair had fallen out of its ponytail, and despite her rigid posture, she looked like a woman who'd been through hell. And he wanted…

God, the things he wanted that didn't make sense to him. He clutched at his shirt, frustrated and lacking the words to express it. "I don't know what this is."

She blinked, *finally* showing an emotion that wasn't haughty disdain. Shock or something like it. Confusion, definitely. She *should* be confused. He was damn confused himself.

"What *what* is?"

"This…feeling. What I feel for you. I don't understand it. I can't say I like it. It's like…a disease."

"I'm a *disease*?"

"That isn't what I meant."

She inhaled carefully. "No, I suppose it isn't." Her eyebrows knitted together, and she studied him. It made his chest feel too tight, and it made him want to do things. Touch her, for one.

She was…she was so much better than him. He knew what he was. What he deserved. It sure as hell wasn't her.

"Reece…" She trailed off, but just his name sounded tortured. Like she was dealing with at least some of the tension he was. But that was stupid, because she was just worried about Henry. About her life.

"I suppose the difference between us," she said after a while, "is I know what I feel, but I can't trust it." She took a step toward him. Her fingertips touched his jaw, featherlight and with some trepidation, as if she might dart away at any second.

He held himself so still he wasn't even sure he was breathing.

Her eyes looked directly into his. "You're a good man," she said firmly. "Against my will, I can't help but trust you. It's myself I don't trust."

She seemed…sad about that, and her fingers didn't fall off his face. She didn't step away. She just…looked at him, like if she did it long enough, something would change.

Maybe he could change it. He could touch her back. He could kiss her. He could change *everything*. Hadn't he done that? Over and over again? Change his life in the face of circumstances that shouldn't have allowed him to change?

His hand settled on her waist with half a thought to draw her near, even as that insidious voice he'd tried to silence his whole life told him he didn't have the right. She didn't step away. She didn't drop her hand. She sucked in a breath, but she didn't turn away.

Without warning, there was the sound of a faint crash, then heavy footsteps, right before a large figure appeared at the end of the hall.

Reece felt like a guilty kid with a stolen piece of candy as he pulled his hand off Lianna's waist. He glanced at her and realized she'd gone stiff and pale as her hand dropped from his face.

"That's Holden Parker," he offered, understanding that the appearance of a stumbling, injured man wasn't exactly the norm for her. "Another operative." One who was sporting a bloody shirt and an unnaturally uneven gait. "Parker, did you get shot again?"

Holden flashed a grin as he stumbled past them and toward his room. "A mere flesh wound, friend."

Reece frowned. Holden looked pale, and there was way too much blood on his shirt. He also didn't stick around to introduce himself to Lianna, which wasn't like Holden at all.

"I think you should go see if he's okay," Lianna said, watching where Holden had gone. "That didn't look good."

"Right."

She returned her gaze to him and then smiled. "Good night, Reece," she said softly, before turning away and disappearing into the room where Henry was asleep.

Reece blew out a breath. He had no idea what any of that…meant. But he figured that was best. He hadn't done anything she'd regret, and he could…get a good night's sleep and shove it all down tomorrow. Focus on the task at hand. Keep her and Henry safe.

No matter the cost.

He strode into Holden's room without knocking. Holden was sitting on his bed, failing at stripping off his own shirt.

"Did you call Betty?" Reece demanded, already knowing the answer. Holden Parker was an explosives expert. He was impulsive and often got himself injured in the line of duty. He also *hated* doctors—not Betty specifically, but any medical attention whatsoever.

"I'm fine," he grumbled predictably.

"You were shot. What were you even doing?"

"Asking the wrong questions of the wrong people, apparently. Someone took offense to me asking questions about the guy who Sabrina tied up earlier. Then I took offense to them trying to 'escort' me elsewhere." Holden flashed a cocky grin. "You should see the other guy."

"You need Betty."

"I'll live. Yet again. Who's the lady?" Holden nodded toward the hallway and waggled his eyebrows.

"Don't worry about it," Reece muttered, knowing Holden was just being Holden and there was no need to get bent out of shape.

"Dibs. I understand."

Offended against his will, Reece shook his head. "There's no *dibs*. Have some respect. She's a *mother*."

"Moms like me," Holden said with a grin. "And I like them."

Reece pulled his phone out of his pocket, pressed Betty's name.

"Don't you—" Holden reached for the phone, but a hiss of pain had him stopping short.

"Bet? Holden's here."

"Did that moron get shot again?" she asked.

"He did. Looks bad. He couldn't even stop me from making the phone call."

Betty swore softly. "I'll get my stuff and be there in a few. Don't let him leave that room."

"Got it." Reece ended the call and shoved his phone back in his pocket again. "If you try to jump out the window, you're only going to earn yourself a trip to the actual hospital."

Holden sneered. "I hate you."

"Yeah, yeah."

Holden's gaze turned sharp and assessing. "Looks like I interrupted a tender moment."

Reece shrugged, refusing to give in to Holden's attempt to irritate him out of the room so he could evade Betty's impending arrival.

"She's the innkeeper, right? The one we're trying to protect."

"She is."

"Never seen you get involved in an assignment before."

Again, Reece shrugged.

"I tell you what. You couldn't pay me to get involved with someone during an assignment. Talk about a disaster waiting to happen."

"Good thing I'm not involved, then."

Holden snorted. "You're up to your eyeballs in involvement, Montgomery. I can't imagine anything worse. Screws with your judgment, your self-preservation instincts. Screws with *everything*."

"Thanks for the pep talk," Reece muttered. He heard the rattle of the medical cart. "Do I need to strap you down so Betty can look at you, or are you going to be a good boy?"

Holden laughed. "I bet I could outmaneuver you even with a gunshot wound."

Reece raised an eyebrow. "Want to try it?"

Betty sighed behind him. "Is there anything worse than fragile male egos?"

Reece moved out of the way so she could push her cart inside.

"I swear to God, Holden, if you fight me, I'm going to sedate you against your will."

There were more grumbles from Holden as Betty got to work. Reece left the room more bothered by the exchange than he'd like to admit.

Couldn't pay me to get involved with someone during an assignment. Talk about a disaster waiting to happen.

Yes, it was. It *was*. So he needed to get himself together. And fast.

Chapter Thirteen

Lianna woke up to Henry whispering her name in an urgent tone.

"I have to pee," he whispered, dancing around by the door. "But I don't know where to go."

Lianna was out of bed and to the door in a flash. She didn't even worry about the fact she was in pajamas as she ushered Henry out the door to the nearest restroom she'd been shown last night.

Henry swooped in and closed the door, clearly making it in the nick of time. Lianna let out a breath of relief. Which ended on an inelegant gasp she couldn't hide when she looked up to see Reece in the hallway, walking toward her.

He was wearing shorts and a sweatshirt, clearly having had some kind of workout, as there was a ring of sweat around his neck. His face was dripping, and he looked at her with a wariness she didn't fully understand.

Much like she didn't understand the shiver of attraction that ran through her when he was grimy and sweaty. It should be a turnoff, but she found herself thinking things she definitely, *majorly* shouldn't. Especially with her son just on the other side of this door.

"Morning," he offered.

"Good morning. Uh. How's your friend?"

"He'll be fine," Reece said gruffly. "He's always just fine."

The door shot open and Henry came out already talking a mile a minute. Lianna stopped him by shooting her arm out to stop his forward progress. "Wash your hands."

Henry groaned and threw his head back, making an epic drama over the short, barely satisfactory handwashing he then performed. Lianna winced at the way he got water *everywhere*.

"Can you play in the arcade with me today?" Henry asked Reece, practically jumping up and down.

Reece's grave expression softened into an affectionate smile. "I will a little bit later, buddy. I've got some meetings this morning. So does your mom."

"Does that mean I can play with Sabrina?" Henry asked hopefully.

"I think Betty is going to play with you this morning. I hope you're ready. She's a tough one to beat."

"I can do it!"

"What about breakfast?" Lianna asked.

"There's a little breakfast buffet of sorts set up in the kitchen. Feel free to help yourself once you're…" He trailed off, his eyes taking such a quick tour of her body she almost thought she'd imagined it. "Dressed."

Heat stole up Lianna's cheeks as she became expressly aware that she wasn't wearing a bra. She tried to *casually* cross her arms over her chest, but it was of no matter. Reece had his eyes on a door farther down the hall. "Take your time with breakfast," he was saying. "We'll meet in the conference room around nine."

Lianna didn't say anything to that. There was no point when he'd disappeared into a room and shut the door.

Henry had already bounded back into the room they were staying in. He was chattering about video games as Lianna handed him his clothes from yesterday to change into. He'd need a change of clothes. Little boys were too smelly to wear the same clothes two days in a row.

But that was a problem for later. She changed back into her own clothes from yesterday and tried to forget everything about Reece and focus on the task at hand. On what she had to do.

She had an idea, but she wasn't sure how to convince Shay and especially Reece it was a good one. A necessary one.

She wrangled Henry to breakfast and fought with him over how much he had to eat before he could play arcade games. It amazed her that even in these circumstances he could be such a...carefree boy.

Thank God for small favors.

At nine, Lianna left Henry in Betty's care and headed for the conference room, pulse beating too hard in her neck. Shay and Reece were already in the room, and Elsie was tapping away at her computer, giving Lianna the impression she hadn't left at all since last night. Sabrina and the man from yesterday—what was his name? Holden, maybe—were sitting at the table, conversing in low tones.

Everyone grew silent when she stepped into the room. It made her feel even more out of place than she already felt. Like she was to blame for all this, when she knew she wasn't. Neither Todd's choices nor this group entering her life were her fault at all.

But that didn't ease her discomfort at being the center of attention.

Reece pulled a chair back from the table and gestured for her to sit. She tried to arrange her face into a semblance of a smile as she took it.

They already had the game room up on the monitor, though the sound was off. Still, she could see Henry dancing around a game while Betty's focus was on the screen of the game.

"We have a variety of options here," Shay said, bringing the meeting to order with an air of control and leadership that impressed Lianna. Everyone's attention was on Shay, and Lianna had little doubt everyone in the room would follow her orders without question.

"None of them are set in stone. We're still in the brainstorming phase, of course."

Lianna didn't have time for brainstorming. Not when Henry needed home and school and…a life. "They think I know something, and unfortunately, me knowing Todd's real name probably only reinforced that belief."

"Yes, we agree. Which puts you in a lot of danger, especially since you *don't* know the information they're looking for." Shay paused for a moment. "Right?"

Lianna nodded. "I've told you everything I know. Unless they're looking for his real name or two of the many groups he was involved with, I'm at a loss."

"And whatever group this guy was working for is…beyond secretive," Elsie said, gesturing at her screen though Lianna couldn't see it from her seat. "Even with the guy's real identity, I'm not digging much up on the group he works for."

"There's nothing your husband might have left you…a banking number, a deposit box key…anything really, that someone might be after?"

"No. I never went through Todd's things. I just tossed them. When Henry and I moved to Denver, I paid someone to get rid of whatever was left. I wanted a fresh start."

"Still, there could have been something in his belongings that connected to them. They could think you have it."

"Maybe, but… Obviously I don't know who came and asked me questions after the murder. Aside from the FBI.

But there weren't questions like those. It was always people quizzing me on what I knew about his work."

Shay drummed her fingers on the table.

"This group had listening devices all over that inn. It's possible they never sent people to question her directly. If they're this concerned about secrecy, maybe they didn't want to risk even asking questions," Reece said, appearing much calmer and more detached than he had at any point yesterday.

Lianna envied him that control.

"If they got devices in the inn, who's to say they didn't have devices everywhere else she lived?" Sabrina suggested.

"But a year of listening to someone is a little over-the-top, even for this kind of a group," Holden pointed out. "They'd want to act. Why haven't they acted?"

Lianna closed her eyes. Her thoughts had been going in the same relentless circles for days. "This is the problem. We don't know. We don't have anything to go on. Which is why..." Nerves assaulted her, but she linked her fingers together and focused on the end result.

A safe, happy life for Henry.

"I have an idea. I'm sure you're all experts at...tactics and whatnot, but I'm an expert at, well, me."

Shay leaned back in her chair. Lianna didn't dare look at Reece. She knew she wouldn't be able to keep the aura of detached calm she so desperately wanted to portray.

"I want to go back to the inn. As soon as possible. No matter what, even if I knew his name, they think I'm stupid. They think they can win. Which means I have to play that role. Just like I did for the FBI and everyone else. The stupid, manipulated wife who didn't even know her husband was some dirty operative for who knows how many criminal groups."

"You aren't that, and you're not going back alone. That's suicide," Reece interrupted. With none of the calm he'd just been using.

"No, I don't want to go alone." Lianna blew out a breath in an effort to settle her nerves. She turned to Reece's dark, furious gaze. "I want you to go with me."

REECE OPENED HIS mouth to tell her there was no way in hell she was going to do this, but then her words sank in.

She wanted him to go with her.

"You see, if I did it once, why not again?"

"Do what once?" Shay asked. Reece didn't like that look. Like she was considering this insanity.

"Fall for a guy. Let him manipulate me into being whatever front or disguise he needed. If I go back to the inn with Reece, and we play it up for the listening devices—that he's trying to get information out of me by pretending to be interested—they'll eat it up."

"They won't come near you knowing Reece is there," Holden said, but it wasn't as dismissive as Reece would have liked. It was more the way they often hashed out a plan.

"If it was only him? Why not?"

"They're patient. Clearly."

"Sure, but I imagine me knowing Todd's real name will speed things along. Especially if we act like I've told Reece something important."

Shay blew out a breath. "I have the utmost faith in my operatives, Lianna, but if they did send in a team to get you—it would be a team. And Reece couldn't fight off an entire team of bad guys, even if he wanted to."

"Depends on how many," Reece muttered. If it had been another assignment, he might have pushed that plan, but this was Lianna. How could he possibly take chances with Lianna?

"You've thought this through," Sabrina said thoughtfully. "You've got a ruse. You've got a well-trained guy to play it out with you. What about the kid?"

"I want him as far away from this as possible," Lianna said firmly. "At first I thought to have him go to my grandparents in Denver, but that would put my grandparents in danger, too, wouldn't it?"

Shay nodded. "Would your grandparents be willing to come here? Normally I'd set everyone up in a safe house, but until Elsie identifies this group, I don't want to take that kind of chance."

"I think they would. If I could speak to them first." Reece watched her shake away the glimmer of doubt. He wished he didn't understand so well that she thought her grandparents might hold her to the mistake she'd made with Todd, might think she was being taken in again.

Because she'd said as much last night. She could put her trust in him, but everything that had happened with her dead husband made it hard to trust herself.

Yet she was the best mother he'd ever seen. Strong in the face of what must have been a yearlong nightmare for her.

"So the plan would be to send you and Reece back to the inn. Playact for the mics that you know something. And wait for them to show up. Then what?"

"Sabrina and Holden can be nearby," Reece said, the plan taking shape in his mind. He still didn't *like* it. He'd rather Lianna and Henry stay carefully holed away for, well, forever. But he understood Lianna's desire to give Henry a real life. Back to school, back to the home he'd only just gotten accustomed to. They both deserved a real life free of Todd Kade and all he'd wrought. "Carefully placed, but near enough to close in once a detail shows up. Return ambush. We're the ones getting intel from them."

"It could work," Holden agreed with a nod.

"With that hole in your gut?" Sabrina asked with a smirk.

Holden only grinned at her. "I could take *you* down with a hole in the gut. Why not some secret group?"

"In your dreams."

"Children," Shay said mildly to Holden and Sabrina. She turned to Lianna specifically. "It's not without risks."

"I understand that," Lianna said. Her hands were clasped so tightly in her lap her knuckles were white, but she pressed on with an impressive outward calm. "I don't think there's a course of action here that doesn't have risks. There's one wrinkle. The listening devices. I imagine they know I know about them. I did take one off the smoke detector."

"Do a sweep and miss one," Elsie suggested, her eyes never leaving her computer. "Make it look like you just didn't know about it."

"That could work," Reece said thoughtfully. "The ones in the common areas were on the carbon monoxide detectors. If they can buy Lianna being dumb, I'm sure they can buy us being inept enough to only find the ones specifically on smoke detectors."

"Risky. They might read through that," Shay pointed out.

"Might. But I'm willing to bet they're going to underestimate until they have reason not to."

"Reece is right," Sabrina agreed. "Besides, if they do read through it, that doesn't change much. They know Lianna knows something. They know she's involved with some other group. To my way of thinking, the worst thing that happens is they *don't* come after her and we need a new plan."

Reece could think of a lot worse outcomes, but he kept those to himself. Because he'd do everything in his power to make sure none of them became an eventuality.

"So? We do it?" Lianna asked. She looked around the room, but clearly everyone was waiting for Shay to agree.

After a pause—dramatic, in Reece's estimation—Shay finally nodded. "We'll make the arrangements with your grandparents and work from there."

Chapter Fourteen

Lianna talked to her grandparents and parents on Shay's secure phone line that was supposed to be completely unable to be tapped on either end. Because apparently they were worried about her family being monitored.

Lianna tried not to let her fear thread through her voice as she spoke with them. As she explained the situation. As she silently *willed* them to believe her, not question her decision.

They had every right to be skeptical of her judgment after what she'd gone through with Todd. But they weren't. They asked questions, they expressed worry, but they didn't act like she was a fool for trusting these people.

"So we'll do a switch," Shay was saying, walking Lianna somewhere deeper in the house. Lianna didn't know where they were going, but she didn't ask. "Your grandfather is going to go shopping. One of our men will meet with him, switch clothes, and that way Henry will have a family member here, and your family will have an operative with them keeping a watch on things."

"How many operatives do you have?"

Shay smiled, opening a door and gesturing Lianna inside. "A variety. Full-time. Part-time. Not as many as we used to, but I have a lot of contacts. I know it's harder to trust someone you've never met, but Sabrina and Holden and Reece are the most experienced operatives I have, and I want them where the potential for danger is the highest."

Lianna tried to find some comfort in that, but she was sending a stranger to stay with her grandmother and parents. Who did that? Who—

Lianna's thoughts stopped short as she realized Shay had brought her into a bedroom. What must be Shay's own bedroom.

"I wanted some privacy. In other words, somewhere Reece wasn't going to come along and interrupt with his macho show of overprotection."

"Oh, he doesn't mean…"

"I know exactly what he means. Reece is a good guy. He cares about you, and before you start protesting that, too, it's obvious. The only person who's been here even close to as long as I have is Reece. I've seen more emotion out of the guy in the past week than I have in something like seven years." She paused before continuing. "A few years ago, our first leader was injured. A guy Reece really looked up to. I *know* it hit him hard, but I never *saw* it hit him hard. If you know what I mean."

"I don't…"

"He's a tough guy. They're *all* tough guys here. They're also good guys, which means sometimes they get all uppity about protecting the womenfolk, but it comes from a good place, an honest place. Even when that makes me want to punch them in the face, I get it."

Lianna was at a complete loss.

Shay glanced at her and seemed to read that. "My point is, Reece will do everything and anything to protect you. As he should, feelings or no. He's a trained soldier and operative, and you're not. That's how it works. That doesn't mean you shouldn't have the means to protect yourself, as well. Do you know how to shoot a gun?"

"Well, yes. My grandfather insisted I learn before I moved to the inn. He taught Henry the basics, too."

"That's good. Do you have a gun?"

"Yes. At the inn. I…keep it locked away and hidden. I don't really want Henry knowing it's there, but you know, safety in such an isolated area and…"

"That's fine for when Henry's there," Shay said dismissively. "But when it's just you and Reece, keep it on you. No matter what Reece says."

"You don't think he'll want me to carry a gun?"

"He's just going to think he can protect you on his own, and he's probably right. But this is about…"

Finally, Lianna was starting to understand what Shay was trying to get across. "It's about standing on your own two feet."

"Exactly. He's going to have a hard time understanding that. Not because he's a pigheaded man, but because he has a deep instinct to protect. He's conditioned to protect. It's what we do. But being a woman, I know that… It's not always the most effective mode of feeling safe. So you carry the gun around."

Shay rummaged around in a drawer and pulled out what looked like a sidearm holster. "Take this one. I assume you don't have anything like that."

"No. No, I don't."

"There. Now you can stay armed and dangerous."

"Thanks." Lianna didn't know quite what else to say. Or why they'd had to come into Shay's private quarters for this exchange. But Shay didn't make a move to usher Lianna back out, which meant there was…more to this.

"Look, I know it's a lot. To trust us. To put your life and your family in our hands."

"I don't really have another choice."

"I guess not. Listen… It isn't my job to tell you what

to do. But it kind of comes with the territory. Being able to analyze people and if they're ready to take on a challenge… I have to be able to do that. For my operatives."

"Reece seems ready to handle any challenge."

"Yes, he is. Even as…invested as he is in this, I think he's capable and ready. I meant you, Lianna."

Lianna let out a laugh, hoping it didn't sound as bitter as it felt. "Another choice I don't have. Ready or not, here it comes."

"Yes and no. You could work on trusting yourself. One of the best ways a woman can be safe, stay safe, is to trust her gut. Listen to it. The gut doesn't lie."

That was never going to happen. Not after all the mistakes she'd made. "My gut lied. I never once thought Todd was…well, what he was."

"I'm going to have to disagree with you."

Lianna's mind whirled around that. This tough woman, who ran some *group* with operatives and men like Reece and Holden looking to her for approval, seemed to think Lianna's instincts were good. "You don't even know me."

"Sure, but you knew that Todd wasn't a good father, right? You told us he traveled to stay away. Your gut knew that wasn't right. Sure, you couldn't have fathomed he was some kind of two-faced, lying bastard, but you *knew* something wasn't right."

Lianna felt like crying, because that wasn't any better. Knowing and doing what she'd done. "I stayed," she said around the lump in her throat, fingering the holster Shay had given her.

"Women have stayed with worse for much smaller reasons. No one goes through life without getting fooled once or twice. No one gets through life without regrets born of…well, all sorts of things. It's kind of part and parcel of being human."

"I find it hard to believe you've been taken in and fooled by a man. Especially a man that was the father of your child."

"No, not the father of my child. But I have my own mistakes and regrets, ones I had to forgive myself for. It took a long time, but I got a lot more accomplished, helped myself and other people a lot better, once I did."

Lianna looked up at her and saw…well, those regrets Shay had spoken of, right there in her expression as she continued to speak.

"We all make mistakes when love is involved. Fathers to your kids. Siblings. Parents. Friends. We all get mixed up and let feelings override reason, or make us ignore our gut feelings. Doesn't mean your gut lies."

"How can you tell the difference?"

"I think knowing there *is* a difference is the first step."

Lianna didn't know how that could be true, but she trusted this woman. Believed this woman. How could she not?

REECE WAS PRETTY sure Henry could spend the next year in the arcade room and only come up for food and bathroom breaks. Maybe a little sleep. Personally, Reece would like to get the kid outside, but he didn't have any say. Not to mention, Henry probably deserved to do whatever he wanted for the time being.

"How long are we going to have to stay here?" Henry asked. His gaze was still on the screen, that glazed-over look to his eyes, but the way he stood had changed. As if he was a little bit more alert of his surroundings.

"It depends, but I have it on good authority your great-grandpa is going to come here to stay with you."

Henry didn't stop his game, but his gaze went sharp and his eyebrows drew together. "Why?"

"Why not?"

"Well, we're in some danger, right? I don't want Gramps to be in danger."

"You and your great-grandfather will be safe here. I promise."

Henry's game character died on the screen. He turned to Reece, expression...very close to unreadable, especially for a seven-year-old.

"Why is he coming here? Really?"

Reece figured Lianna should be the one to tell him, but he could hardly lie to the kid. "Your mom and I are going to..." How the hell did he explain what they were going to do? "We're going to try to get some answers on what's going on."

"You're going to go away?"

"Not away, exactly. We're going to go look into some things. We want you and your mom to be able to go home and be safe. So we're going to make sure we can arrange that." Could he possibly be any more vague or any less reassuring?

"My dad used to go away a lot."

There was an accusation in that sentence. Blame. Reece felt an unaccustomed stab of...hurt. Guilt he would have understood, but how could he be hurt by a young boy's words?

"This isn't like that," Reece said as reassuringly as he could manage. He crouched down so he could be eye to eye with Henry. He put his hand on the boy's shoulder. "It's my job to keep you and your mom safe. Sometimes we have to go away to figure out how to do that, but that doesn't mean we won't come back. It doesn't mean that our goal isn't...going home. Both of you going home and being safe."

"What about you?"

"What about me?"

"Where's your home? You said you didn't live here. Where will you go home and be safe?"

Reece had been shot, been in a building when it exploded. He'd been stabbed. He'd been neglected by his own parents. He wasn't sure anything had ever hurt quite as deeply as that simple question did.

"This building might not be my home, but this group? It's my home. It's what I do."

Henry chewed on his bottom lip. "You're going to keep the bad men away from Mom, right?"

Reece studied Henry. There was something about the boy… A guardedness Reece hadn't seen in him before. "Can you tell me what you know about the bad men?"

Henry shrugged. "It's just… You'll protect her. You'll make sure nothing happens to her."

Reece knew Henry was worried. Scared. Whether he'd had a good father or not, the man had been murdered. It was only natural Henry should have some lingering fears about losing other people in such a sudden, violent manner.

But there was something about those questions, and the direct, imploring blue gaze of the boy.

"I will," Reece agreed, vowed. But he didn't stand up or let go of Henry's shoulder. "Is there something you want to tell me? Something you're worried about?"

Henry was silent and still for longer than Reece had ever noticed.

A ripple of dread skittered down his spine, but he didn't know what to do with it. Because Henry shook his head. Nothing he was worried about. Nothing he wanted to tell.

He'd been through a hard time. Reece was reaching to be reading into his reactions and legitimate fears like this. But long after he'd left Henry under Sabrina's watchful eye, the interaction bothered him.

He packed up what he thought he would need. Packed far more weapons than he'd originally gone in with. It would just be him and Lianna, so he didn't have to worry about the safety of having weapons around a young boy. All he had to worry about was keeping Lianna safe.

It's just... You'll protect her. You'll make sure nothing happens to her. Henry's words, and the careful, almost adult delivery of them, repeated in Reece's head the entire time. All the way up to when he went to seek out Lianna so they could head out.

She was in the kitchen with Henry and an older gentleman. She was smiling at both of them, and even with the worry around her eyes, the *love* in her eyes for the two men around her cut straight through him.

More than want. More than...anything he'd ever known. He thought of last night and the way she'd touched him and he—

Had to focus on keeping her safe. That was the only thing.

"Reece," she said, finally noticing him. She stood and Reece noted she hadn't touched her plate of food. "This is my grandfather. Hank Young. Grandpa, this is Reece Montgomery."

The older gentleman stood and extended a hand. His handshake was firm and his eyes were stern, but his greeting was kind enough. "Good to meet you. I hear you've been keeping our kids safe."

"Yes, sir. I plan to keep it that way."

"Good, good. We're all eager for this to be over."

Lianna walked over to Henry and pulled him into a hug. "Be good for Grandpa Hank and everyone here. I'll be back soon. I promise." She kissed his head, smoothed his hair. Reece watched as she took a deep breath and had to *force* herself to leave her son's side.

That feeling from earlier swelled up in him, threatening to take him completely under.

She walked over to her grandfather, gave him a hug and whispered something in his ear. But Reece hardly had time to recover before Henry bounded out of his chair.

"Bye, Reece," Henry said, flinging his arms around Reece's legs. He squeezed tight and it seemed to squeeze around Reece's heart like a vise.

"See ya soon, kid. No worries, okay?"

Henry let him go and nodded, but there were fears in the boy's eyes. Fears he didn't voice. Reece couldn't help but frown over that as he led Lianna into the hallway.

"Does Henry know something?" he asked quietly, leading her to the front door.

She inhaled, and he knew she was trying to keep her composure over leaving Henry behind. "He's just so smart," Lianna said, somehow sounding proud and sad at the same time. "I'm sure he's overheard things I'd rather he didn't. I'm sure he's put together things I'd rather he didn't."

Reece nodded. That had to be it. Regardless, they had other things to concern themselves with. "Are you ready for this?"

Lianna lifted her chin, a stubborn fighter's light in her eye. "I am."

Chapter Fifteen

The sun was setting as Reece drove her up the familiar drive to her inn. The kind of early-summer sunset that usually gave her a giddy hopefulness that if the world could be *that* beautiful, things couldn't be *that* bad.

Of course, things were pretty bad right now, so it was hard to access her usual joy.

"We're going to do a quick sweep of the area," Reece said, pulling to a stop. "Then the entire building." He sounded every inch the...whatever he was. *Operative.*

"We'll want to check your car, too," he added.

"My car?"

"We're just covering all our bases." She supposed he thought his voice was reassuring, but the way his eyes seemed to take in everything around them didn't put her at any kind of ease.

Still, she appreciated that he said *we.* It somehow made her feel...part of it. Even when she was reeling from the idea of a *sweep* of the area.

"If they can set up listening devices, they could easily set up cameras. So we're going to have to make it look like we're looking, but not too closely. If they're watching, we want to give the impression that we're cautious, but at least a little inept."

"That we're..." Lianna trailed off, irritated that heat

was creeping up her cheeks. "I mean, I think we need to make it look like we're…"

"We're?"

He wasn't going to make this easy on her, and that irritated her enough she straightened in her seat. *"Involved,"* she said icily. "Women do stupid things for men all the time. And vice versa."

He made a noise, not quite an affirmation but not an argument, either. But he got out of the car, so she did, too. He grabbed the duffel he'd packed earlier. Lianna hadn't had anything to pack except the holster Shay had given her.

The evening was almost warm, and everything smelled and felt like summer. The green earth beneath her feet, the colorful pop of color from her gardens.

Lianna wished Henry were here. Wished this had all been a dream. She looked at the man standing in front of his car, waiting for her to close her door and walk to him. Maybe she didn't wish it was all a dream. Well, it was a stupid wish anyway, because this was her life.

He looked at her, and there was something like…confusion in his expression. Like he was at a loss over what to do. It dawned on her that he must not know *how* to look involved.

Now, surely a man like Reece had been involved with a woman before. She remembered how desperate and bewildered he'd been by his own feelings. She understood both those, but he'd never had… She didn't think he'd ever had anyone truly *care* for him, to the point he didn't even know how to fake it.

Unaccountably sad, she skirted the car and slid her hand into his, forcing a smile that didn't show all the sympathy inside of her. His hand was rough and warm, and even though she was talking about *pretending* to be involved, her heart skipped a beat like it didn't know the difference.

"I've still got your keys," Reece said, and she thought he was trying to be cheerful, but there was a rasp to his voice that didn't pull it off.

"Let's take a walk around the gardens first," Lianna said, hoping her forced attempt at cheer didn't sound deranged. "It looks like it rained, but I want to make sure nothing needs to be watered."

"Good one," he said under his breath.

Lianna doubted there would be any listening devices out here, but she felt like they couldn't take any chances for the moment. She'd play a role. She'd learned how to get rather good at that, she thought.

So Reece dumped his duffel on the porch and they walked around the house. Lianna went ahead and checked the soil in her pots and beds, determining nothing needed to be watered. She chattered on about the flowers since she didn't know what else to do, and Reece nodded along as though he was listening.

It felt cozy and intimate and *right*, and Lianna wondered what the hell was wrong with her that she could enjoy something fake, knowing it wasn't real. Knowing she was in danger and her son was locked away with her grandfather just so he wasn't in the cross fire.

Once they'd done a full turn around the house, Reece released her hand. It felt like a loss, and she shivered.

"It's getting a little cold," Reece murmured. "Let's go inside. I didn't see anything that would be a camera or a listening device. I think the outside is clear."

Lianna nodded and they walked up the stairs of the porch. Reece grabbed his bag, then took her keys out of his pocket. He made a move as if he was going to hand them to her, then thought better of it.

He propped open the storm door and shoved the key in the main door's lock. "I have to look like I'm taking advantage of you," he said very, very quietly. "Using you. So I'm going to have to be a little heavy-handed. At least when there's a chance of being watched or listened to."

Lianna nodded silently, because she didn't know what else to do. He unlocked the door and stepped inside, flipping on the lights. Lianna followed. It smelled like home, and she relaxed even knowing someone could have been in here poking around, setting up cameras or more listening devices.

"Nice to be here without your kid, huh?" Reece said, his voice light and flippant and not Reece at all.

Lianna rubbed at the pain in her chest. He was lying, acting. She knew that. Still, she couldn't work it up to agree.

"Why don't you make us some dinner? I've got to go check on some things."

Lianna found this *version* of Reece made her tongue-tied. She didn't know how to get used to him pretending to be someone else. Which gave her the uncomfortable realization that even when he'd lied to her in the beginning, he'd been himself. Maybe he hadn't been out taking nature photographs, but the stories he'd told, the way he'd *been*, was just…him.

"Knock knock," Reece said sharply. "Anyone home? Some of us are hungry."

"Right. Right." She shook her head, trying to get it through her head he was playing a part, and she had to, as well. "Dinner. Let me see what I can whip up."

They parted ways and Lianna moved toward the kitchen. It was home, but she felt so out of sorts now it felt a bit like a stranger's house. Especially without Henry underfoot.

Still, the act of making dinner soothed and settled her. She couldn't fully relax without Henry here or when she knew anyone could be watching or listening and just waiting to strike, but she had a good talk with herself. She had to play her role. Stay in character. Not get flustered when Reece was so utterly un-Reece-like.

She'd finished the quick spaghetti dinner and was setting plates out on the dining room table when Reece finally returned.

"Found a few more of those listening devices in the rooms. Took care of the one you found and the rest."

"I don't know why they'd be listening in to guest rooms," Lianna said, trying to sound a mix of baffled and afraid. "I could lose this place if someone thought I did it."

"This is why it's important you tell me everything you know, Lianna. Who knows what you said without thinking while they were listening."

"I'm sure I've told you everything I remember."

Reece made a disbelieving sound, then prowled around the dining room. He'd said there was one in here, but as he came to take a seat at the table, he shrugged. "Don't see any in here."

"Do you think they'll come after me if you took care of the other listening devices?" She tried to sound scared. A little over-the-top scared. Someone who wouldn't even try to stand on her own two feet.

Then she wasn't standing on her own two feet. In a deft move, Reece had tugged her into his lap. She couldn't bite back the surprised squeak, especially when Reece's mouth moved to her ear.

She could feel the movement of his lips, the warmth of his breath, as he whispered into her ear. "No cameras anywhere. Only the listening devices that were there before. No one came back while we were gone, but with that big window there and the lights on in here, we can't be sure no one is watching."

Lianna tried to *relax*, to act. The idea that someone

might be watching through the window was beyond disturbing, but what really bothered her was that her mind wasn't on that alone. It was on the fact she was *sitting* on Reece's lap. She could feel his body heat underneath her, the tension in his thighs under hers. The thing that shuddered through her was not close enough to fear as it should be.

He eased her off effortlessly and gently, and she had to be about fifty different shades of red. But he went about eating the spaghetti as though this were all *normal*. Because he was good at this. At acting and being someone else.

Which she didn't understand, because he hadn't done that in the beginning. He hadn't put on *this* act with her. The only thing he'd pretended, as far as she could tell, was the nature photography.

But tonight he chatted and ate as if he was, well, Todd Part II. She should have been weirded out, but instead she was almost…relieved. If he could *pretend* to be someone like Todd…didn't that mean he really hadn't been pretending up until now?

They finished dinner and Reece made some condescending remark about letting her handle cleanup. He disappeared again and she tackled the dinner dishes. There was only one window in the kitchen and it was over the sink, but it only had a half blind. Someone could be out there watching her. Someone could…

She closed her eyes and took a deep breath. Reece wouldn't have left her alone if she was in immediate danger. Even for all his acting tonight, she knew that. Believed that.

Trust your gut. She was definitely out of practice when it came to that, but Reece was making it easier. Shay and the whole group of people working to help her made it easier. She didn't even know what to call their group, but she trusted them. With her son. With her grandfather. Basically, her life.

Doubts crept in, because she'd trusted wrongly before, but she just kept repeating Shay's advice. *Trust your gut.* Her gut knew, despite the doubts, she was doing the only thing she could think to do. If it didn't work…

Well, she'd cross that bridge when she came to it.

She went through her normal routine, double-checking doors. She stayed as far away from the windows as she could, and she felt way more tense than usual. Also, there wasn't a baby monitor attached to her hip, none of Henry's snores making the house seem less isolated.

At another time, she might have enjoyed the quiet and the solitude. A vacation of sorts. But with danger lurking, the last thing she wanted to do was be separated from her son.

This is the best thing you can do to keep him safe.

She had to believe that. Had to.

Reece had left the door to the hallway on her side unlocked and open. Lianna had half expected him to disappear to his old attic room, but that didn't make sense, did it? Not that much about this did.

She moved to her room, the tension that already held her muscles tight and her breathing shallow not dissipating any. Because now what?

Her room door was open and Reece was sitting at her desk, tapping away on a laptop she didn't recognize. It was strange to see him here in her room. This had always been *her* room. A girl's space and then a woman's. Even Henry didn't care to spend much time here.

But there was a very large man at her desk who somehow didn't look as out of place as he should.

"Sorry to invade your space," he said, standing up, and

though the move was completely smooth and very *operative*-like, there was a sense that he was…uncomfortable. *Awkward.* Because here they didn't have to worry about listening devices anymore, so he was just… Reece. Normal Reece.

"I don't want you sleeping alone."

WELL, *THAT* HAD come out all wrong. Or maybe there was no right way to say it when he could still feel the way she'd settled into his lap. Warm, perfect curves, that scent of citrus about her. The way her cheeks kept flushing an irresistible shade of pink.

"Sorry. That's not what I…" He cleared his throat. It hadn't been easy to pretend to be some self-absorbed moron out there, knowing people could be watching, but it was harder to pretend everything away when it was just… them. No listening devices. Curtains closed. Here he could be himself, and he could be honest.

And you have to keep her safe.

Safe didn't always equal honesty, but she was here. She hadn't let him handle this…though that still irritated him. But her plan was good and he'd keep her safe.

"The thing is, they didn't break in while we were gone," Reece said. He didn't believe honesty was the best policy here, but apparently the truth was coming out anyway. "They didn't set up cameras or listening devices when no one was here, and they could have. They aren't waiting around for information."

Understanding dawned on her face and the way she went a little pale. "They just want me."

"That's my theory. Now, you don't have to worry tonight. Elsie patched into your cameras—outside and in the hallway there. Someone will be watching around the clock, but I think we should stick close. Like same-room close."

for him? Would *she*? When she had a son to think of far above her own feelings.

"But I want to," he said, and she wouldn't say his words were *certain* so much as a simple truth he didn't know what to do with.

She swallowed at the lump in her throat. "Well, I guess we have to figure out how to do it, then."

Silence stretched between them and too much distance. She wanted to go to him, but…

He frowned and looked at the door. She would have dismissed the sound herself, but his acknowledgment of it made her realize what it had been. The faint sound of a car door being shut.

"Stay put," he ordered, and was out of her bedroom before she could argue.

She scowled at the space where he'd been. No, she would not stay put. She eyed the holster Shay had given her. She would stand on her own two feet. Love and future or not.

THE CAR THAT was parked next to his was sleek, dark and expensive. The man who stood next to it was much the same. Reece didn't know what to think.

On the one hand, whoever was after Lianna and what she knew wasn't just going to roll up in plain view and walk in…alone.

On the other hand, Lianna didn't have any reservations, her website said the Bluebird was temporarily closed, and nothing about this man and his appearance felt *right*.

He heard Lianna enter the living room, where he was watching the man's approach. He frowned. "I told you to stay put." Maybe he'd said that more because he wasn't sure how to find his normal control when she was near.

Last night had been… He couldn't categorize it as a

mistake. Not when it felt as right as anything ever had. Not when she seemed to know who he was and what he needed when he wasn't sure *he* did. But he should have been focused on the *assignment*. Not his feelings.

The look she gave him seemed to say, *I'm not going to follow all your orders*, but she didn't say anything. Hopefully because she remembered they'd left a listening device in the kitchen.

She stood next to him, peering out the window. She leaned forward and squinted at the man. "Dr. Winston," she said, mild surprise in her tone but no sense of alarm.

"Who?"

"My…doctor." She straightened her clothes unnecessarily. "Therapist, that is. From Denver. After Todd…"

She was trying not to seem embarrassed, but he could see the discomfort in her gaze, in the slight pink of her cheeks. "Understandable," he said, cutting off her explanations. Because after what she'd been through, it *was*, and as someone who'd had to undergo his fair share of mental health evaluations either through foster care or the military, he was hardly going to let her be embarrassed over it.

Of course, that wasn't really the image he was trying to portray for whoever was listening. He had to stop thinking about…everything else and focus on the fake persona he was supposed to be. "But what's he doing here?"

"I couldn't say. I haven't spoken to him since I left Denver. He wasn't very supportive of the move. Didn't think I was ready, mentally." She didn't meet Reece's gaze as she spoke quickly. "But look, he's got a bag. I guess maybe he thought he'd…come stay."

"A little blurring of professional lines, don't you think?"

She finally looked at him, expression a little haughty. "I don't know *what* to think, Reece."

"Let me handle him."

She huffed in indignation. "Why on earth would I do that?" She closed her eyes and winced, clearly forgetting herself for a second. Well, at least he wasn't the only one. When she spoke next, it was softer. More pleading.

"I know him, Reece. He's a trained, certified therapist who has nothing to do with this."

"That you know of."

Her mouth dropped open and her eyes went wide, not an act. "Are you suggesting my *therapist* was in on this?"

"Maybe not from the beginning, but anyone watching you could have paid enough attention. Could have considered you might tell your therapist something. This is all about information, as far as we know. Your therapist would be a natural target."

She paled, and he felt like a plodding jerk. Surely there was a better way to tell her that. A better way to do…all of this. He blew out a breath and tried to find it, but she was collecting herself. The way she always did.

"You're right," she said, and though her voice wavered, she was back in control. "You don't think he's in danger, do you? Should we—"

"We should see what the man wants, and once he's gone, you'll tell me everything you ever told him." He tried to sound stern for the listeners.

"Of course, Reece," she said in a conciliatory way that scraped against his nerves. It was an act, but that didn't mean parts of it didn't grate.

A knock sounded on the front door and Reece went to it and answered it, with Lianna at his heels. She quickly swept past him, though, and smiled at the doctor, holding the screen door open so he could step inside.

"Dr. Winston. This is a surprise."

"Hello, Lianna. Not a bad one, I hope."

Reece hated the man. Immediately. If sight had made

him suspicious, the way the man spoke and looked at Lianna made him downright territorial.

Lucky for him, he was playing the role of a man who'd be *very* territorial. And kind of a jerk.

"What's all this, Lianna?"

"Oh." She blinked, and Reece could see clearly she had to remind herself that he was playing a role, but it worked. To someone who didn't know the situation, it would seem like she was what she was going to pretend to be. A woman too involved with an overbearing man. "Reece. This is… Um."

"Reece Conrad," Reece said, sliding past Lianna and holding out a hand.

The doctor looked at it and didn't seem at all surprised to see a man here. Or the inn being closed.

Strike two.

Finally, he shook Reece's hand and Reece made a show out of squeezing too hard. The doctor's expression hardened, so Reece smiled broadly.

He'd forgotten how enjoyable playing a role could be.

"I'm Dr. Winston," the man said. "And you are?"

"Oh, I'm a friend of Lianna's." He stepped back, slung his arm around Lianna's shoulders and gave them a squeeze. "Didn't know we were going to have company. Thought you closed the reservations for the week, hon."

"Oh, I did," Lianna assured him, sounding nervous, like she was afraid of displeasing him. *That* he didn't like so much, but at least he knew it was an act. She slid her arm around his waist as if trying to reassure him.

"My wife and I were on vacation, going up to Devil's Tower and the like. We were so close I just thought I'd stop in and see how Lianna was doing." He smiled. It struck Reece as a cold, calculated smile.

Strike three.

Lianna nodded.

"Lucky for us both, I can sleep almost anywhere, so the floor will be fine," he said, trying to sound…casual. About sleeping in the same room. Which was casual and about the mission.

Lianna blinked and looked at her bed. It was perfectly made, as she'd no doubt left it. Color rose in her cheeks again, but she turned away from him.

Reece took the opportunity to finish the video call he'd been making on the laptop.

"It's so weird being here without Henry," Lianna said, unnecessarily plumping a pillow on the bed.

"Hi, Mom."

She whirled around at the sound of Henry's voice. Eyes filling a little when she saw Henry on the screen. "Hi, baby." Without another thought, she was standing next to Reece, bent over so she could be close to the screen.

Reece nudged her into the chair and settled himself against the desk as Henry babbled happily.

"We had pizza for dinner. Then ice cream sundaes for dessert. Gramps read me the dumbest joke book. Hi, Reece! When are you guys coming back?"

Reece slid a look at Lianna. She smiled brightly and spoke calmly to Henry, assuring him they'd all be back together soon. Yet he could see that under the desk, she was twisting her fingers together, worrying.

There was no way to take the worry away, especially after they'd finished the call with Henry and spoken to Shay and Elsie, finding out there was absolutely no new information.

She still had a placid look on her face when the call ended, but her hands betrayed her, so he put his over hers. "When the mission is more frustrating than you want it to be, you just take it one step at a time. So next step? A good night's sleep."

"That sounds very practical," she said, and he knew she was trying to sound accepting rather than scathing, but she didn't quite make it.

Why did that make him smile?

But she looked down at his hands on hers, and her expression changed. Which he didn't have time to dwell on because she turned her hands in his so they were palm to palm, and that…short-circuited his brain.

He couldn't have said why. It was a simple touch, friendly at best, but… Well, when had he ever had much of that in his life? *Any* of that in his life?

"Why weren't you like that out there in the beginning?" she asked, and her gaze rose from their hands—still joined—to his eyes. She studied him, blue eyes dark and assessing. As if she could see through him. Understand him. In all the ways he didn't.

"Like what?" he asked through a too-tight throat.

"Pushy. Overconfident. It would have made sense."

"No. It wouldn't have."

"I was fooled by one man. I'm sure—"

"You're thinking like someone who goes off one set of facts and makes all their decisions. I'm a trained operative. My job isn't just to go off the information I have. It's to observe and assess. This place was so neat and tidy. Cozy and like a home. The perfect kind you see on TV. Then there you were, and you…you were so competent."

She wrinkled her nose as if that was an insult rather than the compliment he meant it to be.

"When I asked why your name wasn't Young like the history of this house, you gave me this look and demanded to know if I had a personal question to ask about that.

You didn't strike me as the type of woman who would be pushed around."

"And yet…"

"No 'and yet.' You're not. Maybe you made a mistake in trusting Todd Kade, but here you are. Fighting back. For your son. For yourself. Don't pretend like one mistake makes you someone you aren't."

She inhaled sharply, then let the breath go. Her hands squeezed his and she got to her feet. But she didn't move away, or take her hands out of his grasp. She stood there, right in front of him, holding his hands. "I'm starting to think you might be good for me, Reece Montgomery."

"Last night you said you couldn't trust yourself," he reminded her, because this felt like…dangerous ground. Lianna's hands in his. Some unknown battle light in her eyes.

She nodded, a little sadly. "I'm still working on that. It's strange but something about…well, you and your group. You trusted my plan. You're here, and I know you would have preferred to handle it alone. But you all trusted me, and it made it easier to trust you. The easier *that* is, the more I seem to realize… I can trust myself. Or at least try to."

She moved closer, or leaned closer. Somehow she was *closer* and there was a buzzing in his head he didn't know how to stop. Everything inside of him was focused on her. This moment. The mission disappeared. Everything disappeared except *her*.

"Last night *you* said you don't know what this is," she said, her voice barely more than a whisper.

He couldn't pretend not to know what she meant. "I don't. I…"

"It's only because you never had it. No one ever gave you a reason to have it. A lot of people failed you when you were most vulnerable."

Uncomfortable with that word, with her sympathy that he felt drifted a little too close to pity, he shrugged. "I survived." He pulled his hands from hers, but she only reached up and placed a palm to his cheek.

"But survival doesn't give you a chance to care or be cared for." She moved closer, angling her mouth toward his. There was still a wariness there. Doubts, maybe. But her hand was on his face and his heart beat so hard in his chest it felt like a war was raging inside his rib cage. One that would leave him bloody and broken.

He'd never been able to avoid the real kind of war. Why would he be able to avoid this?

"I'm not sure danger and secrets is a great reason for caring about someone, but—"

"You're the only reason." Which seemed to destroy all the reason he'd been clinging to. All the sense. All his control. He closed the distance between them, pulling her against his chest.

And took all the things he didn't understand.

Chapter Sixteen

Reece kissed her like a starving man, and Lianna felt that she was perfectly amenable to being consumed by *this*. His arms banded around her so that it would have taken some serious work to escape.

She didn't want to escape. She wanted to give in to something.

You did this once before and look how that turned out.

But that little voice in her head wasn't as loud as it used to be, and Reece's hands smoothing over her back, molding her to the hard lines of his body, seemed to eradicate it completely.

At worst, mistakes had to be repeated to learn a lesson. Or so she told herself, because nothing about opening herself up to Reece felt like a mistake.

The kiss spun out, deep and consuming, his heart pounding as hard against her hand on his chest as hers was pounding inside her own.

The hands on her back pulled the hem of her shirt up, slowly revealing skin to the heated air around them. It wasn't cold, and still she shivered as she lifted her arms and let him pull the shirt over her head.

His eyes were dark and intense, but there was vulnerability under all that fierceness. He didn't understand it, and he'd probably never admit to being *vulnerable*. But she saw it. Wanted to protect it.

She could be good for Reece, just like he'd been good for her. She slid her hands under his T-shirt, pushing it up and out of the way until he discarded it like he'd discarded hers.

He was pure muscle, scarred skin. She ran her hands over the scars, stomach cramping at the things he must have seen. Endured.

There was a flicker of something on his face. Not embarrassment, but maybe discomfort. Or fear. So she leaned forward and pressed her mouth to one of his scars, to prove they only made him more beautiful. More...*him*.

Then she stretched up on her toes and pressed her mouth to his, wrapping her arms around his neck. She wanted to pour all the confusing, exhilarating emotion inside of her into him. Fill him with it. Until he understood, somehow, something she couldn't have articulated in words.

The kiss went wild, bigger and brighter than she'd ever known. They tugged at each other's pants, undressing the rest of the way, outside world and danger forgotten. He laid her on the bed and still there was such *control* in him, leashing back a desperation she could see in his eyes, feel in his kiss. He didn't seem to know how to let out. So she'd have to show him.

His body covered her like it had been made to. He touched her like he'd known how for years. Every kiss took her deeper and deeper into something she wasn't sure *she* understood. So she held on for dear life. As pleasure ebbed into pleasure, wave crashed into wave, and hope bloomed as pure and simple as if she'd never been hurt, she didn't want to think. She didn't want to worry. For this brief moment in time, she wanted to feel and savor and *enjoy*.

It was a joy, to be with someone like this. To be with

Reece like this. To feel him inside of her, to hold him as he joined her over that edge of bliss.

They stayed there, tangled together, until she dozed off, spent and exhausted and...happy.

When she woke up with the morning sunlight streaming on her face, Reece wasn't in bed with her. She knew he'd slept there for a while because she'd woken up once in the dark and nuzzled closer to him. His arm had come around her, holding her tight.

But now he was up and dressed, bustling around the room. It was...almost as nice as waking up to him. Him moving about, doing things, as if he belonged here. She found she wanted him to belong here even knowing she had no idea how that would work.

Maybe you could have discussed that before... Lianna blinked at the sudden realization. This wasn't so simple as wanting to take care of someone who'd never had that. It wasn't as simple as liking him. This deep, tangled and inconvenient giving in to something she hadn't planned was...something more. Was it love?

No. No, she wasn't being this stupid again. She'd thought she'd fallen in love with Todd at first sight. A week wasn't much better. Especially a week where she'd been threatened. That meant she wasn't thinking clearly.

But she didn't feel muddled. She didn't find that she was talking herself into things like she had with Todd—so desperate for a love that didn't come with the strings of family.

She sat up in bed, frustrated with her own feelings. She didn't have to figure out everything right this second. Yes, they'd slept together, and it had been...wonderful. That didn't mean she needed to immediately know exactly what she felt and exactly what they were going to do about it.

Reece looked up, seeming unsurprised she was awake. "We'll want to drop some hints this morning," he said briskly. "That you know something you aren't telling me. Over breakfast, I'm thinking. You'll say something along the lines of wanting to open the inn, wanting Henry to come home, and I'll be dismissive. We can spend the rest of the morning away from the listening devices. Come back at lunch and I'll escalate the pressure. Bit by bit. We'll give it a day or two, and if they still don't act, I'll really explode. If you have to make something up, we'll figure it out beforehand."

She didn't know what to say to all that. He had plans. He was ready to face the day. She was...naked. She held the sheet up to her chest and tried to follow...any of what he'd said.

Breakfast. Pretending she knew something. Trying to draw someone out to...what? Demand information from her? Try to kidnap her?

This was your idea, remember?

She swallowed. This was the plan, the focus. Last night was the...well, distraction. She had to change gears as quickly as he had.

But when she looked at him again, he was standing at the end of the bed just *staring* at her. She might have felt self-conscious, naked with only a sheet held up to her chest, but she recognized that stare. It was the same look he'd given her in the hallway when he'd said he didn't know what this was. There was just *so much* inside this man that he didn't know how to let out, and she found that her doubts paled in the face of that.

She wanted to help him. She wanted...everything.

"I don't know how to do this," he said, as if each word was dragged across shattered glass.

Lianna felt her own throat tighten up. It felt too close to a goodbye, and she didn't want... Would he walk away because he didn't understand? Because it was too much for him? Would *she*? When she had a son to think of far above her own feelings.

"But I want to," he said, and she wouldn't say his words were *certain* so much as a simple truth he didn't know what to do with.

She swallowed at the lump in her throat. "Well, I guess we have to figure out how to do it, then."

Silence stretched between them and too much distance. She wanted to go to him, but...

He frowned and looked at the door. She would have dismissed the sound herself, but his acknowledgment of it made her realize what it had been. The faint sound of a car door being shut.

"Stay put," he ordered, and was out of her bedroom before she could argue.

She scowled at the space where he'd been. No, she would not stay put. She eyed the holster Shay had given her. She would stand on her own two feet. Love and future or not.

THE CAR THAT was parked next to his was sleek, dark and expensive. The man who stood next to it was much the same. Reece didn't know what to think.

On the one hand, whoever was after Lianna and what she knew wasn't just going to roll up in plain view and walk in...alone.

On the other hand, Lianna didn't have any reservations, her website said the Bluebird was temporarily closed, and nothing about this man and his appearance felt *right*.

He heard Lianna enter the living room, where he was watching the man's approach. He frowned. "I told you to stay put." Maybe he'd said that more because he wasn't sure how to find his normal control when she was near.

Last night had been... He couldn't categorize it as a

mistake. Not when it felt as right as anything ever had. Not when she seemed to know who he was and what he needed when he wasn't sure *he* did. But he should have been focused on the *assignment*. Not his feelings.

The look she gave him seemed to say, *I'm not going to follow all your orders*, but she didn't say anything. Hopefully because she remembered they'd left a listening device in the kitchen.

She stood next to him, peering out the window. She leaned forward and squinted at the man. "Dr. Winston," she said, mild surprise in her tone but no sense of alarm.

"Who?"

"My…doctor." She straightened her clothes unnecessarily. "Therapist, that is. From Denver. After Todd…"

She was trying not to seem embarrassed, but he could see the discomfort in her gaze, in the slight pink of her cheeks. "Understandable," he said, cutting off her explanations. Because after what she'd been through, it *was*, and as someone who'd had to undergo his fair share of mental health evaluations either through foster care or the military, he was hardly going to let her be embarrassed over it.

Of course, that wasn't really the image he was trying to portray for whoever was listening. He had to stop thinking about…everything else and focus on the fake persona he was supposed to be. "But what's he doing here?"

"I couldn't say. I haven't spoken to him since I left Denver. He wasn't very supportive of the move. Didn't think I was ready, mentally." She didn't meet Reece's gaze as she spoke quickly. "But look, he's got a bag. I guess maybe he thought he'd…come stay."

"A little blurring of professional lines, don't you think?"

She finally looked at him, expression a little haughty. "I don't know *what* to think, Reece."

"Let me handle him."

She huffed in indignation. "Why on earth would I do that?" She closed her eyes and winced, clearly forgetting herself for a second. Well, at least he wasn't the only one. When she spoke next, it was softer. More pleading.

"I know him, Reece. He's a trained, certified therapist who has nothing to do with this."

"That you know of."

Her mouth dropped open and her eyes went wide, not an act. "Are you suggesting my *therapist* was in on this?"

"Maybe not from the beginning, but anyone watching you could have paid enough attention. Could have considered you might tell your therapist something. This is all about information, as far as we know. Your therapist would be a natural target."

She paled, and he felt like a plodding jerk. Surely there was a better way to tell her that. A better way to do…all of this. He blew out a breath and tried to find it, but she was collecting herself. The way she always did.

"You're right," she said, and though her voice wavered, she was back in control. "You don't think he's in danger, do you? Should we—"

"We should see what the man wants, and once he's gone, you'll tell me everything you ever told him." He tried to sound stern for the listeners.

"Of course, Reece," she said in a conciliatory way that scraped against his nerves. It was an act, but that didn't mean parts of it didn't grate.

A knock sounded on the front door and Reece went to it and answered it, with Lianna at his heels. She quickly swept past him, though, and smiled at the doctor, holding the screen door open so he could step inside.

"Dr. Winston. This is a surprise."

"Hello, Lianna. Not a bad one, I hope."

Reece hated the man. Immediately. If sight had made

him suspicious, the way the man spoke and looked at Lianna made him downright territorial.

Lucky for him, he was playing the role of a man who'd be *very* territorial. And kind of a jerk.

"What's all this, Lianna?"

"Oh." She blinked, and Reece could see clearly she had to remind herself that he was playing a role, but it worked. To someone who didn't know the situation, it would seem like she was what she was going to pretend to be. A woman too involved with an overbearing man. "Reece. This is… Um."

"Reece Conrad," Reece said, sliding past Lianna and holding out a hand.

The doctor looked at it and didn't seem at all surprised to see a man here. Or the inn being closed.

Strike two.

Finally, he shook Reece's hand and Reece made a show out of squeezing too hard. The doctor's expression hardened, so Reece smiled broadly.

He'd forgotten how enjoyable playing a role could be.

"I'm Dr. Winston," the man said. "And you are?"

"Oh, I'm a friend of Lianna's." He stepped back, slung his arm around Lianna's shoulders and gave them a squeeze. "Didn't know we were going to have company. Thought you closed the reservations for the week, hon."

"Oh, I did," Lianna assured him, sounding nervous, like she was afraid of displeasing him. *That* he didn't like so much, but at least he knew it was an act. She slid her arm around his waist as if trying to reassure him.

"My wife and I were on vacation, going up to Devil's Tower and the like. We were so close I just thought I'd stop in and see how Lianna was doing." He smiled. It struck Reece as a cold, calculated smile.

Strike three.

"You could have called," Reece said, not even trying to be polite.

"I suppose I should have."

"No, don't be silly," Lianna said, looking up at him imploringly. "Reece, Dr. Winston was such a help to me before I moved here."

"What kind of help?"

"Oh. Well…" Lianna looked down at the floor and never finished her sentence, looking perfectly embarrassed.

"Perhaps I could talk to Lianna alone? Doctor to patient? There are confidentiality rules, of course, and I'd like to discuss previous treatment."

Sure you do, buddy. "I don't think—"

"You did say you were going to check on that loose porch railing for me, didn't you? You could do that while Dr. Winston and I have a quick chat, and then I'm sure he'll be on his way, won't you?" She turned a tremulous smile on Dr. Winston.

"Of course."

Reece was loath to leave Lianna alone with this smooth operator, but the hint to go outside was a good one. He could look through the good doctor's car and see what he found, all while keeping a decent enough eye on Lianna. And having Elsie run the man, of course.

Lianna smiled up at him and gave him a gentle nudge out the door. She had her hip to him and patted it surreptitiously.

Underneath the fabric of her T-shirt was a lump of something. She had a gun on her. Well, that was some comfort, he supposed. He couldn't imagine Lianna being one to carry a gun if she didn't know how to use it.

He might not trust the doctor, but if the man had something to do with this whole mess, he wanted information from Lianna. Not to hurt her. Surely he wouldn't be dumb enough to hurt her with Reece right outside.

"All right," Reece agreed, still reluctant. Which he figured fit the profile of who he was pretending to be anyway. He lowered his voice as if he was trying to keep what he was going to say a secret from Dr. Winston. "I'd stay where I can see you, if I were you," he said, with enough threat and a cold look in his eyes to make it look like he really was some kind of pushy abuser.

"Of course," she said meekly.

But she had a gun strapped to her hip. She wasn't meek. She was here because she wanted to fight for her life. For her son's life. So Reece had to give her the space to do it.

And make sure this ended the way they both wanted.

Chapter Seventeen

"Can I get you some coffee?" Lianna didn't have to feign the nerves that made her look ineffectual and weak. This was all so strange. Pretending to be who she'd once been wasn't easy. It left a sick feeling in her gut, and she wanted to explain it to Dr. Winston. He'd been such a help to her.

But Reece was right. This was…strange, at best. If she listened to her gut as Shay had told her to, this was all wrong.

He should have called ahead. He shouldn't be here at all. But he stood in her entryway and she'd let Reece leave her alone with him.

He's your therapist. You don't actually think he's dangerous.

But that was the kind of thing she'd said to herself about Todd. *He's your husband. He doesn't mean it. He's the father of your child. He just needs time.*

She'd never had to remind herself that Reece or Shay or Sabrina had been there to help her. To keep her safe. Her doubts had been the little voice in her head. She rubbed at her temple. Trusting any kind of instincts was a lot harder than Shay had made it sound.

"Where's Henry?" Dr. Winston asked, that pleasant smile affixed to his face. He still held the travel bag clutched in his hand.

Lianna tried to keep her expression passive, but the mention of Henry had all those doubts souring into full-fledged distrust. *Maybe* she could reason away him asking about Henry if it had been summer break, but if things were normal, Henry should have been in school. And wouldn't Dr. Winston default to normal?

Maybe he thinks you're already on summer break. Maybe he wants to make sure you're sane enough to send him to school.

The problem was, she hadn't talked to this man since she'd moved to Echo. There'd been no check-ins. She hadn't even *wanted* to call him, like she'd been afraid she would. Moving to Echo had been good for her and Henry. Running the Bluebird had been everything she'd needed.

So what had brought him here now? What about now made him curious about Henry?

Should she lie? She tried to smile as if she still trusted the man before her. The man she'd told her problems to. Who'd taught her breathing exercises and helped her deal with her anxiety after Todd's death. He'd been good for her. She didn't think she would have been able to move away and find this place without his help.

But she couldn't settle into that old trust. Not with him *here* asking about Henry.

"Lianna?"

"I'm sorry. This is just kind of strange." She locked her fingers together, but let the tremor in them show. Trying to be brave while showing signs of nerves would work for this role she was playing. She hoped. She forced an anemic smile. "And you never answered me about the coffee."

"No, I'm fine. Why don't we sit?" He smiled genially, like he always had. Like he had always put her at ease.

Wasn't this the kind of paranoia he'd warned her against? That being isolated and alone would give rise to the environment where everything would feel fishy, wrong and potentially dangerous.

Then she thought about Reece. He'd been sent here, he'd come back with her, *because* things were dangerous. She'd felt that paranoia rise when he'd been staying here, *because* there'd been something to be paranoid about.

Still, she smiled and nodded at Dr. Winston and led him into the living room. He sat down on the big couch and placed his bag at his feet. The couch was big enough that the polite thing to do would be to sit next to him.

She decided instead to take a seat at the table where she had an old computer guests could use. It created a barrier between them and also made her feel less self-conscious about the gun strapped to her hip.

Dr. Winston sat comfortably on the couch, looking much like he had back in his office in Denver. A well-dressed man with a kind face and easy demeanor. Lianna figured he could make himself comfortable anywhere. Make himself seem like he was the authority in any room.

Even having her suspicions and doubts, she felt like she *had* to tell him everything.

But she didn't. She *wouldn't*.

"I realize it's…unorthodox of me to show up here," he said kindly. "But you know I had concerns about your move. As a mental health professional, I've found it hard to let that go. I wanted to check up on you, Lianna. And I have to say, I don't like what I see."

Nor should he, considering she was pretending to be a different version of herself. Guilt tried to win over, but she caught sight of Reece outside, peering into Dr. Winston's car. A reminder she wasn't in this alone.

"Letting another man take over your life, much like the last one did. And where did you say Henry was?"

Lianna outright frowned at Dr. Winston. This was all

wrong. Guilt or doubts, in her gut, she knew Dr. Winston being here wasn't normal. Asking her about Henry…

Why was he asking about *Henry*? She'd taken Henry to see Dr. Winston once, and Henry had begged to never go back. Lianna had given in to Henry because Dr. Winston had made her leave the room, and no matter how much she trusted Dr. Winston, she didn't like the feeling of being separated from her son when he was so young, so vulnerable.

It hadn't been right, and she hadn't made Henry go back because, overall, the death of his father hadn't changed his life. And he wasn't the one who'd been fooled. *She* was the one who'd needed therapy.

But Dr. Winston had always asked, applying a certain amount of pressure to bring Henry back. Oftentimes she'd leave his office thinking she would, but back home, faced with how well Henry was doing, she'd change her mind.

Why had he been so concerned about Henry? At the time she'd convinced herself it was professional courtesy or interest, but now…why was he asking after Henry again?

She looked up at Dr. Winston, and everything she'd been thinking must have been clear on her face, because his voice hardened.

"Lianna…? Where is he? I know he's not in Denver."

Lianna's heart stuttered, then thudded hard against her chest. In her ears. Her voice wasn't as calm as she would have liked. "How do you know that? *Why* do you know that?"

"Time is running out. I could have played this game for a lot longer if you'd kept your mouth shut. But you had to go get involved with people who would speed things up. I'm not a bad man, but you're forcing my hand."

Lianna slowly slid her hand toward the gun on her hip. Dr. Winston spoke so *rationally*, but the words weren't right. They didn't make sense. *He* didn't make sense. Her heart pounded as she nudged the shirt up so she could reach under and get her fingers around the gun handle.

He stood now, the color slowly rising in his face. Eyes cold and furious. "You told me you didn't know anything. I told them you didn't know anything, and now I'm being held responsible for your lies. It won't stand."

She wanted to look out the window at Reece, but she figured that would send the wrong message to Dr. Winston. *To them.* There was a "them" he was telling things to. It didn't sound like he was a part of what Todd had been doing, but Reece had been right. Dr. Winston had become a target.

Now he was blaming her for it.

She might have felt bad, confessed all, told Dr. Winston Reece could protect him, but the fury in his gaze stopped her. His obsession with Henry stopped her.

He stalked toward the table. Lianna's hands fumbled with the holster, but she didn't let that get to her. She just kept working it until she got the gun free.

Dr. Winston slapped his palms on the desk and leaned in toward her. "Where is Henry?"

THE GOOD DOCTOR had left his slick sports car unlocked, so Reece could get inside to search it with no problem. He glanced at the house. It was hard to see through the windows with the sunlight reflecting off them, but through the big picture windows he could see the doctor's legs. He was sitting on the couch, though his upper body was out of view. Lianna was somewhere hidden by the light's reflection.

He didn't like it. Even after the phone conversation with Elsie, when she assured him she'd dig everything up on Dr. Winston and get back to Reece ASAP, he didn't like being this far away. The doctor could as soon take out a gun and shoot Lianna in the head.

But Reece fought back the urge to run inside. He was a trained operative. He had to think like one. Not like a man…who felt the things he felt for Lianna.

The rational side of his brain understood it made no sense for someone to come this far only to kill Lianna. It made no sense for one person to be behind all of this. It made no sense…

Unless he needs to silence what she knows…

Before Reece could react to that horrible thought, he heard the *snick* of a footstep too close. He didn't pause or think. He acted out of instinct like he'd been trained to do practically his whole life. He whirled in the nick of time to keep a blow from knocking him out completely. Still, the meaty fist hit him in the shoulder and had him stumbling to the side.

He kept his balance, immediately squaring off to fight. He wasn't thrilled to find two men dressed in black materializing from the woods to join the man who'd taken the first blow.

"Three against one aren't great odds," the large man who'd swung at him said with a grin. Which deepened when the two men who'd joined him trained their high-powered automatic rifles on Reece's chest.

"I guess that depends," Reece replied, calculating his moves. He had a gun, but he'd have to unholster it, raise it and shoot before they pulled their triggers. And that wasn't just unlikely—it was impossible. Especially considering their rifles were much more powerful than his pistol.

Three here. He used his peripheral vision to try to get a line of sight on Lianna. Were there more inside? Or had Dr. Winston underestimated Lianna enough to take her one-on-one?

God, he hoped so.

Lianna's cameras wouldn't pick up anything this far away from the house, so North Star wouldn't know he'd been compromised. They'd be able to at least *hear* something fishy in the living room with Lianna and the doctor, but it was very possible Dr. Winston knew that.

Everything was a little too possible.

"Well?" Reece asked of the three men just *standing* around, trying to look threatening. "Are you going to shoot me or what?"

The two with guns exchanged a look, and it was then Reece noticed they had earpieces in. Which spoke of more men. An organized team.

Though he swore internally, he leaned back casually on the car. He flashed a careless grin. "Waiting for orders, boys? That's not going to end well for you." The big one who'd tried to knock him out didn't appear to be armed, so Reece focused his attention on the two men with guns.

They held themselves alert, and the guns were pointed at him, but he noted they did not have their fingers curled around the trigger.

They weren't supposed to kill him. At least not without orders from their earpieces.

Reece didn't plan to wait for them to get any such directive.

Without warning or preamble or any more waiting, he lunged. A shot went off, but he didn't feel any bolt of pain as he'd expected. Which gave him all the opportunity he needed. He grabbed on to the gun he'd been lunging for, sweeping out his legs as he slid across the ground, tripping the other man with a gun.

His only goal was the two guns. Not inflicting damage. Not causing pain. Just get the guns. He could survive everything else these three men could dish out. He jerked the gun he'd lunged for out of the man's hands with a simple elbow to the throat and a tug timed perfectly.

They weren't well-trained muscle, that much was for sure. At best, Reece figured they were probably really good at shooting people and looking intimidating, but they didn't hold a candle to him when it came to hand-to-hand combat.

Lucky for him.

The man he'd tripped had fallen to the ground, but he still had the gun in his grasp and was fumbling to get back to his feet.

Reece swung out and used the butt of the gun he now held to land a nasty blow to the gun-wielding man's temple. He crumpled to the ground.

But Reece didn't have a chance to grab the other gun as the large man tackled him from behind, sending him and the gun sprawling.

The big guy made up for lack of technique with sheer size. He was all bulky muscle, a heavyweight who easily pinned Reece to the ground. He used one meaty hand to shove Reece's head into the dirt below, using his other hand and huge body to keep Reece's hands squeezed to his sides.

Which wasn't smart. He should have tried to cut off Reece's breathing, or rolled him over and started doling out some punches. God knew those ham fists could do some damage.

Reece struggled to breathe as his face was pressed into the soft earth, but all he needed was one perfect blow. One the man clearly wasn't expecting. He couldn't get his hands free, but his legs were mostly unencumbered. His aim had to be perfect, though, or no doubt Reece would be up a creek without a paddle.

He struggled against the dirt enough to keep the man's attention on him, but not enough to lose his breath. He focused, waited and then lifted the heel of his boot to hit the man in his most vulnerable place.

The man howled, and was surprised enough to let up on Reece's head, giving Reece a chance to wriggle and kick himself free.

Reece got to his feet, breathing too hard. His eyesight was slightly blurry from the pieces of mud stuck to his eyebrows and eyelashes. He tried to blink the obstructions away and assess the situation.

The big man was on his feet, though still huffing and puffing and holding on to his crotch. The guns were equally distant from the both of them.

A loud crash had both of them looking at the house. Lianna stumbled out and onto the porch. She had her gun in her hand, but Reece didn't get the impression she knew how to use it. Or at least not well enough to pick off the man he was fighting, from that distance.

Then Dr. Winston stumbled out after her. He looked injured, but not injured enough.

"Run," Reece yelled at her, ducking a fist and taking a few shuffle steps back to balance on one leg and sweep out with the other.

He didn't have the opportunity to watch and make sure she'd listened, because the big man was about to pick up one of the discarded guns, and that could *not* happen.

Chapter Eighteen

Reece had told her to run, so Lianna ran. Into the woods. Woods she'd played in as a child and still knew like the back of her hand.

Sabrina and Holden were placed somewhere in these woods, but in her hurry to escape Dr. Winston, she couldn't think about getting to them. She could only think about getting away.

Because he didn't want her. He wanted Henry.

How could he want Henry? Why would he be after her son? It didn't make sense, but she knew she couldn't allow him to get to her. He could use her as leverage—against Reece, against her grandparents. He could use her in a million ways she couldn't let happen. Not with Henry at stake.

So she ran. Zigzagging through the trees, jumping over fallen logs, skidding and sliding through the wet earth. Her heart thundered in her ears and her breath came in gasping pants that made her chest feel on fire.

She hadn't been able to shoot Dr. Winston, and she considered that a failing. He'd demanded information on Henry's whereabouts, but he hadn't actually grabbed her or tried to hurt her. Just intimidate her. So she hadn't been able to bring herself to get off a shot. She'd simply jumped up from the table and punched him. Giving her enough time to run away.

Then Reece had told her to run and she didn't know what else to do. He'd been fighting more men. Men with guns. She didn't think those men were here just to intimidate her.

Her pace slowed for a second as she thought of Reece. How would he fight off men with *guns*?

He can take care of himself. He told you to run.

She repeated those words to herself as she upped her pace again. She couldn't slow or look behind her, not when Dr. Winston had been so close. Maybe he wouldn't hurt her.

But maybe he would. It sure sounded like whoever he was involved with would. Because he said *someone* was demanding answers. Answers about Henry she wouldn't give. Ever.

"That'll be enough."

Lianna let out a short scream and slid to an inelegant stop as a man appeared in front of her, a large gun pointed right at her.

She didn't recognize him. Had no idea who he was or who he belonged to. But he had a much bigger gun than she did.

He gestured at her gun with his own. "Drop it."

She considered it. She also considered shooting him just to see if she could pull the trigger first. Whoever he was.

But she heard pounding footsteps and looked over her shoulder to see Dr. Winston huffing and puffing behind her.

She was trapped. A gun pointed at her. A man behind her.

Keep calm. You can find a way out of this. Keep your head. Reece is out there. Sabrina and Holden are out here. Be calm. Be smart.

She only had to worry about staying alive.

"*This* is what you thought deserved protecting?" the man said, raising an eyebrow at Dr. Winston behind her.

"She's an innocent bystander," Dr. Winston bit out.

"Then I blame myself for thinking you understood that *innocence* doesn't matter here. Not with this."

Lianna stood very still. She did not drop her gun. Maybe this new man and Dr. Winston would get into some sort of argument and she'd be able to…do something.

But a shot rang out, so loud it drowned out the sound of her own scream. She dropped to her knees, thinking it must have hit her.

But she didn't hurt. She looked up. The man with the gun wasn't hurt, either. Sickly dread curdled in her stomach as she looked over her shoulder.

Dr. Winston lay crumpled on the ground. Completely and utterly still. Lianna closed her eyes against a wave of grief. Perhaps Dr. Winston hadn't been a good man, but he hadn't shot at her, either. He'd called her an innocent bystander, and now…

"I'm going to suggest that when you get back up to your feet, you leave the gun on the ground. If you don't… well…"

Lianna swallowed down the grief and the fear and brought her gaze to the man standing in front of her. "You need me," Lianna managed to say. "You can't kill me."

The man snorted. "This isn't a movie. I can kill you whenever I feel like it and get the information I want elsewhere. But it'll be far more fun to torture the information out of you. To watch you give me everything I want to know, and then realize you'll die anyway. And so will your son."

Though fear drummed through her, she sneered at the man threatening her. "You'll never touch my son."

The man moved toward her. He was tall and very broad.

He looked like an athlete of some kind. Not menacing or evil like bad guys in a movie. He looked more like the dopey football star she'd gone to high school with.

But his words were cold and cruel, and so were his blue eyes as he crouched in front of her, still with the gun pointed at her chest. "Maybe your dead husband shouldn't have been so loose-lipped around a kid."

"Henry doesn't know anything." Her voice shook. *Everything* shook. At least she was sitting, so her legs couldn't give out. What the armed man had forgotten about or didn't seem to care about was the fact she still had her hand on her gun.

Not as big or high-powered as his, and she certainly was no great shot, but he was right there. In front of her.

The man smiled. "Doesn't he?"

Lianna's throat was dry, and swallowing didn't help. Still, she tried to hold on to her last sliver of calm and authority. Because she was Henry's mother, and she'd save him from this. No matter what it took. "Tell me what you think he knows."

"Yes, of course. I'll tell you my whole plan. I'll talk and talk and talk until your friends show up and take me away. Saving you. Are you kidding?"

Todd had taken that tone with her on occasion. It had always felt as much like a physical slap as anything else. She'd cowered when he'd make her feel like he knew so much more than her.

She wasn't that Lianna anymore. "Are you?" she returned, and lifted the gun and shot.

THE BIG MAN Reece was grappling with simply wouldn't go down. Reece had managed to wrestle him to the ground before he'd reached the gun, but all they'd managed to do was roll and roll and exchange painful punches.

At least Reece had been able to roll him away from the guns. Hand to hand… Well, maybe he wouldn't win, but at least he wouldn't die.

The man made a tactical error, giving Reece the upper hand. It took time, and all of his strength, but Reece managed to choke him until the man blacked out, going still.

Tentatively, Reece backed away. Inch by inch, until he was up on his feet and the man was still on the ground, immobile.

He heard footsteps again, inwardly swore, then whirled around, ready to fight. But it was Holden. "What are you doing here?"

"Trying to meet up with Sabrina, but we lost communication. Guess you handled this," Holden said, gesturing at the three motionless men on the ground.

Reece didn't even bother to respond to that. There was no time. He took off in the direction Lianna had gone.

He heard Holden running behind him, hissing his name in an attempt to be somewhat tactical, but screw tactics. Reece had to get to Lianna.

"Reece. Wait. That doctor? He wasn't after Lianna." Holden ran after Reece. Reece didn't slow down, but he did listen.

"What do you mean?"

"Elsie was listening in on the conversation. He wanted Henry. *Demanded* Henry. But he didn't hurt Lianna. Didn't even really threaten her. Just demanded the information for the people he was working for."

Reece nearly ran into a tree as he turned to look at Holden in surprise, sure he'd misheard. "What?"

"Henry. It was all he would talk about. He wanted Henry. Reece, is there any chance Henry knows…something?"

Reece wanted to deny it, but hadn't he had a feeling… an inkling when Henry had asked him to keep Lianna safe, that the boy understood more than they thought? Lianna had waved it off, and Reece had, too. Perhaps because they both didn't want to believe…

"We need to find out what Henry knows."

"Shay and Betty are on it."

"They have to be gentle with him," Reece said, sick with the idea the kid was doing this alone. Without Lianna. Without him. "He's just a kid. I think he's scared…"

"I'm sure they get it, Reece. He's a good kid. No one's going to intimidate him. Not in our group. Besides, Lianna's grandpa is there."

Reece nodded mechanically. Logically he understood that, but his chest still ached at the fact Henry would have to sit there and answer questions without him or Lianna there to…to protect him. Help him.

"Find Sabrina. Three men after me. One man after Lianna. We don't know who else is out there. I know someone was feeding orders to the goons I took on. If Henry knows who's behind all this, we need to make sure our next target is the leader…not just the muscle after us."

"On it. I'll go back to Sabrina's initial point, fan out from there till I find her. You're going after the doctor?"

"I'm going after Lianna. She's priority number one."

Holden didn't say anything to that. He simply peeled off to the west, where Sabrina had initially been planted. Reece tracked Lianna's route. The wet earth made her footprints and sliding slips in the mud easy to track at a decent pace.

The sound of a gunshot echoing through the trees had Reece's heart jumping to his throat.

Lianna.

HENRY COULDN'T CONCENTRATE on the arcade game. His head was fuzzy and he missed Mom. His stomach felt

like a big fat rock. He chewed on his lip and looked back
at Great-Grandpa.

Gramps was sitting on a big comfy chair in the corner,
reading one of his big, boring books. He didn't like the
arcade games, but he always stopped reading to play with
him if Henry asked.

Henry didn't feel much like playing with anybody today.
Not with Mom and Reece gone. No one would tell him everything. He didn't know *what* was going on, but he knew
it wasn't good.

It made him think about his dad. It made him think
about secrets. He tried to never think about either.

He heard voices in the hall, and his stomach hurt even
more. Shay and Betty walked in, and their eyes were on
him. Henry backed away from both of them.

"Henry." Betty's voice was kind and soft, but both she
and Shay moved toward him. Henry scrambled back to
Gramps.

"Did something happen?" Gramps demanded, putting
his book down and getting up out of his chair.

"No, Mr. Young. Not exactly. We've received some information, though. We think if we get some answers, we
might be able to figure some other things out before…"

Shay trailed off, and her gaze was on him again. Henry
wanted to hide behind Gramps, but he couldn't seem to
look away from Shay.

"Henry, do you know something about your dad that
you haven't told us?"

Gramps slid his arm around Henry's shoulders. Henry
wished it made him feel brave. But the rock in his stomach was getting bigger, making him feel sick.

"He's a boy," Gramps said, pulling Henry behind him.
"Why would you question a little boy?" he demanded, his
voice as angry as Henry had ever heard it.

Henry closed his eyes.

"Mr. Young, we think Henry knows something. Something important. Something that could help us keep Lianna safe. We don't want to scare Henry. We just want to ask a few questions."

But Henry was scared. Scared of everything. He kept his eyes closed and his head pushed into Gramps's back. He'd just stay here until they went away. Until it all went away.

"Henry." It was Betty's voice, and Henry felt her soft hand on his elbow. "Sweetie. I know everything is pretty scary right now, but we only want to help. Is there something you need to tell us?"

Henry blinked his eyes open. Betty was looking at him earnestly. Her hand was soft and reassuring on his elbow. Gramps still held him. He was safe here. Mom had brought them here to be safe.

Maybe that meant… "I'm not supposed to tell," Henry whispered. There were tears in his eyes, but he was strong. Like Reece. He'd be strong for Mom and he wouldn't cry.

"Why not, honey?" Betty asked. He liked Betty. She was…soft, but really good at stuff. Like Mom.

"They'll hurt her."

Betty looked up at Shay. Henry could tell Shay didn't like that answer and he hunched even more toward Gramps. Angry eyes. He recognized those all too well. They happened before the yelling. Dad always had angry eyes. And always yelled.

Henry wasn't sorry he was dead, like some people told him he was. Everything was better since Dad had been gone. No more angry eyes.

Reece was never angry. Sometimes he even looked kind of sad. But Shay looked *very* angry right now. Still, she didn't shout like Dad.

She didn't grab him like his father had that one time.

Your mother will die if you breathe a word of this to anyone ever. Do you understand me?

"Honey, I need you to tell me everything you know about what's going on." Betty smoothed a hand over his hair, just like Mom did when he had a nightmare. "Anything about your dad. I know you're afraid. But you know we're doing everything in our power to protect your mom, and this will help."

Reece was with Mom. And Sabrina and Holden. He trusted Reece the most, but Sabrina was pretty cool. And Holden looked strong. They'd all been nice, and they helped.

Betty was nice. Betty was *kind*, and she wanted to help him. Dad was dead. Maybe…maybe he could tell.

"Dad worked for a bad man named Gene Handler." Henry didn't know what to make of the way the adults reacted to that. They all got really, really still.

Henry huddled deeper into himself. "They were selling guns to bad guys. Dad got jobs with good organizations, stole guns, then gave them to Gene."

"Henry," Betty breathed. "How do you know this?"

"I accidentally heard it." He looked up at all the adults in the room. They didn't look angry anymore. So he figured he could keep going. "I couldn't sleep one night and I went to sneak some candy from the pantry. I had my flashlight and I went inside the pantry. I closed the door and got my candy and started to eat it there. But then I heard Dad. He was talking to someone."

Henry remembered how scared he'd been he was going to get in trouble. Then how scared at what Dad had been saying to a man named Gene.

"They argued, and Dad said he'd handle everything. Dad called him Gene once and then Handler once, so I figured that was the guy's name. They talked about guns. At first I thought they were maybe talking about Mature video games, but then I knocked a box off the pantry shelf."

Gramps's arm tightened around him, and Betty smoothed down his hair again, so Henry kept going.

"Dad jerked open the door. The bad man was gone, but Dad was mad. He…" Henry was telling the truth, but maybe he didn't need to tell the whole truth.

"He hurt you?" Betty said, and it didn't feel like a question. It felt like Betty knew. So Henry nodded.

"He picked me up by my shirt. He shook me. He said if I ever said anything to anyone, Mom would die. I didn't think they were talking about video games anymore."

The entire room was silent. The air felt heavy. Henry wanted to cry, but he blinked back the tears. *Be strong like Reece.*

Shay turned and walked out of the room. Henry felt his whole body tremble.

"Am I in trouble?" he managed to ask, even though his throat felt too tight.

"No, baby. No," Betty said. "You just… You are very, very brave and I am so proud of you." Betty smiled at him, but her eyes were bright. "Shay and Elsie are going to work really hard to bring your mom back. Today."

"And Reece?"

Betty drew him into a fierce hug. "Definitely."

Chapter Nineteen

Lianna still held the gun up, but she had her eyes squeezed shut. Which was so incredibly dangerous. She'd shot the gun and nothing on her hurt except her hand and her ears.

Which meant she had to have hit him. Which meant she had to open her eyes and figure out what to do.

It took considerable time to talk herself up to it. To get over the panic and the fear and what she supposed must be shock, as a weird, foggy numbness settled over her.

But this wasn't over. Even if she didn't want to see what damage she'd done to another human being, there were still men Reece was fighting. She still had to get home and safe to Henry.

She managed to open her eyes. Her breath came in short, panicked bursts no matter how well she knew she needed to calm down.

The man she'd shot lay on the ground right where he'd been crouching. She didn't see where he'd been shot, and she could see the rise and fall of his chest. So he wasn't dead.

A new fear filtered through the shock, but still she sat on the wet earth with the gun clutched in her hand, pointing it at someone who wasn't upright anymore.

He *had* to have been shot if he was lying there. He'd been *right* in front of her, so she couldn't have missed.

Run, her mind screamed. *Find Reece. Get out of here.*

The gunshot was still echoing in her head, and she wavered. Should she shoot him again? This unknown man. He'd threatened Henry, but could she…kill?

Just run away.

She managed to get to her feet, though her vision blurred and her balance was off. Shock. Panic. She had to shake them all away and focus on the fact she was fine.

Not that she'd probably killed a man.

She took a deep breath and looked around the woods. Which way had she come from? Which way did she need to go? Everything looked the same, and all those landmarks she usually kept track of on a walk were jumbled in her head.

It didn't matter which way she went, as long as she went. Whether she got back to the inn or walked through the woods until she got to the road, it was better than staying here when the man was still breathing.

Still breathing, and he had a gun. She needed to take it—not just to protect herself, but to protect everyone in these woods. He wasn't holding it anymore, but he was half lying on it. It was possible if she pulled it out from under him he'd wake up. She didn't know how gunshot wounds worked, but she doubted it would knock him out unless it was bad. Unless he was dying.

She should just grab the gun and run. That was what she had to do. She inched closer to the man. She held her own gun pointed at him so that if he moved, she could shoot. She could protect herself.

She grabbed the end of the gun that wasn't hidden under the man's torso and pulled. At first she tried to be gentle. Tried not to disturb whatever unconsciousness he was in, but as the gun refused to budge, she focused more on pulling harder and getting it out than being careful about it.

There was the sound of movement. Then a hand closed around her ankle. Lianna tried to jerk away, but the hand merely pulled as she tried to take off, sending her sprawling forward. She landed hard, a nasty face-plant that had her grip on the gun loosening and her teeth cracking against each other.

A heavy weight fell on top of her. The man. Pinning her to the ground. She struggled, but it was no use. "Did you think it'd be that easy?" he growled into her ear.

Lianna closed her eyes, reaching as hard as she could for the gun that she could still touch but wasn't close enough to wrap her fingers around.

"Oh, I don't think so." He reached over her head, with much longer arms than hers, and plucked the gun out of her grasp. She continued to struggle against his heavy weight. She kicked and wriggled and tried to push herself up out of the dirt.

The man wrenched her arm behind her back, and she howled at the shock of pain that went through her shoulder at the uncomfortable angle he had her arm at.

"Just wait."

Reece. Reece's voice. Calm and authoritative over the sound of her struggle and own harsh breathing. She didn't look up. She was too afraid one move would get her killed before Reece could save her.

Then the man jerked her up out of the mud by her shirt, practically choking her in the process. But that thought was secondary to the fact there was now cold steel pressed to her temple.

"On your feet," the man seethed at her, still twisting one arm behind her back. She slid in the mud but managed to get unsteadily to her feet.

She looked at Reece now. He stood a few yards from them. His lip was bleeding, and she could tell there were places on his face that were already swelling and bruising. Still, he stood tall. He held a gun and looked like…

Her savior.

"We have the kid," Reece said, not making eye contact with her. "She wouldn't be able to get to him if she wanted to. You want the kid, it's me you're after."

"So I can kill her?" the man said, digging the gun harder against her temple.

Reece shrugged negligently. So nonchalantly Lianna didn't know how to believe he was acting. They had Henry. Was that what he'd wanted all along? *Fool you twice…*

"I mean, I don't know why you'd want that kind of cleanup," Reece said. "But that's your business." His voice was flippant, and Lianna…

Stop, she ordered herself. *Think.*

His gaze was steady on the man holding her. Steady and cold. His grip on the gun was tight. His entire posture was rigid, no matter how he shrugged. He'd fought off men with guns to get here. He was *injured*.

And he didn't look at her. Not because she didn't matter, but because she did. And what would a man like Reece do if she became collateral damage? He certainly wouldn't go back to his group and keep working. He wouldn't make sure Henry was okay. He'd simply…give up.

Which meant she had to help herself get out of this mess as much as she had to trust Reece to do the same.

REECE HAD LEARNED from a young age how to deal with terror. He'd grown so used to it, *this* terror was almost new. He didn't know how he'd survive it if Lianna's blood ended up on his hands.

"I didn't kill your guys. Just left them incapacitated for a bit."

"I don't care about those idiots," the man said. He held

the gun to Lianna's temple, but Reece couldn't let himself look at her. If he made eye contact, he'd simply…break.

At this point, what he needed to do was keep the man's attention on him. Once Holden found Sabrina, they would be able to get here and take this guy out without hurting Lianna.

And if Holden disappears like Sabrina seems to have?

Only time would tell. He had to work this through one step at a time. "You want proof I got the kid?"

The man looked at him with narrowed eyes. Reece memorized his face. Square jaw, crooked nose. Blond hair, blue eyes, six-three give or take, and a very solid two-forty. He was built like a linebacker. But there was a trickle of blood running down his face.

Elsie hadn't been able to connect Dr. Winston to any groups, so they were still working blind on who they were fighting. But Reece would commit this man to memory and spend the rest of his damn life bringing him to justice if he had to.

If he got out of this alive. Because he'd do anything—including die—to get Lianna safe.

"You got proof?" the man said suspiciously.

"You let me get my phone out of my pocket, yeah, I got proof."

"Drop the gun."

"You can't honestly expect me to drop my gun. I gotta protect myself, man. I'm not here to hurt you. In fact, I'd be willing to take some kind of buyout. If whoever you're working for can afford me."

The man paused at that. Didn't seem to have anything to say. He wasn't wearing a headpiece like the men Reece had fought earlier had been. It could mean he was the leader, but Reece had a bad feeling he was dealing with another underling.

"I'll hold up my gun, pull out the phone, get the kid on a video call. You just want confirmation or you want what he knows?"

Again, the man holding Lianna was silent, so Reece just kept moving forward. Waiting would give him too much time to think, to despair, to make a mistake where he put his need to get Lianna away from the gun over the reality that he wouldn't reach her in time.

He held up his gun, barrel up, palm toward the man. He pulled out his phone with his other hand and used his secure line to connect with Elsie.

When she appeared on his screen, Reece forced himself to curve his mouth into a smile. As if he was talking to a small boy. "Heya, Hank."

He heard Lianna sob and he had to push the sound away. Freeze it out. He looked at Elsie's face on his screen. She was scrambling with how to respond, clearly. Where was Shay?

"Hi, Reece," Elsie said in some horrible approximation of a child's voice. Reece didn't outwardly react. He doubted the man holding Lianna knew Henry from Adam. Hopefully he'd never met a seven-year-old boy before, either.

"I got a friend I need you to talk to," Reece said, sounding downright jovial.

Reece looked up at the man holding Lianna. The man looked suspicious, but he still stayed yards away from Reece, not reacting. Which was when Reece noticed the man's shirt was wet. It wasn't mud.

Blood. The shirt was a little torn. He'd heard two gunshots go off earlier. "You okay, buddy?" Reece said, nodding to the man's side. It was the side closest to Lianna.

For the first time, he dared look at her. She was pale, streaked with mud from her head to her toes. Her hair was a mess and there was terror in her blue eyes. But not just terror.

Determination.

"Looks nasty, doesn't it?" he said to her. "Maybe he'll let you check it out for him?"

"I don't need anyone to check it out," the man said. "Just grazed me. Show me the phone."

Reece moved slowly. Carefully. He didn't want to make any sudden movements, and he had to make sure it didn't look like he was calculating how to get Lianna out of his clutches even though he was.

"Stop."

Reece stopped on a dime. He held both hands up, though he made sure the phone screen was facing himself.

"Just toss me the phone."

"You're not going to catch it one-handed, bleeding like that," Reece assured him. He crouched carefully and placed the gun on the ground. If he got close enough, the guns wouldn't matter anyway. "Better?"

The man took his time to consider, which tested the last thread of patience Reece was hanging on to. But the gun was digging into Lianna's head, and there was *nothing* Reece could do to make that less of a real, horrible threat.

It wasn't right or fair that she should have to suffer through this. He had to make it end. Here. Now.

Even if it led to his own end.

Chapter Twenty

Lianna's mind was moving in a million different directions. The voice that had come out of the phone was assuredly *not* Henry, but the way Reece had said "Hank" like he usually did had practically cut her in two.

It was another act. So flippant and fake, as if Reece was ever any of those things. But that only reminded her she could put on an act, too.

"Please," she said, letting the fear and a whine into her voice. "Please, let me talk to him. Please. I have to talk to Henry. Please. Please."

The gun dug into her skin and Lianna winced.

"Shut up," the man said.

Reece continued to move very slowly toward the man. He'd mentioned the man was bleeding. Lianna couldn't see it out of her peripheral vision, but she thought if she could figure out where it was, maybe she could hit him there. Would he be able to pull the trigger before she finished trying to hurt him?

That was the part that kept her completely and utterly still. Reece kept moving toward them, the phone in his hand, the gun left behind.

Why had he left his gun behind?

He came to a stop in front of the man. She could have

reached out and touched him. But he didn't look at her. He held out the phone.

Lianna inhaled. Now or never. Either she tried to help or she didn't. He was distracted by reaching out to grab the phone, so she acted.

Everything happened too quickly to fully place into a sequence of events. She knew she ducked and rammed into the man holding a gun to her head. She knew the gun went off, too close to her ears, but no matter the pain in them or how they rang, she hadn't been shot.

She stumbled away, took in the scene. Reece and the man wrestled on the ground, and she knew somewhere in the back of her head that Reece was yelling at her to run. Again.

She'd run last time and it had led her here. Running wasn't a good idea. She had to fight somehow.

Reece and the man rolled and grunted. The man still had his gun and Reece was trying to get out of his grasp. Lianna crept forward, moving for Reece's gun. She couldn't shoot the man while he was rolling around with Reece, but maybe she'd get the opportunity. Maybe she could shoot the gun in the air and create a diversion.

Reece managed to get to his feet, but the man was right behind him. Still, it gave Lianna her chance.

She pulled the trigger, but the man didn't go down. His arm jerked, though. Before she could determine if she'd hit him, Reece pushed her back and she stumbled, hitting the ground with a bone-rattling crash as another gunshot went off.

This time, she held on to the gun, and immediately pointed it at the man again. He was switching guns from one arm to the other, since the hand holding his gun was now a bloody mess. She *had* shot him there.

He glared at her. "You're one terrible—"

Before he got the rest of the sentence out of his mouth, she pulled the trigger again. This time, the man went down.

Lianna whirled to find Reece. He was sprawled on the ground, breathing ragged as he seemed to be trying to drag himself toward her. But he couldn't manage.

Oh no.

Lianna dropped to the ground next to him. "Reece."

He made a noise, but it was an awful noise. "I'm okay," he said, but the words were gritted out and thready at best. "It's okay."

"Reece…" She tried to help him up, but he was too heavy and wasn't trying to get up himself. "Reece, where are you hurt?"

He exhaled in huffs, as if trying to breathe through a pain, but from her vantage point, she had no idea… That was when he rolled over onto his back and she could see the tear of his shirt, the terrifying spurts of blood. So much blood. And a bullet wound, right below his rib cage, that left little to the imagination.

Dizziness threatened but she bit down on her tongue. She had to be brave and figure out what to do about this horrible, horrible thing. Her hands shook but she touched his face. "Shh. It's okay." What should she do? Pressure. They put pressure on wounds in movies. Did she trust a movie? "It's okay," she repeated, because maybe if she said it enough times she'd believe it.

"I'm not so sure about that," Reece gritted out. "Lianna. Get out of here. I don't know what happened to Holden and Sabrina. I don't know… Get out of here. Keep Henry safe. Okay?"

His words were harder and harder to understand, gritted and slurred and *oh, God*. She rolled up the bottom of his shirt and forced herself to put all the pressure she could manage on his wound.

He groaned in pain, but he was going gray. "Reece. Stay right here. Everything is going to be okay."

"Of course it is," he gritted out, squeezing his eyes shut. "But if it's not, it's okay. Everything's okay. I love you."

Love.

A hand wrapped around her arm and Lianna immediately fought it away, pushing and punching against the person who grabbed her.

"Hey. It's okay. It's okay. Lianna. Look at me."

It finally broke through her panic and fear about the blood that it was Holden grabbing her, talking to her.

"Where were you?" she demanded, tears filling her eyes against her will. "Help him."

"We already called in a medic team. Sabrina knows some basic field medicine."

Lianna looked at Reece, and finally realized Sabrina was here, too. Her face was all bloody and she held her arm at an odd angle, but there was no trace of pain in her expression. Only grim determination as she used her good arm to check Reece's pulse, then press a lump of cloth, which Holden handed her, to Reece's bloody chest.

"What happened?"

"She got ambushed by a couple guys," Holden said. When Lianna looked at him, he was checking the pulse of the man who'd shot Reece. He dropped the man's arm and stood. "We took care of them. Just took some time." She could hear the guilt in Holden's tone. Because if something happened to Reece, it was all their fault. "More people coming. Medics. Cleanup."

"He's dead?"

Holden nodded.

Dead. She'd killed a man. The man who'd killed Dr. Winston, the man who'd wanted to kill her. Who might have killed Reece.

She looked at him. If Reece died, wouldn't that be two lives on her conscience? He couldn't die. He couldn't. Lianna crawled back to his side.

"Is he going to be okay?" Lianna asked Sabrina.

Sabrina looked up at Lianna grimly. "I don't know."

Lianna closed her eyes and ran her hand over his hair, his cheek, whispering encouraging things. Anything she could think of. "I love you, too. So you have to live. You have to fight. You have to come back to me and Henry. You have to."

The words kept tumbling out of her mouth long after the medics arrived and took him away.

REECE HAD BEEN here before. In the dark. In pain, or worse, that floaty place where there was no pain. No nothing. Except sometimes memories. Of his parents. Of fear.

Of all the ways he'd tried to make up for what bad his parents had done.

Sometimes he heard Lianna's voice, but it must have been a hallucination, because she'd murmured things about love and taking care of him forever, and that was a dream. Not reality.

But they still made him want…more. More than the darkness. More than the pain.

He came in and out in waves. Sometimes he wasn't sure what was real and what was a dream. Surely Sabrina offering tearful apologies for being too late was a dream? Shay scolding him for not following protocol probably wasn't.

But more often than not, when he thought he opened his eyes, it was Lianna's blue eyes staring back. Warm and loving. And tired.

This time when he woke up, he felt…almost real. No fuzzy dream world. There was a sharp pain right below his rib cage, and there were the annoying beeping sounds he associated with hospitals. The lights seemed too bright and he blinked against them, but closing his eyes didn't send him back into the dark.

That was something. He wasn't sure how long it took him to come to full consciousness. Aware of his surroundings, his body and his own thoughts. This wasn't the first time he'd been shot or injured. He'd had his fair share.

But this was the first time he'd woken up and known there was something…and *someones*…waiting for him.

He looked over at the woman sitting next to his bed. Her eyes were assessing, and she didn't say anything. Just sat there, arms crossed.

"Shay."

"Don't sound so disappointed."

"Everything's okay? Everyone? Bring me up to speed." Everything was a scramble. He'd stopped the bullet from hitting Lianna, hadn't he? She'd gotten away? Henry was safe and…

"This'll be the third time I do that. Think it'll stick this time around?"

Reece tried to shift in his bed, but it sent a wave of pain through him. "How long have I been in here?" he muttered.

"Day five, buddy. But you seem about as alert as I've seen you. Gunshot nicked some organs in there. Surgery's no joke on that. On top of blood loss and the like. But you'll live."

"Well, I guess that's something. Lianna and Henry…"

"Safe and sound. For good. The small weapons distributor Todd Kade was involved with has been taken out. All dead or arrested. They were only out for Henry because he could ID their head guy, thanks to dad of the year. Won't matter now. They basically identified themselves with all this, and what we couldn't pin on them the shrink had kept a record of in his journal. He's the only casualty outside of the weapons dealers."

Reece let his fuzzy brain work through that. Lianna and Henry safe and sound, and for good. The ghost of Todd Kade laid to rest.

"Holden and Sabrina?"

"Banged up, but on the mend. You're the only idiot who jumped in front of a bullet."

Reece let out a breath. The whole thing was hazy, and he didn't fully remember jumping in front of anything, but he knew the feeling that had gone through him. "Couldn't let it be her."

"Yeah. Well, you're okay and getting better now. I know you've all been worried about North Star going under, but we're not going anywhere. This has opened up a new case for us. We've got some weapons to find for our new friends. So you have to get better and fast. We're going to need you." She smiled, but he could see the worry around the edges. The fear. Being this injured had affected their unflappable leader. Just like when Granger had been hurt.

Because North Star was a family. They had become his family. He wasn't sure he'd ever have admitted that to himself if he hadn't flirted with death there for a few minutes. Or days. Whatever it had been. But he cared about each member.

And they cared about him.

But that didn't mean North Star was his life anymore. Even if he could heal as fast as Shay wanted him to—which he doubted, based on all the machines attached to him—he didn't *want* to. "I'm not taking any more assignments, Shay."

"I know you're going to have to be out for a few weeks. Obviously, you'll take your time and get all healed up. Then you'll be good as new, and when you're ready—"

"No, I'm done. Really done." He knew people would doubt him. He was laid up in a hospital bed, after all. Probably pumped full of drugs. But he knew it in his heart. In his soul. "I don't want to fight anymore. I want…"

Shay was very still and looked at him with perhaps a little too much understanding. "A family?"

"Yeah." He'd never thought he'd want something so simple, but he'd never known what family was. Until Lianna and Henry had shown him.

"You don't think you'll miss it?"

Miss it? He'd joined North Star after the army because he'd had a need to…help. To ease something inside of himself. It was never about the *work*. "I've been fighting my whole life. For survival. Then to help people, hoping to fill that hole of never being helped myself. But the only thing that's ever come close is…love. I guess."

Shay snorted. "You *guess*."

"I've survived. I've helped a lot of people. At some point… At some point there's got to be more than that."

"For some people," Shay said, standing.

"It's a young man's game, Shay. Even you can't do it forever. Look at Granger."

"He could do it if he wanted to," she said, a surprising amount of bitterness in her tone for someone who'd gotten to take over in his absence.

"Maybe that's the point. No one wants to forever." Reece closed his eyes against the wave of pain. Soon nurses would be in to inject something else into him, but he had things to say first. "I'm not sure I would have come to that conclusion if I hadn't been this hurt, hadn't had this much not-all-there time to realize… Everyone deserves a chance at a real life. Beyond assignments and missions. No one should have to pay someone else's penance forever." It was true. He'd been trying to make up for the bad his parents had to have done in their gang, but he'd never done it.

Because he couldn't live his life paying for mistakes that weren't his. He didn't feel that mantle of guilt and shame anymore. Not when he wanted something real for the first time in his life.

"Can you get Lianna in here before one of those nurses forces some more drugs on me?"

"She's right outside."

Maybe she hadn't been a dream or a hallucination. As Shay slid out the door and Lianna immediately entered the room, he realized it hadn't been. She'd been here the whole time.

She rushed over to him. She had on what he would call her mom smile. Indulgent but authoritative. "Well, hello there. It's good to see your eyes." She settled herself on the chair and didn't give him the chance to speak. "I'm going to need you to get well enough for them to move you into a room with less restrictions. Henry is beside himself that they won't let children in. School just isn't in the cards until you're better."

Reece frowned. "He should be back in school. Shay said it's safe. He should—"

"My grandfather has been keeping in touch with Henry's teacher, helping him do any work he needs to for the end of the year," she interrupted, popping back up to her feet. She straightened his blankets and the wires on his IV. "He worked everything out with the school, so he's essentially on early summer break without it affecting him adversely. Going home just isn't an option until you can go with us."

"Go with you," he echoed, watching her fiddle with his bed. He never would have believed he'd like someone fussing over him, but it warmed his heart.

"Yes, and I won't hear any arguing," she said primly. "You'll need to be taken care of, and I intend to be the one to do it. I owe you my life."

Ah, well, this all made sense now, didn't it? He shifted in his bed, wincing at the pain. When he spoke, it came out gruffer than he'd intended. "You don't owe me a damn thing."

"Now, now." She leaned over the bed, brushing her hand over his hair. "Don't get worked up."

If he could move right, he would have grabbed her hand and pulled her right on top of him. Show her how *worked up* he could be. But he didn't have that option, he supposed. "I'm not getting worked up. And I won't have you taking care of me because you feel guilty or…or like it's payback or…whatever. No, I won't."

She blinked, and the hand on his hair that had been so…*officious*…gentled. She cupped his cheek, studying his face. He didn't have a clue what he looked like, but it couldn't be good.

"I love you, Reece." She said it quietly and matter-of-factly. "So we'll be nursing you back to health for however long it takes, and we'll deal with the rest once you're well enough to…go back."

This time he did reach up and managed to encircle her wrist with his fingers, thick and clumsy as they felt. "I'm not going back."

"Don't be silly. You'll get better."

"Yes, but I'm not going back to North Star. I don't want to be a field operative anymore."

She sucked in a breath at that, and then let it out slowly. Watching him all the while. "What do you want?"

He thought for a long moment. In his whole life, there'd only ever been one thing he'd ever truly wanted. One thing he'd thought he'd never find. "Home."

She didn't say anything to that, though her eyes filled.

"You could probably use a hand around the inn. I'm handy. I can wash dishes, pick up groceries. I don't require much."

"No, I don't suppose you do." She sighed. "And what about love?"

"I'd give it," he said gruffly, not letting go of her hand.

"And take it?"

"I guess I'd have to."

She leaned closer, one hand still on his face, one hand captured in his. She kept her gaze steady on his and said very seriously, "Yes, you would."

"Lianna, I only want to go home to you and Henry. It's all I want."

"It's all I want, too."

Epilogue

Everyone told Reece he'd change his mind. When he got out of the hospital, when he moved in with Lianna. North Star people, Lianna herself. Everyone.

Reece didn't miss it. Weeks out of the hospital, moved into the Bluebird, living with Henry and Lianna as a family... No, he'd never once looked back and missed his work as a field operative.

He fixed things that broke. He helped around the inn, getting groceries, making beds, greeting guests. He'd been roped into coaching Henry's baseball team, and he found the home he'd always wanted.

He loved Lianna and Henry, and built the life he hadn't known would have been possible a few short months ago.

But most of all, he didn't give up one family for the other. Even secret group operatives could take a break to see a kid's Little League game. As evidenced by the fact Shay and Betty were standing next to Lianna as he and Henry left the field after one of Henry's games.

"Where's Sabrina?" Henry asked, all but dancing on air. He'd gotten his first extra-base hit and hadn't come down from cloud nine.

"She's on assignment, but she'll be at the next game," Shay said, giving Henry a high five.

"But I'll send her video of your monster hit, Mr. Baseball," Betty added, slinging her arm around Henry's shoulders.

Henry grinned. "Cool."

"We've got to get back," Shay said to Lianna.

"You're not coming over for the barbecue?" Lianna asked. "You know you're both welcome. And you can take some leftovers to Holden and Sabrina."

Shay shook her head. "Both out on jobs. Next time we're in between assignments we'll be better, longer guests."

Reece nodded. "Well, you're always welcome."

Some of Henry's teammates came over and dragged him off to the playground. Betty and Lianna had their heads together about something, and Shay just looked at him, shaking her head.

"Can't say I ever predicted any of this, but it looks good on you, Reece."

"Yeah, it does."

"You're really not coming back, are you?"

"Really not."

She slapped him on the back. "Well, I guess I won't ask you to come back anymore. But if you ever change your mind…"

"I won't."

Shay smiled. "Yeah, well. See you later. Come on, Bet."

Shay and Betty left, and Lianna rounded up Henry so they could drive home. Reece barbecued dinner, and they ate together discussing the week ahead. They had two couples coming for a stay, making for a busy week.

Henry ran off to play his hour of video games as Reece helped Lianna clear off the kitchen table.

"Did she ask you to come back?" Lianna asked lightly as she rinsed off dishes and placed them in the dishwasher.

Reece didn't have to ask who or what she meant. He

came up behind her, wrapped his arms around her waist and rested his chin on her shoulder. "Yes."

"And you didn't feel the slightest twinge to agree?" she asked, and though her voice remained light, he could feel the tension within her.

"Not the slightest."

Her shoulders relaxed.

"Come on, Lianna. I thought we were past this."

"It isn't that. It's only…" She let out a breath, then laughed. She nudged him off her and turned to face him. She blew out a breath. "Reece, I'm pregnant."

He stood there, those words echoing in his ears for…he didn't know how long. He opened his mouth to speak, but his throat had tightened up. But Lianna had given him a few lessons along the way. Among them that even when he didn't have the words, he could reach out and find someone to hold.

Which was what he did. Pulled her into his arms. Buried his face in her shoulder. Held her tight until he knew what to say. "We have to get married."

She pushed him away, but he didn't budge, just pulled his head back to look at her. "You said you wanted to wait a year."

"I didn't want to. I thought we should, but now? No. We'll get married. Then we can do the adoption paperwork for Henry. And we'll get it all done before the new addition. So we're not just a family, but legal. Names and everything."

She cupped his face with her hands, studying his face very seriously. "That's a lovely sentiment, but I hope you know we don't need names for that."

"No, but it'll be nice. It'll be official. A baby. Our baby. Our *family*." He shook his head. Too bowled over to say much more. "I don't know how…"

"I know you think we saved you, but you were exactly what we needed, too." She pressed a kiss to his mouth. "We're all exactly where we're supposed to be. All four of us."

Exactly where he was supposed to be. Finally.

* * * * *

COMING SOON!

We really hope you enjoyed reading this book. If you're looking for more romance, be sure to head to the shops when new books are available on

Thursday 13th May

To see which titles are coming soon, please visit

millsandboon.co.uk/nextmonth

LET'S TALK
Romance

For exclusive extracts, competitions
and special offers, find us online:

Get in touch on 01413 063232

For all the latest titles coming soon, visit
millsandboon.co.uk/nextmonth

MILLS & BOON

THE HEART OF ROMANCE

A ROMANCE FOR EVERY READER

MODERN

Prepare to be swept off your feet by sophisticated, sexy and seductive heroes, in some of the world's most glamourous and romantic locations, where power and passion collide.

HISTORICAL

Escape with historical heroes from time gone by. Whether your passion is for wicked Regency Rakes, muscled Vikings or rugged Highlanders, awake the romance of the past.

MEDICAL

Set your pulse racing with dedicated, delectable doctors in the high-pressure world of medicine, where emotions run high and passion, comfort and love are the best medicine.

True Love

Celebrate true love with tender stories of heartfelt romance, from the rush of falling in love to the joy a new baby can bring, and a focus on the emotional heart of a relationship.

Desire

Indulge in secrets and scandal, intense drama and plenty of sizzling hot action with powerful and passionate heroes who have it all: wealth, status, good looks…everything but the right woman.

HEROES

Experience all the excitement of a gripping thriller, with an intense romance at its heart. Resourceful, true-to-life women and strong, fearless men face danger and desire - a killer combination!

To see which titles are coming soon, please visit

millsandboon.co.uk/nextmonth

JOIN US ON SOCIAL MEDIA!

Stay up to date with our latest releases, author news and gossip, special offers and discounts, and all the behind-the-scenes action from Mills & Boon...

 millsandboon

 millsandboonuk

 millsandboon

It might just be true love...

MILLS & BOON
Desire

Indulge in secrets and scandal, intense drama and plenty of sizzling hot action with powerful and passionate heroes who have it all: wealth, status, good looks… everything but the right woman.